FORT SASKATCHEWAN
VOLUME I

PRAISE FOR WINDIGO PLAGUE!

"A grim, blood-soaked, and frightening tale... meticulously researched, feeling authentic to the times. It's a damn good read."

—Tony Tremblay, Author of *Dark Roads Traveled* and *The Moore House*

—

"Spins the truth into a horrific masterpiece... If you love historical stories that delve into far more than just silly jump scares and gratuitous gore, this book is for you."

—Gord Rollo, Author of The Jigsaw Man

—

“An excellent taste of horror on the Canadian Prairie... speaks to the reader through wonderful glimpses of a true story once lost in time... Hard to Put Down!"

—Fredrick LaForge, Author of A Box Full of Tears

—

"Very well written... based on a true tale of cannibalism with some surprises along the way. Highly recommended."

—Gene O'Neill, Author of *Not Fade Away* and *The Hitchhiking Effect*

—

"Checks all boxes. His characters are rich, detailed, fully developed... awesome, gruesome, terrifying moments of true Horror."

—Daniel Lench, Actor, Director, Writer - *Maxxine – Circle – The Lurking Man*

—

"A horrific true story turned into a dark, bleak thriller that had me captivated... For fans of historical horror, this one hits all the high notes."

—Steve Stred, Author of *Mastodon* and *Churn the Soil*

—

"Both a riveting psychological thriller and classic horror novel... meticulously researched and filled with vivid detail."

—Don Sawyer, Author of *The Burning Gem* and *The Tunnels of Buda*

—

"A tale of the supernatural world stepping into the natural world, and that's when things start to go very wrong... hiding within the pages of this superb novel [is] the cold reality of what these troopers were facing."

—Kevin M. Sullivan, Author of *The Bundy Murders: A Comprehensive History*

—

"A historic police procedural with loads of supernatural and creepy elements inspired by a true story... I can't wait to see the further entries."

—James Seamone, Author of *The Belize Experience*

1st Edition

PUBLISHED BY
MJ Preston Thriller and Suspense
Amazon Hardcover ISBN: 978-1-0674900-3-4
Paperback ISBN: 978-1-0674900-0-3
E-Book ISBN: 978-1-0674900-2-7

Story by M.J. Preston

Publisher Notice: While many characters in this book are historical figures, the paths they take, their dialogues and supernatural themes exist only from this author's imagination. Any resemblance to real events or persons, living or dead, outside of historical context, and name is purely coincidence.

Cover and interior art by Marty Croft Concept

WINDIGO PLAGUE

A NOVEL

MJ PRESTON

Author's Note

If you find a typo, it's because I'm human, and that means some of you are still human too.

Written by a human, **<u>not</u>** ~~artificial intelligence.~~

MJ Preston

For Patricia Holycross
So many stories, so little time.

Table of Contents

Foreword by the Author

"When you're writing fiction, everything is on the table."
Gregory L. Norris - Writer/Friend
May 12, 1965 — May 4, 2025

I find myself thinking about Gregory's words, said often to writers, including myself, and how they were as fearless as they were beautiful.

Gregory L. Norris was a writer's writer. He was a champion of scribes, so prolific and so giving, and when we lost him in 2025, it left a hollow place in the hearts of the many writers and readers who knew and loved him.

Gosh, I miss you, Greg.

We live in strange times, and I feel inclined to throw out a few words to the folks who bought this novel and are about to give it a whirl.

The protagonist, Griffith, is fictional, as is his best friend, Marois, but many characters are historical, like Sub Inspector Gagnon and Cree tracker Swift Runner. In fact, the story of Swift Runner and the cannibal murders is true. What I did was wrap a horror novel around it.

I'm not the first writer to do this; there's been plenty.

My first exposure was James Webb's novel, The Emperor's General, in which an aide to General Douglas MacArthur navigates the post-Hiroshima/Nagasaki surrender of Japan, while juggling an affair with two women. It was a great novel, and MacArthur got some fantastic dialogue, which I'm sure he didn't say.

Another would be the collaboration of authors Gene O'Neill and Gord Rollo in their fantastic fable, Voodoo Cowboys. A novel offering up another chapter in the saga of Butch Cassidy and the Sundance Kid, but with a supernatural twist.

What a hoot that was.

In writing this novel, I am guilty of the following: adding a storyline, specific dates, and changing how some things really went down. I used plenty of artistic license writing this novel and wandered significantly off the beaten path of the actual case in its telling, but that's fiction, man.

And that's what I ask the folks who are going to read this novel to keep in mind. I am telling you a story, not reciting history or offering up personal social commentary on such.

I write fiction to entertain readers, and in all honesty, I'm not disciplined enough to write history. My mentor was a historian, and I don't have those chops, so I leave history to the experts.

That said, there are plenty of markers of injustice toward Indigenous people throughout Canadian history. There is mention of some of those injustices in this novel, such as hunters using strychnine to poison buffalo meat after killing whole herds for their hides. This stuff really did happen, and I encourage people to educate themselves. But if you want to know how this country came into being, I advise readers to educate themselves elsewhere.

Certainly not in a horror novel written by moi.

If you've read this far, I'm not going to bog you down with a bunch of information that probably won't make sense until after you have read the book.

It will be there for you in the afterword of this novel.

M.J. Preston
Near Fort Saskatchewan, Alberta

Author Notes
Windigo's and Psychosis

Fort Saskatchewan - Then and Now

—

In 1879, the country we now know as Canada had markedly different boundaries. Fort Saskatchewan was not in the province of Alberta in 1879, because there was no Alberta, at least not yet. Fort Saskatchewan was a part of the Northwest Territories. Not a history lesson, but a minor detail I thought worth mentioning should someone notice different territorial markings in the other two novels to follow this one. **–MJP**

Spelling Windigos and Wendigos

In American culture, windigo is often spelled wendigo. But in the Dominion of Canada, during the 1870s, the reference was spelled windigo. As the story is semi-historical, I chose to use the spelling on which it is based. **--MJP**

Windigo Definition

A **w**indigo is a cannibalistic monster that preys on the weak and socially disconnected. Referred to as: windigo—wihitikow—wendigo—wheetigo—windikouk—wi'ntsigo—wi'tigo, and wittikka. **Other names include:** Atchen—chenoo—kewok. ***–The Canadian Encyclopedia***

Wendigo Psychosis

While famine can serve as a catalyst for the development of **Wendigo psychosis**, it is not a universal driver, as there are cases of nonfamine Wendigo psychosis. ***–National Library of Medicine***

†

Introduction – The Expedition

In the Spring of 1879, a Cree Trapper, formerly employed by the Northwest Mounted Police from Fort Saskatchewan, was alleged to have murdered eight members of his family and dined on their flesh.

His name: *Ka Ki Si Kutchin.* English translation: Swift Runner.

Swift Runner denied the charges, claiming his family had starved to death. He told them he had eaten their flesh only after they had perished. Unconvinced of the story, the NWMP launched an expedition to Athabasca Landing to find Swift Runner's death camp.

This is the unofficial story of that expedition.

Prologue – The Promise

I

March 23rd, 1879
10 Miles North of Egg Lake, NWT

Both father and son were Cree. The boy was ten, a younger, ganglier version of his father who was over six feet tall, barrel-chested, and muscular. The boy had his father's chiseled jaw, high cheeks, mop of hair, and would eventually have his height. He was his father's son except for his eyes.

Those were his mother's, dark and cynical.

They had walked the whole day, stopping for almost two hours to hunt, shooting two ducks.

The father had been brooding until he killed the ducks, then he was pleased—for a while, at least. "You can cook them tonight." He handed the birds to his son, who tied them off and slung them across his shoulder. He gave his son an approving grunt and touched his arm. "You have always been my favorite son."

The boy stiffened but didn't recoil.

They walked in silence, watching the sun slip behind the horizon and taking the day's warmth with it. Cocooned in a state of numbness, the boy didn't speak, hadn't for quite some time. He shifted the ducks from one shoulder to the other and kept his eyes to the south.

"They will not blame you," his father said in Cree.

The boy nodded, head down, and they walked on.

They were going back to Egg Lake, to their people.

As the sun set, they made camp inside a thicket of birch trees, and the boy got a fire going. He plucked and readied the ducks to roast on a spit. He was watching his father, outside the tree line, looking south to Egg Lake, mumbling to himself.

This activity made the boy uneasy.

If not for the ducks, they would have made it all the way.

His grandfather was in Egg Lake.

Tomorrow, the boy thought, wishing they had made it there today.

He adjusted the birds on two spits and leaned them over the fire. The flames were high, and the angle of the spits would make for a fast cook if he tended and turned them regularly.

Behind him, he heard his father coming back into the camp, saw him holding his forehead, heard him say, "My head, it aches." The boy didn't respond and kept to the birds, hiding his terror. The fire cracked and popped, filling the tense silence and adding to the boy's anxiety.

His father shook his head, casting off the affliction.

The boy turned the birds, pretending not to notice.

A few minutes passed.

"You have done well. The ducks are cooking evenly," his father said.

The boy nodded, got up, and turned the ducks again. Oily juices sweating from the meat dripped onto the hot coals and sizzled. He had learned how to cook from his mother.

And now, I am my mother, the boy thought sadly.

"I will take you to Egg Lake tomorrow. Then I will go back to the wilderness," his father said.

The boy nodded.

"Let's have a taste." His father came around him, knife in hand, and cut a small chunk of cooked meat from one of the ducks and sliced it in two. He handed a piece to the boy, then popped the other into his mouth and chewed. "Mmmm. *Mistahiwekasin.*" Cree for "delicious."

The boy placed the piece of meat in his mouth and chewed it absently. His face was an expressionless mask hiding a longing fear to go back to the only home he had ever known.

Before the *wihitikow.*

From behind, his father's giant hands fell on his shoulders, clutching him gently. "The duck is good. Your mother taught you well."

The boy's mask slipped. He began to cry.

"Oh, I am sorry, my son. I shouldn't have spoken of her. The memory is painful for me also." He wrapped his arms around his son and tried to hug him, but the boy pulled away and went back to the birds. The father glared at his son's indifference, a bitter scowl tugging his face, a streak of red in his eyes, and the darkness wanting to come forward.

The father let out a grunt, went to a spot behind the fire, and sat down.

The boy continued his duties.

The fire crackled.

Minutes passed without words.

"*Wepinikewin*," his father grumbled. Cree for "banished." "I had no choice," he added.

This wasn't the first time since the north that his father had spun the lie and waged arguments for the thing which possessed him. It was trying to get out, choosing his father's words, fueling his anger, and assigning blame.

The boy hadn't spoken since the north.

Before the unspeakable.

II

An hour after the duck was eaten, the boy lay by the fire, watching the orange-yellow flames licking the teepee of wood he had restacked on the bed of glowing coals. He was thinking about tomorrow and going back to his people, away from his father and the *wihitikow*.

The boy was afraid to sleep.

Every night, he thought he might never wake up. Or worse, feared what he'd wake to. He didn't think he would be able to sleep, but he had eaten plenty of duck meat, much more than his father, and the exhaustion of the day took its toll.

He just wanted to go home.

Tomorrow, the boy thought.

Then he slept.

III

The father studied his son, watching his eyes open and close, until exhaustion and the abundance of food fell on him like a heavy blanket. His breathing changed to a mild, whistling snore. It had been a hard winter, and they had suffered much. He ate less and let the child gorge himself on the birds. Food was the medicine for sleeplessness.

The father rose quietly and grabbed the stick his son had used to stir the fire. He stabbed it into the bed of coals, sending up a swarm of sparks, followed by orange and yellow flames lighting the night. He looked back at his boy, saw the shadow he cast across the sleeping child.

The shadow was not his, but the *wihitikow*'s, and it waved in the firelight, hands unfurling to jagged claws and eyes glowing red. He gawked impassively, watching the shadow and feeling the *wihitikow* looking out from behind his eyes.

He heard it whisper sickly, "Hungryyyy."

"No!" The father shook his head and moved from the fire, sending the shadow slithering away into the darkness. He tromped out of the camp and to the edge of the tree line. With the fire to his back, he eyed the south, toward the home from which he'd been banished. He had promised the boy he would take him home.

Home?

The father had no home. No family. Just the boy.

"Take him back?" it argued. "To those who caused this? With their *wepinikewin.*"

His head was pounding, and he knew what was coming. "I promised him; he is my last son," the father begged. "Please."

"He is going to tell," the other insisted.

"No, he's a good boy." The father argued.

"He will tell, and they will come for us."

"I told him what to say."

"He will tell his grandfather everything, and they will come and find us."

"I made a promise." But the wickedness was curdling his blood, turning it black, giving rise to ravenous hunger. It was taking over, pushing him to the rear, coming forward.

"It is time to make the offering."

He felt the rifle in his hand.

Then he felt nothing.

***

Chapter 1 - Confessional

I

March 26, 1879
Near Egg Lake, NWT

He was a leaden silhouette moving across the open plain. Behind him, tracks marking his progress disappeared into the flat white light of the day. He didn't want to speak to anyone from Egg Lake, especially the elder, Chogan, but that was who came out to meet him. The others stayed back, watching from different spots in the trees, and he saw three men with guns.

"Where is your family?" Chogan asked in Cree.

"Leave me, old man, I am only passing by." He kept moving.

"Stop," the old man thundered.

He stopped, keeping his back to the elder.

"Where is your wife Charlotte?" Chogan spat. "Where is your mother? Your brother? The children?"

Silence, then he started to walk away.

"Ka Ki Si Kutchin," Chogan roared.

He stopped.

"Where is your family?"

He turned, and in a low, biting whisper through grated teeth he said, "They starved to death."

"Starved?" Chogan spat. "Lies."

"They died in the winter, after you exiled us."

Chogan sniffed the air. "I can smell it on you."

"If you hadn't sent us—"

"Your lies are the symptom of what afflicts you."

"Oh, and what is that?"

"You have the sickness, Ka Ki Si Kutchin." Chogan pointed an accusing finger. "The wihitikow has control of you."

He grinned, but it wasn't his grin, nor his voice. "It was you who sent us out to die, old man. You who killed my family." He took a step toward Chogan.

Chogan moved back raising a single hand. "Take the wickedness you carry back into the forest, or I will have the others shoot you down."

He looked around, saw the others watching, fear in their eyes and rifles in their hands. "You sent us away and you killed them."

"Leave here, you have the plague."

"Are you afraid you will catch it?" His smile widened.

"Yes," Chogan said.

He turned and strode away, calling over his shoulder, "You should be, Old man."

II
Three Hours Later
St. Albert, NWT

With Egg Lake behind him, he stumbled through the snow, focused on the Catholic mission and its steeple. He didn't want to think about what had brought him here or what he had left behind. Nor what had happened in the north or with his son. The farther away he got, the more it seemed muddy and dreamlike. The *wihitikow* was with him. Chogan had been right about that. The *wihitikow* had even tried to haunt his boy, but hunger eclipsed possession.

The mission grew closer.

He pushed those thoughts down and toiled in other lifetimes. He thought about his work for the Hudson's Bay Company. He was an expert hunter and woodsman. He knew the land, where the game was, and how to get it. He had led parties of White hunters and that knowledge got him hired by the Northwest Mounted Police as guide on manhunts.

He had been a good tracker, helping with escaped prisoners, criminals, and he had even saved the life of an NWMP officer. "Constable Ron," he mumbled. The White man's police treated him well, were friendly, and called him by his English name, Swift Runner.

His Cree name was Ka Ki Si Kutchin.

Swift Runner had been a proud Cree.

Then came the *wihitikow*, the whisky, and the madness. They said it changed him, boiled his blood with resentment, made him violent. They didn't know of his affliction. Nobody knew. Except Chogan, and he would tell.

He would have to think about that.

III
Catholic Mission
St. Albert, NWT

Father Leduc was sweeping the steps when he saw a man walking up the hill toward the mission. He knew who it was by how he walked. Nobody carried themselves quite like Swift Runner. He lumbered like a great buffalo, head into the storm, breaking trail for the herd.

But where is the herd?

Leduc had heard of Swift Runner's troubles in Fort Saskatchewan and hadn't seen him since the previous spring.

He doesn't look right, Leduc thought. *Something's off.*

Swift Runner was on the road, halfway up the hill leading to the mission.

"Swift Runner," Father Leduc called.

Swift Runner brought his weary eyes up.

"Come inside, you look frozen." Leduc beckoned with his hand.

"Yes, Father."

They went inside.

Father Leduc led him to his office, a small room behind the pulpit, big enough for a pot belly stove and three chairs, two in front of the father's desk. The room had an aroma of fire and freshly brewed tea. A teapot on Leduc's desk was guarded by two candles, a large Bible, a silver tray with four cups and condiments, and writing tools.

Swift Runner was looking away uneasily, his face twisted into a tortured grimace, and he let out a whimpering cry. Then he rubbed his face and the grimace was gone, but Leduc saw it.

Something terrible has happened, Leduc thought but didn't say. Instead, he went over, lifted the tea pot, and poured two cups. He added two lumps of sugar and cream to each and handed Swift Runner a cup. "That will warm you up."

"Thank you, Father." Swift took the cup.

Father Leduc moved back behind his desk and sat down.

Swift sipped, shivered, and balanced the cup on the arm of the chair.

"What brings you here, Swift Runner?" Leduc asked.

He looked the father in the eyes. "My family was banished from Egg Lake, and we had to leave before the winter."

"Banished? Why?" Father Leduc took a sip of tea.

"The same reason they made me leave Fort Saskatchewan, Father. Whisky and anger." Swift looked down.

Leduc wondered if it was to hide shame or conceal a lie.

"They sent us away, and winter was hard. The winter spirits brought death and disease. There was no game and one by one, they began to die. They starved, all except me."

"Starved?" Father Leduc felt a rush of fear. He knew Swift Runner's family well, had baptized two of his children and his wife. "Swift Runner, are you saying that your family is dead?"

"Yes, Father." Swift Runner raised the cup to his mouth and sipped.

Starvation plagued the Indigenous across the land, especially after the extinction of the buffalo. And not just the buffalo; other wild game had fallen victim to the gluttony and greed of the White man. Leduc knew of the starvation, had heard stories stretching all the way to Upper Canada. He was no stranger to death. As a missionary, he had worked among the Cree during the smallpox outbreaks, his faced markedly scarred and pocked from the disease.

Still, this was harder to accept; he had known this family for some time. He thought of Charlotte and her children starving and clutched the big wooden crucifix he kept in his sash. His hand wrapped around the brass messiah, feeling the crown digging into the soft skin of his palm. He embraced the pain and squeezed harder.

Leduc knew that Swift Runner was lying to him. He was a veteran priest, having counseled and taken the confessions of thousands of worshipers. He had developed an ear and an eye for deceit, and he knew the signs, which included failure to maintain eye contact, nervous mannerisms, or a tick. Whatever Swift Runner wasn't telling him, it had to be awful.

He spoke to Swift Runner in Cree. "Ka Ki Si Kutchin, what have you done?"

"There was no game." Swift Runner bemoaned, "We were starving. I killed my dogs, and we ate them. I removed the hides from my teepee, and we boiled and ate that. Then there was nothing. My traps lay open, and then they all began to die."

Father Leduc leaned in and said in Cree, "Why did you not starve?"

Swift Runner began to cry, shoulders shrugging with each sob. He brought his fist up to his mouth and rocked back and forth, long hair falling across his face.

Father Leduc collected himself and said, "Swift Runner, you're in the house of God. He already knows your sins, but to be forgiven, you must confess to me."

Swift Runner wiped his tears, looked down at the floor, and mumbled, "There was no food—we were starving—I was starving." He brought his eyes up to meet the horrified face of Father Leduc. "I had to eat."

"Eat? You… Ate them?" Leduc's hand unfurled and the messiah glistened with blood. In his open palm, he saw the stigmata. *He ate them!* Leduc gathered himself, keeping his tone empathetic. "Swift Runner, you must confess your sins."

"Yes, Father. I ate my family, but they were dead and"—he looked down—"there was no game."

God have mercy! Leduc wiped the blood from his hand, crossed himself and kissed the wooden crucifix.

Swift Runner stared downward, hiding the lies swimming in his eyes. He didn't look like the sole survivor of famine. His girth was that of a man well-fed, even overfed.

On the flesh of his own, Leduc thought. "How many?"

"My mother, my brother, my wife, and our children."

"How many children?"

"Five."

Jesus, Mary, and Joseph. Leduc crossed himself again.

The temperature in the room plummeted, as if a devil himself had taken up residence. No doubt to collect this man's soul, Leduc mused numbly, then he heard himself say, "May I offer you some more tea?"

"No, thank you, Father. I am so tired; I have walked for many days. May I rest here a while?"

"Yes, of course." Leduc shivered and scanned the room for the other presence. He rose from the chair, fed the stove some more wood, and used the iron poker to stoke the coals.

Should I be afraid?

There was a snort and a gasp.

Leduc turned.

Swift Runner had fallen asleep and begun to snore.

He took Swift Runner's teacup and set it on his desk. Beside the desk was a wooden chest. Leduc opened it, retrieved a woolen blanket, and covered Swift Runner with it.

The chill remained.

He was sure that something else was in the room with them, a presence not wanting to be seen but wanting to see.

But whose presence?

Not Lucifer himself, but perhaps a minion or some Indian devil the Church hadn't yet designated a demon.

Then it hit him.

Cannibalism!

Leduc touched the crucifix again.

Heavenly Father, how are we to save them?

He took in the sleeping Swift Runner. The thought of him doing something horrible to Charlotte and the children made the veteran priest cringe.

He probably killed them.

Leduc retrieved a notebook and a pencil from his desk, quietly leaving the room. He turned back to see if Swift was playing possum. He let out a loud snore and gasped. Leduc stopped and watched him, gathering his thoughts. There was no official police force in St. Albert. Leduc knew that Swift Runner had worked in Fort Saskatchewan as a guide for the Northwest Mounted Police. They were the closest law enforcement.

A full day on horseback. Can I keep him in the church that long? What if he starts getting violent?

Now Leduc was afraid.

He exited the small hallway into the church and saw an altar boy lighting candles. "Oliver, come here, child. I need you to do something."

IV

Eleven-year-old Oliver Halford immediately saw the priest's seriousness and said, "Yes, Father."

"Over here." Leduc pointed and sat down. Then he pulled out the notebook and began scribbling madly. Oliver set aside the match and striker and hurried to the pew.

Father Leduc was still writing when Oliver got there. He motioned for him to sit as he finished up. Oliver sat quietly as Father Leduc read what he had written and let out a grunt. He tore the page carefully from the notebook, folded it over and in half until it was a perfect square.

"I need you to go to the telegraph office and have them wire a message for me." He held the square up. "Then I want you to go right home and tell your mother I sent you home. Do not come back to the mission today, my child."

"Yes, Father," the boy said.

He placed the paper in the boy's hand and squeezed his shoulder firmly. "Listen, Oliver, this is a very important message. Make sure to take it straightaway."

"Yes, Father." Oliver got up facing the priest. "Will you be okay?"

Father Leduc smiled. "I will be fine, my son. Deliver that message. Go home. Say your prayers, and I will see you tomorrow when I come to the school for morning Bible study." He ruffled the boy's hair. "Go change, I will light the candles."

"Yes, Father." Oliver put the note in his pocket. He went to the cloak room, changed out of his alb, and put his coat, hat, and mittens on. He touched his pant pocket to make sure the note was still there.

The dry paper gave a whispery crinkle.

Still there.

Then the room became frigid.

Behind him came labored breathing accompanied by the stench of decay. Oliver saw the shadow cast upon the wall, a high, broad silhouette in which he stood.

Oliver's stomach fluttered.

From behind he heard, "Where are you going, Little Foot?"

Oh my God!

Oliver felt a single squirt of pee splash against his right leg.

"Do not fret, Little Foot. You can turn around."

Oliver turned to find himself staring at a wooden button on the big Indian man's wool overcoat just above the belly. He raised his head slightly, stealing a glance, and recognized him as the man who had come in earlier to see Father Leduc. Oliver had thought he looked like a giant. As it was, he knew quite a lot about giants, as he had a copy of *The Story of Jack Spriggins and the Enchanted Bean.* His Uncle Cillian had given him the little book before his family got on the boat from Ireland.

Giants were monsters that destroyed villages and pulled screaming children from their beds, only to pluck off their limbs and eat them bit by bit as they screamed in agony. This giant gave him a hungry smile.

Oliver lowered his eyes.

"Oh, no, no, no. Look up, Little Foot," the giant said.

But Oliver wouldn't.

Please, please, God, please make him go away.

"Oh, Little Foot, I will not hurt you." The voice was calm, caring. Oliver looked up, and the giant was smiling down at him, his eyes wide, big and brown. "I beg your forgiveness; I smell of the woods."

The odor intensified.

It didn't smell like the woods. It was worse. Enough to make Oliver gag. It smelled like old blood on a slaughterhouse floor. It was an aroma he knew because Uncle Cillian worked at a hog slaughterhouse in Dublin. Oliver and his father had visited his Uncle there. It was a smell he would never forget.

"Stop thinking about pigs, Little Foot."

He felt a rough hand touch his chin, lifting his gaze up to meet the giant's, whose eyes were now glassy black. He could see his own face in those eyes, see the terror. He could feel his will draining out of him.

"Ah, there you are, Little Foot," it soothed.

Pin pricks of red light danced in the giant's eyes.

"Let me in, Little Foot. Let me in, now."

He knew that if he didn't resist, the giant would tear off his arms and legs and eventually his head. Then he would eat him with the indifference of a wild animal, but how could he resist?

Its beckoning transformed into a screeching, enraged rant.

"Let me in, or I'll cut your boyhood off and feed it to you!"

Oliver closed his eyes and began to pray. "Our Father…"

"Stop that! I did not mean it. I would not do that, Little Foot."

"...who art in heaven..."

"Yes, I did mean it you little... Your God cannot help you."

"...hallowed be thy name..."

"Let me in! Let me in, or I will kill you right here!"

"Swift Runner!"

Oliver felt the hand release his chin. Felt the thing in his head slithering back to the darkness. Heard its howl of anger echoing away, then he heard the father.

"Swift Runner," Father Leduc commanded.

Oliver opened his eyes. The giant was smiling, his eyes again that friendly brown. "You should go hunting with me. I can teach you much, Little Foot."

"He's going home." Father Leduc was beside them, gaze sternly fixed on the giant. "Oliver, your father is waiting for you."

"Yes, Father." Oliver scurried from the cloak room, past the pews and out into the open air, and when the dull afternoon light hit him, he let out a strangled cry.

But he didn't stop. He ran for his life.

He had never heard Father Leduc tell a lie. Oliver's father had died after being thrown from a horse six weeks ago. Father Leduc didn't say "mother" because he thought his father would pose more threat.

Oliver wished his father was alive.

Time to be the man, he thought.

He saw the telegraph building in the distance and kept going despite the terror gripping him. He kept looking back, feeling cowardly for running. As he reached the telegraph, he checked one last time and saw the giant coming down the hill.

He's following me! Oh no, please, oh no!

"Where are you going, Little Foot?" the giant called inside his head.

Oliver couldn't go into the telegraph building; the old man working there was no match for the giant. If he went home and the giant followed him, he would kill both his mother and him.

Oh my God, he probably already killed Father Leduc!

Oliver dashed past the telegraph office, ducked down an alley on the other side of the building, and found he had only two options: hide behind a busted-up wagon or a solid-looking feed stall. He chose the feed stall, knowing that if the giant came down here, there was nowhere to run.

He needed to watch.

Oliver saw the empty knothole in the wall three inches above his eye level. Spotting a wooden pail hanging on the trough, he grabbed it, turned it upside down, stepped up, and put his eye to the hole.

Then he waited.

Time was slow, merciless.

He had to pee but was terrified to pull his eye from the knothole, or to step off the bucket and risk any noise. He unbuttoned his fly, pulled out his business, and peed against the wall on an angle to avoid wetting his clothes. He never moved his eye away, blindly he buttoned up.

He heard the giant calling for him inside his head.

"Stop hiding, or I will cut you open right here in the street!"

Oliver kept forgetting to breathe.

Then the giant was there, walking across the opening, eyes straight ahead. Oliver watched in terror, willing the giant to keep going, feeling his heart tighten like an angry fist inside his chest. *"Please, just keep going."*

And the giant did just that, not turning his head once to look down the alley.

Relief.

Oliver let out a breath.

But the giant came back, stopped mid-crossing, turned, and stared at the feed stall.

Oliver was vibrating, pushing down the mounting scream.

No, no, no, no!

"You in there, Little Foot?" The giant was staring right at him.

He sees me!

V

Swift Runner could feel it inside him, demanding to be fed. He marched down the road, looking for the child. When he reached the telegraph office, he kept going, and then he felt something and stopped.

He looked down the road both ways.

"Where are you, Little Foot?"

He could feel him.

Where?

He turned, faced the telegraph building.

Swift Runner sniffed and smelled two things: urine and fear.

He walked back to the telegraph office and looked through the glass. He saw an old man, but no child. Then he turned back to the alley, surveyed the broken wagon, and turned his gaze on the feed stall.

"You there, Little Foot?"

He spotted the child's eye through the knothole.

"Ah, there you are."

Then, from behind, "You, there! Indian! Get out of here! No loitering!"

Swift Runner turned to see a man coming out of the telegraph office. He was an older man, wearing a conductor's hat, limping and waving a cane, barking like a dog, "Move along now!"

Not now! Swift Runner glared at the old man.

He could pull his knife up and spill his guts right there on the road.

But the meat would be old, tough, spoiled.

He turned his gaze to the feed stall.

It was sweeter meat he sought.

Where are you, Little Foot?

"Hear, now, I said, no loitering!"

VI

Oliver almost cheered when Mr. Watts came out and ordered the giant to leave. Almost, but he was so afraid that the giant would kill the old man. For some reason the giant backed down when Mr. Watts held up his cane and did something with it that Oliver couldn't see but would understand later.

"Move along now, hear?" Mr. Watts barked.

The giant paused for a moment and said, "I am going, sir."

Then he walked off.

Oliver watched him disappear from the mouth of the alley, while Mr. Watts watched him go down the road away from his telegraph building. Shifting from one leg to the other, Mr. Watts turned and said, "He's gone, lad," and went back inside.

Oliver stepped down, exited the stall, ran to the road, stopped, and looked both ways.

Gone!

He dashed into the telegraph building.

Coming through the door, out of breath, he blurted, "Mr. Watts, this message is from Father Leduc!"

Mr. Watts said, "Was that Indian following you, son?"

"Yes, sir." Oliver nodded and began to shake.

"Don't move." Mr. Watts came around the counter, locked the front door, turned the sign to Closed, and peeked out the window. "I shooed him away. No worries, lad."

"Yes, sir, Mr. Watts." Oliver handed him the message.

"What did he want with you?" Mr. Watts was moving behind the counter, reading the message. He mumbled, "Huh? Foul play?" and his expression became serious. "Hold that thought, lad, and let's get this telegraph off to the Mounties."

"Yes, sir, Mr. Watts."

Mr. Watts sat down, tapping the telegraph key. It clicked, and there was a beep—Morse code. Oliver wondered how they deciphered the beeping. Each tapping beep sounded too close together for him to understand. He was thinking about this, looking out the window, watching the sky turn ashen. Behind him, the beeping stopped. Then there was a different beeping as Mr. Watts wrote something down.

"Okay, I have confirmation." Mr. Watts read aloud, "Message will be delivered to NWMP."

"Mr. Watts, could you walk me home, sir?"

"Yes, lad, but fair warning, I've got a bad leg, so you'll need to cut your stride a tad."

He closed shop and walked Oliver home.

***

Chapter 2 – The Night Monster

I

Town Telegraph Office
St. Albert, NWT

Swift Runner trailed away from the alley and the barking man.

"No, stop! We need the boy," the *wihitikow* screeched.

Swift Runner brought his hand up to his forehead. The *wihitikow* was beating against the inside of his skull and ranting, *"Go back! Go back! Go back!"*

I cannot.

"You can! Kill the old man! Take the boy!"

Swift Runner kept going but considered going back. There was an appeal, a duality he had with the entity. He craved the shedding of innocent blood, just as the *wihitikow* craved it, but what was being demanded couldn't be delivered without consequence. He couldn't go back. Too many people knew about him—Chogan, Father Leduc, the old man—and soon there would be more.

"I want the boy!"

There are too many people. We can come back later.

It was scratching behind his eyes.

"I want him now!"

It wanted its tribute, and he wanted to give it.

Somehow, he kept going, holding his head, trying to pacify the spirit, yet feeling its need as if it were his own. They argued, madness versus reason.

"We must eat. Feed me! Feed me!"

We can go back for the boy later.

"No! Now! We are starving! We are starving!"

Then through the blur, he saw two little bucks playing on the street. He focused, a carnivorous sneer tugging back his lips. The pounding stopped, the tantrum forgotten. He felt its black blood diluting his own, coming forward, turning him predatory.

"We need food."

"Yes," Swift Runner agreed.

The boys were playing marbles with their backs to Swift Runner, unaware of the looming danger. The day was almost gone, but enough light remained to cast his dark shadow across them and their game.

The younger boy turned and squawked.

"Huh?" The older boy looked up and dropped the marble he had been shooting into the dirt.

Swift Runner was looking down on them, grinning for reasons neither could imagine in their worst nightmares. He bent, passed a hand between them, and snatched up the dropped marble. It was a tiny clear globe with a sail of red suspended in its center.

"Pretty," he said. "But I can make it prettier."

The boys stared as Swift Runner rolled the marble between his thumb and index finger. He was lulling them, just as he had been lulled long ago.

He could taste their innocence.

His stomach growled; mouth wet with anticipation.

Hungry.

He brought the sphere up to his eye and peered through the glass. It appeared to have swelled to twice its size. Swift Runner whispered to them, "Games… I like to play games." The marble began to glow white, its red sail suddenly flapping. Both children stood frozen, eyes fixed to the glow, watching the sail snap, sending spattering dots of crimson inside the glass.

"I like games. There is no greater game than the hunt," he said.

"The hunt?" The older boy stared into the marble.

"Come with me, and I will show you my ways."

"Yes," the younger buck whispered.

"I want to come with you," the older one said.

The red sail had dissolved, filling the globe with blood which now glowed fiery red.

He gave the marble to the older buck.

The boy, entranced by its hypnotic glow, eagerly took it.

Swift Runner stood up, feeling the *wihitikow* crawling beneath his skin, watching from behind his eyes, needing to come out and taste the offering. Down and across the road, a tall man was lighting the street lanterns. The boys were fixed on the red eye glowing in the eldest's palm.

They would have to move fast.

"Children, follow me." Swift Runner began to walk.

They didn't hesitate and followed, side by side, staring down at the glowing talisman.

"I want to learn how to hunt," the younger boy mumbled.

"I want to rejoice in the blood," said the older.

"I will teach you," Swift Runner said.

He quietly led the boys down the road, while conspiring with the *wihitikow* about the act. They would take them to the woods near the Sturgeon River, teach them to build a fire. Then he, Swift Runner, would cut their throats, butcher them, and offer tribute to the master.

He looked back, tasting their innocence, saliva flooding to slobber from the smell of their blood.

The slaughter would be sweet and innocence sweeter still.

The boys trailed, side by side behind him. They were directly across from the lantern man, who had stopped what he was doing and was watching.

Just walk, do not look at him, the *wihitikow* said.

Swift Runner wiped his mouth, watching the lantern man from the corner of his eye. Eye contact would draw him in, but he watched from his peripheral vision, leading the children toward the beckoning darkness.

"Keep your eyes to the front," he whispered to them.

They didn't fuss or complain.

"Do not look at him, and I will show you my ways." He continued leading them. Both boys' eyes were lost in the glowing marble.

"Show us your ways," the older boy parroted.

We only have to get past the man lighting lanterns.

Then they would feast.

II

Mr. Watts had a cane which he didn't lean on but used as a man would a walking stick, trotting it along beside him to a cadence. It wasn't an aid to walking as much as it was a…

…*weapon*, Oliver thought.

Mr. Watts was slower than Oliver, and that was all right because he still felt safer with an adult. Oliver thought that whatever evil possessed the giant didn't translate to adults.

This was Oliver's neighborhood, made up of working poor. He and Mr. Watts walked down a gravel road behind a neighborhood of impoverished tenements.

"Oliver, about that message Father Leduc sent?" Mr. Watts asked.

"Yes, sir?" Oliver replied.

"Did you read it?"

"No, sir, Mr. Watts," Oliver said.

"You're a good lad, Oliver." He ruffled his hair.

"Thank you, sir, Mr. Watts."

They walked for a minute, sequestered to their own thoughts. Mr. Watts's cane tapped a cadence on the compacted earth as they did.

Then Mr. Watts said, "I know him, he's a tracker. He worked for the Northwest Mounted Police out of Fort Saskatchewan. He had a good job, but they sent him back to his people, before the winter."

"Why, Mr. Watts?"

"He liked to drink and that turned him mean, lad. He caused a lot of trouble when he got into the whisky. Picking fights and such. There was an incident with a gun; nobody got killed, but there were threats. The Mounties kicked him back to his people in Egg Lake. What happened from there, God only knows. Remember this, young Oliver: the Devil's nectar can change a man, but never for the better."

"Yes, Mr. Watts." Oliver stopped.

Mr. Watts stopped too. "Is this your home, lad?"

It was a derelict building in disrepair, a dwelling of the poor for transient people to use as a way station. They stood on a walk littered with garbage piled in two mounds on either side.

Oliver nodded. "Would you like to speak to my mum?"

"Yes, lad, I would."

They mounted the steps.

III

They went through the main door into a hall with six dwellings. Oliver led him down to room number six and unlatched the door. "Mum, I'm home, and I'm here with Mr. Watts from the telegraph office."

As the door swung open, Oliver's mom, Jessica Halford, was standing at the counter, her back turned. She was a frail woman wrapped in a pale blue dress that hung on her scrawny frame like a rag of malnutrition. Her hair was tied back in a bun, mostly brown with some threads of gray.

The odor of boiled pig's feet drenched the room.

Mr. Watts knew the story of the Halford widow. Her husband was prospecting on horseback when his horse spooked and threw him. Bad luck would have it, Mr. Halford's head connected with the only boulder in the high grass. According to the other prospector, he was killed instantly when his neck snapped. "It happened so quickly, he probably never felt a thing," said the prospector. This was repeated second- or third-hand during a bull session at the telegraph house, a known repository of local info, both informed and uninformed.

"Good day, Missus Halford." Mr. Watts removed his hat, revealing a shiny crown beneath.

She turned briefly toward them, then away.

Oliver saw she had been crying. His mum cried all the time now. He also cried, but Father Leduc told him that his mum needed him now more than ever to be the man. So, he cried less than his mother, although her weeping was a trigger for his own tears.

He missed his father terribly; six weeks wasn't enough to mourn the emptiness of death. Sometimes he woke up believing his dad was still alive, then he would remember the day the men came and told her. He remembered every word she screamed. "No, please no! No, he can't be! We just got here! No! No! No! We just got here! No, Lord, please no!" Then she just screamed.

Oliver pushed the memory away and came back.

"Pardon my manners," his mum said and managed a weak smile. Her eyes were bloodshot, face flushed. She sniffed and extended a hand. "What brings you to our home, Mr. Watts?"

Mr. Watts took her hand and gave a tender shake. "Sorry for the intrusion. We have a bad Indian out there on the street, whom I expect will be arrested for a horrible crime. He was following young Oliver. I shooed him away, but Oliver asked that I walk him home."

"Dear Lord," she gasped, pulling Oliver closer. "Following Oliver? Why?"

"I suspect, Missus Halford, it was because Oliver was carrying a message for the police from Father Leduc. The Indian wanted to prevent him from sending the message." Mr. Watts looked down.

"What did he do, Mr. Watts?"

Mr. Watts cleared his throat and, in a whisper, said, "He may have killed his family. He's gone mad, got brain sickness." Then he raised his voice. "Keep your door latched, Missus Halford, it isn't safe out there. Don't go out tonight. I sent a telegram to Fort Saskatchewan, and the Mounties will send someone to investigate. Until then, stay indoors, as this Indian is sick in the brain, possibly dangerous. Don't open your door."

"We will, and I won't." She nodded, released Oliver, and said, "Say goodnight, and thank Mr. Watts for seeing you home." She turned back to Watts. "Bless you for looking out for my boy."

"Yes, sir, Mr. Watts, thank you for seeing me home."

"It was my pleasure, lad." He tapped his cane and smiled. "Well, I must be getting on."

"Mr. Watts, aren't you afraid?" Oliver asked.

"I'll be fine." Mr. Watts held up the cane and pulled on it, revealing a long dagger sheathed inside. He put it back together and grinned. "I might be old, young Oliver, but I am always prepared."

"Holy—"

"Holy nothing. Young man, go and change for bed." His mum gave Oliver's earlobe a pinch and paddled his butt. She turned back. "Thank you again, Mr. Watts."

Oliver stood behind the blanket, listening to the adults.

"The Mounties should be here late tomorrow," Mr. Watts said.

"I hope they arrest him," his mother said.

"I expect they will."

Oliver peeked from behind the curtain.

His mother opened the door, and Mr. Watts nodded dutifully, then walked out into the hallway.

"Thank you for watching after Oliver, Mr. Watts. May the good Lord watch over you."

"A pleasant evening and shiny morning to you in your baintreach, Missus."

"Goodnight, Mr. Watts, sir." Oliver waved.

"Goodnight, lad." He called through a closing door.

His mother latched the door and turned around to face him. "Get into your night clothes, and you can have dinner before bed."

"Yes, Mum." Oliver stepped behind the blanket and stripped out of his pants and shirt. Once he was undressed, he felt vulnerable, afraid, understanding what could have happened. He let out a whimper, then began to tremble and it broke loose in great sobs.

His mother pulled back the sheet. "Olly?" She saw the shock and fear in her son's face and wrapped her arms around him, also crying. "Oh, my sweet Oliver."

Oliver cried harder, trying to get it all out, feeling marked by the thing inside the giant.

It had seen inside his head.

Oh my God. He could have…

I could have…

Oh my God.

He was going to kill me!

"Oh my God, Mum."

"It will be okay, my sweet child." She held him, rocking him like he was a newborn.

Oliver shivered, pitching the terror out in strangled moans and whimpers. *I could have died! I could have…* He had seen the monster lurking inside the giant, and that horror was balled up in his guts and needed to be ejected.

"I could have died, Mum!" He shivered again. "He was going to kill me."

"No, no, no, don't say that. You wouldn't have died, Olly, because you did the right thing, and Mr. Watts brought you home, and the police will soon be here." She soothed him, not letting go until the tremors stopped, his crying surrendering to whimpers. "You're safe. I won't let anyone hurt you." She kissed him on the forehead. "They took your daddy from me, but no one is taking you. The door is latched. The police will come and take him."

Oliver looked up at his mum and saw the fresh tears on her face. "I'm sorry, Mum."

"Sorry? Why would you be sorry?"

"I made you cry."

She cried a bit more and let out a little laugh. "Let's get you into your night clothes." She helped him dress, gave him another hug. "I'll warm your dinner. Maybe you can tell me about what happened and that'll ease your mind a bit."

"Yes, Mum." Oliver was trying to think what he could do to ease Mum's mind. As to his own, he doubted anything would alleviate the fear. He followed her around the sheet into the main room. He considered telling his mum that the "Bad Indian" Mr. Watts spoke about wasn't just a man, but a monster. Or had a monster in him that could get inside your mind. He doubted anybody would believe him. It was better to use the story Mr. Watts told, and the police would come and take him away.

Before he came back.

Because Oliver was sure he would.

IV

"Hey there, Indian, where you going with them lads?" the lantern man called while crossing the road. "Hey you, I asked you a question!"

Swift Runner put his hand on the handle of his hunting knife and considered the wihitikow's urging he meet the man in the street, cut his throat, and lead the children away.

"Cut his throat," the wihitikow urged. *"Open his belly too!"*

Swift Runner murmured to the children, "Stop."

They stopped, lost in the glowing marble, ignorant to what was happening around them.

The lantern man was coming, holding an oil torch in his left hand, his right hand resting on a gun set into an unbuckled holster. He was younger than Swift, in his middle twenties, he was strong and showed no fear. "What are you doing with them boys, Indian?"

When they were three feet apart, Swift Runner said, "Good day, sir, a fine job you have done lighting those lanterns." Behind those words, the darkness waited and when the man looked into his eyes, it came forward.

The flame on the oil lantern blew out with a *whup*!

The man's hand fell away from the still holstered gun, and his jaw slackened. u

"That's better," Swift Runner said. "Do you hunt?"

The lantern man blinked, once, twice, and said, "Yes… I like to hunt." He was staring past Swift Runner to the glowing eye the boy held in his palm. "Yes, I like to hunt."

"Come with us," Swift Runner said. "I will teach you my ways."

"Yes, I would like…"

From behind the man came a familiar bark. "Get away from them!"

Swift Runner saw the old man, and he was holding a sword.

He felt the *wihitikow* withdrawing, its influence weakening and leaving him to the consequences.

The lantern man shook his head, stepped back, and shook his head again. "I ah, oh, shit…" Then he buckled over and vomited. It gushed black and foamy, splatting onto the ground, fizzling, and absorbing into the earth. The man wiped his mouth. "What did you do to me?"

Then the two boys also vomited.

"*Pakitinikan*," Swift Runner said. Cree for "seed."

Lantern man didn't speak Cree nor did the barking man, but that didn't matter. Behind him, the older boy dropped the marble in the dirt. The red glow had gone back to clear glass breaking the spell.

Swift Runner watched them run, displeasure on his face. The *wihitikow* would torture him for this. He turned around, remembering the barking man, when he heard a familiar click.

The lantern man had his gun pointed straight at Swift Runner. "Get out of here and steer clear of the little ones, or I'll track you down myself and blow a hole in you."

Swift Runner stepped back.

Then the barking man was beside him, waving the sword. "Get out of here!"

"Move out, Indian. I'll kill you here and now." The lantern man brought the gun up, teeth gritted together, finger tightening on the trigger. "I mean it."

He was no match for a gun and a sword.

"Yes, I will go. I will go." Swift Runner backed away and turned.

The man waved the gun. "Go, now!"

Swift Runner moved away.

"If I see you near any more kids, I will shoot you on sight, Indian." He kept the gun up.

"You'll be talking to your friends from the Northwest Mounted Police soon enough, Swift Runner," the barking man called.

Swift Runner moved off slow.

They had stolen his prize, the sweet innocence of youth.

The beast was pounding against his forehead.

"Now we will go hungry."

Rage began to overtake common sense.

"They have taken our prize!"

His hand reached for his knife.

"They have taken our prize!"

He stopped, deciding what to do.

V

Barking Man and Lantern Man were Mr. Watts and Mr. Buchanan. They were side by side, sword and gun, hurling threats at the withdrawing Swift Runner. Having won the upper hand bred shared exhilaration.

"I will shoot you on sight, Indian," Buchanan finished.

"You'll be talking to your friends from the Northwest Mounted Police soon enough, Swift Runner," Mr. Watts barked.

Swift Runner stopped, and both men's words ran down their legs. Buchanan looked at Watts and back at Swift Runner, who was standing, back to them, like a pondering golem. What was he pondering?

"I might have to shoot him," Buchanan whispered.

"Don't tell me, Mr. Buchanan. Tell him," Mr. Watts said.

"This is your last caution, Indian! Move along!"

Silence.

"I don't think he believes yuh, Mr. Buchanan."

Before Buchanan responded, Swift Runner was moving again, leaving the oily glow of streetlamps and gone into the waiting shadows.

The two men watched for another minute.

He was gone.

"Mr. Buchanan?"

"Yes, Mr. Watts."

"Have you ever shot anybody?"

"No, and I hope I never have to." Buchanan holstered the pistol and asked, "Mr. Watts?"

"Yes, Mr. Buchanan?"

"What in the name of God awful was that?"

"That, Mr. Buchanan, was divine intervention."

"Divine intervention, Mr. Watts?"

"Yes, sir, because if the good Lord hadn't brought me this way and you weren't lighting lanterns, those boys would be gone with him into the wilderness."

"That would be a tragedy, Mr. Watts."

"A repeated tragedy." Mr. Watts sheathed his sword back inside the cane. "Father Leduc thinks that Indian killed his own family. I just sent a message to the Mounties in Fort Saskatchewan."

"My God. What would make a man do such a thing?"

"They're godless people, Mr. Buchanan. Godless people are led in the ways of the Devil. If we are to save them, we must bring them to the table of the Chosen One."

"Aye, Mr. Watts, the Church has much to do."

"It certainly does."

"Do you think he'll come back?"

"I think he might. He was chasing another boy, whom I just walked home."

"Another boy?"

"The boy was carrying the damning message from Father Leduc. I thought he was trying to intercept the note. Now I think his motivation might be worse. If you see anyone, warn them off."

"I surely will, Mr. Watts."

They bid each other a good night.

VI
After Midnight
Halford Residence

Oliver Halford was floating between reality and dream. In his dream, he saw the giant's dark silhouette moving up the alley under the blue light of the moon. He could hear, "*Where are you, Little Foot?*"

Not real.

But it was real. He was hearing the giant's thoughts because…

He's getting closer.

"Come out to play. Where are you, Little Foot?"

Oliver didn't want to open his eyes. He was sure that the giant would be hanging over him. He could smell the stench of sour blood. His heart throbbed in his ears and the giant beckoned, *"Come out and play, Little Foot. The master is hungry. I want to cut you open. Come play in the blood, Little Foot. Come to the hunt. Come to the fire."*

Oliver opened his eyes to a dark room. It had been a bad dream. He didn't smell rot, but the faint odor of boiled pork. He didn't hear the call of the giant, just Mum snoring on the other side of the sheet. Had it all been a bad dream? Oliver slipped from bed and went to the window. He pulled back the thin curtain, stared down the alley, and there he was, a block over, coming up the alley, too far to hear, but Oliver heard.

"Come out and play, Little Foot."

He was stopped in front of a home, probing the occupant's thoughts, looking for...

For me!

The giant knew he lived in this neighborhood.

Maybe he killed Mr. Watts and Father Leduc!

Should he wake Mum and warn her? Then it occurred to him, *What if the giant can hear my thoughts?* He pulled back from the window, stifling a cry.

Shut your mouth and your mind! But how do I do that?

Panic.

Back to the window, he peeked.

The giant looked exactly as Oliver had dreamt.

He was walking again, then he stopped behind the next dwelling. Following behind was the shadowy creature which possessed him. Its eyes glowed red like furnace coal, its body walking directly behind the giant on stilted, bony limbs. It began to clack its teeth, while the giant continued his call.

"Come out to play, Little Foot."

If he comes closer, will he know I'm here?

"Come out to play, Little Foot."

The giant moved to the next house, the night monster following.

They stopped again.

"Come out and we will play in the blood!"

Oliver was in shock, unable to leave the window. Soon it would hear his heartbeat, his thoughts, and then it would come inside and…

Then some of the windows began to light.

A door opened, casting light into the alley. A woman hung out the open door. "What are you doing out there?"

Then a man came out another door.

The giant suddenly looked small.

"Are you stealing?" the man yelled. "Get the hell out of here!"

More lights, more people.

The giant withdrew.

Oliver slept by the window.

***

Chapter 3 – Coyote Winds

I

March 26, 1879 - Telegraph Office
Fort Saskatchewan, NWT

Mr. Watts had been wrong. It would be over two months before the NWMP from Fort Saskatchewan arrived in St. Albert. The telegraph that was sent by Mr. Watts was acknowledged by an operator named Mr. Jenkins, a fifty-five-year-old retired artillery officer who received the alarming telegram.

....

Telegram
St Albert – Fort Sask

Urgent- Stop-Commanding Officer - WD Jarvis -Stop- Northwest Mounted Police -stop- Requesting immediate assistance – stop- Swift Runner - former guide for NWMP claims family perished from starvation -stop- This claim is highly suspect -stop- Also admits to cannibalism -stop- Awaiting your prompt response -stop- Father Hippolyte Leduc – Catholic Mission - St Albert -stop-

-stop- Message received-stop-

Will advise NWMP of request personally -stop- Operator Jenkins-stop-

-stop-Thanks-stop- Operator Watts -stop-

....

The message couldn't wait for morning. Mr. Jenkins dressed and turned the Open sign to Closed. He stuffed the telegram into his coat pocket, locked the door, and started out for the fort.

He was walking against the cutting wind.

He felt strange, not himself, winded.

I must be coming down with something.

It was getting dark.

Murder, he thought. *Cannibalism.*

He heard coyotes yipping in the distance and imagined them dining on the dead, which sent a shiver through him. His left arm had been aching all afternoon. Mr. Jenkins stuffed both hands into his coat pockets and clutched the note in his right. That made his arm slightly better.

The wind was howled..

He saw torches burning at the fort.

Five more minutes.

The coyotes were yipping again.

They're getting closer.

Suddenly, he couldn't breathe. Something was crushing his chest. He was being suffocated by an invisible force. Instinctively, he pulled both hands from his pockets, the telegram still in his right hand. Then his heart stopped. Mr. Jenkins was dead before his face hit the dirt, his spectacles falling off. The fingers clutching the telegraph opened, and the message was snatched and swept away into the night currents.

They found him three hours later.

The coyotes had found him first.

II
April 12, 1879
East of Egg Lake, NWT

—

The sun shone brightly and coupled with a western breeze, was transforming the landscape. Winter snow had contracted into dirty white islands floating on a terrain of decay and rebirth.

It was the Cree who approached the NWMP, speaking with a patrolling constable named Ronald D. Griffith.

Griffith was dark-haired, handsome, with deep-set hazel eyes, and a thin nose over a thick chevron mustache on an oval face. He was long and lanky man, standing over six feet tall.

Griffith had been dispatched with a civilian writer and interpreter fluent in Cree named Keith Kaplan. Kaplan was balding, dog-faced, with a frame hinting that he had once been a portlier man. He had lived among the Cree and knew much about their language and customs. He had also lived with the Algonquins in Upper Canada and understood much of their mother tongue as well.

They were on the plains east of Egg Lake.

"There they are." Griffith pointed after spotting them on horseback, roughly 100 yards away. The Cree party consisted of two young men and an elder named Chogan.

Chogan raised his hand.

Griffith and Kaplan raised theirs.

Chogan turned back to the other two, said something, and then rode in to meet them. Griffith had met Chogan when he brought Swift Runner back to Egg Lake. He had never spoken with the man, but they had seen each other's face.

Chogan was a hard-looking man, weathered by living in harsh elements. Griffith thought he was in his sixties, but he was really forty-eight years old. His skin had faded gray and was etched in wrinkles—on his forehead, around his mouth and nose, and at the edges of his eyes. In stark contrast, his brown eyes didn't have a single smudge of fog making him a formidable presence.

"*Atamiskâtowin*," Chogan called.

"He's saying, 'Hello,'" Kaplan said.

"Hello back." Griffith smiled and nodded to the approaching Chogan. "This is where you earn your pay, Mr. Kaplan."

"Indeed," Kaplan said, and to Chogan, "*Atamiskâtowin*."

Chogan parked his horse in front of both men, almost nose to nose.

"How can we help you?" Griffith asked.

Kaplan translated.

Chogan and Kaplan conversed in Cree.

During the exchange, Kaplan gave Griffith three troubled glances. Midway through the talk, Chogan looked at Griffith and said something

Griffith was sure was about him. When they finished Kaplan said, "He says he's worried about Swift Runner's family."

"Swift Runner? Why is he worried about his family?"

"He says, 'Swift Runner has gone *wihitikow*.'" Kaplan said.

"*Wihitikow*?" Griffith asked.

"It means 'windigo.' It's a—" Kaplan started.

"I know what a windigo is." Griffith nodded toward Chogan, who was listening to their conversation. "What else did he say?"

"He says, 'Swift Runner was possessed by the windigo spirit when you sent him to Egg Lake.'"

"I never sent him to Egg Lake. I was ordered to bring him back."

"I think he means the NWMP."

Griffith remembered.

The Mounties had locked Swift Runner up temporarily for several nuisance offenses of public drunkenness and disturbing the peace in the town of Fort Saskatchewan. Swift was a mean drunk, angry and aggressive, even to women and children. On one binge, it took four officers to get him under control. These benders always ended with the Mounties locking him in a cell until he sobered up. By morning, Swift would be back to his usual self, well-spoken, mild in his words.

The incident that saw him sent back to Egg Lake was an altercation with another trapper. Griffith couldn't remember his name, but the argument between the two had ended with Swift threatening to shoot the trapper and storming off. He returned ten minutes later with his rifle and to show he meant it he fired the weapon, but it went wild. There was a short standoff, and after some tense negotiation, Swift Runner surrendered and was arrested.

He was sent back to Egg Lake.

Kaplan broke Griffith's thoughts.

"He says, 'Someone was bringing whisky to Swift Runner from the outside. He would leave the camp, then after drinking, come back like a rabid bear and run amok.'"

"Amok?"

"It's not a word they use, but close enough." Kaplan said.

Chogan said something else, and when he finished, there were tears in his eyes. He wiped at them before they could spill over.

Kaplan translated, “He says, ‘He was a good man, a good husband, a good father, a good hunter, but the *wihitikow* and the whisky have turned him bad.’”

Griffith nodded at Chogan. “I understand.”

He had used Swift Runner to track a couple different criminals. Horse thieves mostly, but also a killer who had escaped from custody. He had even saved Griffith life, after a thief tried to turn his own gun on him.

Griffith had instantly liked Swift and looked forward to working with him. Unfortunately, that had been another life, before the whisky. “He’s a different man when he drinks.”

“Where are they now? At Egg Lake?” Griffith asked.

“*Wepinikewin*,” Chogan said among other words.

Kaplan nodded. “They banished them.”

“Them?” Griffith asked.

“His entire family.”

“How many?”

Kaplan asked.

When Chogan spoke, he had tears in his eyes again but also anger.

Kaplan said, “His mother, brother, wife, and five children.”

“Eight people?” Griffith raised his voice.

“Nine if you include Swift Runner.”

“Why the hell would they do that?” Griffith frowned.

Chogan asked Kaplan what Griffith said and kept his eyes locked on Griffith while Kaplan translated.

His response was short.

“What did he say?” Griffith asked.

“He says, ‘Swift Runner wasn’t just poisoned by White man’s whisky when you brought him back. *Wihitikow* was already in him; he was already haunted by the spirit.’”

Griffith grunted in disbelief. “How could you turned them all out?”

Kaplan repeated that to Chogan.

He glared at Griffith, a scowl on his face, the tears gone. He spat each word out like venom. The tirade went on for almost a minute. Chogan never looked at Kaplan once; this was directly at Griffith.

Angry, the elder turned his horse and rode back up to the waiting Cree. He shouted at them once more in Cree, and they rode off.

"What did he say?" Griffith asked.

"He said, 'Swift Runner has windigo sickness and would have infected his family and their people. We had no choice but to make them all leave.'"

"It sounded like he said a lot more than that, Mr. Kaplan."

"He did." Kaplan removed a pipe, packed a little tobacco in it, and struck a match.

"Well, why didn't you repeat it?"

"Because you wouldn't have liked his words, Constable Griffith." Kaplan lit his pipe and puffed.

Griffith pulled out a cigar, wet the leaf with his lips, bit off the end, and placed it in his mouth. He lit the cigar, watching Chogan and his two men ride away. Puffing, he said, "I expect I wouldn't." He pulled out a tiny book and scribbled a few notes down.

Chogan's party disappeared behind a cluster of trees.

"Let's go," Griffith said.

They turned their horses to the east and for a while, they rode in silence at a slow trot, dry grass crunching beneath their hooves.

"Mr. Kaplan?"

"Yes, Constable Griffith."

"Why don't you tell me what the old blackbird said."

"Ah, you do know some Cree, Constable Griffith." Kaplan smiled.

"Not much." He took a puff on his cigar. "Chogan means 'blackbird,' I understand that much. I don't understand how they could kick Swift Runner's wife and family out."

"*Wihitikow mohtêwiskâw*, Constable Griffith. They're afraid of the windigo plague."

"Windigo plague… Indian horse puck, Mr. Kaplan. Whisky is Swift Runner's nemesis, not Indian spirits."

"There have been many reports, all across the land."

"It's superstition; he's probably gone crazy. Bad whisky or cabin fever."

"They don't live in cabins, Constable Griffith."

"You get the gist, Mr. Kaplan. Now, are you going to tell me what he said?" Griffith put the cigar in his mouth and adjusted himself on the saddle.

"He blames us for Swift Runner. He thinks we poisoned his mind with our ways."

"Our ways?"

Kaplan pointed his pipe at Constable Griffith. "He said that White hunters killed off their food supply and poisoned the meat. The bison are gone. The deer are gone. Whisky has turned their men and women into slaves. Disease is everywhere. The *wihitikow* seeps from Mother Earth, drawn to the fragility and suffering."

"Fragility and suffering?" Griffith chuckled. "You're telling me that Indian said all that, Mr. Kaplan?"

Kaplan grinned. "I may have used a little artistic license."

"A little?" Griffith smiled, and then his face became serious. "I don't disagree with what the old Indian says, but I'm a servant of the queen and have a job that doesn't include politicking. As to the nonsense about *wihitikow*, that's what it is, Mr. Kaplan. Indian superstition."

"It isn't just the Cree who believe in the windigo. The Algonquins have reported similar cases in Upper Canada. There have been reports of windigo madness from coast to coast. I wouldn't disregard what the Cree elder said."

Griffith smiled. "Nonsense."

"Then what is it?" Kaplan asked.

"We're all animals, Mr. Kaplan, and animals will eat their own in times of starvation. It's desperation, hunger, and madness… This is starvation, not windigo plague."

"Hardly reassuring, Constable Griffith."

"Not meant to reassure; it's just the reality."

Kaplan smiled, but it was a grim smile.

Before coming to the prairies, Kaplan had become a believer when he saw a windigo spirit in an Algonquin village. He didn't speak of it in the circles of White men like himself. They would have laughed at him. Though he liked Griffith, his views were very black and white, and so that story remained untold. "Are you going to report it?"

"I'll do one better, Mr. Kaplan." Griffith tapped his cigar.

"And what would that be?"

"I'm going to investigate it."

Mr. Kaplan chuckled.

III

In the shadow of the accusations, the NWMP led three separate parties in search of Swift Runner, his family, and the camp. For weeks, they combed the region north of Fort Saskatchewan, but the prairies were so vast and the forest dense, and though they searched, there was no sign of them. A return trip was made to Egg Lake, but Chogan had taken ill and, fearing tuberculosis, the camp was quarantined.

Griffith and Kaplan were turned away.

They continued searching without evidence of any crime. It seemed inconceivable to many of the officers in the NWMP who knew Swift Runner. He had a problem with the whisky.

But murder? Cannibalism?

There was speculation that Swift Runner and his family had just moved on. They had been banished from Egg Lake, so why stay? It was a good theory, but there was no evidence to support it.

The search for Swift Runner and his family wasn't the only business of the NWMP. Therefore, the missing was just that, until a man came by horseback to Fort Saskatchewan from St. Albert.

IV
May 26, 1879
Superintendent WD Jarvis' Office
Fort Saskatchewan, NWT

Sergeant Richard Steele was waiting to see his commanding officer, Superintendent WD Jarvis. He was being called in about the investigation into Swift Runner. Steele had come to the NWMP after a distinguished career in the military. His two brothers, Samuel and Godfrey, also served in the newly formed national police, but at different forts.

Steele was standing at ease by the door. He had been here for almost a half hour after being summoned. Inside, Superintendent Jarvis was speaking with Sub-Inspector Gagnon and a civilian he didn't recognize. Steele looked out across the yard, pondering what they were talking about.

The door opened.

Gagnon stuck his head out. "Sergeant, we're ready for you."

"Yes, sir." Steele came to attention and wheeled right and through the door, which Gagnon held open. He marched up to the desk, came to attention, and saluted Jarvis.

"At ease, Sergeant," Jarvis said.

"Yes, sir." Steele went from attention to at ease. His boot cracked against the wood floor. His eyes remained firmly to the front, breathing controlled, chest out, a monument of discipline.

"Stand easy, Sergeant," Jarvis ordered. Steele relaxed and brought his eyes to meet his commanding officer. "Sergeant, we have reports that Swift Runner has been sighted in St. Albert."

"St. Albert?" Steele raised an eyebrow. "I thought we were looking for him in the north, sir?"

"We were." Jarvis sighed. "Fill him in, Severe."

Sub-Inspector Severe Gagnon looked to the civilian.

He was a bald, stout man, holding his hat in two hands and looked like a farmer. "Sergeant, this is Mr. Robert Boseman."

Boseman rose and held out a hand.

Steele shook the man's hand. "Good day, sir."

Gagnon said, "Mr. Boseman, could you please tell Sergeant Steele what you told Superintendent Jarvis and myself?"

"Why, yes, sir," Boseman said to Jarvis, then to Steele, "The man you're looking for, the Indian tracker they call Swift Runner, he's in St. Albert."

"St. Albert? How long?"

"He showed up end of March, said his family had perished from starvation. Seen him two or three times, myself. He didn't look like no man who was starving to death. There's been stirrings that he might have killed his family. I was asked by Father Leduc to contact you and find out why you haven't come to St. Albert to investigate this? He sent a telegram at the end of March."

"We don't know anything about a telegram," Jarvis said.

Gagnon interrupted. "We checked on that. Mr. Jenkins was found dead between the fort and the telegraph office. We now think there is a possibility that he may have been bringing the message by hand."

Steele remembered. One of his subordinates, Constable Griffith, had mentioned the scene, which had been bloody, as the coyotes had dined on Mr. Jenkins for a few hours before he was found. "It's been almost two months. Why didn't the father send another message?" Steele asked.

"Father Leduc has been on a pilgrimage to British Columbia," Boseman said. "He hasn't been in St. Albert since the beginning of April and only returned yesterday."

"I see. Please continue, Mr. Boseman," Steele said.

"He's luring Indian kids, and there were reports that he's done it to some local kids too," Boseman said.

"Luring them for what purpose?" Steele asked.

"I don't know, Sergeant, but Father Leduc said to express that Swift Runner is a very real threat to the locals."

"Threat how?"

Superintendent Jarvis interrupted. "Sergeant Steele, it would seem the Cree are just as afraid and have also requested our help. They fear Swift Runner, not just for what he's done, but for what they think he will do."

"Yes, sir."

"I think there's enough credible evidence to bring Swift Runner in for questioning. I think we need to find his camp and investigate the allegations," Jarvis said.

Gagnon got up and placed a hand on Boseman's shoulder. "I'm afraid you'll have to excuse us, Mr. Boseman. You can return to St. Albert and reassure the good father that we'll be sending investigators by the morning. But first, there are legal and logistical matters to attend."

"Yes, I understand." Boseman stood, and Gagnon led him to the door.

"Mr. Boseman," Sergeant Steele said.

"Yes?" Boseman turned to face him.

"We'll probably be in St. Albert by noon tomorrow. That is all I want you to tell Father Leduc, and please, keep this in your strictest confidence. We don't want Swift Runner alerted and leaving the area. He'll do that if he knows we're coming, and that will make it harder to take him into custody."

"Yes, Sergeant, I'll only tell Father Leduc." Boseman was at the door.

"Thank you for coming all this way to alert us," Steele said.

Superintendent Jarvis shook Boseman's hand. "We'll be along soon enough, Mr. Boseman."

"Thank you, Mr. Boseman," Gagnon said.

Boseman nodded and smiled.

Gagnon closed the door.

V

With Boseman gone, Jarvis rose and shook Sergeant Steele's hand. "Richard, it's good to see you."

"Thank you, sir." Steele grinned. He, Jarvis, and Gagnon had history. If there were two men Steele felt he could trust, it was these men.

Jarvis said to Gagnon, "Pour us a drink, Severe, and we'll discuss this nasty business."

"Coming up." Gagnon opened the liquor cabinet and poured them each a drink. "How are your brothers, Richard?"

"Last I spoke to them, they were well," Steele said.

Superintendent Jarvis said, "I've heard good things about Sam and Godfrey. More about Sam, though. He's making quite a name for himself."

"Sam is certainly getting the assignments," Steele agreed.

Sergeant Sam Steele had recently been assigned to meet with Chief Sitting Bull. The Sioux leader and his band had come into the Northwest Territories to escape the U.S. Cavalry after the Battle of Little Bighorn. Sam had been there, along with U.S. Army Major General Alfred Howe Terry. Both Steele and Terry had tried to convince Sitting Bull to leave the NWT and return to the United States. Though they had been unsuccessful, the story had afforded his brother some celebrity.

Gagnon came over and handed them both a drink.

"To Her Majesty, Queen Victoria," Jarvis said.

"Her Majesty," Gagnon said.

"The queen," Steele said.

They raised their glasses and clinked.

Then there was a minute of silence, each man pondering the crime they were now sworn to investigate. Jarvis took a sip and said, "My God, cannibalism."

"It's everywhere," Gagnon said.

Steele said nothing. Severe Gagnon was right. It was everywhere and the truth was, the government was starving the people off their traditional hunting grounds.

"Richard, you'll need to ride in the morning," Jarvis said.

"Yes, sir."

"This could be a rumor." Gagnon sipped his drink.

"One can only hope," Jarvis said.

Steele nodded but doubted it was rumor.

"Horrible business, Richard," Jarvis said. "Take the complement of men you think will be necessary to arrest Swift Runner." He turned to Gagnon. "Severe, what's the name of the corporal assigned to trial that new jail wagon?"

"Corporal Hood, sir," Gagnon said.

"Richard, you take Corporal Hood and his jail wagon for a ride."

"Jail wagon?"

"I keep forgetting the name," Jarvis said.

"They actually call it a Paddy wagon," Steele said.

"Odd name," Gagnon said.

"Nickname, sir. It started in England. There was usually an Irish driver, so they called it a Paddy," Steele added.

"I don't think Hood is Irish," Jarvis said.

"Yes, sir. Jail wagon it is." Steele chuckled.

"Richard, are you having me on?" Jarvis grinned.

"Just a little, sir," Steele said.

"You got anybody in mind, besides Hood?"

Steele did. "If possible, in addition to Corporal Hood, I would like Constables Ron Griffith, Fredericke Marois, and Daniel Crane."

"Why these men?" Gagnon asked.

Steele scratched his chin. "They're friendly faces. Griffith has prior knowledge and is closest to Swift Runner out of all of us. Marois would be second closest, and Crane third. Both Griffith and Marois were involved in the hunt for the Gypsy who robbed the dry goods. Swift Runner killed the robber. Griffith was also the one who talked Swift Runner down after the incident with the rifle last year. Griffith is a good man. I trust his judgment and his experience. Same with Marois and Crane."

"Isn't Griffith getting promoted?" Gagnon smiled.

"Oh?" Steele raised his eyebrows.

"You never heard that, Sergeant." Gagnon winked.

"Of course not, sir," Steele replied with a smile.

"Take whoever you need." Jarvis placed his glass on the desk. "Ugly business, Richard, and such business draws negative attention, so be discreet and quick."

"Yes, sir."

***

Chapter 4 - Dog and Pony Show

I

May 26, 1879
Fort Saskatchewan, NWT

After the meeting, Steele went out into the day and saw the men lined up for the mess hall. He spotted a corporal named Bagley, and called, "Hey, Bags, do you know where Corporal Hood is?"

"He's playing with his toy, Sarge." Bagley had thick, dark hair, an oval face, and was of average build. "Behind the stable, I suspect."

Steele spotted Griffith and Marois in the lineup.

"You two. After chow, come down to the stables for a briefing," Steele ordered. "Either of you know where Crane is?"

"Already inside eating, Sergeant," Marois said.

"Make sure you grab him and get him to the briefing. I'm going to get Corporal Hood. Let's say, 1830. That'll give me a chance for a bite before we get this dog and pony show organized."

"Yes, Sergeant," both Griffith and Marois said.

"Enjoy your chow, see you at 1830." Steele marched off toward the stables.

Marois said to Griffith, "A dog and pony show, *mon ami*?"

"It must be about Swift Runner," Griffith said.

Marois was of average build, but he was blond with pale blue eyes and wore a pencil-thin mustache that didn't extend past the edges of his upper lip. Upon their first meeting, Crane had remarked, "You're so bloody handsome it's sickening. You going to leave any ladies for us?" Although Griffith was his best friend, Marois liked Crane's sense of humor. Crane was right. Marois's good looks, coupled with his French charm, thrilled many of the ladies in and around Fort Saskatchewan.

Griffith and Marois where shuffling up the line when Griffith spotted Crane coming out the door. Danny Crane was gauntly tall, dark-haired, had gray eyes, a crooked nose, and thin red lips on an acne-pocked, oval face.

Griffith called, "Danny!"

Crane searched the lineup, walked over, and said, "Hey, what's going on?"

"You're cordially invited to an orders group with Sergeant Steele at the stable at 1830 hours," Griffith said.

"What is it all about?" Crane asked.

"Dog and pony shows," Marois chirped.

"As I suspected." Crane laughed, but he was shifting around uncomfortably.

"We don't know what they have going. It might be about Swift Runner," Griffith said.

"Nothing like a good *mystère*," Marois added.

Crane made another uncomfortable shift. "I'll see you there. I gotta take a shit." He wandered off with some haste.

"I hope that isn't because of something he ate," Griffith said.

Crane was now running.

"Enjoy your shit!" Marois called.

II
1830 Hours
Fort Saskatchewan, NWT

The arresting party consisted of five men: Sergeant Steele, Corporal Hood, and Constables Griffith, Crane, and Marois. Steele met them in the stables with Corporal Hood. They stood in a semicircle, Sergeant Steele out front. He adjusted his cap and gazed around at each of them.

"A warrant has been issued for the arrest of Ka Ki Si Kutchin, who we know as Swift Runner. As of now, he is a suspect in the disappearance of his entire family."

There were mumblings.

Steele sighed. "I know that all of you know and have worked with Swift Runner. I know him as well and feel much as you do, but he's suspected of murder." He cleared his throat. "Multiple murders, in fact.

Gentleman, there are also accusations of the most horrific nature." He turned to Griffith. "Ron, tell them what that elder said."

Griffith cleared his throat, feeling all eyes upon him, and said, "The Cree think Swift Runner may also have resorted to cannibalism."

"He ate them?" Crane looked skeptical.

"Yes, that is what is alleged and backed up by a message from a priest in St Albert," Steele said. "The primary purpose of our mission is to arrest him. He's been seen in and around St. Albert. Witnesses put him there at the end of March and, according to one local, he's been tempting both Indian and town kids to go hunting with him." Steele's eyes moved from one man to the next. "Gentlemen, we may well have a homicidal lunatic on our hands." Then he paused again, letting them think about it, and finished with, "Any questions?"

"Did he get any?" Crane asked.

"Any? Kids? I don't know. The allegations aren't proven; therefore, it's up to us to investigate the matter. Our immediate mission is to ride to St. Albert, locate the accused, place him under arrest, and bring him back to Fort Saskatchewan for questioning. Any other questions?"

There were plenty.

Steele went over what they would do when they got to St. Albert. He also went over the sensitivity of it and to remember the last time they had tried placing irons on Swift Runner. "You know him the best, Ron," he said. "That's why I want you out front when we find him."

"Yes, Sergeant." Griffith felt a combination of guilt and pride at Sergeant Steele's words. There was a rumor of promotion in the springtime. Griffith tried to ignore the chatter. Mounties with time on their hands were as gossipy as a sewing circle. They had been placing him in leadership roles, and he was getting exemplary reports. A few weeks back, Superintendent Jarvis had said to him, "I'm hearing favorable things about you, Constable Griffith. Keep up the good work."

Steele interrupted his thoughts. "Reveille is at 0500 hours, breakfast is at 0515. I want you men formed up by 0550 and ready to ride." He turned to Hood. "Corporal Hood, we ride at 0600 hours. Stragglers will not be tolerated."

"There will be no stragglers, Sergeant," Hood assured him.

"Good. I'll leave you to it, Corporal." Steele left them to chat among themselves.

III
May 27, 1879
Fort Saskatchewan, NWT

The morning was cool, the sky smothered by iron gray clouds promising a prairie downpour. The only uncertainty was when it would happen. The men had breakfast together and formed up fifteen minutes before the departure time.

Crane and Marois were side by side on their horses. Behind them, Corporal Hood was doing a pre-trip inspection on the jail wagon and horse team. Beside him, on the rider's perch, hung a coiled bullwhip.

"Morning, Danny, Fred," Griffith said as he joined them.

"Morning, Ron," Crane said.

"Ron," Marois said, "I haven't seen you since breakfast. How have you been?"

"A lot can happen in ten minutes," Crane chimed in, and they both busted out laughing.

"You two are hysterical." Griffith rode past them and to the wagon. He gazed down at Corporal Hood, who was hunkered down, checking the front wheel. Hood was a thirtyish, stout, square-headed man with a face that was all business. His blond hair was brushed with streaks of gray.

Griffith asked, "You need help with anything, Corporal?"

"Nah, I'm ready to roll, but thanks just the same." Hood pulled a rag from his pocket, wiped his hands, stood, and adjusted his uniform.

"Quite a beast to be pulling across the countryside," Griffith said.

"In England, they call it a Paddy wagon," Hood said. "Genius invention, if you ask me."

"It's better than putting a prisoner on a horse," Griffith agreed. "A man on a horse can get up to all sorts of nonsense."

"Indeed. A bit more upkeep than a horse, though. You gotta keep them axles well-greased and the locks and chains well oiled." Hood smiled a little, clearly proud of his charge. He looked past Griffith and said, "Here comes Sergeant Steele. You best get into formation, Ron."

Griffith turned his head and saw Steele. "Best get, indeed." He moved his horse, Gunner, past Marois and Crane, both grinning at him like kids. "Knobs."

They snickered.

NWMP horses were local breeds, mostly brown and white. Gunner was a gray mustang gelding, just over fifteen hands, with black ears and mane, cool dark eyes, and a pink snout marked by white streaks that looked like they were painted on with an artist's brush. His tail, also gray, had a silky, corn shade causing it to shine like his overall coat.

"Good morning, Ron. We ready to go?" Steele said.

"Morning, Sergeant. Ready when you are."

"Excellent." Steele aligned his horse with Griffith's and yelled over his shoulder. "Corporal Hood, do you have the pride of the Northwest Mounted Police ready to travel?"

"Yes, Sergeant," the corporal called back.

"Outstanding! Keep your spacing," Steele said. "Constable Crane, the wagon will be slower, so you keep an eye on it, and if you have to slow down, we'll follow suit by keeping an eye on you."

"Yes, Sergeant," Crane said.

Steele waved his arm, signaling. "Move out!"

Steele and Griffith began to lead the way, a space of twenty feet between each pair of horsemen. Corporal Hood and the jail wagon rolled thirty feet behind Marois and Crane. They jockeyed toward St. Albert on a still developing road that connected the communities. Steele estimated that they would arrive in St. Albert before noon. The terrain between the two places was relatively flat, but the road gave way to open ground as they traversed around the Sturgeon River.

Two hours later...

Griffith looked back over his shoulder.

"Lagging?" Steele asked.

"They are so, but not too bad."

"To tell you the truth, Ron, I'm more worried about them storm clouds," Steele said. "They bust open and this will be a miserable ride."

"Could it be more miserable?" Griffith asked.

"Look, I like Swift Runner as well. We're on an errand that is indeed miserable, but we're the law in this land and bound by duty," Steele said.

"Yes," Griffith agreed, but there was sadness in his heart.

"Maybe we'll collect him and get back before those clouds bust and piss all over us?" Steele winked at Griffith.

"I had no idea you were such an optimist, Sergeant." Griffith winked back.

"Some might say…" Then there was a plop on his shoulder and another, and Steele muttered, "Well, shit."

The sky unburdened itself in bone-drenching cascades of rain, soaking them and turning the road into sludge. Corporal Hood's Paddy wagon fell farther behind. The spoked wheels dragged the muck like an anchor, slowing the horse team's progress.

They slogged on for another half hour.

"They're falling way back," Griffith said.

Steele pulled back on his reins, and the horse halted, sliding slightly in the mud.

Griffith halted beside him.

"I wasn't keen on dragging that thing to St. Albert, but here we are." He motioned to Marois and Crane and waved his arm in a circular gesture.

They saw the signal and rode in.

When Marois and Crane joined them, Steele was watching Hood struggle. "We're going to give those horses a break until the rain blows over."

"Don't you mean 'if,' Sergeant?" Crane kidded.

"That's exactly what I meant." Steele pointed. "That stand of trees right there will do just fine as a harbor. Constable Marois, you go back and give Hood a hand, and we'll get things set up here."

"Yes, Sergeant," Marois said. He rode back to help Hood.

The rest dismounted and led their horses into the dense forest, finding relief under the canopy. They tied them off to a fallen tree.

"Hey Crane! See if you can't find some dry wood and get a fire going," Steele said.

"Yes, Sergeant," Crane responded.

Griffith was looking at the map.

"How far?" Steele looked down at the map.

"I think we're here," Griffith said, pointing.

"I agree."

"It will probably take us another three hours," Griffith suggested.

"Unless it snows."

Griffith snickered.

They set up a camp, stringing a couple tarps in the tree branches overhead to offer the horses some relief. Crane stood up from the fire, which had begun to crackle and spit, and said, "Just what the doctor ordered."

"That was quick." Steele hunkered down, warming his hands in front of the flames licking the outside of the stacked wood.

"I have a secret weapon, Sergeant," Crane said.

"Huh?" Steele looked up.

Crane reached in his pocket, produced a shiny flask, and spun off the cap. He offered it to Steele. "A taste to get the wet cold out of your bones, Sergeant?"

"I have my own." Steele produced a flask.

"This is homemade." Crane held up the flask.

Steele leaned in to give it a sniff and immediately recoiled. "Oh, my Jesus."

"It's got a bite," Crane said.

"Bite? It smells like paint thinner."

"Great for starting fires." Crane capped the flask. They looked at Griffith, who smirked and produced his own identical flask.

"It's a little early in the morning," Griffith said.

"A rum ration's worth won't impair us," Crane said.

The fire was crackling away, radiating heat against the cold.

"As the ranking NCO, I say we wait until Hood and Marois get here," Steele said. They nodded putting away their flasks, and warmed themselves around the fire.

Ten minutes later, Marois led the way as Hood's marvel of modern law enforcement trailed through the mire behind an exhausted horse team. Griffith showed Marois where to tie up his horse. The team pulling the wagon couldn't be moved to cover. To do so would have meant disconnecting and reconnecting the team's harnesses and gear.

By happenstance or divine intervention, the rain stopped almost the instant Corporal Hood dismounted the wagon.

Hood looked up and saluted. "Thank you, Lord," he said. He marched across the field and into the trees to the makeshift camp.

"You know what that is there, Constable Griffith?" Steele nudged.

"What's that, Sergeant?"

"That is what a career corporal looks like." He chuckled.

"And proud of it, Sergeant." Hood grinned and leaned into the fire, warming his hands; he was drenched. "Thank goodness the rain stopped."

"This'll warm you up." Steele removed his flask, uncapped it, and offered a nip to Hood, who raised a toast. "To the marvels of modern law enforcement. I best not hear a snicker or a snark."

They erupted with laughter and more flasks came out.

"Constable Crane!"

"Yes, Sergeant?"

"Give us a taste of that paint thinner."

"Aye, Sergeant."

Steele took the flask, looked at his men, had a shot, and stepped back. He made a strange face and there was laughter, then he pulled out his own flask and took a sip of rum. "Constable Crane, that is the most flammable concoction I have ever tasted."

The flasks were put away.

The clouds broke up and rolled to the west, replaced by sunshine and a breeze, drying things up a bit.

"Still going to be a shit ride," Griffith said.

"Better than rain," Steele said.

Crane asked, "You think Swift Runner did it?"

Steele took a deep breath, looked around at his men, and said, "I think it's highly probable. As to the cannibalism accusation, I don't rightly know."

"*Mais comment?* How could he…" Marois's face was nightmarish with wonder. He turned to Griffith. "We worked with Swift. Shared food and camp."

"If he did what they said, he's gone mad," Griffith said.

Hood snickered. "I've seen a fox chew off its own leg to get out of a trap. These Indians are uncivilized. They're like wild animals that ain't been tamed yet."

Crane said, "You don't have to be Indian to turn on your own. Remember that group of settlers in California that got cut off in the mountains and ate their own?"

"Donner Pass," Steele said. "Remember?" He chuckled. "That was a long time ago. That nasty piece of business happened in the late forties. I was just a toddler, while all of you were still riding around in your daddies' balls."

This brought plenty of laughs.

"I'll tell you one thing," Hood said with a sly grin. "If we ever get cut off in the mountains, I ain't eating you, Crane. You look like tougher chewing than woodpecker lips."

Steele let out a barrage of guffaws, setting the rest of them off. When it was over, they were quiet for a spell and Marois said, "It feels like we're going to arrest a friend."

"Yeah, I know, that's exactly how it feels," Griffith said.

Crane nodded in agreement.

"I don't feel nothing. He ain't my friend," Hood said.

"How we feel is irrelevant to the law," Steele reminded.

"*Bien sûr*," Marois said.

"Yes, of course," Crane said.

Griffith said nothing.

IV
Two Years Earlier…

Griffith couldn't remember the store owner's name, and that made him feel guilty, but he remembered that day because he hit the ground running. He was posted to Fort Saskatchewan from Fort Macleod, which was over 300 miles to the south. He was riding in when saw Marois riding out to meet him.

"Well, there's a sight!" Griffith laughed and stuck out his hand.

Marois took it and they shook vigorously. "Welcome to Fort Saskatchewan, *mon ami*."

"I'm so happy to see you, Fred." Griffith smiled ear to ear.

"*Moi aussi, mon ami.*" Marois smiled back. "I rode out here because the old man wants to see you immediately. We're going out on a patrol."

"What happened?"

"Armed robbery and assault. A tramp came into town and robbed the dry goods store," Marois said. "He beat up the store owner with his own cashbox."

"How bad is he?"

"He'll live. He lost a few teeth and his jaw is busted. Nose too."

"Who is leading the patrol?"

"You are, *mon ami.*"

"Me? I just got here." Griffith laughed.

"*Oui.* You're the senior constable. The old man wants to see you right away."

They turned their horses and rode in toward the fort at a gallop. When they got to the stable, they dismounted, and Griffith straightened out his uniform. "How is it here, Fred?"

"The food isn't bad. The leadership is good. But winter is a cold, heartless bitch. No warm breezes in February up here, *mon ami*, just bitter cold. That, I miss most from Fort Macleod."

"What's the old man like?"

"He's fair. I don't think the higher ups care for him much, but he's good to the men. One of Steele brothers is being posted here as well."

"Which one? Can't be Sam."

"Not Sam. I don't know which."

"I guess I better go see him, then."

"We'll be waiting."

Griffith started for the CO's office.

Marois went to ready the patrol.

V

The meeting with the CO was a brief affair. Superintendent Jarvis was at his desk when Griffith entered the office, came to attention, and saluted. "Constable Griffith reporting for duty, sir."

"At ease, and stand easy, Constable," Superintendent Jarvis said.

Griffith stood at ease, then relaxed and looked at the commanding officer.

Superintendent Jarvis was an average-sized man. His face was egg-shaped and he had receding, short brown hair streaked with gray. His most distinguishing feature was a thick, brown mustache that curtained a gray goatee, which extended two inches below his chin.

"Welcome to Fort Saskatchewan, Constable Griffith," Jarvis said.

"Thank you, sir."

"Normally, I'd be a bit more formal in welcoming you, but as you've no doubt heard, there's been a robbery, and I'm shorthanded, and although you just rode in, you're the senior constable."

"Yes, sir," Griffith said.

"Did Constable Marois fill you in?" Jarvis asked.

"Yes, sir."

"Good, now you know as much as I do. Get on the trail, Constable."

"Yes, sir!" Griffith came to attention.

"Dismissed."

When Griffith reached the stables, Marois was waiting with another Mountie and an Indigenous man. Marois pointed to the Mountie. "This is Constable Serge Langois."

Langois was a thin man with a narrow face decorated with wire-rimmed spectacles that made him look like a banker. There was a gloss of ginger in his light brown hair.

"*Bonjour, monsieur.*" Langois stuck out his hand and they shook.

"Ron Griffith," he said and added, "Two Frenchmen in my patrol. Whatever will we talk about?"

Marois replied, "Well, *mon ami*, we could talk about food, music, art, or French culture as a whole."

"Yeah, yeah," Griffith said chuckling.

They laughed and Marois continued, "Constable Griffith, this is Swift Runner, our Indian guide."

Griffith took in Swift Runner. He was a big, square-faced man, barrel-chested, with immense forearms and hands. When their eyes met, he was armed with a friendly smile. "Good day, Constable Griffin."

"Constable Griffith," he corrected with a smile.

Swift Runner frowned. "I beg your pardon, Constable Griffith, my English is still not yet fully learned."

"No pardon required." Griffith tipped a nod. "Your English isn't bad, and if you keep using it, it will just get better."

Swift Runner's smile grew, and he said, "Thank you."

Griffith nodded, then turned his attention to the others. "All right, gentlemen, I was briefed by the old man, and as I understand it, our fugitive robbed the dry goods store and made off with the cashbox? So, what else didn't he tell me?"

"He's got one eye, and he's gone east, Ron. We have a witness account he's on foot too. So, he won't get far," Marois said.

"He's got a two-hour head start," Langois said.

"Unless he goes into the woods." Griffith was watching Swift Runner. "What do you think, Swift Runner?"

Swift Runner smiled. "There are White men who live along the path he went. Men who camp and are travelers?"

"Tramps," Marois suggested.

"Yes, tramps. I know of this man with one eye. He lives in the woods with bad people. People who take what is not theirs," Swift Runner said.

"How many in the group?" Griffith lit a cigar.

"Five men, two women. There were six men, but one man left the group," Swift Runner said.

"Do you know the location of this camp?"

"Yes, I sometimes hunt near there. The one-eyed man, we crossed paths many mornings ago, maybe twelve or fourteen. I was hunting for game so when he saw me, he also saw my rifle. He was walking toward me when he passed, and he stared right at me. I did not speak to him or bring my eyes to meet his, but I was glad to have my gun."

"Why?" Griffith asked.

Swift Runner adjusted himself on the saddle. "I felt him thinking bad things against me."

"You felt?"

"Yes, I felt. I felt the same thing any creature feels when the predator is watching. I felt he wanted to hurt me."

"But he didn't?"

"No, but only because his friends were not around, and I had my rifle."

"Okay, Swift Runner, you lead the way, and we'll talk about it more on the trail," Griffith said.

"I will show you the place."

VI

The thief's name was Declan Gallagher. A decade before, three years into a ten-year sentence, Gallagher had escaped an Irish prison known as the Kilmainham Gaol, in Dublin. Then he stowed away on a ship bound for the New World. Since coming to Canada, Gallagher had robbed hundreds of people and killed five.

Presently, he was alternating between the road and the woods. He was thinking about the old man in the store who didn't want to give up the cashbox. The old prick had reached into his apron and offered him one dollar and a shilling.

Gallagher took the money. "Where's the rest?"

"There ain't no more. We work mostly on credit," the old guy said.

Gallagher didn't believe it. "Don't lie to me!" He slapped the old man.

"Stop, please, I… I… I'll get it for you," he said.

Gallagher hit him one more time. "Get it… Now!"

The old man fumbled out his keys with trembling hands, unlocked the padlock, and set it on the counter. He opened the cabinet, revealing satchels of tobacco and small sacks of tea and coffee. He pushed the coffee aside, exposing a small tin lockbox.

Gallagher snickered. "Credit, huh? You sneaky old prick. Bring it over here."

The old man removed the box and set it on the counter, all the while keeping his eyes on Gallagher.

Gallagher opened the box and counted the cash. There were nineteen new Canadian dollars and four shillings. He put the money into his pocket, came around the counter, and pointed with the gun. "Get down on your knees."

The slaps had turned the old guy's face was tomato red, but his eyes were still defiant, locked on Gallagher.

"What you looking at?"

"You got your money, now go," the old man said.

"I'll go when I fucking well please," Gallagher said and thought, *He's burning my face into his head.* He holstered his gun, picked up the cashbox, and smashed the old man in the face. There was a sound of metal and gristle colliding and cracking. The box had caught the old man across the bridge of his nose, turning on twin faucets of dark blood.

Then he hit him again. And again…

And he fled.

The old man was probably dead.

He had hit him plenty hard, broken his nose, knocked out his teeth, and smashed his skull.

Probably dead.

He should have hit him a few more times to make sure.

There was nothing he could do about it now.

Gallagher veered off the road and into the forest, and none too quickly. He heard men talking and horses snorting. They weren't that hard to spot. Three men on horseback approaching. Two were Mounties, clad in red jackets with buttoned fronts and pillbox hats. The third rider was an Indian who looked familiar to him, and he remembered him from a couple weeks back, when they met on the road.

I guess the old man isn't dead.

Gallagher was above them, fifty feet away, looking down from a berm where the southern wood line rose above the road. There were three of them, but he had the high-ground advantage. He cocked his handgun, thinking that if he'd had a rifle, he could pick them off in about five seconds.

Only forty feet away.

He would have to kill them all, because they would never stop looking, but he needed them closer.

He aimed and got ready.

VII

Swift Runner spotted the broken branches as they made their way down the road. There was also a footprint. Griffith and Swift Runner dismounted and studied the woods. Someone had gotten off the road in this spot.

"Was this the place you met him?" Griffith whispered.

"No, their camp is about three miles farther." Swift Runner stared at the tracks leading off the road and up a bank. Most of them were scuffles, as the snow was over their ankles, but one print was preserved. "That is his foot size, and this is his hunting ground."

"Hunting?"

"For people to steal from."

Griffith nodded. "Good eye, Swift Runner. I think I would have wandered right by."

"Thank you, Constable Griffith. Do you want me to follow the trail?" Swift Runner asked and that was when Griffith felt his first affection for the man. He was ready to go up that trail and lead the charge against an armed maniac thief because in this moment, he was one of them.

Griffith found this admirable and almost agreed, but instead said, "I have another idea."

"I hope it includes us," Marois said.

"What do you want to do, Ron?" Langois asked.

Griffith smiled. "I'm going up that trail, and you gentleman are going to follow the road. If he comes back my way, I'll run right into him."

"Sounds risky. What if he's waiting on the trail with a gun pointed on you?" Langois said.

"That's why you boys are going to keep going and draw that gun onto yourselves."

Marois laughed. "That is very thoughtful of you, *mon ami*."

"Can I come with you, Constable Griffith?" Swift Runner asked. "I am a good shot."

Griffith patted Swift Runner on the shoulder. "I bet you are, but I'm faster alone and will make less noise as one. Besides, I need you to take care of these two and keep them out of trouble."

"I will do that." Swift Runner mounted his horse.

Griffith tied his horse off. "You boys get moving." Then he went up the trail.

VIII

Gallagher trained the sight on the chest of one of the Mounties. That would be the order of the kill—both Mounties, then the Indian. He needed them just a little closer.

"Come on," he whispered under his breath.

He heard a click, and a voice say, "Lower that hammer, put the gun on the ground, and hands up."

He couldn't see who the man behind him was, but he felt the gun barrel against the back of his head.

"I didn't even hear yuh."

"You hear me now?" the man asked.

"Aye, yes, sir, I hear you loud and clear."

"Put the gun on the ground," the man ordered.

Gallagher lowered the hammer slowly, placed the weapon on the ground and raised his hands. Behind him, the man got closer and kicked the weapon down the embankment.

"Okay, I'm going to get you to stand up, and we're going to walk down to the road. My friends are down there, and they know about you. If you try to run or anything, they have orders to shoot." The barrel nudged him. "Understand?"

"Yeah." Gallagher nodded.

"Stand up and don't run."

Gallagher stood up, hands only raised at his sides.

"I have him, we're coming out!" the man behind him called.

One of the men called back, "Come on out!"

Gallagher felt a wave of anger roll through him. Why hadn't he gone the other way? Why had he put his gun down? They would hang him for the murder of the old man or the others, should they find out. And while he stewed in some cell waiting to be hung, it would be torture. He couldn't go back. He wouldn't. He wouldn't! Gallagher spun and grabbed the policeman's gun.

IX

The prisoner was in front of Griffith, and they were working their way down the slope. Then the prisoner turned and grabbed the barrel of Griffith's revolver, and the fight for life began.

The one-eyed man wasn't big; Griffith had at least six inches and about fifty pounds on him. But he had strong, vicelike hands that were twisting the revolver around and up.

Griffith tightened everything in his body and fought to regain control of the weapon, but the man was stronger and the barrel kept twisting, an inch at a time, coming up and almost aligned with his chest. Then, in the ball of four hands wrapped around that gun and each other, one of the prisoner's fingers was burrowing like a worm toward the trigger.

He's winning, Griffith thought desperately.

They grappled, and Griffith lost his footing and stumbled backward. Then the prisoner was over him and that finger was parting his fingers, and the gun was almost in line with Griffith's head. The burrowing finger found its way to Griffith's own finger on the trigger and began to hook around it and squeeze.

I don't want to die, Griffith thought, looking into that one green eye. "No," he said.

"Yes," Gallagher said, squeezing, and then his only good eye detonated like a hen's egg.

Griffith felt a yolky substance splatter his cheek and the pressure on his trigger finger released.

Then he heard the gunshot.

The man fell on him, hands relaxing.

Griffith pulled the gun out, pushing the man off, and scrambled like a crab out from under him. As he did this, he stared into the bloody cavern of the man's eye socket, and he shoved the body away. Griffith looked down the hill and saw Swift Runner lowering his rifle.

Marois and Langois looked shocked.

"You okay, Ron?" Langois called out.

Griffith touched his cheek, drew back his fingers, and saw a speck of blood. "I'm hit."

"What?" Marois jumped from his horse and scrambled up the bank.

Griffith remembered the eye flying into a panic, searching for a handkerchief, but there was nothing, and he cried, "Get it off me! Get it off!"

Then Marois was there, rag in hand, wiping his face. "It's gone. There wasn't much."

"You sure?" Griffith reached up, checking his cheek.

"Wait," Marois said. "Hold still."

Before Griffith could protest, Marois grabbed him and said, "Don't move." Then he used the handkerchief to scoop something off Griffith's shoulder and tossed both it and the hankie away.

"What was it?" Griffith asked.

"It was most of that dead guy's eye," Langois said. "Looked like a sparrow egg staring skyward."

"Ah, shit!" Griffith buckled over and threw up.

"*Ferme ta gueule*, Langois," Marois barked, patting Griffith on the back. "Get it out."

"Sorry about that, Ron," Langois apologized.

Griffith nodded, took a couple breaths, and wiped his mouth. "It's okay."

Swift Runner was there, rifle slung, looking down at Griffith and the dead man.

"Thank you, Swift Runner," Griffith said.

"I did not want to shoot him," Swift Runner said.

"I'm glad you did. You saved my life. Thank you," Griffith said and stuck out his hand.

Swift Runner took it and they shook. "You are welcome, Constable Griffith."

"Swift Runner, I'm in your debt."

"Maybe you will save my life someday, Constable Griffith."

"It would be my honor," Griffith said. "We're friends now. Please call me Ron."

"Others might think it disrespectful if I use your first name," Swift Runner said.

Griffith began to protest.

"I will call you Constable Ron," Swift said.

Langois said, "I'll go get your horse, Constable Ron." He went back to his horse, mounted up, and rode down the trail.

Marois searched the dead man's body as Griffith and Swift watched. He found the money stolen from the cashbox, but no identification. Gallagher had a sizeable knife still in its sheath.

"Was that the man you met?" Griffith asked.

"Yes, he was the one-eyed man." Swift Runner said.

"Now, he's the no-eyed man," Marois interrupted.

Having just escaped with his life, feeling like he had held his breath for too long, Griffith was the first to crack up. Laughter erupted from him with the zeal of baked bean flatulence. He laughed and buckled over, grabbed his breath, and then it came again.

He thought they must think him crazy, but that passed when first Marois, then Swift joined in the laughter. This went on for a couple minutes, and when it looked like they were getting it together, one or the other would start laughing again. The dark amusement faded to a lengthy disquiet between them, lasting until Langois returned with Griffith's horse.

"Guess we'll have to leave him here," Griffith said. "We'll have to bring back a wagon and collect the body."

"What if someone takes it?" Langois remarked.

"I can't see anyone stealing a dead body," Marois said.

They marked the spot and returned to Fort Saskatchewan. The next day, the body of the unknown thief named Declan Gallagher was collected and brought back to the Fort. The shooting was deemed justified, and he was buried in an unmarked grave.

The old man recovered and would die a year later from heart failure.

X

May 27, 1879
St. Albert, NWT

Corporal Hood waited on the outskirts while Sergeant Steele led the rest of his men into town. The red uniforms would already draw attention from every bystander, so they parked Hood and his marvel of modern law enforcement on the east side.

"I'll send someone back for you when we got him," Steele said.

"Okay, I'll be here twiddling my thumbs," Hood said.

They rode up the hill to the Catholic mission.

Griffith was thinking about the man who had saved his life and how he was here to arrest him for murder. He tried to be indifferent to it, to be a police officer first, but his heart was drowning in shame. He tried to be as detached as he had when he spoke with Mr. Kaplan after their encounter with Chogan. Griffith couldn't connect his friend, Swift Runner, to the crimes for which he was accused. Even with the whisky binges, even with the rampages.

They reached the mission, tied off their horses.

"I'm going up to see the father. Keep an eye for him." Sergeant Steele went up to the church and left them loitering by row of bushes.

"I can't believe were here to arrest Swift for murder," Crane said. "It feels odd, dreamy, not real."

"How you feeling about this, *mon ami*?" Marois asked.

"This?" Griffith asked back.

"You know, Ron."

"Yeah, I know." Griffith said, Swift's words echoing in the back of his mind. *"Maybe you will save my life someday."*

"Mon ami?"

"I'm fine, Fred." Griffith looked past Marois to the side of the Catholic mission, where the sisters were setting up tables, putting up pots, and stacking plates.

"What are they doing?" Crane asked.

"Meal line," Griffith said, "for the poor folk."

Marois pointed. "There's the sergeant and the father."

Sergeant Steele appeared in the doorway of the mission with Father Leduc, and they chatted. Griffith saw a large wooden cross tucked in the sash on Leduc's robe. He only saw half of Leduc's face, the other half obscured in the shadow of the doorway. Although none of them could hear the conversation, it was clear that the priest had a lot to say because his lips moved the most. Steele listened attentively and nodded. There were more nods and shaking of heads, and finally, Steele and Father Leduc looked their way and gave a wave.

They waved back.

Steele came down the path. "Father Leduc says he usually comes to the mission for a meal."

"Looks like they're setting up," Griffith said.

"We're going to draw attention out here. Let's tie up the horses and wait in the bushes to see if he shows up," Steele said. They moved the horses behind the church and tied them off. Then they positioned themselves in the foliage surrounding the church.

Twenty minutes passed.

"Here he comes," Steele whispered. "Alert the others."

***

Chapter 5 – The Arrest

I

May 27, 1879
Catholic Mission, St. Albert, NWT

Griffith whispered to Marois, "He's coming," who then passed it on to Crane. They followed Steele's pointing finger to Swift Runner, who was lumbering up the road toward them.

At least six others were also coming to the mission, but they kept their distance.

"Are they afraid?" Griffith mumbled.

"He probably stinks." Steele was looking through a small telescope. "It doesn't look like he's bathed in a while." He tossed the telescope to Griffith, who looked through it and found Swift Runner. He staggered like he was drunk or hung over. Griffith hardly recognized him. His face was blank, his eyes withdrawn, hair unkempt, hanging in twists and tangles to his shoulders. His shirt hung open, like dirty, stained drapes framing him from neck to belly button.

"What's he got all over him?" Griffith took his eye from the scope.

"Mud maybe, or blood?" Steele said.

"Blood? Whose blood?" Griffith felt a rush of exhilaration.

"I don't know," Steele replied. "Maybe we can ask him."

Swift Runner stopped before the tables and stood there. People were gathering in groups, women and children among them. He was an island unto himself as the other groups steered away from him.

He certainly stinks, Griffith thought.

Before taking up their hiding spots, Steele said, "When we take him into custody, don't draw your guns unless he brandishes a weapon. We don't want a scene; let's try and keep it civil and take him quietly."

Griffith was eyeing Swift, trying hard to see his friend, but he didn't look at all like himself.

"Let's go," Steele said.

They stood up—four NWMP officers in red jackets, gray breeches with a yellow stripe, and pillbox hats. Hardly inconspicuous. Marois and Crane were positioned farther down the line. Swift Runner had passed them on the dirt road. They were now behind him, while Steele and Griffith approached from the side of the mission.

It didn't take long for them to catch the attention of the other gatherers.

There was chatter and even a gasp from the spectators.

Swift Runner remained still, seemingly unaware.

As they closed in, they could smell him, and the type of stench dawned horror, given the allegations. Steele and Griffith were twenty feet away, Marois and Crane about the same on the other side and closing. Fifteen feet, then ten. Swift Runner remained oblivious to their approach, golem-like, eyes vacant, only tatters of his hair and shirt dancing in the mild breeze.

"You smell it?" Griffith whispered to Steele. "I think you're right; it's blood."

"Yeah, I think so," Steele whispered back. "I said he would stink."

On the other side, Marois gagged, covering his mouth as did the others.

Griffith breathed through his mouth and it helped, but barely.

They had Swift Runner surrounded.

Steele said to Griffith, "Okay, Ron, you got the lead."

Stench aside, Griffith moved in a little closer. He was filled with sadness. He leaned in, inches away from the Swift's face, and gazed into those blank eyes.

The smell! Oh my God! The smell!

Griffith cupped his mouth and nose, inhaled, then whispered into Swift Runner's ear, "Ka Ki Si Kutchin, it's me, Constable Ron."

He stepped back and stood beside Steele, who shrugged.

They waited. Five seconds, then ten.

Swift Runner suddenly blinked and mumbled, "Constable Ron?"

"Yes, it's me."

Swift Runner stared through Griffith.

"We need to speak to you, Swift," Griffith said.

"Speak to me about what?"

"About your family."

"My family?" Swift Runner slurred.

"Yes."

"All dead, Constable Ron."

"All dead?" Griffith whispered. "How?"

"They took all our food."

"Who took your food?"

"White men took our food, Constable Ron. You White men."

"I'm your friend," Griffith said.

"I have no friends. White man banished me from Fort Saskatchewan. Chogan banished my family from Egg Lake. Now, you come to blame me with your White man law," Swift Runner said.

"We came to find out the truth," Griffith said.

"Truth?" Swift Runner scoffed. "You do not want truth."

"Yes, we do. That's why we've come."

"The truth is White man took all the food for White man."

"That's enough of that," Steele barked. "Marois, Crane, put the irons on him. Swift Runner, I'm placing you under arrest under the authority of the federal government and Her Majesty, Queen Victoria,, for suspicion of foul play."

Marois and Crane got on either side of Swift Runner, locking the iron bracelets on his wrists.

"Foul play?" Swift Runner asked. "What is foul play?"

"Murder," Griffith said.

"You and Chogan murdered my family with your *wepinikewin.*"

"We didn't murder anyone," Steele growled.

"What the hell is the matter with you?" Griffith shot back.

"I save your life, now you come to take mine," Swift Runner retorted.

Griffith felt the words cut through him.

"Shut your mouth, I'm not done!" Steele roared.

All of them, including Swift, were quiet, and Steele finished with the Order of Arrest. Following that, he folded it over, put it into his pocket, and they escorted Swift Runner behind the church, away from the onlookers.

"All right, Swift, where is your family?" Steele asked.

"All dead," Swift Runner mumbled, looking through Steele rather than in the eye.

"How did they die?"

"We had no food to hunt. They all starved to death. The buffalo are gone."

"Why didn't you starve?" Steele asked.

"I almost died, but I did not," Swift Runner said.

Steele shot Griffith a sideways glance.

"Where are you taking me?" Swift Runner asked.

"We're taking you back to Fort Saskatchewan," Steele said.

"Fort Saskatchewan." Swift Runner closed his eyes. "Many bad memories in Fort Saskatchewan."

"How did you get that blood all over you?" Steele asked.

Swift Runner told them.

II

On the main road leading out of town, two boys came scurrying out from between the buildings and were almost trampled. Griffith pulled back on the reins, yelling, "Move off, lads! Whoa, Gunner! Whoa." The horse halted, almost throwing Griffith as the boys reversed course and went back the way they had come. Griffith let out a chuckle, watching them run away. "Little shits, that was close."

The horse snorted in agreement.

Griffith looked to the road and nudged Gunner's sides with his heels. Then they were galloping once more, the cadence of hooves pounding the road dirt, bouncing off the buildings. Soon they were out of town, and the road devolved into an overgrown trail shouldered by black spruce and clusters of paper birch trees.

When the trail was gone, they traversed a grade that descended toward the Sturgeon River.

"At the bend in the river is where you will find it," Swift Runner told him.

"Find what?" Griffith asked.

"The bridge."

When Griffith reached the river, he followed the bank, looking for the bend. That was when he saw the hundreds of ravens circling above the woods across the river. *That must be it,* he thought. They were riding through the waist-high yellow grass, stepping deliberately, until Griffith saw a gopher hole. "Whoa, Gunner."

He dismounted and led Gunner the rest of the way.

When he reached the bend, he saw the makeshift bridge, but it was the sound of the birds. They were now close enough to hear. Unlike crows, ravens didn't "caw," but argued in a discordance of gurgling croaks. In this case, hundreds of gurgling croaks, knocking, and cackling. This abundance of ravens was considered a treachery, meaning only one thing.

"Death," Griffith said, unpleasant thoughts poking him.

Is that where Swift's family is? Are the bodies of his family across the river lying in those trees rotting?

If that was the case, they would be bones by now, long past the interest of a treachery of ravens. Too many for a scattering of bones, or buttons, or other souvenirs of the dead.

So, why the hell are they there?

Griffith remembered Sergeant Steele saying that Swift was luring kids, both local and native. Could there be new victims? Was that the source of the awful stench floating across the river?

The idea made him shiver.

If so, why aren't the ravens landing?

The ravens continued their mad deafening symphony, croaking and cackling..

Griffith tethered Gunner to a piece of deadfall, stroked his neck, and said, "The only thing I don't understand is, why aren't the ravens landing?"

The horse gave a low snort, which Griffith understood as expressing concern. They didn't speak each other's language, but they understood each other all the same.

"Why, Gunner? Why aren't they landing?" Griffith could feel the fear crawling up his legs, softening the mettle in his bones. He gazed over at the circling ravens and paused to consider the reason for them being here.

Gunner gave a snort.

"I know, I don't want to go over there." Griffith laughed, but it was laced with fear. Laughing was how he dealt with fear, but it didn't seem to be working, so he said, "It's my job. I gotta go. I won't be long."

Gunner didn't respond.

Griffith went to cross the river.

III
Catholic Mission
St. Albert, NWT

While Griffith was crossing the Sturgeon, Marois went to get Hood and the jail wagon, leaving Steele and Crane standing five feet from a shackled Swift Runner.

Steele curled his nose. "Wait here."

"Huh?" Crane looked up.

"The smell of him," Steele grumbled.

"Yeah?" Crane didn't understand.

"I'm going to see about getting him bathed. Keep an eye on him."

Swift Runner didn't raise his eyes.

"Good idea, Sergeant. He stinks a might," Crane agreed.

"Glad to have your approval, Constable Crane." Steele grinned, and before Crane could reply, he turned and left.

"It's a good idea!" Crane called after him. Steele waved his hand and kept going, disappearing around the corner of the mission. "Oh boy," Crane scolded himself.

"It knows," said a strange voice from behind.

Crane turned to see Swift Runner looking down at him.

"Swift, you gave me a start," Crane squeaked.

"It knows," Swift said again, a carnivorous smile climbed up his cheeks.

Crane took a defensive step back.

Swift's eyes darkened and then began to glow.

Crane heard chanting inside his head, but not in any language he knew.

"*Wibitikow* is coming," Swift Runner mumbled and let out a painful moan. His pores began to sweat out, expelling beads of ichor that enveloped him, blotting him and transforming him further. His eyes dimmed, dulling to pinkish-gray, and his skin became grizzled and cadaverous. The thing was climbing from its host—a dark shadow of churning blood and smoke, its hair hanging in tangles, eyes burning like iron rivets.

It was a specter of pure darkness and infinite suffering.

Crane wanted to scream, to run, but for those burning eyes.

Now completely free of its host, it rose up, a shadow thing with long, bony limbs and claws to roost. In red glow, he saw an outline of its emaciated face. Beneath the floating entity, Swift Runner was inert.

It twisted and turned, unfurling claws, but Crane couldn't move.

Then it detonated like coal dust, engulfing both Swift Runner and him in blinding darkness.

Crane thought he had been struck blind.

He heard the beat of its icy heart—slithering echoey voices, crawling over each other. *"Danny Crane. I know what you did! Know what you did! Let me in! Let me in or I'll tell!"*

"What I did?" Crane said.

"Let me in! Or I will tell. I know what you did. I know what you did. I know what you did!"

The beast was inside his head.

It knows, Crane thought.

Then there was another voice, shouting, "Crane!"

Crack!

Then stinging pain.

IV
Near the Sturgeon River
South of St. Albert, NWT

The horse, Gunner, loved the man and was content to travel to places and things that concerned him. The man often spoke to Gunner on the trail and in the stable. Sometimes the man came to the stable smelling of fermented fruit, slurring his words. The man would put his cheek against Gunner's and whisper. "I love you, old friend."

Gunner understood many of the man's words and was communal to his moods. If the man was happy, Gunner was happy. If the man was anxious, Gunner was anxious. Today had been one of great unease, anxiousness and fear.

Animals, including horses, see things that men cannot. Gunner didn't know the name of the specter watching the man cross the river to the place of death. He was almost on the other side, unaware of being watched. Gunner had seen these things before, hiding in the shadows. He had heard their ranting, turning men mad, turning them to murder.

They were darkness, and darkness was everywhere.

There were many others, but this one was more powerful than the others.

Gunner snorted and whinnied a warning, but the man was too far away.

Already across the river and onto the bank, moving through the high grass and toward the trees.

Darkness melted back into the woods.

Gunner whinnied again, but the man was gone.

He could only wait.

V

The ravens circled over the forest like a giant black wheel in the sky. Griffith stared up into the vortex, overwhelmed by the amplified discord of competing croaks. He was moving through the grass toward the wood line, mouth hanging in awe at the anomaly. That was when the stench of rotting flesh hit him in a thick wave, curdling the air, making him gag. He gazed down and saw the copper drag marks in the flattened yellow grass.

Oh, shit, blood trail, he thought, looking back up.

He followed the path, pulse hammering, horrified at what he would find. He told himself he shouldn't be worried, that their prisoner was in chains, and whatever lay decaying in those trees was no threat to the living.

Then why do I have my gun out? Griffith wondered.

It was a good question, and he had a good answer.

The ravens and rot, and whatever horror lay ahead was plenty good reason to have his gun out. He was afraid, and that was a damned good reason.

He couldn't see Gunner anymore.

Stay safe, my friend, he thought and followed the path.

When he reached the entrance to the camp, he found a rotting deer head tied to a tree. Both eye and nasal sockets were charged with squirming maggots. The exposed flesh was jellied around the already exposed bone, which ran the length of the nose. There were plenty of insects buzzing, crawling, and squirming about. He held his hand over his mouth and turned his attention to the twine used to hang the ghastly thing up. Swift Runner had used the same twine over the years he had known him. The binding was gray, tightly wound by a single golden tinge.

It looks like a gatekeeper, Griffith thought.

He looked up through the canopy and could only see part of the bird vortex. He turned his eyes up the path. Whatever lay ahead would be worse, because the smell from the woods beckoned like an invisible hand, daring him to come and see. He holstered his weapon, removed a hankie from his pocket, and tied it around his face.

Griffith looked skyward. The opus of croaks was almost deafening.

Maybe they're warning me to stay away?

He unholstered his gun and got going.

Every step, every beat of his heart, the awful dread of what was in those woods deepened.

Oh my God, the stink, he thought. *What if there's a bunch of dead kids in there?*

He felt his guts contract and he spit up a tiny bit of vomit. He pushed it down, held his breath, lifted the rag, and wiped his mouth with his sleeve. He readjusted the mask. Griffith, who thought himself to be an atheist, crossed himself, raised his gun, and ventured into the camp, thinking, *Lord, if you are there, please protect me.*

Death was everywhere, drowning Griffith's sense of smell in competing states of decay.

The first body was a decapitated deer strung between two trees, its belly slit open and emptied of the internal organs. He guessed the deer was the rightful owner of the gatekeeper head. Below the deer, there was no viscera anywhere on the ground.

Why would he take the viscera and leave the meat to rot?

There were more.

Ten feet to the right lay an eviscerated coyote, belly open, entrails also gone, but the head intact. Next to that was an opossum, and as Griffith turned to look at each animal, he realized he was turning entirely around. There was a much smaller deer, a fawn, and a dog beside that, all of them covered by myriad carnivorous insects. In between the animal corpses, random bones of smaller creatures hung in clusters on branches like grisly charms, twisting in the breeze, some clicking together like skeleton teeth. Griffith felt numb, turning from corpse to corpse.

Above the macabre scene, the treachery continued to circle, but the croaks had stopped.

Griffith felt something else, a sensation that he wasn't alone. He slowly cocked his pistol and turned.

Nothing.

Just clicking bones.

Stop being paranoid, he scolded himself. *This is Swift's doing.*

Griffith let out a sigh, then took in a slow, deliberate breath and turned his eyes to the nucleus of the madness in which he stood. A large cooking pot hung from a spit over a firepit. He moved to it, gazed in, and immediately recoiled. "Oh my God!" The stench was more concentrated than the surrounding carcasses. Griffith gagged and almost threw up.

He pushed the cloth hankie against his face, trying to filter the odor and suppress the urge to vomit while assembling his nerve. Slowly, he leaned in for a second look, this time with nose pinched and breath held. The pot was half full of brown, coagulated blood, and in that, ropy intestines rose and fell like a jaundiced sea serpent.

Griffith stepped back, gun still up, and felt the hairs rise on the back of his neck.

Movement to the left!

He spun in that direction, gun aimed.

Nothing.

A twig cracked.

He turned and yelled, "Who's there?"

Whispering, "I know who you are."

Griffith spun in the voice's direction.

Nothing, only empty forest and hanging carcasses.

Hissing, the voice taunted, "Have you come to play, Constable Ron?"

"Who's there?" Griffith hollered.

Mad mimicking hisses. "Who's there? Who's there? Who's there?"

Above, the spinning wheel disintegrated into charcoal smudges, and the ravens began to descend and land on the branches and bushes, shaking the foliage, bowing tree limbs, lining up like legions of black angels all around the camp. Griffith had underestimated their number, which had to be in the thousands. They poured from the sky, wings flapping, gliding to take up a spot in the forest of death.

Even the mysterious voice was silenced by the arriving birds lining the trees. Griffith only heard the tempest of wings, only saw the darkening forest. They kept landing, filing along the branches, surrounding Griffith and the camp.

Were the ravens here to devour him?

He didn't think so. Or hoped not anyway, and speculated their quarrel was with the invisible spirit calling to him from the woods. Swift Runner's *wihitikow.* It had mimicked him but not shown itself. Griffith considered this when the last raven landed, and he found himself encircled by thousands of them.

Black angels, he thought.

All at once, they broke their silence, and sanity was obliterated by the chorus of opposing croaks. Griffith brought his hands up to his ears, including his gun hand. When he covered them, it barely stifled the volley of eardrum-piercing psychosis.

Griffith had seen and heard enough and ran for the path. When he cleared the camp, he didn't look back to see the darkness standing at the entrance. But he heard it, even over the mad arguments of the gathering birds.

"Come to the fire, Constable Ron! Come to the fire, and we will feast like kings!"

He didn't dare look back.

Just kept going.

VI

Griffith was running for the river, but he felt numb, out of his body. His world was dream-like and strangely devoid of color. He passed the gatekeeper head, was into the tall grass, across the bank, and onto the tree bridge, gun still out. Halfway across, he almost fell into the river. Only then did he holster his weapon, thinking it was probably useless against an invisible Indian spirit, but it was all he had. He steadied himself and carried on across, using the branches on the fallen tree to keep from slipping into the water. Once across, he jumped onto the bank and knelt.

What was the matter with his vision? Why was he suddenly colorblind?

Back across the river, the sound of rioting croaks and rasps continued.

Griffith felt a shiver of fear and drew his gun yet again.

His hands were quaking. He let out a watery moan to relieve some of the anxiety crushing his chest. "Oh my God. Oh my God," he half whispered and whimpered.

Never had Griffith been so overwhelmed or terrified.

He eyed the entrance, saw nothing, but then he hadn't seen anything to begin with. It hadn't shown itself, just whispers in the forest.

It knew my name, Griffith thought dimly.

That got him moving again.

When he reached Gunner, reality realigned, tunnel vision widened, and the color returned to his world. His senses sharpened, and he heard the wind whispering in the grass. He still heard the ravens across the river, feeling like he had just come through a doorway into hell. He wrapped his arms around Gunner's neck, embracing him, needing the security of his warmth and the sanity of the world.

The horse gave him what he had.

Griffith let loose a sobbing moan expelling fear, shame, and cowardice. He began to shake, something that often happened when he was in moments of high stress. After he collected himself, he gazed across the river but saw nothing. Heard nothing. Even the shouting croaks of ravens had lessened.

I didn't see it, he thought. "I didn't see anything," he said to Gunner.

But he had heard it.

Gunner, who did see the darkness standing at the entrance, gave a whinny and a snort.

"Yeah, okay, loud and clear, time to go." Griffith untethered Gunner and led him out of the high grass until there was nowhere to hide a gopher hole. He climbed into the saddle and gazed back across the river one last time. He lost sight of the entrance after leaving the bend.

Gunner shook himself uncomfortably, giving a grunt.

"Okay," Griffith said, and they rode back to town.

On the way, he decided what he would and wouldn't tell them. He would tell them about the macabre display of animal death. He would mention the ravens' presence, even the magnitude. He wouldn't tell them about the invisible thing in the woods calling his name or how thousands of ravens had come down to save him from said invisible thing.

Is that what they were doing?

He wouldn't talk about the colorblindness or running like a coward and hugging his horse while sobbing like a frightened child. He had an image to maintain. Halfway back, he decided that he had accomplished his mission. He had confirmed that the blood on Swift Runner wasn't human, and there was no sign of Swift Runner's family or any human victims.

Probably murdered them somewhere else, Griffith thought.

But he wasn't going to say that either.

VII
Catholic Mission
St. Albert, NWT

"*Esti de tabarnak*, what is wrong with them?" Marois asked Hood. They were standing on either side of Crane and Swift Runner. They were a foot apart, eyes locked and in stupor.

"I don't know," Hood said and leaned into Swift Runner. "What did you do to him?"

Swift Runner didn't even twitch.

Hood snapped his fingers.

Nothing from either.

Crane's face decided Hood's next move. It was a mask of terror, frozen in time. It was clear who was holding who. Hood motioned with a nod for Marois to keep an eye on Swift Runner. Then he pulled his hand back and slapped Crane hard across the cheek.

He brought his hand up to hit him again.

Crane gasped, shook his head, recoiled, and brought his hands up defensively. "Stop! No more!"

"What's the matter with you, Danny?" Hood lowered his hand. "What's that Indian done to you?"

"I, uh, oh…" Crane's eyes widened, then he buckled over and vomited out a glut of black foam that hit the ground, bubbled like seltzer, then was sucked into the earth.

Marois and Hood stared where the vomit had been.

No one spoke.

Thirty seconds became sixty.

Swift Runner was coming back.

Hood turned to him. "What did you do to him?"

"*Wihitikow*," Swift Runner mumbled.

"Tell me now, Indian," Hood demanded.

"I'm all right," Crane said. "I just had something that didn't agree with me. I'm all right, Corporal."

Hood looked hard at Swift. "Are you sure, Danny? You didn't look all right."

"I'll be fine." Crane stood up. "It was a bad spell, that's all."

"Okay, Danny," Hood said. Then to Swift Runner, he added, "You sit your ass down."

Swift Runner sat without a word.

Sergeant Steele arrived then, asking, "Any sign of Griffith?"

"Not yet," Marois said.

Sergeant Steele was carrying two water pails, with four nuns in tow, also carrying water, rags, and food. He looked down at Crane. "What's wrong with you?"

"I'm not feeling well, Sergeant," Crane said.

"Everything under control here, Corporal Hood?" Steele called.

"Yes, Sergeant, everything is under control," Hood said, shooting Crane a sideways glance.

"Good," Steele said and walked up to Swift Runner. "You going to give me trouble, Swift?"

Swift Runner shook his head. "No trouble."

"Good. We're going to get you cleaned up. After that, we'll have a feed. I want you to get out of those bloody clothes so the nuns can wash you down." Steele looked at the restraints and said to Marois, "Get the chains off him."

Swift held his hands up obediently.

Steele leaned in and said, "I like you, Swift, but you mind them nuns and let them do their work. You mind them plenty. Do we understand each other?"

"I will give you no trouble, Sergeant."

"Good." Steele smiled. "After you get cleaned up, we'll eat."

They unchained the prisoner, he undressed, and the nuns went to work. When they started washing the blood off him, one nun stepped back, excused herself, and threw up. She was a young woman, new to the parish. She cleaned her mouth and returned to work without further issue.

Swift's clothing was washed in two buckets, then hung to dry in the mild breeze, while he waited wrapped in a blanket. The Mounties helped the nuns by dumping the buckets, the bloody aroma transplanting itself to the pails of pink, foamy water.

Marois and Hood almost barfed, but Crane seemed indifferent to the stink.

Finished, the nuns were off to feed the less fortunate, leaving the oldest, Sister Martha, to take care of the officers and their prisoner. She opened a hamper and served venison stew swimming with potatoes and root vegetables. Still wrapped in the blanket, Swift Runner was put into the jail wagon and given a spoon and a bowl of stew. The food lightened the mood and brought friendly banter between police officers and the elderly nun.

All except the sickly Crane, who stared at the jail wagon like a confused dog.

"Here comes Griffith," Steele said.

***

Chapter 6 – Oliver's Struggles

I

May 26, 1879
Halford Residence, St. Albert, NWT

Dr. Fraser was fortyish, spectacle-wearing, round-faced, clean-shaven, and of average build. He wore a charcoal suit and thin black tie, and a gold watch chain hung from his jacket pocket. The doctor had come by on a house call to examine Oliver.

"You're awfully pale," the doctor said. "Are you eating?"

"Yes, I'm eating," Oliver said.

"Not enough," his mother called out.

"Let's give you a good examination." Dr. Fraser checked Oliver's eyes, his neck and mouth. He even stuck his finger up his bum and said, "You pooping regular, Oliver?"

"Yes, Doctor." He didn't care for the bum part.

"I don't feel any bullets in the chamber," Dr. Fraser said. He withdrew his finger, pulled a handkerchief from his pocket, and used it to clean off his finger. After a few twists, he nodded and placed the hankie back in his pocket. "Now, why aren't you sleeping?"

"I don't know," Oliver lied.

"Are you having bad dreams? Night scares?"

Oliver felt he had to give the doctor something. "I just get... can't shut my brain down."

"Ah ha, and what is it you're thinking about?"

I can't tell him about the giant! Or his demon, Oliver thought.

He needed a lie, and Dr. Fraser gave him one in a whisper. "Are you thinking about your father?"

Oliver's face bunched up.

Can't make Mum cry!

He brought his finger to his lips, glassy eyes indicating the curtain.

The doctor nodded and whispered, "I lost my Pa when I was your age."

Oliver nodded and listened.

"It isn't easy, I know. The only medicine is time. Right now, not feeling sad might seem like an eternity away, but as time goes on, it will hurt less and less."

"It hurts so much," Oliver whispered.

"Come here." Dr. Fraser gave the boy a hug, and he did cry then, but low and muffled. "Listen, Oliver, you have to turn your thoughts off when you go to bed." He leaned in. "Tonight, when you go to bed, I want you to push them away one by one."

"I'll try," Oliver said.

"Good boy. Now, I gotta speak to your mum," he said and stepped behind the curtain.

Oliver listened.

"What's wrong with him, Doctor?"

"I believe he has insomnia," Dr. Fraser said.

"Insomnia? Is that…" Mum's voice wavered. "Is it…"

"Calm down, Missus Halford, Oliver will be fine. It's a sleeping disorder. This is a temporary thing that some children suffer. Not uncommon given the tragedy that has befallen your family."

"How long will he have this insomnia?"

"Oh, I suppose it could last a few days, maybe a week or more, until his body overrides his mind and puts him to sleep. Keep the food and water in him. Maybe a shot of spirits before bed will ease him?"

"I have some rum," his mother said.

"That will do," Dr. Fraser said.

"Goodnight, and thank you, Doctor."

"Goodnight, Missus Halford."

The door closed and his mother latched it. A moment later, she came in with a capful of rum.

It tasted like tainted fire and burned from Oliver's throat to his belly. "Oh, Mum, that's awful."

"It will help you sleep," Mum said.

II
May 27, 1879
Halford Residence, St. Albert, NWT

Oliver's body didn't override the insomnia because there was no insomnia. His clock was backward;, he had been sleeping in the day, hiding in the light.

At night, he stood watch.

The giant came around every other night, calling from the shadows in his mind. Moving in the darkness. Oliver imagined the giant wanted to take him away, kill and eat him. That's what he feared when the giant followed him to the telegraph building.

They were supposed to take him away.

"By tomorrow," Mr. Watts had said.

That was more than a month ago.

Oliver had been locked up in their little dwelling since Mr. Watts walked him home. The giant had come, but the neighbors chased him off, and he disappeared. Oliver had hoped for good. Maybe he had moved on? Or the Mounties had taken him? Maybe he had decided just to leave St. Albert?

He sure hoped so, and with every new day, he began to think it, until the eighth day when all hope dissolved. He was awakened by the giant's voice in his head.

"Little Foot, where are you?"

Careful not to wake Mum, he snuck to the window and saw nothing in the alley. He went to the corner room and peered out, and a block over he saw the silhouette of the giant staring up at another residence.

Not gone, just searching other neighborhoods.

Moving home to home.

"Where are you?"

Since that day at the Catholic Mission, something was different inside Oliver's head. He could hear the giant's thoughts, and the closer the giant was, the clearer those thoughts became. He had burrowed into his brain like an earwig seeking to nest its brood. Worse, he shared the giant's senses. Oliver felt the coppery taste of blood dancing across his tongue, and it stirred in him the same sensation as the giant.

Craving and hunger.

Oliver knew the giant's real name, Ka Ki Si Kutchin, and he knew that he was possessed by a demon called a *wihitikow*. When they were close by, he would hear them arguing in his head. The *wihitikow* wanted Oliver more than Ka Ki Si Kutchin. The *wihitikow* wanted his innocence; the giant wanted him for meat.

They called for him to stop hiding and accept his fate.

Oliver didn't respond.

The probing, the arguments, the calls in the night continued and days became weeks, then a month, and still nobody came to save him. Not Father Leduc, not Mr. Watts, not the Northwest Mounted Police. Oliver had been abandoned by everyone—by his father in death and his mum in life, taking all of the sorrow for herself and leaving him alone to stand watch as the monsters closed in.

"We are coming for you, Little Foot," called the giant.

"You had better come out or we will come in," said the *wihitikow*.

"Then we will kill and eat her in front of you," both said. "*Are you listening?"*

Oliver vomited up more of the black stuff into a wash pail by the door.

It's already inside me.

He brought up his nightshirt and bunched the cloth into his mouth, muffling the cries. He remained that way until panic gave in to resignation. He stared at the pail. He would have to dump it, but not tonight. They were still out there looking for him. He was afraid to go outside right now. He stood, straightened his nightshirt, and picked up the pail. On tip toe, he snuck past Mum, gently set it by his cot, and climbed back into bed.

I'll dump it when I wake up.

Farther away, he heard, *"Come out, you little bastard!"*

The voices faded with the rising sun.

Oliver drifted off.

III

A while later, Oliver was awakened by Mum when she placed a cool hand on his forehead. She was leaning over him, looking down sadly. "Oh, Olly, you're still not feeling well?"

"No, Mum, I'm tired. I need to sleep."

"Food will help you. I'll cook an egg."

"I'm not hungry."

"The doctor said—"

"I'll just throw up. I'll eat later." Oliver turned away.

"Okay, sweetheart." She rubbed a hand on his back. "I must help Mr. Dumfries at the market again today. I have a fresh chicken on the counter that I'm going to boil for dinner when I come back. Maybe you'll be hungry later?"

"Maybe," he said.

"Are you sure I can't—"

"I'm just tired, Mum," he interrupted, while thinking, *Tired of being afraid. Tired of being the man. Tired of being locked up while you're out there with Mr. Dumfries. Just go away!*

He felt her eyes upon him, trying to read his face.

"I'll try and get some sleep." He managed a smile.

"Good boy." She kissed his forehead, stood, and flattened her dress.

Mum had been working for Mr. Dumfries quite a lot since Oliver's father died. He had yet to meet the man who seemed a little too willing to help them out.

"Latch the door," she said.

"Yes, Mum," he said.

He followed her from the bed and locked the door behind her. On his way back to bed, he saw a pot with a tea towel over it. Mum had got it from a man in the street. The man came every other day with a wagon of caged hens, and he slaughtered them there with a sharp cleaver.

Oliver went to the pot and lifted the towel, revealing a plucked and washed bird.

From a circular clot, scarlet tendrils branched out like arteries in the clear fluid puddling in the bottom of the pot. He touched his finger to the clot and brought it up to eye level.

Maybe this would stop the black vomit.

Maybe?

Oliver stuck his finger into his mouth, licking it off, and immediately wanted more. He was thinking about the man with the chickens and how the decapitated heads rolled off the execution plank and into the wood bucket swinging below.

Maybe?

He removed the chicken, set it on the counter, brought the pot to his lips, and canted. The puddle, which was an amoebic muddle of animal fat, water, and blood, glided from pot to mouth and down his throat.

His nausea eased slightly.

Oliver had no idea how long he stood beside the counter holding the empty pot in his hands. He was thinking about the bucket of chicken heads, the bloody necks, and how suckling the blood from the open necks would ease the darkness nesting inside him.

Then a wave of nausea hit him, and he ran for the pail and vomited.

More darkness.

"It is in you," the giant whispered.

He returned to the kitchen, replaced the chicken, covered it with the towel, and got dressed.

Attired, he picked up the pail and moved cautiously outside into the day. He scanned the alley; sometimes the giant showed up in the daytime. The coast was clear, so he crossed the alley to the sewage ditch on the other side, which reeked of urine and feces.

There were two men standing side by side, urinating in the ditch.

One was tall and skinny, the other, short and fat.

Oliver waited, unintentionally eavesdropping.

"You hear about the arrest at the mission?" Tall asked.

"Yep, arrested themselves a cannibal Indian," Fat said.

"You should see the size of him." Tall laughed. "He's humongous, like a colossal man."

"Colossal, that's a big word for a Gypsy." Fat laughed.

"I ain't no Gypsy," Tall said. They put their stuff away, turned around, and saw Oliver standing there staring, pail in his hand. "You snooping on us, lad?"

"No, sir." Oliver lowered his eyes.

"Good, because I don't like snoops," Tall said.

"Leave the kid alone, Barney," Fat said.

Tall looked back at his fat friend and grinned, then hunkered down in front of Oliver. "They got him in a cage at the parish. They say he killed and ate his whole family. The Mounties are gonna take him back to Fort Saskatchewan and fit him for a noose."

"Knock it off, Barney, you're gonna give the kid the night scares," Fat urged.

"Too late for that, sir," Oliver said.

"Careful where you walk, boy, he likes your kind. Indian's been chasing the kids for a meal, he has."

"I know," Oliver said.

"Huh?" Then Barney's face became serious. The joke was over. "What's the matter with you?"

"I'm one of the kids he's looking for," Oliver said.

"Oh, geez," Fat said.

Barney frowned. "I'm sorry, kid."

"I've been hiding from him since the end of March."

"Aw, geez, I bet you're happy they arrested him. He'll not be bothering you again. I suspect if he did what they say he did, he'll be not long for this world."

"I need to see him go," Oliver said.

"Barney, we're gonna be late," Fat said.

Barney turned to his friend and nodded, then to Oliver, he said, "I heard they'll be leaving after lunch. If you want to catch a glimpse, head for the east side of town and wait."

"Thank you, sir."

"I gotta go." Barney gave him a pat and followed Fat.

Oliver went to the bank and dumped the pail. The black bile splashed against the earth. The slick fizzled and foamed and vanished into the ground.

He wondered why it hadn't evaporated in the pail and thought maybe it had to touch the earth.

God up above, Devil down below.

"The evil must return to Hades," Oliver mumbled.

It was the creature's blood he was vomiting.

The giant had cursed him.

Oliver returned the bucket and headed for the east side of St. Albert.

It was time to look the Devil in the eye.

***

Chapter 7 – Funeral Procession

I

May 27, 1879
Catholic Mission - St. Albert, NWT

When he brought Gunner to a halt, Griffith saw Steele coming out to meet him. He also noticed Swift Runner watching him from the jail wagon. Avoiding eye contact, he dismounted and tethered his horse to a hitching post. He gazed past the approaching Steele, at Marois and Hood, who were eating under a tree. Crane sat away from them, staring at the jail wagon.

"Well, what did you find?" Steele asked, but there was a strange look on his face.

"I found his camp. No bodies. No people. No kids. The blood was from dead animals," Griffith said in a low voice.

Steele stared at Griffith for a few seconds before saying, "Well, I suppose that's good news, but it doesn't solve the mystery."

"It wasn't just a hunting camp, Richard."

"What do you mean?"

"I, ah, don't…" Griffith took a breath. "I've never seen anything like it. There were dead animals everywhere. Deer, dog, coyote, racoons, opossum all hanging in the trees like ornaments."

"Ornaments?"

"Eviscerated ornaments. He never touched the meat, just ate the viscera..."

"He ate the guts?" Steele curled his nose.

"Yeah. There was a pot full of innards."

"Jesus." Steele turned his eyes to the wagon. "He has to have gone completely mad."

"I think so," Griffith agreed.

Except that didn't explain the voice or the thousands of ravens. Only yesterday, Griffith had been an atheist who scoffed at the existence of

God. Now he was entertaining Indian demons. He pushed the thought away and pulled focus to see Steele's alarmed face.

"What? Why are you looking at me like that?"

"I didn't say anything when you got here, but…"

"But what?"

"Ron, you look like you've lost three pints of blood."

"Three pints of…" Griffith didn't understand.

"It's probably shock from what you saw. I saw another man struck gray by shock. He was the sole survivor of an ambush. Four men around him were killed and he had not a scratch, but he was gray like you. Your body does some weird thing and contracts all the blood to the extremities. You need to get some grub into you, my friend. I don't need you passing out."

"After what I saw, I haven't got no appetite."

"Appetite or not, you need some food in your belly."

"I don't..."

Steele stiffened. "Constable Griffith, do not mistake this for a request. It's an order. We need to get a move on, and I don't need you dropping off your horse. Get some grub into you." He raised his voice and called to the old nun, "Sister Martha, would you be so kind as to serve Constable Griffith here a bowl of that fine venison stew?"

"Certainly, Sergeant Steele." Sister Martha was a fortyish, grandmotherly woman of substantial girth and comparable strength. She had carried the heaviest of the load down from the mission. "Come and eat, Constable Griffith."

"You heard the sister," Steele said. "Get some grub in you, Ron. Make sure she gives you lots of meat so you can up that blood count." He turned toward the wagon and raised his voice. "You want another bowl of stew, Swift?"

Griffith peered toward the wagon. At this angle, he couldn't see the bars or Swift Runner. Just the back of the wagon, which was a black iron plate covered in rivets with a padlocked, with a windowless iron door.

A hand fell out from between the bars holding the empty bowl. "Yes, please, Sergeant."

"I got it, Sergeant." Marois stood up, grabbed Swift Runner's bowl, and went up to see Sister Martha, who ladled out the stew.

"He's eating normal food now," Steele said of Swift.

"You think I'm lying?" Griffith suddenly felt defensive.

"Of course not. I just said he's eating normal food."

"Maybe."

"Maybe what?" Steele asked.

"Maybe he only eats the guts when he's under its spell?"

"Spell?" Steele chuckled. "Maybe you should go get some grub like I said and save the disgusting talk about eating guts for later?"

Griffith reached into his tunic, removed his flask, and took a big swig. The whisky burned all the way down, setting fire in his chest. He grimaced and said, "I'll be back for that rum ration."

"I'll be here waiting with it. Now go dog up." Steele grinned.

On his way, Griffith met Marois, who made the same face Steele had and asked, "Are you sick, *mon ami*?"

"I'm fine."

"No, Ron, you aren't fine. You look like a ghost." Marois frowned. "What was there?"

"No people."

"What did you see?"

"Nothing good, but I'll tell you later."

"Okay." Marois didn't look okay; he looked spooked.

"The sergeant says I'm in shock and that some grub will fix me up," Griffith said.

"You coming over to eat with us?" Marois asked.

"I think I'll do the eating part alone. I don't want to barf around you guys—or him." Griffith pointed toward the wagon.

"Okay, come over when you're done."

"I have to see the sergeant first."

"We need to talk," Marois said.

"We will," Griffith said.

"Later," Marois said and carried on toward the jail wagon with Swift's filled bowl.

"Give him a big helping, Sister," Steele said from behind.

"Aye, Sergeant," she called back. "We also packed a food hamper for your trip."

"You are angels of mercy, Sister." Steele bowed. "The Northwest Mounted Police is in your debt."

Sister Martha smiled and blushed.

When Griffith reached the serving table, she handed him a heaping bowl of stew. He was certain the smell of boiled meat would turn his stomach, but to his surprise, it didn't. The aroma was so inviting, he could almost taste the tang of venison chunks floating along with the potatoes and carrots in a thick brown gravy, spiced with floating peppercorns.

"Thank you, Sister." Griffith tipped a smiling nod. "It smells good."

"You're welcome." Sister Martha smiled back. "If you want more, come back."

"I will."

She nodded and gave him the same look as Steele and Marois. Did he really look that bad? Had the thing he felt watching him stolen his color? Had the camp's world of black and white rubbed off on him?

One thing at a time, he thought. *I have a bowl of stew to eat.*

After picking a spot under a seventy-foot spruce, Griffith set the bowl down on the ground and cleared away some pinecones and other debris. Satisfied, he sat back against the trunk, reached over, and picked up the bowl.

It's excellent, he told himself.

Not once did he think of the eyeless deer, or gutted dog, or dead coyotes, or the intestinal horror swimming like a sea serpent in the coagulating blood of a battered fire pot. He had one mission: eat a bowl of stew without puking his guts out.

He dug in. Spoon from bowl to mouth, back to bowl.

Chew and swallow.

He concentrated on the taste, which was as appealing as the smell.

The meat was tender, salted perfectly, and peppery.

He burped, venison and whisky. Then he was scraping the bowl clean.

That'll keep the sergeant happy.

Griffith stuck the spoon into his mouth, pondering, *If that was what he did to a bunch of animals? What did he do to his own?* He pulled the spoon out and dropped it into the bowl. He thought about the camp and the horror hanging all around and the voice of the thing operating just outside the peripheral of sight and sanity. He remembered the interpreter, Kaplan, and how he, Griffith, had been so flippant about talk of windigos.

Kaplan had wanted to tell him something, and he had dismissed it. Now, after all he had seen and heard, he wished he had been less dismissive. It wasn't the dead animals that had stolen his color; it was the beast in those woods. Griffith looked down at the empty bowl. He still had Steele to contend with. He got up and went to return the bowl to Sister Martha, who was cleaning up.

"Thank you, Sister, that was excellent."

"Would you like some more?"

"Thank you, no, I'm quite full, and we have a long ride. But this should give me my strength back." He tried to hand her the bowl.

Sister Martha frowned. "You didn't like it?"

"No, Sister, I liked it just fine. It was very—"

"It's fine, Constable, not everyone likes venison stew." Her words were soft, but there was an edge that put Griffith on the defensive. She was going to guilt him into another bowl of stew.

"It was good. In fact, it was probably the best venison stew I've ever had."

"Then have some more. You need to get your color back." Sister Martha smiled triumphantly.

Defeated, Griffith held up the bowl.

She filled it up, and he went back to his spot.

Scoop, chew, swallow, repeat. He didn't scrape his bowl the second time.

"Thank you, Sister Martha." Griffith turned to go.

"Place it on the table, Constable." She was helping the other sisters pack up.

"Thank you, again." He set the bowl down.

II

When he reached Sergeant Steele, there was an offering of dark rum. Griffith waved it away. "I'm okay, feeling a bit overstuffed with stew at the moment."

"You got some color back already." Steele offered him a cigar, which he took, and Steele lit. "Must have been the shock of what you saw."

"I guess?" Griffith felt a little better.

"A man sees something terrible, and it changes his appearance," Steele said.

"I don't know what I looked like," Griffith said.

"You looked like a ghost."

They puffed away quietly for a time.

Marois and Hood tended to Swift Runner.

Crane just sat there, partially eaten bowl of food cast aside, staring at the jail cart.

"You all right there, Constable Crane?" Steele called out.

"Yes, Sergeant, just a little under the weather."

"Keep your distance, *mon ami*," Marois joked.

Griffith puffed away. "What's wrong with Crane?"

Hood left Marois to guard Swift Runner and came up to meet them.

"The Indian did something to him," Hood said.

"What? Did something?" Steele turned around. "What are you talking about?"

"The Indian had him under some kind of spell."

"Spell?" Steele looked to Crane, who had returned the bowl and was making his way back.

"Like a mesmerist?" Griffith interrupted.

"Mesmer? I don't even know what that is," Hood said.

Steele raised a hand to silence Griffith. "Then what was it?"

"I don't know, but he had Danny in some sort of daze," Hood said.

"Why wasn't I told about this before?" Steele complained.

"I meant to tell you, but—" Hood started.

"Can I join this conversation?" Crane interrupted.

He was right behind them. All three turned to face him awkward and embarrassed.

Steele broke the silence. "Of course, Danny." He gestured the wagon. "But let's move a little farther away."

"That suits me just fine," Crane said.

III

They huddled in a half-circle scrum out of Swift Runner's hearing range. Crane stood at the head, facing them, stealing glances at the jail wagon. He was afraid and sickly-looking.

"What happened to you?" Steele asked.

Crane said, "I don't rightly know, Sergeant. I got to talking to him, and I sort of fell under his spell without knowing it."

"How do you mean 'spell,' Danny?"

"It was like one minute I was talking to him, and then I was in a dreamy state." Crane was looking through Steele, tugging at his memory. "Nothing seemed real, and I could hear him inside my head."

"Did he blow anything on you?"

"Blow anything?"

Steele explained that there were some tribes in Africa who used strange potions to disable or disorient their enemies. This could be accomplished by blowing hallucinatory powder from an open palm or delivered in a poisoned dart.

Crane pondered this. "I don't recall him blowing anything at or on me or pricking me with any needles. He just lulled me into a waking sleep, and then he was inside my head."

"Inside your head? What do you mean by that?" Steele asked.

"I don't know, Sergeant," Crane said. "He was talking to me, trying to influence me to do things."

"What things?"

"I can't explain. It was like a dream. I was there but not there. Floating in darkness, and he kept saying inside my head, 'Let me in. Let me in.' I could hear him as clear as day."

Steele shook his head. "It had to be your imagination."

"He was right out of it, Sergeant," Hood said. "I had to smack him just to bring him back. Come to think of it, the Indian was all trancey too."

"That brought me back," Crane said, touching his cheek.

"You're welcome." Hood grinned.

"If it happens again, shake my shoulder instead?"

"You wouldn't have responded to a shake, Danny," Hood said.

"Please try, my cheek feels like a hunk of frozen liver."

Hood snickered. "If it happens again, I'll shake you first."

"Thanks," Crane said.

"Are you okay now, Danny?" Steele asked. "We can leave you at the mission, and when you feel better, you can ride back on your own."

"No, Sergeant. I'm ready to ride. I'll shake it off. It just feels like I've been on a bender. It won't stop me from performing my duties." Crane tried to be convincing.

"Maybe it's the paint thinner yer sipping?" Steele suggested.

"I've been sipping that stuff for years," Crane said. "I won't slow you down on the way back, Sergeant. I promise. I just want to get back to the fort."

Griffith didn't think Crane looked healthy enough for travel, but he understood. Crane didn't want to be left behind, and the fort was their home. Whatever Swift Runner had done to him, home among the NWMP was the safest place to be.

Steele yelled to the wagon, "Swift Runner, finish your grub. We're going back to Fort Saskatchewan."

A second later, the hand reappeared from between the bars holding an empty bowl. "Yes, Sergeant."

Steele said to Crane, "I think you should stay."

"I just want to get back to the fort," Crane almost begged.

"We all do," Griffith added sympathetically.

"Okay, Danny, have it your way," Steele said and announced, "Gentleman, we have lollygagged long enough. Marois, go grab Swift's clothes."

Marois collected Swift Runner's clothing and exchanged it for the bowl, which he returned. Hood and Griffith grabbed the hamper of food and secured it to the jail wagon. Crane got up onto his horse and waited for them to finish their duties. When they were done, they formed up, and Steele positioned himself out front with Griffith and called to his men, "Is everyone ready?"

There were four responses of, "Yes, Sergeant."

Then Swift Runner said, "Yes, Sergeant."

All eyes went to the wagon.

"He's one shifty Indian," Hood said with a toothy grin.

Everyone laughed.

Everyone except Crane.

IV

"Forward, march!" Steele decreed, and they rolled out of the Catholic mission like a slow funeral procession. Swift Runner peered out between the bars and saw Father Leduc watching from the mission steps.

He raised a hand and waved.

Father Leduc waved back, solemn faced.

They worked their way down the hill upon which the mission stood, the same piece of road Swift Runner had arrived on. As they rode, people gathered along the side to catch a glimpse of the caged devil rumored to have killed his family.

Among them stood a portly man, his rake-thin wife, and their young daughter. Griffith guessed the girl for eight or nine. Ripe pickings for an accused murderer alleged of luring children. The mother had her left arm and hand curled protectively around her daughter's chest, the right shielding the child's eyes. Griffith was annoyed that a parent would bring their child to such a spectacle.

Do they want the kid to have nightmares?

"Hello." Swift Runner waved to them, chains clinking against bars.

The mother brought her right hand up to stifle a dramatic cry. For the benefit of her husband or the Mounties, Griffith thought. But in doing so, she unshielded her daughter's eyes, which found Swift Runner's.

"Hello, little one." He waved.

The mother covered the girl's eyes again.

And the child cried out.

"Sit back and keep quiet, Indian," Hood warned.

Swift Runner sat back.

Farther on in town, they came upon six men standing in a circle. The group was working class, no bankers or lawyers in this bunch. The largest and most easily identifiable was a butcher. He still wore his bloody apron, which didn't cover his mammoth arms. The rest wore bib overalls or work attire and were of average builds.

They were gathered on the right side of the road.

"We might have a problem," Griffith said to Steele.

Steele perused Hood, Marois, and Crane, who acknowledged the tiny mob, and turned back at Griffith with a smile. "Nah, this won't be a problem."

Griffith watched Steele take a deep breath through his nose, filling his lungs and reaching down into the pit of his gut. That was where a commanding roar, only possessed by drill sergeants, was waiting to be unleashed. Steele had a blusterous roar rumored to have blown back the hair of any man on the receiving end his wrath. He gave Griffith a wink and let the beast out. "Pay attention here, you gang of halfwit flapdoodles!"

The gawkers eyed Steele.

"You best stow that rummy fire in yer bellies, lest you want to ride back to the jail in Fort Saskatchewan with lumps on your heads courtesy of the finest officers in the Northwest Mounted Police!" And before anyone could respond, Steele gave the command, "Detachment! Halt!"

They halted.

One of the horses let out a snort.

No one moved.

"They don't think we're serious, gentlemen." Steele looked around with a grin on his facc.

"Oh, we're serious, Sergeant," Griffith said, then, "Move off! Or join him in the cage!"

"Get out of the road," Hood added.

"*Éloignez-vous, enfoirés*!" Marois spewed, which no one understood.

"Corporal Hood!"

"Yes, Sergeant!"

"Ready that wagon for six imbeciles," Steele snarled.

"Ready when you are, Sergeant!" Hood jingled the key chain.

Steele spied the butcher, pegging him for the leader, and zeroed in. "Listen here! The next order I give is to dismount, and once given, it won't be taken back until every one of you is in irons." He lowered his voice. "Then you get a ride to Fort Saskatchewan, but you'll be walking back after your sentence is served for obstruction of justice."

"Come on, let's go," one of the men said.

"We're leaving," said another.

There were mumblings of retreat.

The group dispersed.

All except the butcher.

V

The butcher's name was Jack Hitch, and things had all started in front of his shop. They had gathered on that morning, sipping coffee with a shot a whisky for a warmup. The coffee ran out and was traded for a bottle. More men came over, drinking, smoking, talking about the Indian they suspected of murder and of luring children. By the time there were seven of them, the first bottle was emptied, a second came out, and even more whisky spilled over bibulous, fiery words.

"Luring kids, and they're saying he might've killed his whole family and ate 'em," John Beavertown said.

"Ate them," Charlie Spector gasped. "Goddamned savages!"

"How do you eat your kids?" Beavertown said.

"It's because they got no God," Craig Edwards said.

"Mounties got him in a cage," Gord O'Neill said.

"Good place for him," Gene Rollo chipped in.

"Hanging from a tree would be better," Hitch said.

This was met by approving grunts of the primate variety. The bottle continued to circulate. They were feeling self-righteous, at least Hitch was, and his gang seemed to approve of what he was proposing. "We oughta drag him out of that cage," he heard himself say, "and string him the hell up."

"You mean, like take him from the Mounties?" Gene Rollo asked.

"That's exactly what I mean," Hitch said with a grin, and there were cheers.

"Let's not be hasty," Gene Rollo said.

"Hasty?" Hitch wiped his mouth with the back of his hand and on his bloody apron. "We'd be doing the town a favor."

"He's in the custody of the NWMP," Rollo said.

"So. You think they care about that Indian?"

"Hitch, you're drunk."

"You a goddamned coward, Rollo?"

"I have an aversion to getting shot," Rollo said.

"Sometimes being a man takes courage, Gene."

"You're mistaking courage for drunken stupidity, Hitch. I am drunk, but not that drunk. I suggest you put the bottle away and go take a nap."

Rollo looked around at the rest of them. "I'd suggest the same for all of you." He stepped away from the storefront and went back up the road.

And then there were six of them.

"Boy, you think you know a guy," Gord O'Neill said.

"Piss on him," Hitch said and passed the bottle. More whisky lit fire in their bellies, and the smoke poisoned their thoughts. Then they were marching up the side of the road through a fog of self-righteous bravado. The Indian was luring kids, after all, and they would be saving the government the trouble. It was a great idea, a noble idea, and Hitch felt like a general leading them up the road to glory.

Then came the Mounties and their leader's thunderous roar, all growling and threatening. Hitch felt the ranks of his noble idea pulling apart and thinning until there was only Gord O'Neill left, who said, "I'm leaving, Hitch."

Hitch mumbled, "Hey, Gord."

"Yeah?"

"Boy, you think you know a guy," Hitch slurred, then O'Neill was gone. Now he was alone and staring through the milky haze of inebriation at the toughest man he had ever seen in his life.

VI

"Cowards left me," the butcher mumbled.

He was tanked. They could smell the whisky from their horses and, as the ranks thinned, Steele's face softened and he grinned. He leaned down and said, "Butcher man."

"Huh?" The butcher's head floated under Steele's gaze.

"Listen, you don't want to fight me," Steele said. "I can guarantee you that I've killed more men in my lifetime than you've laid women."

The butcher was thinking.

"You've had too much to drink," Steele said sympathetically, "something all men do at one time or another. As one man to another man, I'm telling you to go home. Tomorrow, you will wake up and be glad you listened."

"You're not going to beat me up?"

"Not if you go home." Steele smiled.

"Yeah, okay. I'm going…" The butcher shuffled away toward his shop, mumbling and counting on his fingers how many times he had been laid.

They watched him disappear around the corner.

Griffith started laughing.

"What?" Steele asked.

"You wouldn't make that bet with Marois."

Steele let out a bark of laughter and then gave the command, "Forward! March!"

They were moving again.

There were fewer gawkers now and no vigilantes.

Clip clop, clip clop.

The road had emptied of onlookers. Steele's showdown with the mini mob was already being gossiped about around town. Almost everyone was gone, except one. Griffith saw the boy before Steele. He was around ten years old, standing beside the road like a sculpture with faraway, blank eyes, and he was sickly—like Crane.

"What's that kid doing over there?"

"I guess he came to see the monster," Steele said.

"What's wrong with him?"

Then the boy yelled something at Swift Runner, who went crazy.

VII

"Take it back!" the boy shouted at Swift Runner. "I don't want it. Take it back!"

"Ahh, Little Foot, there you are!" Swift rose from the floor, the wagon shifting slightly as he moved to the bars. "He lives in us, Little Foot!" Swift ranted, both arms out between the bars and hands clawing at the air. "Only *wihitikow* can take it back. You cannot sick it up! It is in you, Little Foot."

Griffith saw the boy buckle and vomit up something dark.

What's wrong with him?

The boy straightened, mouth agape, eyes like frozen meat.

"See you in your dreams, Little Foot."

Griffith saw the darkening stain in the child's crotch, and that infuriated him. He steered Gunner up the opposite side of the wagon and barked, "Stop that!"

Swift Runner ignored Griffith, his hands reaching through the bars, clawing the air in frenzy, while sputtering a patchwork of Cree and English.

"Swift Runner!" Griffith screamed at him.

"Come to the fire! Come to the fire!" Swift Runner was holding the bars, spittle spraying from his mouth, rocking the wagon, ranting, "*Wihitikow* lives in me and—"

Crack!

Griffith watched Swift Runner pull his hands back.

"Shut yer flap, Indian," Hood barked, coiling the whip. "Shut it closed! Or I'll shut it for you."

Swift Runner pulled back and lowered his head, sulking.

They rode past the boy, who kept his eyes locked on the departing Swift Runner. Griffith rejoined Steele, looking back, catching glimpses of the boy, smaller in every glance, until he and St. Albert were gone. The ride was quiet, except for the steady *clip clop* of horses' hooves, an odd snort, and the spring breeze whispering secrets in the trees.

***

Chapter 8 – The Last Leg

I

Afternoon - May 27, 1879
East of St. Albert, NWT

Steele and Griffith talked on and off about the kid on the road, about the butcher, and about Crane. They didn't breach the subject of Swift's camp, and Griffith wasn't forthcoming with anything about the *wihitikow* or the ravens.

"I'm worried about Crane. He barely reacted back there," Steele said.

"What do you think is wrong with him?" Griffith asked.

Steele smirked. "Do I look like a doctor?"

Griffith offered, "Maybe what Hood said was right? That Swift put him under some kind of Indian spell?"

Steele chuckled. "I don't believe in such things."

Griffith stole a glance at Crane, who was bobbing along, mouth unhinged, skin almost gray. "Then what is wrong with him?"

"I don't know, but it isn't Indian magic. Whatever is wrong with Crane is medical. Maybe he has influenza or possibly food poisoning. Marois said he puked something up. Maybe he ate some spoiled meat? Did I mention that I'm not a doctor?"

"You did," Griffith said. "But it's not food poisoning."

Steele shot him a quizzical eye. "How do you know?"

"Because, Sergeant Steele, we all ate the same breakfast and lunch, and nobody else is sick. Also, Crane hasn't shit himself."

"Yes, and thank goodness for that." Steele chuckled.

"I got food poisoning twice. Puking and shitting yourself is mandatory," Griffith said.

"Mandatory?" Steele was laughing.

"Pretty much." Griffith peered sideways and offered one of his cigars to Steele.

"Thank you," Steel said.

"Welcome."

They puffed away quietly for a bit.

Griffith removed the cigar from his mouth and asked, "You've never had food poisoning?"

"No, not once, but it sounds charming." Steele puffed. "Especially the shitting part."

"How is that even possible?"

"Just lucky, I guess." Steele gave him a smile. "I got the clap twice. Does that count for anything?"

Griffith busted out laughing.

"It was, I'm sad to report, from the same woman," Steele said.

"Stop, please stop!" Griffith didn't know what had broken the dam and sent him down the path of skittish abandon, but it was a welcomed relief.

"She said she was all better."

Griffith exploded in a fresh fit of laughter.

Clearly amused, Steele went back to puffing his cigar.

Griffith croaked, "Enough, enough!" Then he was trying to rein it back in, until he said, "Same woman," and flew into another round broken by, "No more! No more," and deep breaths, then "Okay, okay, okay," and more deep breaths.

Steele puffed on his cigar, waiting for Griffith to go off the deep end again.

Griffith regained control, turned, and said, "Crane doesn't have food poisoning."

"Must be Indian magic, then." Steele grinned.

"You never saw the camp, Richard. That's not our friend in the cage. Not the man I knew and worked with. The things he said, blaming us for his family. Look how he acted with that boy. The Swift Runner I knew might have gotten drunk and belligerent, but the camp was a playground of madness."

"Ron, sometimes men go crazy. Women too. Sometimes the brain gets sick. Just as a dog can become feral, so can a man. In this case, that is the most likely culprit."

Griffith pushed off elaborating on the camp. Steele's indifference seemed an impossible obstacle. Still, he asked, "What about Crane, then?"

"Maybe Swift scared him. Shocked him the same way you were shocked by the camp," Steele said. "But got into his head? Made him sick? I doubt Swift has such an ability."

They were quiet again. Griffith thought of his own reaction to Kaplan, and now he was getting the same treatment from Steele. Come to think of it, he and Steele had very similar views about such things. Until the camp. Until the invisible man in the woods. Until Crane.

Steele brought him back. "What was all that stuff back there about a mesmerist?"

Griffith remembered. "I saw a man once at a traveling show called The Remarkable Doctor Ranvier: Mesmerist Extraordinaire. He claimed to be able to influence people's actions." He took a puff on his cigar, exhaled the smoke through his mouth and nose. "I watched him put audience members into a trance and make them do things up on stage."

"What kind of things?"

"He made a man cluck like a hen," Griffith said. "He also convinced him that he had no clothes on, causing him to run around crazily. It was very entertaining, and funny, but also a little unnerving."

"Unnerving how?" Steele asked.

"The idea that someone could strip you of your will and make you do things against your own judgment is quite unnerving. Wouldn't you say?" Griffith asked.

"Yes, I suppose. You didn't step up to be mesmerized?" Steele asked.

"No, I might have if I hadn't been in uniform."

Steele laughed. "That's what I like about you, Ron. Sensible."

"Would you have?"

"No, of course not. It's not dignified to cluck like a hen when you're in uniform." Steele took a puff, exhaled, and added, "I might have tried it in a private setting."

"So, you think it's possible?"

"I have a question for you. Are you sure the man wasn't an actor?" Steele asked.

"He wasn't an actor." Griffith shook his head. "He was a farmer."

"Some of these con men pay people," Steele said. "I've been to one of those healing tent revivals. It's a show, all right, watching people coming in on crutches and the healing hand of God, and—"

"He wasn't an actor. I'd seen him before; he came into town with his wife and seven kids often on a horse pulling an empty hay wagon." Griffith stared back at Crane, who was bobbing along. He looked completely out of it. "After the show, I caught up with the farmer as they got up on the wagon to go home. I asked him if he remembered anything of what he'd done up on stage."

"What did he say?"

"He said, 'I don't remember nothing,' and he snapped the reins, and they rode off."

"That don't prove much," Steele said.

"We're in a different world here, and while we might claim to have some moral or religious superiority, we know little of the Indian customs."

"So Swift Runner is a mesmerist?"

"Maybe," Griffith said.

Steele chuckled.

"He's different, Richard. I don't see a whole lot of the man I used to know. I'm neither religious nor superstitious, but I felt something evil in that camp. Like I was being watched, but it was all around me."

"Murdering your family is an evil act," Steele said. "Hanging dead animals and eating their guts is both evil and repugnant." Griffith was going to respond, but Steele raised his hand gently and continued, "Swift was covered in blood; the allegations against him are horrific and evil. You were fired up when you rode down there, expecting the worst, and it hit you hard enough to turn you gray. I have no doubt that what you saw was evil, but evil spirits, or an Indian mesmerist, isn't something I'll be filing in any official report."

Griffith turned to face Steele. "Mesmerist or not, I don't think any of us should be alone with Swift Runner."

"On that, we agree," Steele said. "Go back and ride with Marois for a bit, and send Crane up to see me. I want to talk to him more about what happened and see if there's anything he might tell me in private."

"You think he's holding something back?"

"I don't know, but I'm sure you're itching to go back and jaw it up with your pal, Marois. So, send him up."

"Yes, Sergeant." Griffith steered Gunner right and rode back past the jail wagon. He felt Swift looking at him but kept his eyes on Crane. He rode past them, circling back up on their left. "Danny, Sergeant Steele wants you to join him."

"Why?" Crane asked.

"He wants to talk about what happened to you."

"God, I just want to get home," Crane complained.

"We all do." Griffith touched Crane's arm. "Danny, when you ride up, don't look at Swift Runner. Don't talk to him, even if he calls to you."

"Oh, don't worry, I won't." Crane rode away, keeping eyes right until he was past the wagon.

"Did the boss demote you, *mon ami*?"

"They would have to promote me to demote me." Griffith winked. "I'm just a lowly constable in the NWMP like yourself, *mon ami*."

"Of course." Marois smiled, tipped his hat.

"Same thing for you, Fred," Griffith warned. "Don't let yourself be alone with Swift."

"Oh, I know. I won't ever be alone with him."

"What happened, Fred? What did you see?"

"Swift Runner did something to Crane. I saw it. After Hood slapped him, he puked up something black, and it melted away like steam. It didn't even leave a stain on the ground."

"That kid back there. He puked something black up too," Griffith said.

"Really? I didn't see that. I saw he peed his pants."

"I'm thinking maybe Swift Runner is a mesmerist?"

"*C'est quoi ça? Mesmériste*?"

"Someone who beguiles people."

"*Oui, ça, il l'est.*" Marois understood.

"You never heard him say anything to Crane?"

"It was already happening when we came along. Danny and Swift were standing face to face, but whatever happened before that is a mystery," Marois said.

"Did either of them say anything during the exchange?"

"*Non.* They were just staring at each other."

"Can you elaborate?"

Marois thought about it, gave a short nod, and said, "Swift Runner was like clay. Nothing on him was moving, not his eyes, not his nose. I didn't even see his chest rising or falling. I'm sure he was breathing, but it looked like he was suspended in time."

"Anything else?"

"*Oui.* The smile on Swift's face, it was a lunatic's smile."

"What was Crane doing during all this?"

"Crane was also still. Barely breathing, nothing moving, but he wasn't smiling. He was staring into Swift Runner's eyes, his face… It was frozen in a mask of terror, like he wanted to break the bond, but he couldn't. I've never seen a man look so frightened."

You should have seen me a few hours ago, Griffith thought but instead said, "Crane still looks scared."

"*Oui*, he does," Marois agreed.

II
1700 Hours
May 27, 1879

The clouds returned, but no rain fell on the way back to Fort Saskatchewan. Hood was all business, clutching the reins, keeping the horses on course. Coiled beside him, the whip waited to be called upon, like a sleeping viper. Steele and Crane maintained the lead, while Marois and Griffith brought up the rear. Swift Runner was still brooding about the boy and Corporal Hood's whip.

After two hours, Steele ordered, "Detachment! Halt!"

Everyone stopped, still spread out tactically. Nobody thought they would be ambushed, but anyone who got ambushed usually thought that and paid dearly. Steele kept them spread out, just in case. "Five-minute break. Stretch your legs and do your business, gents." He dismounted and began to urinate at the side of the trail.

The rest followed suit.

Hood climbed down from his perch, stretched out his back, and said, "Hey, Indian, if you gotta piss, do it now. I don't want no filth inside the carriage." He moved to the back corner of the wagon and began relieving himself.

Griffith was one hundred feet away, watching Hood pull out his pride and piss unapologetically. He would have turned the other way, but Hood was waving with his free hand and grinning ear to ear. "Hey, Ron?"

"Yeah?" Griffith called back.

"If you can guess what I got in me hand, I'll let you have a lick." Then Hood laughed hysterically.

"Yer a sick man, Corporal Hood," Griffith hollered back.

"Bravo, Caporal Hood," called Marois, laughing.

Then Griffith saw a golden stream rising between the bars, reach its pinnacle, arch down, and splash on top of Hood's head. It took a second for everyone to realize what was happening, including Hood, who turned skyward, piss flooding into his left eye. "What the…" His mouth. "Ffff… ahhhh."

Hood bounded away, still confused.

"Oh my God," Griffith said, mounting Gunner.

"What?"

"Swift just pissed on Hood!"

"Pissed? *Quoi*?" Marois climbed up on his horse.

"Come on! Before he kills him." Griffith turned Gunner, leaned forward slightly, and they were gone in a gallop.

"Get up!" Marois prodded his horse and raced after Griffith.

III

Following his hasty retreat, Hood began to understand what had happened. He smelled the urine, felt the sting in his eye, the taste of it in his mouth, and saw tiny golden droplets glistening on his bangs.

Piss!

Hood's eyes, the left one slightly bloodshot, burned their way back to the jail wagon and the kneeling Swift Runner, who was smiling. "You… You fucking pissed on me! You fucking pissed on me!" He slicked back his hair, then examined his wet hand. "You fucking pissed on me!" Not just on him but all over him, in his hair, in his eye, and in his fucking mouth.

The stench of it!

Swift Runner grinned, rattlesnakes dancing in his eyes, and in a strange voice said, "How do I taste, Corporal?"

"Huh?" For Hood, being mocked was almost worse than being pissed on. "You think you're funny?" he yelled. "It'll be funny when you're swinging from a noose with shit in your pants."

"If you like, I will let you have a lick, Corporal." Swift's voice was venomous, burrowing into Hood.

"I'll show you funny," Hood barked. He stomped toward the jail wagon to get his whip.

Then Griffith was there. "Wait! Stop!"

"Fucking savage pissed on me!" Hood grabbed the whip, stepped in front of the cage, began unfurling it, and aiming between the bars. He drew his arm back, ready to snap.

"Corporal Hood, stand fast!" Steele commanded.

Hood froze.

"Put away the whip."

"He pissed on me, Sergeant," Hood complained.

"Corporal, we are officers of the law. There will be no frontier justice on my watch. His actions will be noted, but you won't be whipping him." Steele handed Hood his canteen. "Clean yourself up."

Hood took the canteen and used a rag to clean up.

Steele turned to Swift Runner.

"Now, you listen to me, Swift. If you pull another chicanery like that, I'll tie you to the back of that wagon, and you'll run all the way back to Fort Saskatchewan."

Swift Runner's grin faltered.

"You understand what I'm saying?"

Swift nodded and settled against the back wall.

"That's it?" Hood handed the canteen back.

"It will be noted in the record of investigation. A charge of assault against an officer of the law."

Hood's dagger eyes pointed at Swift Runner.

"Form up, we got a few hours ahead of us yet."

They got back into formation and carried on.

Hood was separated from Swift Runner by the seat and the iron wall. He was in a silent rage, his discipline holding him in check. Disobeying the order of a superior was out of the question for him, so he pushed it down.

An hour later, Steele rode back to the jail wagon and peered between the bars. He saw that Swift was sleeping. He might have been playing possum, which Steele thought possible, but the snoring sounded genuine. He moved his horse in line with Hood and in a low voice said, "You okay?"

"Yes, Sergeant," Hood replied, also in a low voice.

"Good," Steele said. "You understand why I stopped you?"

"Yes."

Swift Runner let out a succession of snorts.

Steele gazed toward Hood, grinned, and said, "I had a guy piss on me once."

"Is that so?" Hood smiled.

"A drunk Frenchman. He'd climbed up a tree and refused to come down. I turned my back for a second, next thing I feel warm piss hit my right ear and shoulder." Steele gazed over at Hood.

"What did you do?"

"I wanted to kill him." Steele grinned.

"But you didn't." Hood grinned back.

"No. I didn't. I wanted to, but I didn't."

They were quiet for a bit.

Hood said, "How did you get him out of the tree?"

"I got an ax and chopped it down."

Hood laughed.

"It wasn't a real big tree," Steele said with a grin, and they both laughed. When that settled, Steele looked over and said, "The incident, if you want, we can keep it off the record."

Hood nodded. "I'd prefer that."

"What happens on the trail stays on the trail," Steele said.

"Yes, Sergeant."

"I'll make sure no one talks about it."

"Thanks, Sergeant." Hood's mood lightened considerably.

"Gotta go." Steele winked and rode away as Hood watched, a smile still on his face. The incident was weighing heavily on his mind. He felt better about the whole thing, humiliating as it was. He liked Sergeant Steele; he was a good leader, considerate.

"Hey, Corporal, I'll keep it quiet too," Swift Runner whispered from behind.

Hood stood up, swung around to look. Swift Runner was fast asleep.

But he had heard him. He watched for a second and retreated to the bench seat.

No more words from behind or inside his head.

IV

Two hours later, the road became mucky, and their progress was again slow. The horses on the wagon were given a rest at the location they had used on the way to St. Albert.

"Last leg will be the hardest," Griffith said.

"No harder than it was coming in," Hood said.

"It might be a bit better; there's been no rain since this morning." Steele re-lit a half-spent cigar. "We're losing daylight. I don't want any loitering; let's chow down and get moving."

There were nods of agreement.

"Marois, get him some food." Steele pointed to the wagon.

"I'm not hungry, Sergeant." Swift was curled in a fetal position, facing them through the bars.

"I don't want any food either," Crane said.

Griffith thought Crane looked even grayer than before.

"Suit yourselves," Steele said. "The rest of you, dog up."

The hamper contained cooked chicken and bread rolls cocooned in cloth, sealing in the warmth, and it smelled wonderful. Griffith's appetite had returned, whether from the ride or being farther away from the horror he had encountered.

He, Steele, Hood, and Marois all ate the meal prepared by the nuns.

Crane sat with his back against a tree.

Out of earshot, Swift Runner watched from the jail wagon.

While they ate, Steele talked about the incident involving Hood and Swift Runner and said it wasn't a matter of official record. "As officers of the Northwest Mounted Police, I expect that you will not speak of this again."

Hood's eyes were moving from man to man, looking for a sneer, a snicker, any indication that the secret wouldn't be kept. There was none, and all agreed to forget the incident.

"I appreciate your discretion," Hood muttered.

That was the end of it.

They ate, mounted up, and were moving again.

For over three hours, they slogged through the muddy trail until they made it back to dry road. It was easier going east, but not a whole lot. Hood didn't fall back this time; the detachment of men and their prisoner moved at a slower but uniform pace. There was even a bit of light left in the prairie sky when they got back onto dry ground.

V

When the light was gone, Griffith found himself stewing about Swift Runner. Feeling the sting of the accusation, he said, "You took our food, Constable Ron." In Griffith's time as a Mountie, he had arrested plenty of criminals—some petty, some hard-boiled. Career criminals almost always had an excuse or someone else to blame. Blaming others wasn't that unusual.

However, Griffith had never seen that side of Swift Runner.

"White man took all the food for White man," Swift Runner echoed.

Griffith recalled slaughtered bison, killed only for their hides. Left on the plain were whole herds, reduced to giant mounds of meat rotting in the sun. They were inedible to anyone or anything, as the hunters had poisoned the mounds with strychnine. Griffith agreed that Swift was right about the things that had happened to his people, had heard him grumble when the drinking took over. But surely, even starvation was no excuse for murdering your family and eating them? If that was what he had, in fact, done.

"Ain't that a sight for sore eyes," Sergeant Steele called.

"There she be," Hood agreed.

Marois and Griffith were leaning forward, looking for the light.

"There she is," Steele called.

"*Le voilà*," Marois said.

Griffith was leaning forward, staring into the darkness. "Ah, I see it now."

"Finally," Swift Runner mumbled.

Hood was the first to laugh, then the rest joined in, even Crane.

They had reached Fort Saskatchewan.

VI

2210 Hours
May 27, 1879
Fort Saskatchewan, NWT

The garrison was a welcome sight. Torches burned at the lookouts, amber light flickering against the log walls of the fortress. Sergeant Steele and Crane rode on ahead to get the gates open and ready the jail, while Griffith and Marois got up on either side of Hood.

"*Bienvenue à la maison*," Marois said.

"I, uh, don't speak French," Hood said.

"Welcome home," Marois translated.

"Welcome home, ah yes." Hood smiled, but it was uncertain, still thinking about the piss incident.

Griffith picked up on it and said, "What happens on the trail stays on the trail."

Hood looked at Griffith, then Marois, who nodded.

"I am appreciative," Hood said.

"Forget it."

Hood nodded, smiled, and said, "I intend to." That brought laughter. "Ron, you're going to have to get out of the way. I gotta swing a wide right to line her up on the gate."

"Yeah, okay." Griffith pulled back on the reins and whispered, "Whoa, Gunner." The horse slowed, and the wagon pulled away as they steered behind it, until it swung right.

He got up beside Marois.

"Oh Ron, I'm tired, *mon ami*," Marois said.

"I was thinking you and I might go off for a nightcap," Griffith said.

"Night cap?" Marois took a moment. "Maybe one to put me to bed."

"The stable, just be us in there."

"What about the sergeant, and Crane, and Corporal Hood?"

"The sergeant is going right in to see the old man. Hood will tend to his wagon. Crane is headed for the infirmary. Besides, I want to have a private talk."

"All right, Ron, but only one drink."

"Maybe two?" Griffith smiled.

"Maybe two," Marois agreed and grinned.

They rode in to help Corporal Hood.

VII

Griffith had been right. Steele ordered Crane to stable his horse and go to the infirmary. A moment later, Griffith and Marois rode up to assist him. Steele pointed at the guard room. "I had Crane open the cell door. The keys are hung back up. I sent him to see the doc. You gents, get him into his cell. I am going to see the commandant and report our arrival. Make sure Crane's horse and mine are properly stabled."

"Yes, Sergeant," Hood said.

Marois and Griffith dismounted and tethered their horses. Hood watched them do so, purposely ignoring Swift Runner, not wanting to stir up the anger in his belly. It had been humiliating, but everyone had agreed to keep it quiet. If the story got out, it would spread like wildfire and before long, someone would nickname him something like, "Piss head" or "Piss eye." He would never live it down; it would ruin him. He was glad when Griffith and Marois said they would forget about it and he wanted to believe they would, though it made him no less wary. Hood was a proud military man who had come to the service of the NWMP after leaving the army. The line share of Mounties were recruited out of the combat units, and many were gunners from the Royal Canadian Horse Artillery. Hood had been an infantryman, and though welcomed by the others, he still felt a bit like an outsider. Gunners were a tight-knit bunch. Hood pushed the thought away. It was time to move the Indian.

"Prisoner, we're going to move you," he said. "You mind us! Understand?"

"Yes." Swift Runner nodded and started to rise.

"Sit down, Swift Runner," Griffith said.

Swift Runner gazed at Griffith.

"Sit down, Swift. We'll tell you when to get up." Griffith looked to one side, then back.

"You pay attention!" Hood grunted.

Swift Runner sat back down.

"Good." Hood unlocked the padlock. There was a click, and the shackle popped open. He removed it and swung the door open. "Prisoner, stand up!"

Then he stepped away and placed his shaking hand on his sidearm. "You come on out, and the constables will help you into yer new home." Hood gave his sidearm a tap for Swift Runner to see. "Give them no trouble! Understand?"

"No trouble."

Hood kept his hand ready. "Come on out, Indian."

Swift Runner stood, his chains clinking on the floorboards. The wagon leaned as he moved toward the door. He stepped down, bare feet finding the cool earth.

Marois and Griffith got on either side of him.

Swift Runner lowered his head and began to sob.

Hood gave the order, "Prisoner and escorts… March!"

They escorted Swift Runner from the wagon to a waiting cell. He didn't resist, continuing to weep as he went. When they reached the cell, Swift Runner had to duck his head. Once inside, Griffith removed his restraints. He kept his eyes down while Hood stood in the doorway with his hand still on his gun.

"Where is your family?" Griffith asked.

"I am tired." The cot creaked under his weight.

"Where is your family, Swift Runner?" Griffith repeated.

No response.

Griffith stepped back.

Marois closed and locked the cell.

***

Chapter 9 – Charlotte

I

2215 Hours
May 27, 1879
Fort Saskatchewan, NWT

With Crane off to the infirmary, Steele reported to Superintendent Jarvis's office. When he returned fifteen minutes later, they were standing in a semicircle outside the officers' quarters for a debriefing.

"Corporal Hood, is everything buttoned up and put away?" Steele asked.

"Yes, Sergeant, the prisoner has been secured," Hood reported. "We'll stable the horses after the orders group."

"Good. There are four officers posting guard this evening, so that is taken care of." Steele glanced toward the cell. "For tomorrow, we'll tend to our horses and equipment. Reveille is at 0700 hours, after breakfast report to the stable."

Hood nodded. "Yes, Sergeant."

Steele turned his attention on all of them. "Gentlemen, you did an outstanding job today. I informed Superintendent Jarvis of your conduct, and there will be a write-up added to all your personnel files. Are there any questions?"

Griffith raised a hand.

"Go ahead," Steele said.

"Sergeant, did you inform the guard shift not to engage with Swift Runner individually?" Griffith asked.

"Yes, I informed them that they are not to converse with the prisoner," Steele said. "Anything else?"

"No, Sergeant." Griffith thought Steele had probably warned them but omitted Crane or the boy in St. Albert. He probably hadn't mentioned it to Superintendent Jarvis either. No point fighting it; talk of mesmerists and windigos had passed.

"Well, gents, it's been a long day. If yer thinking about a choir practice in the stables, keep your duties and the time of those duties in yer mind." Steele stepped back.

"Why don't you join us, Sergeant?" Hood offered.

Griffith and Marois looked at Hood and at each other, then at Steele, who said, "Tempting as that might be, I'm going to be writing reports for the next while. Don't let it get out of hand, Corporal Hood."

"I won't, Sergeant."

Hood just invited himself, Griffith thought and laughed.

"Something funny?" Hood asked.

"It has been a long day. Marois and I were talking about a sip in the stable and didn't know if you'd want to join us. You clearly do and I found it funny. No offense, Corporal."

"None taken." Hood grinned.

"I'll be in meetings with Superintendent Jarvis, discussing today's events and the investigation late into the morning. I'll be over to check your progress before the lunch hour. I want written reports from all of you after your maintenance is completed," Steele said.

"Yes, Sergeant," everyone responded.

"Good work and good evening, gents." Steele marched off into the darkness.

Outside the guard room, an officer took his post.

They went to the stables, tended their horses, and helped Hood disconnect his own horses from the jail wagon. With that completed, they finished stabling Steele and Crane's horses.

II
2310 Hours - The Stables

They were well into their cups. They were tired, but the booze perked them up. Marois was trying to translate a French joke into English that neither Hood nor Griffith understood but still found hilarious.

"Ze chicken was holding a gun on ze pig and..."

When the flasks were emptied, Hood produced a bottle from his saddlebag. "Look what ze chicken robbed off ze pig."

More laughter.

They drank into the bottom of the hour. It wasn't all chicken and pigs. They spoke about Crane and Swift Runner, and the mesmerizing. Griffith withheld what had happened to him at the camp. He wanted to tell Marois, but he didn't know Hood all that well and wanted it kept in confidence.

"What I think is that he's one of those witch doctors, like in Africa," Hood slurred.

"A shaman," Griffith corrected.

"Same thing."

"I think he's possessed by a *démon*," Marois said.

"A windigo," Griffith said.

"That's what he might call it, but…" Marois hiccupped and burped. "Their *démons* are still our *démons*."

"Demons that make you eat family?" Hood snickered.

"Human sacrifice," Marois mumbled. "I think he met *le diable*—the Devil—in the north and killed them all."

"Maybe they died of starvation," Griffith said, "like he said."

"Yeah, sure." Hood snickered again.

"The investigation will reveal more," Griffith slurred.

"The investigation will reveal that he most likely killed them and probably ate them." Hood stood up. "There's something wrong with him. I saw what he did to Crane. Maybe Marois is right: their devils are our devils." He straightened his uniform. "I do know I'm gonna have me a piss and bid you gentlemen all a goodnight."

"Goodnight," Griffith said.

"*Bonsoir, Caporal*," Marois said.

"I'll see you in the early hours."

"You will," they agreed.

When he was gone, Griffith looked at the equally drunk Marois and took the last swallow of Hood's whisky.

"Why didn't Steele talk about what happened to Crane?"

"I don't know. What I do know is that we were supposed to stop after two drinks, and we are on duty in…" He removed his watch from his pocket, looked at it, and cussed, "*Tabarnak*."

"What time is it?"

"It's 0145 hours."

They stumbled outside.

"All the time I wasted in that stable drinking could have been put to better use, Ron," Marois complained and unbuttoned his fly. "We could have snuck into town and got laid."

"You mean you would have gotten laid," Griffith corrected him grimly.

"She's not coming back, *mon ami*," Marois said.

"Why you gotta bring that up?"

Marois was talking about the woman who had broken Griffith's heart. He had fallen hard for her, even though Marois knew she hadn't for him. Her name was Tasha Larson, and she was a gorgeous, curvy dirty blonde with blue eyes, fair skin, and a wildness about her. She was intoxicating and seductive, manipulative and sadistic. The affair between them had only lasted three months, and in that time when Griffith was on the trail, she tried unsuccessfully to take Marois to her bed. He never told Griffith and was secretly relieved when she left him for a prospector named Jack Sool. Tasha and Jack had taken off three months ago in search of Yukon gold. Griffith was still carrying a torch for her.

"You need to get laid," Marois said.

Griffith ignored the question. "So, who was on the menu for tonight?"

"Probably Gertrude," Marois said.

"Gertrude?" Griffith's most up-to-date intelligence provided by Marois was that he had five ladies in the area whom he frequently visited. Four were beautiful young women, all drawn to Marois's boyish good looks, blond hair, and French charm. "Is that the ugly one?"

"No, that's..." He was speaking of a Scottish woman named Flora, who was the least pretty, but for reasons he wouldn't divulge, his favorite among all his lovers. They finished their piss and stumbled drunkenly back to the barracks, discussions of women, windigos, and chickens with guns forgotten.

III
0322 Hours - May 28, 1879

Griffith awakened to the sound of coyotes howling outside the walls of the fort. He brought his hand up and squeezed the bridge of his nose. He was still drunk, but there was a monster hangover looming in the shadows. More howling in the early morning dark.

There must be fifty of them.

He sat up, rubbed his eyes, and the sound of howling coyotes transformed into the screams of a raving lunatic. The commotion around him drew him from his stupor.

Marois was there, shirtless, hoisting up his pants. "It's Swift Runner!"

Griffith stood up, swayed, sat down, got up again, and began searching for his pants.

Everyone sleeping in the bunk house were up and heading out the door to see what the furor was. Oil lamps were being lit. Griffith and Marois stumbled out of the barracks. They were moving around the building, a mob of men, most of them in their underpants, marching toward the guardhouse to a man surely being flailed. At the front of the guard shack stood two officers facing the building.

Hood was already there, looking quite unhappy to be awakened. "What in the name of B'Jesus is going on in there?"

"He won't shut up," the guard said. "He started weeping, and I told him to go to sleep. Then he started bawling. Then he was arguing."

"Arguing? With you?" Hood asked.

"No, with whoever he thought was in there with him. He just got louder and louder, and now…"

Swift Runner was yelling in Cree at the top of his lungs.

"What the fuck is he on about?" Hood barked.

"It's nonsense," Marois said.

Is he arguing with the thing from the forest? Griffith wondered.

Hood stepped through the door. "I'm telling you to shut yer goddamn trap, Indian."

Swift Runner ignored Hood, shouting at the wall in Cree. Griffith could barely see him through the door. Hood spun around and came back out and called, "Galli, go get a bucket of water."

"Sure thing, Corporal." Galli turned to go.

Hood saw Sergeant Steele stomping across the yard. He was dressed, but unbuttoned and untucked, and looking mighty unhappy to be so. He was wearing his side arm.

Hood called, "Wait! Galli, stop, forget it."

"What is going on here?" Steele demanded.

Before Hood could answer, Swift Runner broke into a fresh rant.

"Everyone get the hell out of the way!" Steele marched forward, the crowd spread, he unholstered his gun and stepped onto the boardwalk. When he reached the doorway, he pointed the gun skyward and fired.

Everyone except Steele flinched.

Swift Runner stopped, mouth hanging partly open.

"Shut yer bloody mouth! Do you understand?"

Swift Runner gasped, sucking in quick breaths, exhaling, trying to cool down, rocking the madness back to sleep like a two-year-old coming off a temper tantrum.

"Swift Runner," Steele roared. "I asked you a question!"

Swift Runner turned to face Steele, tears glistening in the lantern glow, and asked, "Do you not see it, Sergeant?"

Steele holstered his weapon, staring where Swift was looking. "I don't see anything, Swift."

"He cannot see you," Swift Runner said in English to the wall. "Only I can see you."

Steele softened. "Listen, you probably had a bad dream."

"He thinks you are a dream," Swift said to the wall.

Steele sighed. "It has been a long day, Swift. Go back to sleep. We'll talk in the daylight."

"Yes, Sergeant." Swift leaned back into the shadows.

Steele stood there a minute longer, pondering, then abandoning some thought. He stepped out of the doorway and back around to face the audience of half-dressed Mounties. "Thank you for attending the evening's festivities. This concludes our show, so back to the barracks in an orderly fashion." He then turned to the guards. "If he pulls this horse puck again, get as many men as you need to hogtie his ass up and mute him."

"Yes, Sergeant," they both replied.

"Don't abuse him, but don't wait until it turns into a fucking dog and pony show like tonight!"

"Sergeant Steele," Superintendent Jarvis called from the window of his quarters.

"Ah, shit." Steele rolled his eyes and called back, "Yes, sir."

"Did you shoot someone?"

Steele rolled his eyes again. "No, sir!"

"Is it all in hand now?"

"Yes, sir."

"Good night, Sergeant."

"Good night, sir." Steele looked back through the door at Swift Runner. "Not another peep out of you."

There was no response.

That night, there was none.

IV

Swift Runner's wife Charlotte was the mother of five, and a devoted wife. She was soft in some ways and hard in others. She was into her thirties and should have been carrying weight after bearing five babies, but she was thin and strikingly beautiful, with mahogany almond eyes set above knife-edged cheekbones curtained by raven hair threaded with silken gray. Her hardness came in her terse criticisms of Swift's drinking and threatening to leave him. Charlotte often traveled from Egg Lake to St. Albert with her children to sell beads and crafts, while Swift Runner worked for the Hudson's Bay Company and the NWMP.

Swift was a nomadic husband. He would be gone for a week or more, working his traplines or working with the Mounties or as a guide for the Hudson's Bay Company. Then one day he came back, the smell of whisky on his breath and resentment in his heart. The drinking and the absences increased and with that, the rages and the violence. The last time, Charlotte hadn't seen her husband for three months, resulting in a whisky binge that ended in his jailing.

Swift Runner threatened to kill a White trader, whom he had branded a cheat and a liar. He stumbled away, only to return a few minutes later with his rifle to make good on the threat. He fired at the man, but the whisky betrayed his aim, sending the bullet wild.

Swift Runner was arrested and put in a cell.

Goodwill and diplomacy on the part of the NWMP kept Swift Runner from remaining in jail. The trapper agreed to drop the charges if Swift Runner apologized. He did so the next day, but there were more consequences. The Hudson's Bay Company and the NWMP had deemed him unemployable. He was ordered back to his people in Egg Lake and was no longer welcome in Fort Saskatchewan.

Griffith was assigned to escort him back.

V

Swift Runner was riding a loaned horse. Once delivered to his people, the horse would go back with Griffith. It was an awkward ride, and one-sided. Griffith tried to talk to Swift Runner but was met with indifferent silence.

"You need to stay out of trouble," Griffith said. "You need to stay away from the whisky, Swift. It changes you, makes you angry, turns you into someone else."

No response.

More silence except for the sounds of the ride.

Clip clop, *clip clop.*

"You don't want to talk to me? Fine. That doesn't mean I have to stop talking to you." Griffith smiled. "In fact, if I want to talk to you all day long I will, and if you want to play the mute, you go right ahead."

Swift Runner frowned at Griffith.

Griffith smiled, pulled out his cigar case, and offered.

Swift considered, took the cigar, rolled it between his lips, and bit off the tip. He reached in his pocket, produced a match, and lit the cigar.

Griffith lit his own, and they rode in silence.

"You know what I think? You need to go back to the land and to your people. It will be good to have you there to provide. You're the best tracker and trapper I've ever known. You need to find your way back to that, Swift. You don't need the booze."

Swift Runner stayed quiet.

"Suit yourself," Griffith said with a sigh.

They rode quietly for a spell, and then Griffith tried again.

"My mother liked to drink. But when she drank, she changed too, and not for the better. I don't think she knew how it changed her, but she was mean to me as a boy. Said mean things. Said I was the reason my father left." Griffith looked over at Swift Runner and continued.

"My father left because of her and the booze, but he also left me, so maybe she was half right. When he was there, she would drink and insult him. Then one day he wasn't there ever again, and before long, I took his place."

They stopped to relieve themselves and carried on.

More silence.

Clip clop, clip clop.

"You don't know how lucky you are," Griffith said. "A lot of people went out of their way to help you, including the trapper you shot at. They could have charged you with attempted murder."

Swift kept his eyes straight ahead, on the trail, face hard.

Griffith felt a pang of guilt.

VI
Egg Lake, NWT

Charlotte had a baby in her clutch, and behind her, a gathering of little ones of varied ages and sexes were playing and laughing. She saw her husband, saw the Mountie accompanying him, and frowned.

Griffith looked from Charlotte to Swift.

The air between them was tense.

She knows, this is it, Griffith thought. The baby fussed, and she offered it a breast. Griffith saw the exposed breast and turned away while he and Swift dismounted.

"Goodbye, Constable Ron." Swift handed over the reins.

"Take care of yourself, Swift," Griffith said. "And good luck."

"Luck is a White man's word," Swift said, walking away, past Charlotte's angry stare. He said something to her in Cree and kept on toward his children.

"*Ohtâwîmâw*," his children called gleefully. Cree for "father." "*Ohtâwîmâw*! *Ohtâwîmâw*! *Ohtâwîmâw*!" They ran to him, encircling him. Swift Runner sat down, and they crawled over him like he was a mountain. He lifted one of his sons up over his head and let out a bear's roar. The boy roared back; they were all laughing, Swift Runner included.

He's better off here, Griffith told himself.

He finished readying the follow for the horse, securing a knot and giving it a shake to test it. He climbed aboard Gunner, glancing back at

Swift Runner playing with his children. Beyond the children, the elder named Chogan watched disapprovingly. Word of Swift Runner's exploits had reached the ears of his people from elder to wife. Charlotte was still facing Griffith, eyes drilling into him as her husband and children played and giggled behind her. Why was she staring at him? He gave her a cursory nod and turned to go, until she said something in Cree and he understood, although he shouldn't.

He turned back to face her.

"Pardon me?"

"You have delivered death upon us," she said.

VII

Griffith opened his eyes. Charlotte's accusation tumbled away into the withdrawing dream, while reality was awakened by a smell. In the bunk across from him, he heard a man snoring while letting out the occasional gasp. The snoring was a precursor to the gasp, almost a warning, then a pause, then the gasp and another snore. The farts, which were acidic, biting and rancid, had no precursor of a toot or trumpet or even a poof. Silent, deadly.

Griffith turned, cupping his nose, and his attention was drawn to dust particles floating in a ray of light coming through the window. He watched the little particles; they looked like microscopic sea life floating in an ocean of light.

Griffith thought about Charlotte and the dream.

Was it a dream? Or was it a memory? Griffith mused.

It was both.

Everything Griffith remembered from the dream was what had really happened on the day he escorted Swift Runner back to Egg Lake, except for a few details. He did see Charlotte, and she was as he remembered from the dream. He had seen Chogan as well, watching with impatience. That was real. But he never spoke to Charlotte, never heard her voice because she had never said a word.

So, why? Why the accusation? Is it guilt?

It made sense. He felt guilty about Swift Runner, he did bring him back, and they did banish him, so Griffith thought he bore some responsibility. Was Charlotte pointing an accusing finger at him from the grave? The guy behind him snored, gasped, and there was sound accompanying the gag-inducing flatulence of a man who might have had a dead animal fermenting inside his rectum.

Griffith sat up, held his breath, put his boots on, and stomped outside to have a piss. In the cool morning air, the urgency to pee increased, so he half walked, half jogged to the designated pissing area, DPA for short. This was a term coined by Marois and used by all as an inside joke.

Once there, he found a spot, unbuttoned, and began to relieve himself.

A septic stench permeated from a collection of buckets of undisposed poop five feet to his left, and this made him nauseous. There was a duty detail that took care of feces. Somehow, Griffith had managed to dodge that assignment. If the rumors of his promotion had any validity, he wished they would get on with it before someone realized he hadn't done a turn. Corporals didn't do poop patrol, another term coined by Marois.

In his mind, Charlotte repeated, "“You have delivered death upon us”

Why? Why would I dream that?

"It was the booze," he whispered.

He put himself away and walked back toward the barracks. Along the way, he spotted the bugler making his way to his post. By the time Griffith got back in the barracks and was dressing, the bugler had begun to play the morning reveille.

***

Chapter 10 – Enter Gagnon

I

May 28, 1879
Fort Saskatchewan, NWT

Griffith, Marois, and Hood furnished their handwritten reports to Sergeant Steele. He looked over each chronicle, nodding, grunting, and placing them in his pocket when finished. "Very good." He smiled at the three men. "You gentleman look a tad green behind the gills."

"Feeling just fine, Sergeant," Hood assured him.

"Yeah?" Steele turned to Griffith. "You look like you ate the ass out of a dead moose and need to take a shit, Constable Griffith."

"I feel like a moose shit on my head, Sergeant."

"How about you, Marois?"

"I never ate no moose ass, Sergeant."

"Could have fooled me." Steele winked at Hood, and they all laughed. Hangovers aside, the mood was good, and Steele didn't give them a hard time. "Overall, good reports on the events of yesterday. One slight criticism goes to Marois. You need to work on giving more details."

"Yes, Sergeant."

"Talk to Griffith. He knows a bunch of fancy bullshit words that I don't even know. I don't know where he gets them." Steele smiled. "Probably out of his ass."

"That's why you can't shit, Ron?" Hood laughed.

Steele snickered and carried on. "Writing a detailed report is vital to every investigation. Observe what you see and report it on paper."

"Yes, Sergeant." Marois nodded.

"You're a damn good officer, Freddy, but I want you to be better because I know you got it in you."

Marois perked up and smiled. "I will do better."

"Maybe you can help Griffith take a shit," Hood snarked.

Everyone cracked up.

"What about Crane's report?" Griffith asked.

Steele sniffed and turned to face Griffith. "Crane is in the infirmary and in no shape to write reports. I won't need his; your combined testimony will corroborate what I wrote in my report."

"What about what happened to him?"

"Interesting you should mention that. I went down to see the doc, and he says Crane cut his back on a rusty fence nail in the stable. That happened about ten days before we went to St. Albert. He said the wound, which isn't much bigger than a penny, is infected. He's suggesting that is what made him throw up that black stuff and has turned him so pale."

"A nail?" Griffith wasn't sure he believed this, but Steele never gave him a chance to question it.

"I'm heading back to see the CO, and I'll add your reports to mine. Then we're going over to the cell to do a proper interrogation of Swift Runner. Maybe then, we'll get to the bottom of this. I'll be back later to check on your progress." Steele left them and went back to meet Superintendent Jarvis.

II

Before questioning, Jarvis cautioned Swift Runner of his rights while standing outside his cell. "Swift Runner, it is my duty to inform you that anything you say will be written down and used against you should charges be laid. I would advise you to request legal counsel before speaking with officers further. Do you wish to seek counsel?"

"Counsel?" Swift Runner shook his head.

"A lawyer," Jarvis said.

"No counsel," Swift Runner replied.

"I will further caution you that anything you say may be used should a trial arise from the allegations against you. Do you understand, Swift Runner?"

Swift Runner nodded.

Steele questioned him, and he maintained his story that his family had perished from starvation.

"Don't be telling stories, now," Steele urged. "Tell us the truth. Where are they?"

Swift Runner said, "All dead."

"How? How did they die?" Steele pushed.

Swift Runner looked down, contemplating.

"Did you kill them?"

"*Wihitikow* killed them," Swift Runner said.

"*Wihitikow.*" Steele rolled his eyes.

"It is here now, watching us." Swift Runner looked toward the corner of the cell wall, and both men stopped long enough to look. There was an odd shadow in the corner, slowly dancing in the flickering flame of the oil lamp.

"Can you feel it?" Swift Runner asked.

Steele paused, then shook it off and barked, "Enough of this! Tell us where they are!"

Swift Runner turned away. "I am done speaking."

Jarvis tapped Steele and gestured toward the door.

"Very well," Steele said. "We'll discuss this again."

They exited the guardroom.

"Sir, I, uh…" Steele started.

"Follow me," Jarvis said and stepped off the boardwalk. Steele followed him. When Jarvis reached the center of the yard, he turned around to face Steele. "Ask your question now."

"No disrespect, sir, but you're advising him to seek counsel?" Steele smiled. "How are we to extract a confession if you're advising him not to talk?."

"It's the law," Jarvis said. "This case is going to be a big deal, Richard. There'll be newsmen and politicians looking to make sure that every 'i' is dotted and every 't' crossed. We're already under the scrutinous eye of our friends in Upper Canada. What we don't need is a scandal. Swift Runner is to be advised of his rights every time he's interrogated or for requests to give a statement."

"Yes, sir."

Jarvis changed direction. "That aside, you're sure he killed them?"

"I'd say so, sir." Steele nodded. "Yes, sir."

Jarvis removed a pipe from his pocket and lit it. "Dead or alive, we need to find his family and solve this."

"Yes, sir." Steele lit a half-smoked cigar.

Jarvis's words came out in puffing clouds of pipe smoke. "You tell the men I won't tolerate the jabbering nonsense about Indian spirits spreading around the fort. There's going to be eyes all over this. I want the family found, and if there has been foul play, we'll bring justice to the victims. That includes informing the prisoner of his rights and making sure that warning is recorded."

"Yes, sir."

"He'll talk, Richard, it's only a matter of time."

"Yes, sir."

"Sub-Inspector Gagnon will be back today. He'll be leading the investigation."

"Best man for the job, sir." Steele respected Gagnon.

"Oh, yes, I almost forgot. I'm reassigning you."

Steele raised his eyebrows and pulled the cigar from his mouth. "Is there an issue, sir?"

Jarvis grinned. "There's no issue, Richard. I've received another assignment for you and Corporal Hood in Fort Macleod."

"Sir?"

"They need a prisoner brought back to Edmonton to face murder charges. The killer's name is Jonathan Collie. He killed two sisters and defiled them after burglarizing their home in Edmonton. He was apprehended in Fort Macleod and needs to be brought back for trial. He poses a serious escape risk and isn't afraid to mix it up. He broke a guard's ribs and nose while trying to escape custody."

"Sounds like a bruiser," Steele said.

Jarvis pointed his pipe. "That's why I'm sending you, Richard."

"Yes, sir." Steele held his gaze.

"If it wasn't for this, you'd be the sub-inspector's right-hand man in the investigation. But this is a job where I need your brains and brawn."

"Yes, sir."

"Take Corporal Hood and the jail wagon. When you get down there, Fort Macleod will be providing two escorts. You can roll down, pick him up, and bring him back to Edmonton to face charges."

"Yes, sir."

"I will have your written orders and the proper authorities for the Fort Macleod transfer ready in a half hour. I don't expect to see you for a few weeks."

"Yes, sir, that sounds about right," Steele said. "Regarding the ongoing investigation, I would like to recommend Constables Griffith and Marois. They're both solid officers who will be an asset to whatever task is required. Besides, Griffith has a connection with Swift Runner."

"I'll pass their names on to Sub-Inspector Gagnon once we figure out how to get Swift Runner talking. How's the other officer doing? Crane?"

"He's not feeling well at all, sir. Doc Herchmer thinks he's got blood poisoning from a rusty nail." Steele was coating the truth. Herchmer had said, "It might be connected," and he had also omitted what happened with Swift Runner at the Catholic mission.

"Is that serious?" Jarvis asked.

Steele was about to say something but didn't want to dig in any deeper. "I… I think you should consult the doctor, sir. I know nothing about blood poisoning." He stubbed out his cigar.

"Of course, I'll do that."

"Unless there is anything else, I best get to my duties, sir."

"One more thing. The quartermaster has already put together supplies for your trip."

"Yes, sir."

"I'll have those orders ready within the next thirty minutes. Go about your duties, Richard."

"Yes, sir," Steele said and left the older man behind. He was confused as to why Jarvis spent so much time schooling him about the letter of the law if he, Steele, was being reassigned.

Bloody officers, he thought, shaking his head.

Jarvis would probably end up giving an identical speech to Sub-Inspector Gagnon.

Maybe he was warming up on me?

Steele chuckled and muttered aloud, "Bloody officers."

He went back down to the stable to meet Hood outside and brief him.

"Where are we going?" Hood asked.

"Fort Macleod, prisoner transfer. Head on over to the QM; they've got supplies waiting for us."

Hood went to get the supplies.

Steele briefed Griffith and Marois. "Corporal Hood and I are going to Fort Macleod for a prisoner transfer. Sub-Inspector Gagnon will be taking over the investigation. He'll want to speak with both of you."

They nodded.

"Sub-Inspector Gagnon is a good man," Marois said.

"I couldn't think of a better man to lead an investigation," Steele said. "Other than myself."

There was laughter.

"You gents give a hand rigging up the horses on Hood's contraption?" Steele pointed. "Hood should be back with supplies, and he can check your work."

"Yes, Sergeant," Griffith said.

They went to work while Steele readied his own horse. Hood came back with another officer, each carrying an armful of supplies. They loaded that up while Steele reported back to Superintendent Jarvis.

Half an hour later, Steele returned, and they climbed onto their respective horses and jail wagon.

"See you in a few weeks," Steele said.

"Safe travels, Richard," Griffith said.

"*Au revoir*," Marois said. "Farewell."

Steele winked and gave his horse a nudge.

Hood leaned down from the wagon and chirped, "Hey, Ron?"

"Yeah?"

"Don't be eating any moose ass while we're gone. We want to see you do that."

"Maybe he wants to watch that. I personally do not." Steele laughed.

"What else am I supposed to do?" Griffith snorted.

"You can eat Marois's ass." Hood rolled away, tittering as he went. "Give him a taste, Freddy!"

"Not happening," Marois called.

More laughter.

Then they were gone.

III

Sub-Inspector Severe Gagnon was a man of average build whose thinning hair line was compensated by a beard which hung to his belly. The dark mane was so thick that he couldn't secure the chin strap on his pillbox hat. Instead, Gagnon tucked the chin strap up into the cap and balanced it on his head, canted to dress policy. Not once had it come off in the presence of anyone in the NWMP.

There were theories about how it was secured—hooks, pins, horse glue?

But none were proven.

Gagnon was French but also spoke and wrote fluently in English. He was a experienced and respected officer, noted for his intelligence and approach to even the most difficult of tasks. He was also a Fort Saskatchewan original.

Sub-Inspector Gagnon and Superintendent Jarvis had traveled over 900 miles from the east, driving horses and wagons of goods along with settlers. Gagnon had commanded "A Troop," and at the time, his sergeant major was Sam Steele, Richard's brother.

Gagnon rode into the fort late that afternoon, where a Constable Galli met him at the gate with a message to report to Superintendent Jarvis immediately. "I'll stable your horse, sir," Galli offered.

"*Merci.*" Gagnon dismounted, taking the offer and proceeded directly to the superintendent's office. He knocked, entered, and they met behind closed doors.

Two hours later, Jarvis and Gagnon emerged for dinner.

IV

Griffith and Marois were talking about another officer named Corporal Fred Bagley, with whom Marois had shared a guard duty or two. Marois remarked that Bagley was an insufferable know-it-all and a braggart. "The man doesn't know how to shut his mouth. He knows everything about the NWMP, and Indians, and any other topic you should want to breach."

Griffith knew about Corporal Bagley, who had also been on the march west to Fort Macleod, an unforgiving trek that saw their horses dying five a day. Corporal Bagley was very well thought of in Fort Macleod, and by the leadership here in Fort Saskatchewan.

"He might be a braggart, but he earned those corporal stripes honestly," Griffith said.

"Honestly?" Marois laughed. "His mouth is a fertilizer factory, *mon ami*. And as far as bullshit goes, he's bags full."

"You're both named Fred, you'd think you'd get along." Griffith laughed.

"Only you get to call me Fred."

"Okay, Fredericke."

Later, Griffith wondered why Steele had dismissed the story about Crane being mesmerized by Swift Runner. He had said he didn't believe in such things, yet he agreed that the guards shouldn't engage with Swift Runner, and he also kept them off the guard list.

Not that Griffith wanted to be near Swift Runner.

He thought about Crane's words: *"He was trying to get in."*

Trying? Griffith thought. In Crane's case, Swift did get in.

He didn't believe the blood poisoning story either. Swift had done something to Crane.

Maybe he got into my head at the camp, and that's why I'm having nightmares about his wife? He thought about that for a while and found no resolution.

A hand fell on his shoulder.

"It's lunchtime," Marois said.

V

Griffith and Marois were eating in the dining room when they saw Sub-Inspector Gagnon and Superintendent Jarvis step inside to greetings and smiles from subordinates.

After waiting for all the men to be served, the commanding officer and his sub-inspector each took a plate of food and came to Griffith and Marois's table.

"May we join you for dinner?" Gagnon asked.

"Of course, sirs." Griffith gestured. "Please join us."

"*Merci beaucoup*." Gagnon and Jarvis took their seat.

Superintendent Jarvis smiled. "How is the chicken?"

"Good, sir," Griffith replied.

"Well, it certainly smells good." Jarvis picked up his cutlery.

Marois asked Gagnon a question in French.

Gagnon answered in turn while smoothing down his beard, making a path to his plate, declaring, "*Bien oui*!"

Griffith listened, picking up a little, but they were speaking much too fast for him to translate. For all his ignorance, he thought French was the most beautiful of all languages, poetic and musical.

"I think they're talking about us." Jarvis was cutting into his chicken and gave Griffith a wink. "Marois, are you and Sub-Inspector Gagnon talking about us?"

Marois smiled. "But of course, sir."

Gagnon let out a chirp of laughter, and everyone joined in. They ate, and there was relative silence, but Griffith and Marois knew they weren't just there for dinner.

Eventually, Superintendent Jarvis broke the silence.

"Sergeant Steele has informed me that you gentlemen were instrumental in the capture and detention of Swift Runner." Jarvis raised his fork with an carrot impaled on it. He was looking at Griffith, but he was talking to both. "Well done and noted."

"Thank you, sir," said Marois and Griffith.

"I think you gentlemen will prove an asset to the next phase of the investigation." Jarvis stuck the forkful of carrot in his mouth.

"Sir?" Griffith. "What is the next phase?"

Chewing, Jarvis said, "Severe, why don't you tell them what you're thinking."

"Yes, sir. Gentlemen, our mission is to find Swift Runner's camp. Once we do, there should be ample evidence to prove or disprove the allegations against him."

"Has Swift Runner told you the whereabouts of the camp?" Griffith set his knife and fork down and dabbed the corners of his mouth with his napkin. "Has he said anything?"

"Not so much. He still maintains that his family starved to death, but he won't tell us where the camp is." Gagnon lifted a glass and took a drink.

"Where do we come in, sir?" Marois said.

"Sergeant Steele mentioned you were friendly with Swift Runner, both of you," Jarvis interrupted.

"Is this true?" Gagnon asked.

Griffith and Marois looked at each other.

"Once we were friendly. But now?" Griffith tapped his temple. "He isn't right. He isn't the man I knew before."

"Yes, I agree with Griffith, sir. He's quite different," Marois added.

"Lunatic," Jarvis interrupted.

Gagnon swallowed, moved his tongue to the corners of his mouth to check if he had missed anything, and nodded. "Yes, lunatic is the exact word, sir." He smiled and used his fork to make a whirling gesture beside his temple. "That aside, we need him to tell us where the camp is."

"We've tried that so far, and nothing," Superintendent Jarvis said.

"Yes, sir. That is because he sees us as his jailers and tormentors. We need to remind Swift Runner that we're still his friends." Gagnon grinned.

Jarvis chuckled. "We're to befriend a cannibal lunatic?"

Gagnon looked down, contemplating, checking his beard for errant crumbs. Finished, he brought his eyes up and said, "He will confess to a friend, even if it doesn't change his circumstances. Many of the men here in Fort Saskatchewan were friendly with Swift Runner."

Superintendent Jarvis seemed to consider this. "You might have something there." Then he turned to Marois and Griffith. "You boys were friendly with Swift Runner?"

"Yes, sir," Griffith said, realizing this was a performance. "How do you think we can help?"

Jarvis said, "Sergeant Steele said you're a straight-to-the-point type, Griffith. He also said that you and Swift Runner were more than just friendly on the trail. You know him probably better than anyone here."

"I knew him, sir. I don't know the man in the cell."

"That is the point," Gagnon interrupted. "Marois, *mon vieux*, you were also friendly with him? *Non*?"

"Yes, I liked him, but he isn't right."

"Well, gentlemen, you're going to talk with Swift Runner, and I want you to remind him of the happy times. Remind him how you were and that you are still his friend. You aren't the only officers. I've spoken with three other officers. When you guard Swift Runner, I want all of you to engage him. Show him that you're his friends."

Superintendent Jarvis had his arms crossed. Even under Gagnon's spell, Griffith felt the older man's eyes on him, so he held Gagnon's gaze. "We just talk to him when on guard?"

"Exactly, and I think if all of you continue to speak with Swift Runner about the good things he did, you may draw him out. His family is dead. The Cree turned him out and say he's a killer. The elder told you this himself. We, gentlemen, are the only friends he has left."

Griffith thought Gagnon might be onto something but also about how sick Crane had become and what he had seen and heard at the camp. "May I mention something that I believe is important?"

"*Bien sûr*," Gagnon said. "Of course, please proceed."

Griffith told them about the incident with Crane and almost everything that had happened on the trail, including an modified version of what happened at the camp, going easy on the ravens and omitting the voice he had heard.

That would have been too much.

"Are you suggesting he's possessed?" Jarvis's tone was clear; he didn't like this.

"No, sir, but there are reports of shamans manipulating subjects. I believe that Swift Runner may possess an ability to beguile. I would suggest that guards not engage eye to eye with the prisoner. Crane is sick after interacting with Swift Runner. Both Corporal Hood and Marois witnessed this beguiling."

Jarvis looked at Marois, who nodded, then back at Griffith. "I was told Crane has some kind of blood poisoning from a rusty nail." He lowered his voice, inviting Griffith to come closer. "Are you suggesting some Indian hocus-pocus, Constable Griffith?"

Griffith chose his words carefully. "Sir, I'm suggesting, whether it's Indian myth or not, that we not take the chance." Jarvis was staring back. It was clear he wasn't happy with Griffith's response, so he added, "And of course that suggestion is with due respect, sir."

Jarvis began to open his mouth to say something, but Gagnon interrupted.

"It's a good idea, sir. Probably nothing will happen, but why risk being wrong?"

Jarvis considered this and nodded. "You may have a point, Severe." Then he turned his eyes on Griffith and Marois. "You gentlemen, listen to me now. I don't want this windigo nonsense leaving our circle. We have enough to contend with based on what he's accused of. Windigo talk is a crazy man's excuse for doing something unthinkable. If there is foul play, he'll say the Devil made him do it."

A devil maybe, Griffith thought, *but not the Devil.*

Sub-Inspector Gagnon pulled him from the thought. "You, gentlemen, will also accompany my search party."

"Search party?" Marois asked.

"Swift Runner will show us where his camp is." Gagnon winked at Jarvis, then turned back to Marois. "Sergeant Steele recommended you accompany us to keep him calm."

"Yes, sir," Marois and Griffith said together.

Griffith felt his spirits rise at Steele's recommendation. He and Marois shared a glance. He thought about Swift Runner and the thing in the camp and the ravens and Crane, and the accusation leveled by Swift's dead wife. He was nervous about Marois and him getting too close to Swift. He thought, *I should go see Crane and talk to him about this.*

But he never did because he was afraid of catching whatever Crane had.

Nor would he ever speak to Swift on guard duty.

They finished their dinner, and Jarvis and Gagnon went back to his office.

Marois went off to see Gertrude.

Griffith had thought about joining Marois, who had suggested that Gertrude had a pretty, red-headed friend named Mae. It was tempting, and the afternoon was theirs, and getting next to a woman might be just what he needed. Except there was Tasha, but it wasn't how Marois thought. Griffith wasn't carrying a torch for her. He was past that and had moved on to the pissed off portion of a bad relationship. He wasn't angry at her but at himself, for letting her string him along. Griffith had always been a pushover when it came to women, and he had always been attracted to the type of women who hurt him. Before Tasha, there had been others, and they had always hurt him. He wasn't ready to meet Mae or any other woman, so he went to the barracks for a nap.

***

Chapter 11 – Corporal Bags

I

June 8, 1879
Fort Saskatchewan, NWT

Gagnon stood before the six officers assigned to watch over Swift Runner. "Gentlemen, I have handpicked most of you because of your unique connection to our prisoner, Swift Runner," Gagnon said. "Using that relation, I want you to try to connect with him, be his friend. Don't talk about the crimes that he's accused of or the whereabouts of his family. Instead, I want you to talk about the work you did with him."

"How are we supposed to find out about his family if we don't be asking, Sub-Inspector?" Corporal Bagley asked.

Griffith remembered Marois's "Bags" comment, feeling a grin tugging at his face.

"An excellent question, Corporal." Gagnon turned to all of them. "This is what I'd advise. Make friends with the prisoner and find commonality. Talk about the weather. Be a friend, because a friend will eventually tell you his secrets if you don't interrupt him with rudeness."

"Oughtn't we just beat it out of him?" a young constable said.

"Taylor, you're an imbecile," Bagley scolded.

Bags went up a point in Griffith's book.

"Constable Taylor, do you know what a beaten prisoner will tell you?" Gagnon asked.

Taylor shook his head.

"If you beat him, as you suggest, all he wants is for the pain to stop. He'll tell you anything you want, except the truth. He'll lie to you. He'll confess to whatever crime you accuse him of even if he didn't do it. We don't beat confessions out of prisoners." Gagnon gave him a second to digest it. "Understand?"

"Yes, sir." Taylor looked humiliated.

"Dope," Bagley scolded.

Gagnon turned his attention back to the group.

"I have read the reports from the search parties, and we don't have months in which to scour the endless woods. If his family is *morte*—uh, dead—then we only have so much time before nature consumes the evidence." Gagnon referred to the ravens, coyotes, wolves, bears, and even insects making a meal of the discarded bodies. Even bones would be dragged away and eventually absorbed back into the earth. "Gentleman, our mission begins here," he continued. "We must find the camp, and Swift Runner is the key to that. Don't ask him about it. Let him tell you."

II

It only took a few days, and it happened in much the way the French-Canadian sub-inspector had predicted it would. Swift Runner began to converse with his captors, especially Corporal Bagley, whose fluency in Cree put Swift at ease. Bagley might have been a know-it-all, but he was a jovial sort and had a gallows humor. After each guard shift was finished, a written report outlining the discussion was reviewed by Sub-Inspector Gagnon. Swift Runner's rapport with Bagley was by far the best connection. The other officers didn't have much to report other than the Swift's demeanor and conversations about the mundane. Griffith never saw a guard duty with Swift Runner, nor did Marois. Bagley began to assume longer duties, spending many hours at the cell door. Swift was at ease, and that comfort seemed to calm the affliction that nobody was allowed to speak of. There were no nightly rants or screaming fits; the *wihitikow* was haunting elsewhere.

In the interim, Bagley read Swift the newspaper, translating it into Cree, and he chatted about everything from traplines to preferred hunting rifles, NWMP history, and the vanishing buffalo. "What is the farthest shot you've made?" Bagley asked.

Swift pondered the question. "I once shot a buck at about four hundred yards."

"Four hundred, you don't say," Bagley marveled. "Was there any wind?"

"No wind."

They talked some more. Bagley told him a story about a horse thief he had chased all the way to Athabasca Landing. He said in Cree, "I got him at the river bend. He had nowhere to go."

"There is much muskeg up in that part," Swift Runner said.

"Yeah, spongy wet ground up there. Gotta be careful where you walk, else you might end up to your waist in the keg, and that's how I got him. He must have figured I picked up his trail and was far enough ahead that he was able to dismount and was setting himself up to pick me off. Unfortunately for him, he stepped into one of those soft spots, and Swifty," Bagley chuckled. "He was in it up to his tits."

From the shadows, Swift let out a chuckle and said, "It must have been a sight."

"Oh, Swift, it was indeed." Bagley leaned back on his stool, which creaked, and crossed his boots. "I was looking down at this sad sack, up to his neck in mushy plant life and frog semen, the barrel of his rifle sticking out of the hole. I leaned down, snatched the rifle out, and said, 'What were you going to do with that?'"

Bagley finished the story, and they sat quietly for a minute.

"You ever been up 'round the river in Athabasca, Swift?"

"Yes, I have hunted there for many years."

"I bet there's some good trapping in the muskeg."

"There was beaver and muskrat, but no more," Swift Runner said.

"Why?"

"The muskeg is sour now, the woods empty."

"Sour?"

"No game, just death."

Then there was a lingering silence as Bagley searched for a way to continue. Gagnon believed there would be a breakthrough and had told Bagley to act when he saw an opening. This was as close as he was ever going to get. Bagley took a leap of fate and asked, "Is that where your camp was, Swift?"

Swift Runner was quiet.

"Is that where they are?"

A minute passed, and Swift Runner remained mute.

Then Bagley, his voice sympathetic, said in English, "Come on, Swifty, tell yer old pal, Corporal Bagley, what happened to your family? We need to investigate so to erase any doubt."

Swift Runner was thinking.

Bagley went back to Cree. "They won't let you out if you don't help us. They'll keep you here."

"Will I ever be let out?" Swift Runner asked.

"That depends on whether you help us. We must see the bodies and confirm how they died. If you help us do that, and if it is as you say, we'll be able to close the case."

Swift Runner considered.

"Show us where they are," Bagley said. "I'll be right there with you, Swift, I promise."

In Cree, Swift said, "It will be many hard miles. Come for me when you are ready."

"You going to take us to the camp?" Bagley sounded surprised.

"Yes, I will show you."

"Good, okay, okay…" Bagley looked through the bars and gave Swift a great big grin. "Thank you, Swift."

It wasn't returned, but Swift said, "You are welcome."

When his shift was over, Bagley went out to meet his replacement.

"Keep an eye on him, Taylor," he said.

"Did he say anything?" Taylor asked.

"Just keep an eye on him and don't rile him up." Bagley felt a dizzy spell and placed a hand on his stomach.

"Are you okay?"

"Yeah, yeah, I'm fine," Bagley said. "Keep an eye on him. Don't let anything happen to him, or I'll hold you responsible."

Bagley reported to Sub-Inspector Gagnon and related the story, and from there they went to see the Superintendent Jarvis. Gagnon had Bagley repeat the conversation he had with Swift to Jarvis, whose pleasure with the breakthrough came with the slow emergence of a smile. "Severe, it would appear that your plan has worked."

"Yes, sir, it would appear so." Gagnon didn't smile, but he was still pleased. "Thanks to Bagley." He and Jarvis did most of the talking while Bagley listened.

"Let's head over to the mess hall and have a bite before they shut down, and we can discuss this further," Jarvis said. They did that, and they arrived late to the meal as there were only three officers left eating in the hall. Jarvis gave a quick nod to the men, and they got their food.

Tonight, it was pork, potatoes, carrots, and beets.

"I'm not much for the beets," Jarvis said.

"You can get the cart ready," Gagnon told Bagley.

"Yes, sir," Bagley said. Then his eyes widened, he stood up, turned his head into the aisle, and puked a sizeable glut onto the plank floor. "Oh my gosh, sorry about…"

Then his bowels let loose.

"Oh, fuck no…"

III

Having finished his guard shift, Taylor arrived at the mess hall minutes before Bagley and company entered. Preoccupied with Jarvis and Gagnon, Bagley hadn't said anything but shot him a stern glance, to which he nodded back. Then he was puking and shitting, and Taylor watched as they carried him outside. While they cleaned up the vomit, he finished his own meal, thinking the beets were the best part. Then he went to the stable, where Griffith and Marois were tending the horses.

Griffith was checking Gunner's mouth for issues, pulling back his lips with his fingers. There was no resistance by Gunner, who was at ease with the ritual. He checked his gums and teeth, thinking about the time a sliver of hay had gotten under the horse's gum and caused a small ulcer.

Finishing the examination, Griffith wiped his fingers on a rag and gave the horse an apple from a bag hanging by the stall. He was still looking at Gunner when he heard the stable door open and felt a presence behind him.

"Bagley's sick," Taylor said.

Gunner chewed, the apple crunched and popped.

Griffith turned to face Taylor. "What's wrong with him?"

"He has some kind of bug. He hurled his dinner and is tarring his skivvies." Taylor smirked.

Marois came over to join them.

"Was he acting strange?" Griffith asked.

"Strange?" Taylor asked. "How do you mean?"

Griffith ignored that, turning to Marois. "Crane didn't shit himself?"

"Not as far as I know," Marois said.

"Crane?" Taylor looked confused.

"Did you see him throw up?" Griffith asked.

"Sure did. I saw him puke his dinner all over the dining room floor." Taylor's smile widened.

"What did it look like?" Griffith asked.

"What did what look like?"

"What color was the puke?"

"Was it black?" Marois added.

"No. It was puke color," Taylor said. "With carrots and beets."

"I don't think they got the same thing," Griffith said.

"He probably picked it up in town," Marois said.

"I sure hope we don't catch it," Griffith said.

"Serves him right, calling me an imbecile," Taylor said.

Griffith and Marois turned back to Taylor.

"You even know what an imbecile is?" Marois asked.

"No," Taylor admitted.

"You want to know?"

"Yes." But Taylor didn't look so sure.

"An imbecile is a very stupid person," Marois said.

Taylor looked to Griffith, who nodded.

He stewed on this for a second. Then, through gritted teeth, he said, "I hope he shits until his asshole falls out."

Griffith and Marois shared a glance.

Marois leaned in. "Suggesting beating a confession out of a prisoner to a sub-inspector is very stupid."

Taylor looked at Griffith, who nodded.

"I guess," Taylor agreed. "He's still an asshole, and I still hope his asshole falls off."

Marois grinned and said, "*C'est très bien.* Just don't mention it to the sub-inspector or Corporal Bagley."

Then it was Griffith's turn. "I'm surprised they haven't thrown you off the detail for saying something so…" He searched for the word, turning to Marois. "So?"

"Imbecilic," Marois suggested.

"Exactly." Griffith turned back to Taylor. "I'm going to tell you something. Swift Runner was our friend, and most of us feel pretty bad about this whole thing."

Taylor nodded.

"If I ever hear that you put a hand or any implement on Swift Runner, I will drag you out to the woods and beat you senseless."

Taylor wasn't smiling anymore.

"And when he's done, it will be my turn," Marois said.

"Understand?" Griffith asked.

"Yes," Taylor mumbled. "I didn't really mean it anyway."

"If you don't mean it, don't fucking say it."

"Okay, okay."

"Now, tell us about the puke again," Griffith said.

IV

The absence of Corporal Bagley presented a problem: they needed an interpreter. As luck would have it, a trapper named George Washington Brazeau had ridden in from Redwater. Brazeau was a big man like Swift Runner, bearded, broad-shouldered, and barrel-chested. He was of mixed blood, Cree and French, and fluent in English, French, and Cree. He was attached to the NWMP as an interpreter, but he was also a trapper employed by the Hudson's Bay Company.

After hearing of Brazeau's arrival, Superintendent Jarvis dispatched an officer to retrieve him from the town. Brazeau was ushered into a meeting with Jarvis and Gagnon, who skipped the pleasantries, explained the charges against Swift Runner, and asked him to join the expedition.

Brazeau had crossed paths with Swift Runner and suggested he might know where the death camp was. "As I recall, he was partial to the muskeg. Up toward the trading post in Athabasca Landing. I remember seeing him with one of his boys in the autumn, hunting up in that region. He had a rifle on his shoulder."

"Could you find the camp without Swift Runner?" Gagnon asked.

Brazeau thought about it. "Maybe."

"No disrespect, George, but 'maybe' isn't good enough." Gagnon turned to Jarvis. "We'll have to bring Swift Runner."

"I agree," Jarvis said.

Gagnon turned to the map spread out on a table in the commandant's office. "I still need you, George. You know him, and you speak his language. Show me where you think his camp is."

Brazeau stepped up to the map, oriented himself, and traced his finger from Fort Saskatchewan northward, until it reached a spot just southeast of the Athabasca River. "I was up in this region when I saw him and the boy."

"This is a big help, George." Gagnon marked the map, and Jarvis stepped up for a look.

"We had a patrol up in that region," Jarvis said.

"I'm not surprised they didn't find anything," Brazeau said. "Pretty big area, lot of dense forest, easy to get swallowed up in."

Gagnon was hanging over the map, his beard brushing the paper. "*Caporal* Bagley was conversing with Swift Runner in Cree. He seems more at ease in his mama tongue." He turned his head to face Brazeau. "Maybe, George, you can put him at comparable ease."

"Maybe," Brazeau said.

"Welcome to the expedition," Gagnon said.

Bagley was out and Brazeau was in. They agreed on payment for services, but it was morbid curiosity rather than monetary gain that drew Brazeau in. He would have done it for nothing.

Brazeau had to return to his home in Fort Saskatchewan and gather his gear, and when he came back there were further delays. The Red River wagon was a two-wheeled wagon pulled behind a single horse. The wagon wasn't built for prisoner transportation; it was built for goods, and it needed a new wheel, and after much grief, they changed it. When the wagon was fixed, they had to rig it with a restraint system. Taylor was assigned to take care of the horse pulling said wagon and their prisoner. This was an interesting feat because he would also be riding a horse of his own.

"Who steers the wagon?" Taylor asked.

"The prisoner," Gagnon responded.

"The prisoner…" Taylor was about to say more.

Gagnon raised a hand. "He will, of course, be shackled, Constable Taylor."

"Yes, sir."

"And surrounded by men on horseback with guns."

Taylor smiled at this.

"Get this wagon rigged up, make sure it's ready to go because I'm told the ground will be rough. I'm counting on you to get it ready." Gagnon winked.

Taylor stiffened. "Yes, sir, I'll give it a good going over."

"Good. I'm off to see the inspector. Get it done, Horace."

Gagnon reported to Jarvis to update him.

"How's it progressing?" Jarvis inquired.

"I'm waiting for the doctor," Gagnon said.

Dr. Herchmer was tending to his patients and giving instructions for his absence.

"We need to get this moving," Jarvis said.

"Sir, the dead will still be dead," Gagnon said. "Whether it be three days or four."

"Yes, I know, Severe," Jarvis replied. "The day is pretty much shot."

"What would you suggest, sir?"

"Push back the departure until tomorrow morning," Jarvis said.

"Yes, sir," Gagnon agreed.

***

Chapter 12 – The Offering

I

June 10, 1879
Just Before Dusk
35 Miles North of Fort Saskatchewan

The expedition consisted of Sub-Inspector Gagnon, Dr. Herchmer, George Washington Brazeau, and three NWMP constables: Griffith, Marois, and Taylor. Out front, Gagnon, Herchmer, and Brazeau rode together. Behind them, Swift Runner stood in the wagon, holding the reins to a single horse. Griffith and Marois were twenty yards on either side of the wagon, and Taylor brought up the rear. They crossed the North Saskatchewan River that morning, and the expedition moved slowly north.

Swift Runner was bumping along to the beat of uneven ground. The ride was an uncomfortable, noisy affair, with the wagon groaning and creaking and axles squeaking. At his front, the horse's tail flapped, swatting at insects, and occasionally lifting to drop manure into the mix. Swift Runner's face was like granite, one meaty hand holding the reins, the other hanging out of sight below the wagon's headboard.

II
Six Hours Later...

The ride was indeed rough, and there were numerous slowdowns and setbacks, including finding their way around woods so dense, it was impossible to ride or even lead a horse through them, let alone a prisoner in a wagon. Then they ran into a swollen creek. They stopped while Marios and Griffith searched for a shallow crossing, which they found. The day was slipping by without having gone the miles they had hoped. Swift Runner had been compliant but quiet, and when they hit open prairie, there was a relief that they were making some progress.

"Stop! Stop him!" Taylor was hollering. "He's escaping! He's escaping!"

Swift Runner had jumped from the wagon and was running.

Griffith was first to react. He prodded Gunner, leading the rein, and the horse reacted, turning right and breaking into a gallop. Swift Runner cut diagonally between Taylor and Griffith toward the forest. Griffith heard the others calling but didn't see them. He was in rhythm with Gunner, rising and falling with the charging horse, zeroed in on his prey.

Swift Runner bounded across the field, chain slung over one shoulder, swinging like a pendulum. Griffith was gaining, but he had to beat him to the wood line.

If he gets in there, it'll be a foot chase.

Griffith pressed Gunner's sides, and the horse galloped harder. They rushed past Swift Runner and without prompting, the horse turned left, bringing Griffith back and cutting Swift Runner off.

"Whoa!" Griffith ordered, sitting back in the saddle, his revolver out.

The horse stopped.

"Halt!" Griffith fired a warning shot.

Swift Runner was still coming.

Griffith cocked the hammer back and aimed. "Stop or I will shoot you dead!"

Swift Runner stopped.

"Get your hands up!"

Swift Runner raised his hands.

Griffith kept the gun on him, face flushed, he let out an adrenaline-laced gasp. "What were you thinking, Swift? I could have shot you."

"I wish you would have shot me, Constable Ron," Swift Runner said.

"Then why did you stop?" Griffith asked.

"I want to die, but the *wihitikow* wants me to live."

"What the hell are you talking about?"

"You know what I speak of. You should kill me before it spreads," Swift Runner said.

"Spreads? I don't know what you're talking about."

"Please, Constable Ron, before they come, pull the trigger."

Griffith was staring down the barrel, sight trained on Swift's chest, pressure on the trigger. A hair more, and the gun would decide the rest.

Something inside him told him he should shoot Swift, but he pushed it away.

"What will spread?" he demanded.

Then everyone was there, horses and men, surrounding them—all except Brazeau, who had gone to retrieve the horse and cart.

"Secure that prisoner!" Gagnon was livid.

Taylor was already off his horse when Marois dismounted.

Both were red-faced.

Taylor came around and grabbed Swift Runner's left arm as Marois got the right. Swift paid them no mind, his eyes riding the barrel of Griffith's revolver, urging him. "Do it."

"Constable Griffith," Gagnon said. "You can lower your weapon now."

Griffith glanced around.

Everyone was staring.

He eased the hammer down and holstered his weapon.

Swift was still looking up.

Then Gagnon turned his attention to the prisoner. "I'm losing my patience, Swift Runner."

Brazeau came up then, horse and wagon in tow.

Swift Runner turned to Gagnon and said something in Cree.

"What did he say, George?" Gagnon asked.

"He said, 'I can't go back,'" Brazeau translated.

"Well, you are going back," Gagnon said to Swift. "You will keep your promise."

They got off the horses and inspected the wagon. There was a hole where a lag bolt securing the chain to the main headboard should have been.

Brazeau stuck his pinky in the hole and said, "It looks like he just kept wriggling it until he made the hole big enough to pull the nut and bolt right out."

"Probably at it since we left," Taylor said.

Gagnon grumbled, then to Taylor, "Shorten the chain, move the locks, and find a better anchor point!"

Dr. Herchmer asked, "Was anyone hurt?"

"Nobody is hurt, Doc," Brazeau said.

"George, Doctor, keep an eye on the prisoner. If he tries to escape, shoot him in the ass," Gagnon said and growled at his officers. "You three, follow me."

They mounted up and followed.

"Somebody's gonna get a talking to," Brazeau said.

"You're right about that, George," Herchmer agreed.

Gagnon led his officers approximately 250 yards away. They lined up knowing what was coming. Gagnon was out front. "Does anyone here have an explanation for what just happened?"

"We were watching, just not close enough," Griffith said.

"If he'd gotten to those woods, we'd still be chasing him now. The only one paying attention was Taylor! So, maybe… Maybe you should watch closer? That way, we won't spend a whole fucking day looking for him when we're supposed to be looking for his dead family?"

"Yes, sir," Griffith said.

"Yes, sir," Marois said. "Good job, Taylor."

"Thanks." Taylor started to grin.

"Marois, *ferme ta gueule*," Gagnon snapped.

Marois shut his mouth.

"Understand this, gentlemen. I'm not going back to Fort Saskatchewan and reporting to the commandant that our prisoner escaped from a party of six men. I'll shoot all of you and disappear before I do that."

"Where would you go?" Marois asked.

"Far away from you, lover boy!" Gagnon had made his point. He peered up at the darkening sky and sighed. "There is a storm coming, and it's getting late. We'll set up camp over in those woods."

"What about Swift Runner?" Marois asked.

"Tie him to a bloody tree," Gagnon muttered.

III

They reached the woods, tethered their horses, and although the black clouds took the daylight, it didn't rain. Sooner or later, it was going to rain hard, and the trees offered little shelter, so they began to gather wood and constructed a lean-to from deadfall and spruce branches.

Marois and Griffith tied Swift Runner to the only pine in a cluster of birch. It would offer fair shelter from any downpour. Marois remained on guard duty, while Griffith collected wood and gave Gagnon a hand getting the fire going.

Brazeau and Taylor tended to the wagon.

Dr. Herchmer moved about the small camp, checking the state of Swift Runner, making small talk, helping where he could.

An hour later, they had shelter.

The prisoner was secure.

A fire was in full blaze.

And still no rain.

"I thought it would be pissing by now," Gagnon said.

"You sound disappointed," Griffith said.

Gagnon chuckled. "*Non, non, pas du tout.* Not at all."

"I saw rabbit tracks coming in. If the weather holds, I was thinking about getting us some fresh rabbit for dinner."

"How far back?"

"Quarter mile. I won't be more than an hour, if that. If there's nothing to shoot, I'll come right back." Griffith wanted to do something other than sit around the fire, chewing on venison jerky and smoking.

"No more than an hour," Gagnon said.

"An hour."

"Bring something back. I'm already sick of jerky."

"That's my plan." Griffith took off as the others went about their business.

Gagnon and Brazeau broke out the map, estimating the distance and obstacles for the next day.

Taylor attempted to refasten the chains, locks, and irons to the wagon, but he had issues. He rubbed the chain across the main beam and watched the sawdust fall. "Well, that ain't worth a shit."

Taylor came back to the main camp as Gagnon folded the map, looked up, and smiled. "Constable Taylor, you look like the bearer of bad news."

"I'm afraid so, sir. The wagon ain't looking so good," Taylor said, his voice low. "There's only one crossbeam, and I secured it, but he could still break loose. The wood is full of dry rot. You could cut it with a butter knife."

"Secure it the best you can," Gagnon said.

"Yes, sir."

A shot rang out in the distance!

"That would be Griffith with our dinner," Gagnon said.

Another shot.

"Taylor, do what you can," Gagnon said.

"I'll do my best, sir."

Then there was another shot.

Taylor went back to work on the wagon.

IV
40 Minutes Later…

Griffith came back with six rabbits. He had set four snares, and three were bountiful. He dropped them on the ground. "That ought to feed us."

"*Magnifique*," Gagnon said.

"Mmmm. All the makings of a fine rabbit stew," Brazeau said.

"All except time, George," Gagnon said. "A good stew must simmer more hours than we have."

They skinned the rabbits and roasted them on a spit, frying up potatoes and carrots brought from the camp. Marois guarded Swift Runner while Taylor finished the repairs and joined them at the fire.

"Well?" Gagnon asked.

"I made some modifications." Taylor was looking at the rabbit. "It still isn't great, sir."

"Good work, Taylor. We'll keep an eye," Gagnon said. "Get some food."

"Time to eat," Griffith said.

All the men had a mess set consisting of utensils, a tin plate, and cup. Even Swift Runner had a set, provided courtesy of the quartermaster. Griffith prepared the food and brought Marois and Swift Runner their meals.

"*Merci*, Ron." Marois took the mess tin. "Could you watch Swift Runner for a few minutes? I need to talk to nature."

"Sure." Griffith smiled.

Marois set his mess tin down. "I'll be right back."

Swift Runner was on his butt, legs crossed, rope wrapped around him and the tree. His hands were cuffed by irons, and he was staring down at the ground.

"Are you hungry?" Griffith knelt beside him, extending the plate.

Swift Runner took the tin plate. "Thank you, Constable Ron."

Griffith stepped back, running his tongue around his mouth, feeling a small chunk of meat lodged in his back teeth. Reaching into his pocket, he removed an apple intended for Gunner. Keeping an eye on Swift Runner, Griffith polished the apple, brought it up, and took a bite. The fruit was sweet, crisp, and he felt it cleaning his teeth as he chewed it up and swallowed.

Lips curled back, Swift Runner picked up a hind leg and bit into it, tearing the meat from bone and holding it between his yellowed teeth. Something about him had changed; he was more animalistic. Realizing he was being watched, Swift pushed the meat into his mouth, chewed, and said, "The rabbit is good."

"There were plenty, about a mile back," Griffith said.

Swift Runner tore away another bite, holding a chunk of meat between his teeth.

Griffith took another bite of the apple, holding the piece in the side of his mouth.

Did he do that with his children, after he slaughtered them?

Swift Runner pushed the meat in, chewed, and swallowed. "Yes, I did."

"What did you say?" Griffith met his eyes.

"You asked if I did that with my children after I slaughtered them." Swift Runner's eyes darkened, and by the time Griffith understood what was happening, it was too late. Something black came out of Swift and pulled reality away, casting Griffith into darkness. At first, he wondered if he was dead, that maybe Swift had overpowered him. He touched his face, clasped his hands, his belly, felt the ground below his feet. If he was dead, he thought, he wouldn't feel physical things like touch.

What has happened to me? Am I blind?

"You are not blind, Constable Ron," Swift Runner said.

"Where am I?" Griffith asked.

"You are in my dream, Constable Ron."

"I don't understand."

"Yes, you do."

Then darkness gave way to a flash and a pop and a blinding white light.

Griffith shielded his eyes with his hands.

Slowly he uncovered them, and his eyes began to adjust. He saw his feet first, felt them crunching in the snow, then his hands when he realized he was walking beside Swift Runner. As with his visit to Swift Runner's other camp on the Sturgeon, Griffith was again colorblind, his world a moving canvas of blacks, whites, and grays. He was on a forest path, marching against a merciless wind, cold pinching the skin on his face. Swift Runner was beside him, facing forward, hands gripping a rope slung over his back.

Griffith felt his head pondering that rope, eyes moving to see.

"No, Constable Ron... Do not look past my shoulder," Swift warned.

"Why?"

"It will be easier if you do not see, until you have to."

"Where are you taking me?" Griffith asked.

"To the place of seeing," Swift said.

A gust of wind lifted the snow from the forest floor, sending it crashing into them. Shards of ice crystals scraped their faces, while the wind howled like an arctic ghost. When Griffith turned to shield his face, he caught sight of the tiny horror slung over the Cree trapper's shoulder.

Griffith turned away, moaning, "Oh no, dear God."

"I told you not to look." Swift grinned. "Keep walking."

"What have you done?"

"What is done cannot be undone."

Griffith took a deep breath. "Where are we going?"

"To make the offering." Swift Runner shook the rope.

Then a horrible, jagged shriek came ricocheting through the forest, sending winter creatures to their hiding spots and shaking the snow from the tree branches.

"What the hell is that?"

"The *wihitikow* is near," Swift Runner said.

They were on their way to meet Swift Runner's Indian demon and, worse still, Swift Runner was offering up his murdered child as a meal. Griffith had shot a few men in his day. He had seen bodies as a police officer, but he was now faced with an unspeakable horror. "No, I can't do this!" He tried to stop but couldn't. No matter the surreality, biting cold, crunching snow, howling wind, or the beating of his terrified heart, he lacked the key component of reality.

Free will.

This was Swift Runner's dream, not his.

A nightmare, really, and he wanted no part of it.

"Please, Swift, I don't want to see!"

"You must see this," Swift Runner said.

Then came the sound of distant cracking branches in the forest, followed by another shriek.

"Please, Swift, I don't want to see this," Griffith begged.

"You should have shot me, Constable Ron." Swift was indifferent, emotionless.

To this, Griffith had no response. The smell of decomposition crawled into his nose and mouth. It was worse than the animal death camp. Hand on mouth, Griffith gagged and almost vomited. The scent of death wasn't coming from the dead child; instead, it rode the frozen breeze coming from the place of offering.

Swift Runner inhaled. "It is almost time."

"We should be running away! Not walking to it!"

"Soon, it will be time for the offering."

"Please, Swift Runner, you can still stop this," Griffith croaked.

"You cannot stop what is already done, Constable Ron."

Griffith wondered about the other members of Swift's family. Had they already been offered? Was this child the last? Hopeless, Griffith began to weep. "Please, Swift, I don't..."

Swift Runner turned to him. "Do you feel lucky, Constable Ron?"

"What? I don't understand."

When they reached the camp, they found a fire burning brightly at its center. Griffith stopped, but only because fate decided to let him. Swift Runner continued until he reached the fire. It dawned on Griffith that the snow, for as far as the eye could see, was stained in crimson splatters and splotches, and the horror wasn't restricted to the snow alone. Blood was smeared and splashed across the white birch bark, and scarlet icicles hung from the bare branches.

Griffith didn't want to see this, but the cruel hand of fate controlled his eyes and feet. He watched Swift Runner lay the body of his baby on the frozen earth. "Sweet Jesus, no, Swift... Please..."

Swift peered back and said, "It makes you do things you could never imagine, Constable Ron." He removed a line from around the baby's neck, and Griffith saw his pale, dead face. Mercifully, the child's eyes were closed. There were no bullet holes, no knife slashes; the child had died by asphyxiation.

"Oh, Swift, how could you?" Griffith moaned. "My, God, Swift... How?"

Swift Runner was about to respond when a blood-curdling screech shook the snow from the trees, and the source of his madness stomped into the camp and took its place at the fire.

The windigo was gigantic, almost fifteen feet tall. It was human-like in that it had the appendages of a human—head, arms, legs, and torso. But that was where the similarities parted between man and monster. Its face was the worst, covered in rotting, desiccated skin wrenched over its misshapen skull and sucked into its black eye sockets. It had no nose—rotted away, or lips—ravenously chewed off. Black ichor seeped from lacerations and sores in its flesh. Long tangles of its hair floated in the fire's updraft like black, silken cobwebs. Its body was a rickety frame of starvation with deformed, elongated, bony limbs anchored to claws rather than hands or feet. It was sickly indeed, but worse, it was hungry.

It ogled Swift Runner, anticipating its offering, breathing in gasps, lungs crackling like old newsprint. Swift looked up at his master and spoke in a language that was neither Cree nor English. The thing looked down on him, listening, eyes beginning to burn red, and the only sane witness was Griffith, who wanted to turn and run more than anything he had ever wanted in his entire life.

Swift Runner brought out his hunting knife.

Black drool spilled out over the windigo's jagged teeth.

I don't want to see this! I don't…

Then the knife came down.

Griffith saw it all, from disembowelment to offering and, like a branding iron, it burned part of his soul.

Swift Runner knelt before the monster, eyes lowered, holding up a tiny octopus of bloody viscera in his clutch.

The offering.

The windigo's dry breathing increased. Black drool spilled from its lipless mouth, rolled down its chin and into the fire, where it hissed. It brought up its massive claws and plucked the viscera from Swift Runner's hand. What followed was a sickening serenade of tearing flesh, scraping teeth, convulsive gulps, and whistling gasps.

Then it was Swift Runner's turn.

God, no, I… I… I… Griffith thought.

Cutting, Swift Runner said, "When the *wihitikow* is inside you, you have no remorse, only hunger, only craving. You will do things for that hunger. Things from your worst nightmares." He took his part and ate, then licked the blood from his hands. "When they kill me for my crimes..."

The beast finished the offering and shrieked for more.

Swift Runner picked up the knife.

I'm standing in a doorway to hell, Griffith thought numbly.

Swift was cutting, pulling, and removing the offering. "When they hang me, I will be dead."

The windigo shrieked impatiently.

Swift Runner exacted what the master demanded.

"Dear God, please, no more," Griffith cried.

"When I am dead, I will be free, and the *wihitikow* must go back to the earth." Swift Runner rose up, the last of the offering hanging in his clutch.

The creature snatched it away, gobbling it down, and turned its attention to Griffith and snarled.

It sees me!

The beast swallowed the last of the offering and stepped over the fire.

It was coming toward him. Griffith tried to move, forgetting about fate's hand holding him in place. He wanted to run, wanted to scream, but he couldn't even cry out. He heard its bones, cartilage gone to dust, joint grating against joint, with each step. Then it was standing over him, looking down on him like a bug through its burning eyes. The creature turned back to Swift Runner and said something in its devil tongue. Griffith guessed it was telling Swift to bring his knife for another offering.

Then he heard Swift say, "Ron."

The windigo turned back and hunkered down, its face inches from Griffith. "Ron," the windigo said in a slurring whistle. Then it added, "Breeeaaaathe."

Breathe? Griffith thought, then realized, *I can't breathe! I can't breathe!*

He was suffocating, heart beating in his ears, pumping blood, but no oxygen, and darkness was coming, the windigo, Swift Runner, the campfire, all fading to black.

Why can't I breathe? There is no passage.

Then blooming pain and…

V

Marois returned to find Griffith face down on the ground. He turned him over, finding that his eyes were open, but they were blank, and his skin had a cyanotic hue. He turned to Swift Runner. "What happened to him?"

Swift Runner turned away, ignoring Marois.

"What did you do to him?" Marois accused.

Nothing.

Marois focused on Griffith and gave his face a light slap. "Ron!" *He's not breathing!* "Breathe." He shook his friend by the shoulders. "Ron, breathe!" He slapped him on the back. "*Respire*! Breathe! Breathe!" He opened Griffith's mouth and saw something white behind his tongue.

Griffith was slipping away.

He's going to die!

"Forgive me, *mon ami*." He stood Griffith up and socked him high in the guts, where his ribs met. The white thing launched from Griffith's mouth onto the forest floor. Marois put him down.

Griffith gasped, trying to refill his lungs and make them work again. It took several attempts, but he caught his wind, managing short, sharp breaths. His eyesight was clearing. Marois was leaning over him, face full with fear and shock.

Griffith reached up and took Marois's hand in his own.

Swift Runner remained indifferent.

The sky was black.

Griffith could only breathe.

The others were coming.

***

Chapter 13 – Shriek of the Mutilated

I

Gagnon, Herchmer, and Brazeau hung over Griffith, staring down. Their faces charged with curious concern as he stared back up, feeling the uncomfortable claustrophobia of being surrounded and gawked at.

Sensing Griffith's angst, Dr. Herchmer said, "Let's give the man a little air, gents."

"*Bien sûr*," Gagnon said, nodding to the others.

They all stepped back, but only a little.

Standing outside the circle, Marois alternated between staring at the ground and stealing glances at Griffith. He wore a mask of fear. Griffith didn't want to think himself flippant, but he had just witnessed Swift Runner butcher his child and dine on the guts with a giant monster.

Dr. Herchmer interrupted the thought. "You're a fortunate young man, Constable Griffith. You could have choked to death on that apple."

"App—" Griffith stopped, clearing his throat.

"Take your time," Herchmer said.

"Did you say 'apple'?" Griffith's voice was raspy.

"Yes, a fair-sized chunk of apple," Herchmer said, holding it up for Griffith to see.

Griffith looked at the apple chunk, which was dirty and yellow. Then he looked back at Marois and understood why Freddy was spooked. "I don't remember choking."

"Not surprising. It might come back to you. I'll tell you one thing, if it wasn't for Constable Marois, you probably never would have. You were asphyxiating and undoubtedly would have died if he hadn't found you, He saved your life," Dr. Herchmer said.

Griffith gave Marois a nod, feeling shame for his flippancy.

"Constable Griffith," Herchmer interrupted.

"Yes?" Griffith turned back to the doctor.

"Let's have a look. Open your mouth wide, please." The doctor leaned forward and peered inside. "Uh-huh. Yeah, as I suspected, your soft palate is a little swollen. You'll probably have a hoarse throat for a day or so." He stepped back. "You can close your mouth now."

"Thank you, Doctor." Griffith closed his mouth.

"You're welcome." Herchmer smiled and patted him on the shoulder. "Just be sure to chew your food before you swallow."

"Yes, Doctor." Griffith still didn't remember choking.

"Constable Griffith," Gagnon said.

"Yes, sir?"

"I will be very unhappy if you do that again."

"Don't worry. I won't."

"*Très bien.*" Gagnon gave a wan smile, patted him on the shoulder, and turned to Marois. "Constable Marois, I want four shifts on guard. Set that up between the three of you but leave the last hour for me."

Marois nodded. "Yes, sir."

"Marois, *êtes-vous malade*?" Gagnon asked.

"I'm fine, sir," Marois said and stared over at Griffith, who was staring back.

"No more apples, Griffith," Gagnon said.

"Yes… uh, no, sir."

"Marois, get that guard list made up and I'll send Taylor up to relieve you," Gagnon said.

Then Gagnon, Brazeau, and Herchmer went down the trail to the main camp. A minute later, Taylor came up the path, and they went down to meet him, putting distance between them and Swift Runner, who appeared to be dozing.

Taylor recounted how an uncle of his had choked to death on a fish bone. "Salmon bone it was, killed him right there at his own dining table."

"You don't say?" Griffith was looking at Marois.

"My aunt won't even touch fish. She's a spinster now."

"How old is she?" Griffith asked.

"Forty-five, I think," Taylor said.

"Forty-five is old." Marois looked at Griffith and gave him a nudge.

"Anyway, I best get to my post. I'm glad you're okay, Ron."

"Thanks, Horace." Griffith acknowledged Marois with his eyes, then took Taylor's arm and whispered, "Horace, don't talk to Swift Runner on your shift."

"What?" Taylor looked at him strangely.

"Just do as I say, okay?"

"Okay." Taylor looked worried.

They left him, Marois leading, Griffith following until they left the woods and walked out into an open field.

Marois stopped, turned, and said, "Ron, you're my closest friend, and you're not allowed to die."

Griffith said, "Thank you for saving my life."

They shared a hug.

"You were blue, *mon ami*," Marois said. "I thought you would die for sure." He shivered. "*Esti de tabarnak*, I prayed to St. Jude."

"St. Jude being the patron saint of the lost cause," Griffith joked.

"It's not funny, Ron," Marois said, letting out a squeak of laughter. "Don't do that again. *Promis*?"

"I won't. I promise."

They were quiet for a minute. Griffith was deciding whether to tell Marois what he had seen. He wasn't sure if it had been real or a nightmare brought on by choking. He needed to think about it. Had the thing at the camp on the Sturgeon River been real? Had he been jumping at shadows? He didn't know, at least not enough to divulge anything.

"What did you say to Taylor?" Marois asked.

"I told him not to talk with Swift Runner."

"Why?"

"I'm still putting that together, Fred," Griffith lied.

"I don't understand, *mon ami*."

"Give me a little time to think about this."

"Did Swift Runner do something to you, Ron? Like Crane?"

"I don't know. Maybe, but I need to figure that out."

"That's not the answer I was hoping for."

"I'm still recovering from what happened. Some of my thoughts are missing from the incident. I need to think about it. Try and get them in order. I'll talk to you about it tomorrow." Griffith patted his arm. "I promise, Fred."

"*D'accord*, but if something is happening…"

"You'll be the first to know, Fred."

"I have to go back and see Taylor for a second," Marois said.

"I'll come with you," Griffith offered.

"*Non*! No, you go to the main camp. I just forgot to give him a copy of the guard list." Marois didn't want him going back; Griffith saw it in his face.

He knows it was more than an apple.

Griffith clutched Marois's shoulder. "Don't talk to Swift, Fred."

"I won't, and I'll repeat that to Taylor."

"Okay, I'll see you at the camp."

They went their separate ways.

II

At the main camp, a fire crackled happily as the aroma of roasted rabbit and smoke lingered. Griffith surveyed the inhabitants when he entered the camp. Sub-Inspector Gagnon was snoring. Dr. Herchmer also appeared to be sleeping.

The only one awake was Brazeau.

"Didn't take long for those two," Griffith remarked.

"They went down like nothing," Brazeau agreed. Griffith sat down across from him, warming his hands, seeing Brazeau's face lit in the tawny glow of the fire. "You tangled with an angry apple."

"Yes, angry indeed." Griffith tried to be nonchalant, even as Swift's voice echoed, *"You should have shot me, Constable Ron."*

"Did you see anything?" Brazeau asked.

"Anything?" Swift Runner's child's lifeless face floated before his mind's eye.

"Did you see anything strange?"

Like a baby who had been hung?

Griffith shook his head. "Strange?"

Like a man and his windigo dining on the dead baby?

"Sometimes when men brush close with death, they can have a vision," Brazeau said.

"Is that so?" Griffith averted his eyes. "I don't remember anything."

Brazeau studied him for a long moment. "I've worked side by side with these Indians for many years and learned that some of the things they speak of aren't superstition."

"Some might say you are Indian, George." Griffith smiled.

Brazeau smiled. "My mother was plains Cree, I was raised in both worlds."

"I mean no offense," Griffith said.

"None taken," Brazeau said.

"I choked on an apple, George," Griffith said.

"Okay, I understand."

"Understand?"

"You don't want to talk about it," Brazeau said.

"I—" Griffith started, but thankfully, Marois interrupted.

"Taylor is on until midnight. You got him from midnight until two, and I'll take two until four. Sub-Inspector Gagnon is taking the four to five shift. Before reveille, he wants to have a *tête-à-tête* with Swift Runner about any further escape attempts. He wants all of us on the trail by five."

"I guess some shut eye is in order." Griffith got up from the fire. "I'll be up to relieve Taylor at midnight."

Marois looked from Brazeau to Griffith; he had something else to say.

Griffith stopped him, saying, "I'm okay with the shift, Fred. I'm also good after what happened with the apple." He didn't want them looking at him like they had looked at Crane. "I'm plenty good to do my part, just a hoarse throat."

Marois nodded.

Gagnon muttered, "*Bonsoir*, Constables."

"*Bonsoir*, Inspector," Marois said.

Brazeau said, "Goodnight, gents."

They went to sleep.

III

Just before midnight, the clouds unburdened themselves and rain cascaded down for almost a half hour. Swift Runner was the least affected because he was sitting upright and only had to cross his legs to avoid getting wet. Taylor hid beneath another pine and kept mostly dry. When the rain stopped, the trees still held onto part of the downpour.

Taylor took Griffith's advice and avoided conversing with Swift. He had heard about Crane, which he had initially blown off as barracks gossip. But Griffith's warning had spooked him. There was an edge of fright in his words, like he had seen something he shouldn't have. Also, Swift tried drawing him into a conversation.

"I want to tell you a story, Constable Taylor," Swift said.

"I ain't interested, Swift, go to sleep."

"Are you afraid, Constable?"

"No, I'm not afraid. Why would I be afraid?"

"You are afraid of the *wihitikow*, that it might steal your soul as it did mine."

"I'm not afraid."

"Griffith is afraid. Crane was afraid."

Taylor suddenly grasped that he was doing exactly what Griffith told him not to do. "Listen here, I don't believe in Indian demons. We have a lot of miles ahead of us, and I'm not up for any stories. So shut up and go to sleep," he said.

"It is okay, Constable. The *wihitikow* is not here right now."

"Go to sleep, Swift." He sat in silence, stealing glances at Swift Runner.

Taylor had worried that Griffith and Marois would shun him over his comments about beating a confession out of Swift. He didn't think they much liked him after that. But today, he had earned back some respect during the escape. Marois even threw him a compliment and Griffith, whom he thought hated him, called him by his first name twice. He still didn't like Bagley for calling him an imbecile, but it had been a stupid thing to say. Taylor did that sometimes—opened his mouth and inappropriate words tumbled out. He didn't know why it happened, a nervous reaction perhaps, but he was working on conquering it. Taylor loved being a Mountie and hoped that he would find the type of friendship he saw with Griffith and Marois. Maybe they would all be good friends someday?

Taylor heard a snort and saw Swift Runner was beginning to snore.

That was good; no more talk about Indian demons, or Griffith being afraid, or Crane.

What did he mean by he was afraid?

That was his last thought as the fatigue began to creep in. He got up and fidgeted, splashing a little water from his canteen on his face. He even pinched himself a couple times. Feeling slightly refreshed, he sat back down, assured himself he was fully awake, and began to doze. He started to close his eyes for a second, maybe two, then open them, then close them again while mingling with questions.

Eyes open. *How could he kill his family?*

Eyes closed. *How could he murder his children?*

Open. *How can he sleep like a baby?*

Closed. *How could he eat them?*

Open. *How long did it take to eat them?*

Closed. *Someone catches me sleeping on guard duty, I'll be ruined.*

Taylor's eyes snapped open to find Swift Runner staring. "What?"

"You're all wet," Swift said.

"Huh?" Then Taylor felt a single cold plop splash on top of his head. He looked up, and the rest came in buckets, soaking him from head to toe. He dashed for the shelter of the pine but by the time he got there, it was over. The trees had unburdened themselves of the earlier downpour.

"Aw, shit! I'm soaked!"

Swift Runner laughed to himself.

"Yeah, real funny," Taylor grumbled.

IV

In the main camp, Griffith sat staring into the flames, exhausted yet unable to sleep for obvious reasons. He was pondering the vision he had refused to admit to Brazeau and still hadn't told Marois. Griffith had no desire to return to that place and was terrified at the prospect that sleep might deliver him there.

Whatever the event had been, it was now broken into segments, and he hadn't lied when he told Marois he needed to put it together. He sat in front of the fire, thinking about the mutilated thing shrieking as they entered the camp with Swift Runner's offering.

Not an offering, a dead baby, Griffith thought. The same baby Charlotte was holding when he brought Swift back to Egg Lake. He had heard Charlotte say, "You have delivered death upon us."

That wasn't real, it was a dream.

Griffith left the fire, went back to his bedroll, and lay there quietly as minutes passed. After that, there was a succession of wind gusts that shook the trees. With the canopy they had strung up, everything remained dry. Then Griffith heard Taylor cursing and knew why, and that made him smile.

Across the fire, Marois let out a chuckle.

Then all was quiet, excluding the crackling fire, the snoring of men, and the occasional fart. Griffith mused that there truly was no such thing as complete silence. A few miles off, coyotes yipped excitedly, the wind howling against the prairie night. But as Griffith listened, the howl began to sound less like a howl at all, and more like the shriek of the windigo.

He lay there, eyes closed, listening as the coyotes continued their tirade, which was followed by another definable shriek.

Not the wind.

In the theater of his mind, he saw the starved beast surrounded by snarling and yipping coyotes and towering over them.

The coyotes continued their taunt.

It shrieked again, and Griffith was sure he could see it swiping at them.

The coyotes had surrounded and were tormenting it.

Maybe it only has influence among men?

More yipping.

Maybe some creatures aren't afraid of it?

It shrieked again.

Griffith heard Marois stir.

Fred isn't dreaming; he heard it too.

Griffith realized that the shriek was backward, being pulled over picket rot teeth, down its festering throat, and into vapid lungs. It was bone-cutting, ear-piercing, and it was wrought with rage and pain.

The coyotes continued their harmony of torment.

It's telling them, Griffith thought, *leave me alone!*

Then the shriek became a lethal growl and a coyote yelped in pain, followed by an even deeper growl.

The coyote yipped in agony.

The other coyotes continued their tirade.

It's begging for its life.

Yip—yip—yi…

And no one stirred.

The coyotes howled in retreat, as the beast devoured its kill. Griffith continued listening, but the vision faded, and he lay there as the night sounds returned to farting and snoring. Randomly, he remembered Swift Runner calling to the boy in St. Albert, "See you in your dreams, Little Foot."

What had happened to the boy? Was he recovering now that Swift had been taken away? He was also thinking about Danny Crane and felt bad for not being able to visit him. Dr. Herchmer had him quarantined.

Maybe the boy and Danny are recovering, he thought.

But he doubted it.

There were no more shrieks or coyotes yipping. No more sounds except the crackling fire. Griffith lay there, listening, knowing it wasn't his imagination. The thing was out there, and he had heard it kill one of the coyotes.

He checked the time—ten past eleven—still fifty minutes before his shift. He thought maybe he would go up and spare Taylor off early. Once Taylor went to ground, he would confront Swift Runner and find out what he had done to him. If he tried anything, he would shoot him dead.

2345 Hours

Taylor had started a small fire to dry himself out. Swift Runner was sitting cross-legged, the bindings holding him upright, chin on chest, and appeared to be sleeping.

Taylor poked the fire with a stick, looked up and saw Griffith standing there "You're here early."

"I couldn't sleep," Griffith whispered. "In my hooch or here, I'm awake. You can grab an extra fifteen minutes on me."

"Thanks, I can use it." Taylor stood up and led Griffith down the path to the same spot where he, Marois, and Griffith had spoken the night before.

"How long has he been out?" Griffith pointed to Swift Runner.

"An hour, a bit more," Taylor said. "Thankfully."

"Why?"

"He was messing with me."

"How was he messing with you?"

"He was mumbling a bunch of stuff in Cree I didn't understand. And in English, he kept saying I should let him tell me a story."

"What did you say?" Griffith asked.

"I said I wasn't interested. Told him to shut up and go to sleep."

"Did he go to sleep?"

"Not for an hour. He was persistent, but I ignored him and finally, he closed his eyes. It was all good until the rain and that thing with the coyotes."

Griffith grabbed his arm. "Thing with the coyotes? You… heard it?"

"Yeah, I heard it. Now, let go of my arm."

Griffith let go. "What do you think it was?"

"It wasn't the wind, I'll tell you that," Taylor said. "I don't need to—"

"*Wihitikow*?"

"That's what Swift said. He asked me if I was afraid of the *wihitikow*." Taylor rubbed his chin.

"You heard it? The thing with the coyotes?"

"Hell, yeah. I told you I heard it, and every time that thing screeched, Swift Runner moved around like he was there with it."

"What do you think it was?"

Taylor thought about the question. "That thing with the coyotes wasn't no wind."

"No, Horace, it wasn't no wind."

"Can I ask you a question?"

"Go ahead," Griffith said.

"What are we going to do about it?"

"Do? I don't quite know, Taylor. I guess we do as the inspector says and find the camp."

Taylor was nodding, eyes were far off, thinking about something else.

"Taylor?"

"Yeah, I guess you're right, we need to find the camp."

"I'll take the watch. You go and get sleep."

Taylor nodded. "Thanks." He started away and stopped and turned. "Ron?"

"Yeah?"

"Be careful."

"I will. Thanks, Horace."

Griffith watched him go and took a spot at the fire.

V

"I know you're not sleeping," Griffith said just loud enough for Swift hear. "Come on, Swift, open your eyes and let's talk." He reached into his pocket and pulled out his last two cigars. "Would you like a smoke?"

Swift Runner opened his eyes, raised his head, and grinned. "A smoke would be agreeable."

Griffith came around, handed the cigar to Swift Runner, and lit it for him. He puffed a couple times.

"Mmmm, red wine," Swift Runner said. "What I would give for a drink. Have you any spirits, Constable Griffith?"

"No, just enjoy the cigar."

"Okay, I will." Swift puffed, contemplating.

They stayed like that for a few minutes. Then Griffith said, "What did you do to me?"

Swift Runner took another puff, brought his hands up, and cupped them when he exhaled. He held one hand up in the light and unfurled his fingers. The smoke clung to his hand, tiny wisps licking the air.

Dirty smoke, Griffith thought.

"The *wihitikow* was in me long before I took White man's drink, Constable Ron. I drank to get the poison out. I would get angry, yell and even fight, but the poison had to come out."

"Was that what I saw tonight, Swift? The poison?"

"Yes," Swift Runner said.

"And where is it now?"

"It is listening to us talk."

Griffith looked around, into the darkness.

"No, not out there." Swift Runner closed his hand into a fist, squashing the cloud, and pointed to his temple with his index finger. "The *wihitikow* is inside me—looking at you—listening to us—making plans for after."

"After?"

"You will hate me for what I have done. Everyone will hate me, and I will die for my sin against Mother Earth and her children. But that is not the end for the *wihitikow*. It is in me, in the marrow of my bones, poison drawn to poison—always waiting."

"Waiting for what?"

"*Macâtisiw*," Swift Runner said.

"Evil?" Griffith knew the word, had heard it cross Chogan's lips when conversing with Kaplan.

"*Macâtisiw* is everywhere now, across the land."

"Where did it come from?"

"The *wihitikow* has always been here, roaming the forest, in search of misery. I was angry all the time. Anger turned to hate, and that burned a hole in my heart and made a nesting place for the *wihitikow*."

Griffith interrupted. "Where did it come from, Swift?"

"White men conjured the *wihitikow* with your lies, your gluttony, your sin. It was you who plagued my people," Swift Runner said.

Griffith stiffened. "How dare you accuse me! I was your friend; I never lied to you!"

"All White men lie, mostly to themselves."

"You're saying you weren't responsible? Horse shit, Swift."

Swift Runner looked across the fire at him. "I tried to fit into your White man world, but your people take and take and take, until there is nothing. Then I began to have bad thoughts."

Griffith tried to remind himself that Swift was a murderer and likely a liar. Assigning blame elsewhere was what murderers usually did. Steele had said the same. He had considered this before and it sounded reasonable, offering a sliver of hope that what he had seen and heard were figments of nightmarish imaginings.

Reasonable, except for everything he had already seen.

Swift Runner continued, "There was a voice inside my head, telling me to do bad things. My only comfort was in the whisky. It dulled the *wihitikow*, silenced it for a time."

"You're blaming everyone but yourself. The White man, the *wihitikow*, the trader you shot at. Who took a shot at that trader, Swift? You or your *wihitikow*?"

"That was me. The trader was a cheat."

"You had a good job. A good life for your family."

"I was drunk and mad, and the poison had to come out."

"What happens if the poison doesn't come out?"

Swift was blowing smoke rings across the fire. He sent one floating out and instead of being sucked into the updraft, it hung above the flames. "You saw what happens when the poison does not come out."

"Yeah, I saw."

"But you never saw everything, Constable Ron."

Griffith's eyes were locked on the smoke ring, listening to Swift's words. Then Griffith was blinded by a flash, and he heard a craclking sound. He felt the transition, heard the raspy breathing, and knew that when he opened his eyes he wouldn't be at the fire.

His world was again colorless, the camp, his vantage point, the same. The windigo was hanging over Swift Runner, black, yolky drool spilling from its lipless, ragged mouth. It was all so awful, but this second time around, Griffith's eyes wandered, and that's when he saw the boy.

He was maybe ten, eyes wide, watching from behind a fallen tree. It was one of Swift Runner's many children. Griffith recognized him from Egg Lake. The child was staring in horror as his father defiled the body of his baby brother in offering to his master. When it was done, the windigo began to dematerialize, changing from the physical to dark smoke, settling onto Swift Runner and being absorbed. He was on his knees, staring into the fire, mouth unhinged, eyes vacant. The smoke became liquid, and the darkness beaded on his skin, absorbing through his pores. Then it was just him and the evidence of the crime.

But the horror didn't stop there.

Swift Runner turned to the woods and called to his boy in Cree. "Come to the fire."

The boy was peeking over the log, eyes wide, fearful.

Swift Runner called the boy's name. "The *wihitikow* is gone now, come to the fire."

The boy began to rise.

No, no, don't get up! Griffith thought.

The child was moving from behind the log.

Run away, boy! He'll kill you! Run away! Hide!

The child had hidden from his father during the family massacre. He had gone into the woods for a pee, under the flap of the teepee. This was to avoid the loud arguments of his mother and father at the fire. Just as the boy finished peeing, the shouting exploded into violence. His mother was screaming, then gunshots, his siblings wailing, and one by one their lives were extinguished while he hid. Griffith didn't know how he knew this, but he did.

The boy entered the camp and took his place beside his father.

Griffith gave up trying to warn him. This was the past, in which he had no voice.

Swift Runner placed a hand on his child's shoulder. "You have always been my favorite son."

The boy said nothing. He began to build the fire up while his father prepared their meal.

Before Griffith could bear further witness to the atrocity, there was another crackling pop and blinding flash. When he opened his eyes, he saw Swift Runner staring back at him, still tied to the tree. "What did you do to me?"

"I promised him I would take him back to Egg Lake," Swift said.

"What happened to him? What happened to the boy?"

"When the *wihitikow* came, he hid. I tried to be strong."

"You killed him? My God, Swift, how—"

"I tried to be strong, but the *wihitikow* is stronger." Swift Runner grinned, eyes flashing pinpricks of red light, his voice a sickly snarl. "His flesh was sweet. Soon, I will be coming for you, Constable Ron."

Griffith recoiled and brought up his revolver.

"Do it," Swift Runner begged.

Griffith stared down across the fire and knew what the consequences of his actions would be.

"Do it! I do not want to go back."

I could end it here. Just shoot him in the head.

"I am coming for you next, Constable Ron."

"No!" Griffith squeezed…

"Ron?"

Griffith looked up and saw Marois was standing on the path, looking at him strangely. He turned his head to the fire. Swift Runner was sleeping.

"What the hell just happened? What are you doing here?"

"It's two; it's my shift."

I haven't been here two hours.

Griffith turned from Marois back to Swift Runner, who appeared to be fast asleep. The fire had burned down. He looked at his hand. Where was his gun? It was in his holster. *What the hell is happening to me?*

"Anything to pass on?" Marois asked.

"Yeah, a couple things," Griffith said and nodded toward the path.

He led Marois away, and they stopped where they could talk but still watch Swift. When they stopped, Marois asked him, "Did something happen?"

"Yes, something happened. I don't remember two hours slipping by. We had a cigar, and I asked him some questions, but not for two hours." Griffith shifted his gaze to Swift Runner, who still appeared to be sleeping. "He did something to me. The same kind of thing he did to Crane, I think."

"Could you have fallen asleep?"

Griffith thought about that. "I don't think so. Was I sleeping when you showed up?"

"No, you were standing up, but you looked strange, like Crane, staring off into space. Did he mesmerize you, *mon ami*?"

"Yes, I think so." Griffith yawned then.

"Have you slept at all?"

"Not since yesterday." He yawned again.

"Fatigue. You need to get some sleep."

"Fred, don't—"

"Don't worry, get some sleep," Marois said.

"Don't talk to him, Fred. Don't even look him in the eye. Something's…" He yawned again. "There's some weird stuff going on. I had a vision, but…" He yawned.

"I won't. You're exhausted, go lie down. I'll come and get you at reveille. You can tell me about it tomorrow."

"Don't talk to him, Fred." Then Griffith went back to the main camp, pulled off his boots, and set them at the foot of his bedroll. He lay down, rolled onto his right side, and closed his eyes, wondering if he was losing his mind. Why had Fred looked at him so strangely?

He thinks I'm a madman.

He wasn't.

At least not yet.

***

Chapter 14 – Whiskey to the Devil

I

June 11, 1879
Expedition Camp
32 Miles South of Athabasca Landing, NWT

The next day, and into the evening, several incidents occurred, but it all started with an orders group held away from Swift Runner. The five of them gathered, Gagnon at the head, Swift Runner roughly 200 yards away, tethered to his tree.

"Good morning," Gagnon greeted.

The greetings were acknowledged in mumbles.

"Today, we have a big day. Our prisoner has already tried to escape once. Constable Taylor tells me we must watch him very closely as the wagon's wood is kaput. The restraints probably won't hold him if he tries to run again," he said, then to Brazeau and Herchmer, "The duty of guard is normally assumed by junior officers, but today, I'm asking both of you to assume a shift."

They both nodded in agreement.

"Good. Constable Marois, make up a guard watch," Gagnon said.

Marois nodded. "Yes, Inspector."

"Gentlemen, if possible, we must try to reach our objective today. Failing that, I want to get close enough to camp overnight and begin the search in the morning." Gagnon stopped, eyes drawn to Griffith, and then they were all looking inward.

"What?" Griffith looked around.

Dr. Herchmer reached into his satchel, produced a small mirror, and turned it so Griffith could see his face.

Gagnon and the others contained their shock. Griffith couldn't. "Oh, my God," he whispered. His complexion wasn't just pale, but milky gray and slick with perspiration.

I look like Crane, he thought. "What the hell is happening to me?"

"Are you having trouble breathing?" Herchmer lowered the mirror and put it away. The others were immediately uncomfortable with the doctor's supposition.

"I'm not having any breathing issues," Griffith said. "I'm tired. I only slept a few hours."

"Relax. I don't think you have tuberculosis, Constable Griffith."

Gagnon leaned in and whispered, "You don't look well, *mon vieux*. I think maybe you should ride back to Fort Saskatchewan. I can send the *docteur* with you?"

"We're almost at the camp," Griffith argued. "I would prefer to see this through, sir."

"I don't think it's a good idea, Ron," Gagnon said.

Griffith lowered his voice and leaned in. "Please, Severe, I think I need to see this to its end."

Gagnon thought about it. "*D'accord*, but from this point on, you're on light duties. Marois!"

"*Oui*, Inspector?"

"Griffith is on light duties. Strike his name from the guard watch." He turned back to Griffith. "I hope my decision isn't wrong."

"Thank you, Severe," Griffith said.

"I'm only doing it because you ask. If you had been someone else, you would be going south," Gagnon whispered. Then he raised his voice. "Gentlemen, there is also something I want to talk about."

All eyes moved to Gagnon.

"I'm not a superstitious man, but there have been some strange occurrences these past days. Constable Crane became sick after being in the company of our prisoner, Swift Runner. Dr. Herchmer... You reported that Crane had possible blood poisoning after catching a rusty nail in his back. Is this not true?"

"It is, and at the time, it seemed the most likely diagnosis," Herchmer said.

"I'm not a doctor, but I don't think a rusty nail is our culprit. What do you think, Doctor?"

Herchmer glanced at Griffith. "It's plenty debatable now."

"Yes, plenty debatable." Gagnon gazed to where they had left Swift Runner tied. "The rest of you, don't speak to the prisoner from here on. Don't look in his eyes or listen to his words. Whatever is happening somehow goes back to him."

He paused, sighing. "Last night, I heard the thing quarrelling with the coyotes. You think the inspector was sleeping, but I heard it yelling at the prairie wolves. I have traveled this land for years. I have heard bears and wolves and once even an angry wolverine, but what I heard last night was something worse. I suspect the thing is connected to the prisoner."

"I heard it too," Brazeau said.

Marois, Taylor, and Herchmer concurred.

"Gentlemen, may I suggest something?"

Gagnon nodded. "By all means, *Docteur*."

"Perhaps the nature of the crime is causing a mass illusion," Herchmer suggested.

"I don't think so, *Docteur*."

"We should report it, Inspector?" Griffith asked.

"Report what?" Gagnon asked. "What would you have me write, Ron? Our prisoner is possessed by an Indian spirit that fights with coyotes at night. They'll think we were out here drinking ourselves silly and baying at the moon. Nobody will believe us."

Griffith thought about it and said nothing.

Gagnon placed a hand on Griffith's shoulder. "I know that I believe what I see and what I heard."

Griffith considered telling them everything but remained quiet. He saw how they were looking at him. There was fear in their faces; he was repelling them. He would talk to Marois first.

"Constable Griffith," Herchmer asked.

"Yes, Doctor?"

"Whatever is afflicting you isn't physically contagious; otherwise, we'd all be infected. I would be just as sick as you. And Marois too."

"I don't understand," Griffith said.

"You and Marois were with Constable Crane, all the way from St. Albert to Fort Saskatchewan. I was the one who examined Crane. If he was contagious, we would all be as sick as you. Inspector Gagnon is also right about Crane having a scrape from a rusty nail, but he looked exactly like you, Constable Griffith."

"Gray," Griffith said and asked, "Am I going to die?"

Herchmer frowned. "You'll probably be fine."

"You don't really know, though, do you?" Griffith was scared.

"No, I'm sorry, I don't know," Herchmer said. "But whatever you and Crane were exposed to came from Swift Runner. I agree with Sub-Inspector Gagnon. We should all keep our distance from the prisoner. Especially you."

"I'll do that," Griffith said.

Marois smiled weakly, like someone trying to be strong at the deathbed of a loved one.

And he's looking right at me.

"I got a question," Taylor said.

"What?" Griffith asked.

"If it comes from Swift Runner, why isn't he all sickly looking?"

It was a good question.

No one had an answer. Griffith thought he might know why but didn't share. *Maybe he looked like me before he committed mass murder and indulged in cannibalism? Maybe all that blood and guts put the color back into his flesh?*

"Gentlemen," Gagnon interrupted. "I would remind all of you that our primary mission is to investigate the allegations of murder and to gather evidence. We'll finish what we set out to do, but as a precaution, don't talk to the prisoner or meet his eyes. In fact, I don't want you to even fart in his general direction."

There were some chuckles, and Griffith gave an obligatory smile. Gagnon dismissed them, and everyone went about their duties, except Griffith, who mounted Gunner and waited for the others.

Before setting about his own duties, Gagnon said, "Maybe absence will make you well again."

"Yeah, maybe," Griffith lied.

Taylor and Marois got Swift Runner into the wagon, and they formed up.

Swift Runner tried to catch Griffith's eye.

Marois saw this and parked his horse between them, blocking the view.

Gagnon took up the lead.

They were pushing north again.

The guard was rotated every half hour. When noon arrived, everyone had done two or more shifts, except Griffith, who brought up the rear.

Brazeau kept them on course for Athabasca Landing. "When we get there, we'll need Swift Runner to find the camp," he told Gagnon.

"Get us as close as you can. Then we'll deal with Swift Runner," Gagnon said.

Marois rode beside Griffith. "How do you feel, Ron?"

"Tip top," Griffith said, but he looked like a starved vampire.

"So? That is better?" Marois smiled.

"Better?" Griffith laughed. "I don't know about better. There's something eating my energy."

"He mesmerized you?" Marois shook his head angrily. "Didn't he? Just like Danny Crane?"

"Yeah," Griffith admitted. "Twice."

"Twice?"

"The apple, that was also Swift Runner. I was talking to him, and then I was pulled into his world, Fred. His nightmare world."

"Nightmare world?"

"He… he…" Griffith lifted a shaking hand to his mouth, took a gulp of breath, and gathered himself. "I saw him butcher his own child, like a slaughtered piglet. He disemboweled the body of his baby, and the windigo fed on the entrails."

"Windigo?" Marois cocked his head.

"I know it sounds crazy, but Swift Runner is telling the truth about that. I saw it, Fred. I saw it eat his child's entrails. That is what we heard last night quarreling with the coyotes."

"I heard it," Marois said.

"I swear, Fred, it's real," Griffith said.

"I don't have to look any farther than you to know that something is happening. But what do we do? What if it's waiting there for us?"

"I don't think it can harm us as a group."

"*Non*?"

"No, I think the threat will come from within."

Marois's eyes grew wider. "The threat?"

Griffith grinned.

"Don't joke."

"I'm not joking," Griffith said. "I wish I was."

"Don't talk like a…" Marois stopped.

"Like a madman?" Griffith finished. "The windigo got into him, Fred, but before it did, it shadowed him, whispering in his head, fanning the flames of rage, and feeding on him like a pariah."

"This is hard to—" Marois started.

"To believe? We heard it, Fred. You heard it. Brazeau and Taylor heard it. Gagnon, the doc, they heard it too. You saw what happened to Crane," Griffith said. "Look at me, Freddy!"

"Yes, yes, I believe you, Ron." Marois looked at him. "I know you're not crazy."

"Yeah? That makes one of us."

"You're not," Marois said. "What is this windigo? Is it the devil, a *démon* of unknown origin?"

"You're asking the atheist?" Griffith asked. "I only know that Swift Runner killed them all, and we're going to a massacre, Fred."

"We need to tell Severe," Marois whispered.

"Not yet, Fred. They're already looking at me strangely. The weird thing about that is I understand how they feel. I felt the same about Danny Crane, and he probably felt exactly as I do now. If I tell them what I told you, they'll—"

Taylor was yelling. "He's out! He's escaped! Stop him!"

Swift Runner was running again.

Dr. Herchmer had been the man on guard.

Marois went after Swift Runner.

II

Three Hours Later
22 Miles South of Athabasca Landing

Sub-Inspector Gagnon made good on his promise. Swift Runner wouldn't be escaping from the cart again. They wrapped him in rope from his biceps to ankles. One dignity they left him was to keep his hands bound within reach of his fly so that he would be able to relieve himself. That was only because no one among them, including Gagnon and even the doctor, wanted to deal with that.

Gagnon was looking down from his horse, his accent thick and matter of fact. "I warned you. Don't make me angry, Swift Runner. I say that the ride will be more uncomfortable. But do you listen? You think the sub-inspector is a softy? Now, you see the extent of the bondage I'm willing to apply."

Swift Runner was brooding.

Gagnon sneered. "Go ahead. Escape! Flop-flop-flop like a halfwit sucker fish all the way to the Athabasca River. No need to tie him down, just throw him in the cart."

Swift Runner grunted, "Why did you not just kill me?"

"Are you going to show us where your camp is?"

"Inspector, I beg you. Shoot me."

"No, Swift Runner, my job is to investigate a crime, not shoot you. You promised you would help us find your camp. You were an honorable man once. Are you not now?"

Swift Runner remained defiant.

III

As they bound Swift Runner, Griffith climbed down from Gunner, tethered him to a branch, and gave him an apple. He lit a cigar, took a puff; even they tasted different. He found a spot and sat down, back against a tree. He watched them go about their work of restraining Swift Runner. Griffith felt sick but not queasy. Just run down.

"But I haven't eaten anyone," he said under his breath.

Not yet, he thought and took another puff.

He wondered again about Crane.

He's probably dead.

"He's not dead," a voice much like his own said in perfect English to his right.

Griffith turned to see the windigo sitting cross-legged beside him. It was looking down into its lap. It was less physical than what he had seen in his vision, made up of oily smoke churning out the ghostly thing beside him. The windigo raised its mutilated face, teeth clicking behind an open drapery of blood and rot, long hair floating in the air like silken cobwebs.

"Hello, Ron," the windigo said. It was looking from him to Swift Runner and back. "He was a good host and provider. You will be as good or better."

"I will not be hosting you," Griffith managed.

"Oh, but you already are," the windigo said.

"I'm not afraid of you," Griffith said.

It cackled. "Oh, yes, you are. If you are not, you are a fool for sure, and I know you are not one. Ka Ki Si Kutchin is finished, and I am going to need you to start thinking about that feeling you have."

"Feeling?"

The windigo sighed. "Do not be coy, Ron. You know exactly what I am talking about." The words slithered out in whispers, "Unease, emptiness, despair, that is your soul eating itself. That can only be filled by one thing, and you know what that is." It tried to smile and failed without lips.

Griffith did but said, "I will not!"

"They all say that. I will not do it, I will not, but in the end, there is always blood, and I always get what I want." It moved in front of him, nose to rotted nose. Its face fading in places, solidifying in others, blood and smoke churning beneath an invisible membrane. Its was in flux, changing, from Griffith's to Swift Runner's and back to a face of death with glowing eyes. "There is an easy way and a hard way, Ron. Kill them all, and we will feast by the fire. Pledge yourself to me, and we will eat like kings!"

"I will not!"

It moved closer, its rot stinging his exposed skin. "I know you feel it inside you."

Griffith stared down, seeing only its horrible mouth talking in perfect English. How could this be? How could an Indian spirit sound like a…

"Like a White man?" The creature cackled. "Oh, Ron, I am in all places and in all men. That feeling inside you is me. You feel it? Like something is eating you?" It reached up one claw and tapped its head. "That is the ache of starvation. Before long, it becomes agony. Then agony will feed hunger and obsession."

Griffith smelled the odor of its breath, a stench worse than rotting flesh. He gagged.

"You will dine with me, Ronald Griffith. You will bow down to me, or you will sustain the agony of my curse." The *wihitikow* pointed to the wagon. "Just like he did, just like your friend Danny Crane. You are my possession."

"No." Griffith found his forgotten cigar, took a draw, and blew smoke into its face. The smoke blew through it, and Griffith knew that it wasn't strong enough to hurt him. *Not yet anyway.* "You can kill me with whatever sickness you put upon me, but I'll never kill for you or dine with you."

"That is what your friend said." It pointed.

"What are you?" Griffith asked.

"I am you." The windigo's face became Griffith's.

"You aren't me."

"I am the killer of little children, the eater of their hearts, the corrupter of their parents. I am born of man's sin. I am the *wihitikow*, I am the windigo, I am the regulator, I am the Holy Ghost. I am your child waiting to be fed. I am the messiah of blood and death."

"You aren't welcome here," Griffith said.

"I have never been welcome anywhere." It cackled again, the sound grating on Griffith.

"Then why are you here?"

"Time for you to get back on your horse," the windigo said. It began to fade, ink to translucence, smoke to light. "Kill them all, Ron! Swift Runner too."

Then it was gone.

"Constable Griffith, mount up," Gagnon called. "We're moving.

Griffith turned to see Gunner staring at the spot where the windigo had been.

"Did you see that?" he asked the horse.

Gunner had. Griffith was certain of it.

He mounted up and followed them north.

The closer they got to Athabasca Landing, the more apparent it became that Swift Runner had misled them on the map. When they stopped to resection, he corrected their course. He did this three times, leading them off course each time. There was no camp to be found, but plenty of wasted time. The third time, Gagnon's patience thinned and that came out in his words.

"Why are you playing games?" Gagnon barked.

Swift Runner stared straight ahead, like a soldier.

"Sooner or later, we're going to find the camp!"

Nothing.

This went on for a few minutes, until Gagnon said, "No matter how much you lie and mislead, we'll find it." He steered his horse and rode away from the cart, tapping the top of his head, yelling, "Gentlemen, orders group!"

Everyone rode in to meet Gagnon, again out of earshot of Swift Runner. Marois had been guarding the prisoner, and he was also pulled in. He needed no guard, as there was no chance of escape now. He was completely immobilized.

Gagnon waved for Griffith to join them. They circled their horses and discussed what to do next.

"He's not going to show us. He's been misleading us," Brazeau grumbled.

"I guess this proves he killed them," Taylor said.

"It doesn't prove a thing. We need to find the camp," Gagnon barked. "We won't leave until we have located it."

They talked for another ten minutes.

"Give him whisky," Griffith suggested.

"I don't think getting the Indian drunk is such a good idea," Dr. Herchmer said.

"I disagree, Doctor," Griffith said. "Swift Runner told me that he used the alcohol to numb the windigo's influence. Maybe if we get him drunk and numb whatever influence he thinks the windigo has over him, he'll help us."

"Might loosen his yap," Brazeau agreed. "Maybe we mix up some *mus-kee-wah-bwee.*"

"Might turn him violent," Marois said.

"How violent can he be when we have him tied up like that?" Griffith argued.

Gagnon let out a bewildered sigh. He glanced back at Swift Runner and then at his men. "Set up camp. I don't like doing it, but we're going to try Griffith's plan."

IV

Brazeau concocted a drink he knew Swift Runner enjoyed, called *mus-kee-wah-bwee*, which was whisky with a large helping of plug tobacco. He took a sip of it to check its potency and smiled. "This will loosen his tongue."

Griffith stayed back, but not so far that the windigo's presence wouldn't have stirred his comrades. He watched Swift Runner as Brazeau offered him the drink, and he took the cup willingly and drank and drank and drank.

What they saw at the fire was a metamorphosis.

At first, Swift was polite, pleasant, and he joked with them. But as the whisky concoction thinned his blood, his mood darkened, and he became a raging, raving maniac.

He spoke in Cree mostly, which Brazeau translated.

"He says we're swines," Brazeau said. "He says that we killed his family."

"He says the Hudson's Bay Company is evil."

"He says that he loved them."

Brazeau asked a question in Cree and Swift Runner replied, and an argument in Cree erupted between the two. Whatever was said made Brazeau angry enough to place his hand on his gun. He took a break, and Gagnon spoke with Swift Runner about hunting. "Where is the best hunting around here, Swift Runner?"

"Your mother is a whore," Swift Runner said and snorted.

Gagnon ignored the question. "Are there moose up here?"

"The moose have flown away, you French twat." More snorting.

"You don't hurt my feelings, Swift Runner. I know you're afflicted with this thing you've done. It must feel like you're carrying a buffalo upon your shoulders."

Swift Runner ignored him and motioned Brazeau. "*Mus-kee.*"

Brazeau gave him another drink.

He cried for a time, inconsolable, mumbling in Cree, once saying his wife's name. Brazeau hung on every word; his own face lit with emotion. Swift Runner stared into the fire, brooding, ranting, blubbering, and they continued feeding him whisky for over three hours until he asked for Griffith.

Griffith came to the fire.

"Will you drink with me, Constable Ron?" Swift Runner asked.

"Will you tell us where the camp is?" Griffith asked.

"One more drink." Swift Runner's eyes drooped with intoxication.

"I will have one drink, if you tell us where the camp is."

"Bring the drink," Swift Runner said and mumbled something in Cree.

Brazeau brought the cup to his mouth, and Swift Runner sipped.

Griffith brought out his flask.

"No," Swift Runner protested. "We must drink from the same cup."

"Fine," Griffith said and put away the flask.

Brazeau poured the last of the whisky into the tin cup and offered it to Griffith. He didn't want a drink but thought of duty. He brought the cup to his lips and sipped. The whisky was bitter on his tongue. He handed it back to Brazeau, who gave the rest to Swift Runner.

"Tell us where the camp is," Griffith said.

"*Wahabankee Keezikow*," Swift Runner said and closed his eyes.

"What does that mean?"

"Tomorrow, I show you," Brazeau whispered.

***

Chapter 15 – Death Camp

I

June 12, 1879
Last Expedition Camp
13 Miles South of Athabasca Landing

The windigo didn't come to haunt as it had the night previous. Griffith managed to sleep about four hours, broken by horrible thoughts chipping away at his hope and humanity. There had been an unsettling revelation. The windigo had been right about the craving. Griffith wasn't a fiend. He still cared for his comrades, and he wasn't considering the creature's demands. Not yet, but he could feel the sickness inside him, dissolving his principles a little at a time. He tasted phantom blood in the back of his throat, a sickening throwback to when he had been punched in the nose during an arrest. It had tasted like copper and mucus, muddying his senses and making him feel ill. This was like that, but what had once sickened now beckoned.

Hit by a sudden wave of nausea, Griffith rose rom his bedroll and stumbled out of the camp into the forest with his hand over his mouth. He buckled over and vomited, looked down, and felt his heart sinking into despair.

Black, he thought, wiping his mouth, seeing beads of ichor on his palm, then repulsively shaking it off. The black vomit sizzled and fizzed and sank into the earth.

He looked around; no one had awakened.

He went back to his bedroll, hearing the voice of the windigo whispering, *"Kill them all, and we will feast like kings. Kill everyone, Ron, including Swift Runner."*

I won't kill anyone! I'll kill myself before it comes to that.

But would he really?

Yes.

He would have to warn his fellow officers about the risk. It was the right thing to do. He had to do that soon or there wouldn't be much left of him. First thing in the morning.

Just need a little bit more sleep.

He closed his eyes, only to be awakened by the sound of men moving around the camp. He opened his eyes to daylight in the sky, and the others packing up their gear. Where had the time gone? Hadn't he just gone to sleep? He got up, packed up his bedroll, and dressed for the ride. After putting on his weapon, he felt another wave of nausea.

"Ah, oh, no!" Griffith ran for a bush and threw up.

Marois came over and patted his back. "Get it out. Sick it up."

Griffith watched the foamy stuff disappear into the earth. It was leeching from the marrow of his bones. He didn't know how he knew this, but he did, and he also suspected it was the windigo's blood.

Marois stared down at the black vomit and said in a sad voice, "Oh, *mon ami*."

I guess I won't have to tell Fred, Griffith thought.

"What's going on here?" Gagnon was behind them.

Marois got up, turned around. "Uh, Griffith isn't feeling well."

Griffith wiped his chin before turning around, still wondering if there was a black stain on his face. He decided that it didn't matter and turned to face him. "Sub-Inspector Gagnon, I'm respectfully withdrawing from the search."

"Withdrawing?" Gagnon's face was unreadable.

"I believe I may pose a danger to myself or others due to the same blood poisoning suffered by Constable Crane." Griffith slowly unholstered and offered his pistol, butt first.

Everyone, including Swift Runner, was watching.

"Are you sure about this, Ron?" Gagnon asked.

"Yes." Griffith pushed the gun a little closer.

Gagnon frowned, took the weapon, unloaded it, and replaced one bullet, then handed it back to Griffith. "I will not leave one of my officers defenseless to the elements."

"Thank you, Severe." Griffith took the weapon back. "I think the closer I get, the sicker it makes me. I don't trust myself to find out. I don't think I can go there. I'm not myself, Severe." He was shaking. "I think if I go…"

Gagnon took his right arm. "Ron, you stay here. We'll go to the camp, and we'll finish what we started. Swift Runner says it isn't far, a few miles. You stay here, keep the fire going. I'll call out to you when we get back. Don't shoot anybody." He grinned, but he wasn't joking. He confirmed that with, "Including yourself."

"I won't."

"We'll be back by early afternoon to pick you up, and we'll head home to the fort."

"Yes, sir."

Marois looked at Taylor. "Let's get him some firewood."

Taylor nodded, giving Griffith an awkward smile.

"You know, Ron, it's because of you," Gagnon said.

"I don't understand," Griffith said.

"Giving Swift Runner whisky." Gagnon said. "That is the reason we'll find Swift Runner's camp today. Once we find the camp, we'll get as far from these haunted woods as God will allow us."

"Yes, sir."

"Mount up!" Gagnon gazed sadly upon Griffith. "I should have sent you south."

"It was my choice. You did the right thing," Griffith said.

"So did you, Ron," Gagnon said, and he got ready to ride.

Marois hung back. "Don't do anything stupid."

"Only in your presence." Griffith smiled weakly.

"Funny guy." Marois smiled back. "We'll be back soon, *mon ami*."

"Be careful."

"You as well," Marois replied and rode off to join the others.

Griffith watched his fellow officers on horseback cross the field surrounding the wagon and its prisoner. The farther away they got, the less of them there was, until the low morning fog took them completely and he was truly alone.

At least he hoped he was.

II

They rode for an hour, moving through the fog, until they reached a densely wooded area.

Swift Runner pointed and said, "In there."

"Party, halt," Gagnon ordered and gazed in the woods. "I see nothing to indicate a camp. What is this?"

Swift Runner murmured something in Cree.

"He says his oldest son's body is buried in there," Brazeau translated.

Gagnon dismounted and called, "Doctor, will you please join me?"

Herchmer cleared his throat and said, "Yes, of course," and dismounted.

"Keep an eye on the prisoner," Gagnon said to Marois and Taylor.

They walked to the edge of the treeline. Herchmer saw the depression before Gagnon and pointed. "There!"

They enter the woods, and ten feet they found a shallow grave. The earth was sunken, covered by forest debris, a fallen branch, broken twigs, dried leaves, a scattering of tiny pinecones, and mossy overgrowth. What lay beneath the collection of forest reject was a body. Gagnon and Herchmer got down on their knees and gently began to unearth the corpse by hand.

What they disinterred was the emaciated, mummified body of a boy.

Herchmer said, "The body is in good condition given how long it's been out here."

"He doesn't look that good to me, *Docteur*." Gagnon smiled bitterly.

"He should be bones. I guess the animals missed him," Herchmer remarked.

"How old would you say?" Gagnon asked.

"I'd say younger teens." Herchmer began to examine the body from head to toe as Gagnon watched in silence. When he finished, he let out a sigh and said, "I don't see nothing."

"Nothing?"

"No bullet holes, ligature marks, broken bones. I don't see anything to indicate violence."

"Then how did he die?"

"They all starved to death," Swift Runner called from the cart.

They looked back at Swift Runner.

Gagnon made a hand gesture to lower their voices.

"He's probably telling the truth, Severe," Herchmer said in a whisper. "This boy shows nothing to indicate violence. None that I can see. It's very likely the teen died of natural causes, if starvation could be considered natural."

"Do you think they all starved?" Gagnon whispered.

"I wouldn't be able to say until I see the bodies, but unless he poisoned the boy, I think it's possible he's telling the truth about this one," Herchmer whispered back.

They covered the body up and returned to Swift Runner.

"This is one body," Gagnon said firmly. "Where are the rest?"

"They all starved," Swift Runner insisted.

"We'll need to see the rest."

"This is the proof you wanted," Swift Runner complained. "I have done what you asked."

"Where is the rest of your family?" Gagnon demanded.

Swift Runner's face hardened, but no words came.

Gagnon got into his face. "Where are the rest of them?"

"I have—"

"You have shown us one boy!"

"I showed you."

"*Bon sang*! We're going to see your camp." Gagnon gritted his teeth together and said, "We're not leaving until we find the truth. Enough bullshit! Take us to the camp!"

Swift Runner replied in Cree.

"He says the route to the camp is too hard for a wagon," Brazeau translated.

"How far?"

"A few miles."

They left the wagon and Swift Runner rode bareback, hands bound in front of him and ankles tethered together beneath the horse's belly. The horse had no bridle, only a lanyard of rope around his neck to hold onto.

"If you try to escape, the horse will trample you," Gagnon warned.

Swift Runner said, "I will not try to escape."

"If you do, the horse will step on your face, or your balls, or your kneecap. If he doesn't, I'm going to shoot you in the foot so you can't run, and you'll be hopping back to Fort Saskatchewan on one foot."

"You really want me to say that?" Brazeau asked.

"I wouldn't have said it if I didn't mean it," Gagnon growled.

Swift Runner waved Brazeau off. "I know what he said."

"I hope you do, because I won't be run in circles, Swift Runner," Gagnon warned. "Try to escape and hop, hop, hop, all the way back, following a horse on tether and stepping in its shit."

"I will take you," Swift Runner said.

III

The horses were the first to sense the horror waiting for them in the woods. They became stressed when they reached the edge of the forest, slowing and spooking at nothing and even stopping. They would have to go in on foot.

"Dismount!" Gagnon ordered. To Marois and Taylor, he added, "Get him off that horse and keep him under heavy guard."

"Yes, sir," Marois said.

They got Swift Runner down from the horse and secured him.

"Can you hear that?" Brazeau asked.

"Hear what?" Gagnon asked back.

Brazeau cupped his ear. "Listen."

They all listened, and what they heard was nothing. Not a chirp of bird, a wisp of wind, nor a cricket's serenade.

"Can you smell it?" Dr. Herchmer asked.

"*Oui*, *Docteur*, this odor is not new to me," Gagnon said. "But surely, the bones have been picked clean by now."

"One would think," Herchmer agreed.

They chatted a bit about decomposition to pass the time.

"The elements are the key," Herchmer said.

"But the summer has been dry, *Docteur*," Gagnon said. "The blood and the flesh should be no more."

"Unless he buried them. That boy back there was well preserved," Herchmer said.

"I guess we'll see," Brazeau interrupted.

They had Swift Runner up and ready.

"Swift Runner, you will lead us in."

"Yes, Inspector," Swift mumbled.

They had Swift Runner on a tether of rope tied around his waist at a length of twenty feet. The area was surrounded by muskeg, the ground spongy, and there was plenty of standing water. Gagnon stepped into a grass patch and pulled his foot back after submerging his boot to the shin.

"Not so dry here," Herchmer said.

"You're correct, *Docteur*," Gagnon said, kicking the mud from his boot.

They were following an overgrown trail through the woods, the stench hitting them hard now. When they crossed a clearing before the camp, Swift Runner stopped and let loose a glass-shattering shriek that echoed out across the plain. They recognized the sound as the shrieking thing arguing with the coyotes from two nights previous.

"What the hell was that?" Gagnon shouted at Swift.

"The *wihitikow* is gone from here," Swift Runner said and led them into the camp.

He was obedient and morose as they moved up the trail. The camp itself was at the center of intersecting paths. Gagnon recognized the other trails set for traplines and hunting game. The landscape began to reveal its secrets. On either side of the opening, he saw both small and large traps hanging indiscriminately from the tree branches. Some of those traps had the skeletal remains of small animals in their jaws.

At their feet, Gagnon saw what he thought was a bone.

Then Taylor saw another and another. "Oh, my God."

And the stench of death only got worse.

They stopped.

There were more bones ahead, but these were human.

"The animals," Swift Runner mumbled.

"What animals?" Gagnon seethed. "You said there was no game."

Swift Runner didn't answer, and they continued.

In the camp, they saw the teepee folded up neatly on a log, not eaten by his starving family as Swift Runner had related to Father Leduc. Gagnon would have questioned Swift Runner about the lie, but he saw two ribcages broken in half.

Marois crossed himself and puked, barely avoiding soiling his boots.

And it only got worse.

The ground was littered with femurs, mandibles, backbones, hip bones, clavicles, fibulas, and tibias. Gagnon's eyes followed the trail of bones all the way to a tiny skull. "*Docteur*!"

"I see it," Herchmer replied.

They knelt and examined the skull.

"A bear," Swift Runner lied.

Gagnon picked up the skull, handed it to Herchmer, and they both stood. Stuffed into one eye socket was a petite child's rolled-up sock. Gagnon's revulsion turned to anger and he hissed, "A bear scattered all these bones, that is what you say? How can this be, Swift Runner, as it was you who said there was no game to eat. No game! I see traps hanging in trees.... Mixed among these human bones are animal bones. Muskrat, opossum, no bear, although your trap hangs empty on a stump. Where was this so-called bear when your family was starving?"

Swift Runner didn't respond.

Herchmer held up the child's skull. "Did a bear stuff this sock into the child's eye socket?"

Swift Runner remained mute.

They continued scouring the ground, finding more bones and skulls. Some of the skulls had bullet holes, but two were broken apart.

Gagnon held it up. "What did this?"

Swift Runner was quiet.

"Probably used an ax," Herchmer said.

They moved to a large firepit that held a steel cooking pot hanging from a roasting spit made of wood and twine. Taylor looked in, and the scent of cooked human fat permeated up into his nose. He turned and retched.

Dr. Herchmer began tallying the number of skulls and trying to marry them to the four victims. One adult and three children.

"Where are the rest of them?"

Swift Runner didn't answer.

Gagnon took a long deep breath and exhaled. "Constable Taylor, stay with Doctor Herchmer and guard Swift Runner," he ordered.

"Where are you going, sir?" Taylor's voice trembled.

Gagnon tried to smile. "We're going to walk the perimeter of the camp and check to see if there is any other evidence."

"Yes, sir," Taylor said.

"We won't be long, Horace," Gagnon assured.

They followed the trail and their noses toward the source of the stench. Along the way, they found intestinal tract and viscera that had been turned to leather in the summer heat. They also found another child's skull on a tree branch using the eye as the hooking point. The jawbone had broken away from the skull on one side, hanging only by thin threads of tissue.

Gagnon turned the skull to see that it also had a pencil-sized hole in the cranium.

"Executed," he said.

Brazeau and Marois looked on in shock.

They carried on following the trail and found more bones, but no more skulls. "When we come back, I want that skull picked up and brought to Doctor Herchmer."

Marois and Brazeau nodded.

They carried on until they found an opening to the standing muskeg. If the bones weren't enough, standing at the center of the opening was a meat pole, lashed together with rope and birch logs, stained with copper. At its center was a crossbar for hanging game. The pale birchbark was plastered with layers of old blood, and in the dirt below, a large blotch marked the bloody mélange of innocents.

"He hung them like game," Brazeau gasped. "My God."

"*Mon Dieu*," Gagnon agreed.

Marois kept crossing himself. "This is an evil place."

All three men had one hand over their mouths.

"He killed them and butchered them like deer," Gagnon said.

"I don't think you need any more proof, Severe," Brazeau said.

"How do you do this to your family?" Gagnon was incredulous. "There was game. Why do this? *Pourquoi*?"

"*Le windigo*, *Inspecteur*," Marois said.

"*Le windigo*." Gagnon turned, hand on mouth. "What do we tell them? That Swift Runner wasn't responsible, that this was an Indian demon as he suggests? *Mère Marie et Jésus le charpentier*!"

"Can I make a suggestion?" Brazeau asked.

"By all means, George," Gagnon said.

"How about we talk about this somewhere else? I'm about to toss my breakfast."

"We never had breakfast," Gagnon reminded him.

"*Dieu merci*," Marois said, sending them drawing uneasy laughter.

"I was talking about yesterday's breakfast," Brazeau said, and there were more laughs through cupped mouths. The moment passed, then only silence and lingering death remained.

Marois said something that stuck with all of them. "He killed them in the winter; the camp would have been blanketed with snow. Could you imagine the bloody horror that would have painted the scenery?"

All of them could, conjuring the nightmare of blood and snow in their own minds.

Gagnon took a last look around, burning the scene into his head, making mental notes to record later. "Remember everything you saw here, gentlemen. We'll be responsible to recount it."

As they walked, Marois stole glances at Gagnon's face. His eyes were full of rage. They retrieved the hanging skull and returned to the main camp. Gagnon brought the skull over to Herchmer, who added it to the collection, raising the number to five.

"We're missing one kid and two adults," Herchmer said.

"The boy in the grave?" Gagnon asked.

"No, there were supposed to be five kids, so we should have four child skulls."

Gagnon went back to the bone collection and retrieved a small child's skull, not knowing whether it was a girl or boy. He carried that skull and sat down and presented it to Swift Runner. "What demonic possession was powerful enough for you to do what you did here?"

"They starved. I was the last," Swift Runner said.

"And in the face of all this damning evidence you still weave lies, Swift Runner." Gagnon leaned forward, pushing the skull closer to Swift. "This was your little baby child!"

Swift Runner began to sob.

Gagnon watched for a bit, stood, and put the skull back. "We're finished with this part of the investigation. Gather up all the skulls, some of the bones, and we'll bring them as evidence."

Under the direction of Dr. Herchmer, Marois and Brazeau carefully wrapped the bones in a makeshift bag fashioned from a horse blanket.

It was heavy.

"Who's going to carry them?" Brazeau asked.

"We'll have to carry them until we get back to the wagon. Then you can put the bones in the wagon with their killer," Gagnon said through clenched teeth.

"I'll carry them," Taylor said.

"Mount up!"

When they got back to the site of the first body, Swift Runner was transferred, along with the bones of his family, into the waiting wagon, which they hitched to the horse.

Swift Runner stared into the woods and said to Brazeau in Cree, "The *wihitikow* has taken everything. Even my favorite son."

"He was your favorite?" Brazeau replied in Cree, pointing to the woods.

"My favorite son's body is near Egg Lake," Swift said.

"Inspector," Brazeau called.

Gagnon joined them and Brazeau translated.

"You killed your other son near Egg Lake?" Gagnon asked.

"The *wihitikow*," Swift Runner corrected.

"What became of your brother and your mother?" Gagnon asked.

"When the *wihitikow* took over, they ran away into the storm. I went to look for them after but found nothing. I did find my favorite son. I hid him when the *wihitikow* came, but the *wihitikow* found us near Egg Lake. I will take you to the place where I left him."

"We don't have enough supplies," Gagnon said. "And I'm not dragging a sick constable all that distance when we've accomplished our mission. We have more than enough evidence. Maybe we'll go and seek out the boy's location after we return to the fort, but we're not going to Egg Lake now."

IV

The sickness had sapped Griffith's energy; he was slipping in and out of consciousness. He forced himself to get up and check to see if they were coming back.

Nothing.

Just fog.

He checked his watch.

They had been gone over two hours.

He stood there dutifully, exhaustion dragging him down, perusing his childhood past and dozing on watch. Tasha passed through his mind, then he thought about his first true love. Penny. He and Penny were two years apart, she the elder. She was dark-haired and tomboyish, but she had freckles and a wonderful smile. He had a child's crush on Penny because she treated him like he was special. She didn't even call him Ron. She called him "David," which was his middle name.

"I like David better. David was a king," Penny insisted. "David slew Goliath."

He called her "Pen" and "Penny" when he really wanted to get her attention. Penny's father, his Uncle John, was a widower, and he and Ron's father worked adjoining farms in Wales. The Griffiths were descendants of Welsh farmers all the way back to the 1200s. His father and uncle would go off to work the fields after dropping Penny off. She would come to his house and Griffith's mother would send them out to play.

He and Penny were left mostly to their own devices for reasons that Griffith was only beginning to understand. She kicked the kids out so she could drink alone.

"Why is your mom so sad, David?" Penny asked.

"Sad? She's not sad, Pen. She's mad… She yells at me and at my dad for nothing," nine-year-old Ron Griffith said. "She changes when she drinks."

"She drinks, David, because something is making her sad." Penny said this with such confidence that he could only believe her.

Lying here waiting for them to return, he thought perhaps his mother had been plagued by her own windigo madness, as it seemed a shadow would cross her face when the transformation occurred. He felt no love between his parents, only duty. The love he sought came from Penny.

When Penny was eleven, she complained about a bad pain. That was the beginning of the end of happiness for Ron Griffith and his first true love. First, the adults just said she was sick, then they said she was very sick, but no one said she was going to die. With every visit, the disease took a little bit more of her. She lost so much weight, her clothes hung on her, shoulders bowing like tired tree limbs. Worse still, her eyes were sunken, faded, tired, and her skin was pale.

Pale like me.

Griffith opened an eye, looking over at Gunner, who was tied up only a few feet away. The horse was standing guard, watching for the darkness that plagued him. "Thank you, Gunner."

The horse snorted an acknowledgement

He stared out into the fog, searching for movement.

Nothing yet.

He closed his eyes and went back to Penny. Back to remembering how the disease ate her from the inside and her beautiful, freckled cheeks seemed to melt away to skin and bone. No one had said the word "dying" until Penny did. "I got something wrong with me, David. I'm not going to get better. The doctor says I have a type of blood cancer, and it can't be cured. Everyone has been praying."

"I've been praying too," Ron said.

"I know you have, David, but I'm not going to get better. I'm dying."

"No, Pen. I don't want you to go." He couldn't say "die."

"Don't cry, King David." She spread her frail arms, and he gently leaned into her bony embrace.

"Please, God, please, make Pen better," he cried.

"Oh, God has a plan for me and you, David. I'm going to see my mami in heaven, and we're going to watch over you every day until you become a man."

"No, Penny, no, please. I love you," he sobbed, and she soothed him and told him it was going to be okay while she was being eaten from the inside. It wasn't fair, and he felt selfish for crying and taking her strength.

He saw her one last time before they took her away.

He went to Uncle John's farm. She was in a wagon, looking weak and pale, and she smiled for him and whispered, "I'll watch over you, King David."

He kissed her cheek. It was cold. "I love you, Pen."

"You'll slay your Goliath." She winced a little and closed her eyes. "Oh, Daddy, it hurts."

Griffith stepped back, buried his face in his father's belly, and cried harder than he had in his whole life, as Uncle John rolled Penny away in that wagon.

He saw Penny once more—at her funeral.

She had been two inches taller than him. An inch for each year. She tickled his chin with buttercups, she ruffled his hair, and she made him feel like a king. Then she was in a box, her gaunt face powdered by the undertaker's brushes, trying to bring life to death. Griffith didn't say anything, not a prayer. He didn't think she was in heaven, didn't believe. A loving God wouldn't afflict children to die as his Penny had. No God, no heaven, no hell. Only darkness. Blood cancer.

Griffith opened an eye. Checked the fog.

Nothing yet.

Closed the eye, and thought, *I have a blood disease too, Pen, but it's worse than cancer. It isn't just killing me but eating my soul. I need to keep an eye out for them.*

Penny whispered, *"Go slay your Goliath!"*

Then came the hideous shriek of the windigo.

Griffith opened both eyes, scanning the fog. He thought the shriek came from the same direction that they had gone with Swift Runner.

Have they come face to face with the beast?

He watched, feeling his eyes closing and opening, listened for almost two minutes. Nothing, but not just nothing. No gunfire, and that made him happy. No gunfire meant that everything was fine.

Maybe the monster is on its way here?

He thought about that.

Better here than there.

He still had that one bullet.

Griffith took a last look, sat down, and rolled over on his side, unable to keep his eyes open any longer. He closed them and felt himself falling, down into the endless darkness. Drifting toward a dream or maybe a vision. The darkness withdrew, revealing the camp through colorless sight. Griffith was with them—not physically, but he was there—watching as Gagnon and Dr. Herchmer stopped to examine a small skull.

The scenes passed from one to the next in blinding flashes.

Griffith was watching Taylor peering into the camp pot, his revulsion, and he was vomiting.

Flash!

Then Herchmer gathering the bones and organizing them by size.

Flash!

They were standing in front of a meat pole, the earth dark with old blood. Griffith watched Marois at the water's edge, witnessed the blood leeching into the muskeg.

Marois vomited.

Flash!

Gagnon pulled out his compass and map, orienting the return bearing to the camp.

"Taylor, Marois, keep an eye on the prisoner. Everyone else, stay in a tight formation," Gagnon said as he led them back into the fog.

There were acknowledgments.

"Yes, sir."

"Swift Runner," Gagnon called. "I will not appreciate any outbursts or shenanigans."

"Yes, Inspector," Swift Runner mumbled.

They started back through the fog at a slow gait, leaving the death camp behind, melting into the haze. "Can't see a damn thing," Dr. Herchmer complained.

"Halt," Gagnon ordered and checked his compass and map.

Without warning, Taylor drew his gun and started shooting at them.

Brazeau was hit first, but before he could drop from his horse, the windigo came out of the fog and dragged him away. Brazeau screamed, but the cry was cut short by a crunch.

Then Taylor shot Herchmer, declaring, "Dinner is served!"

The windigo returned, carrying Brazeau's headless torso in its right clutch. It snatched the still alive Herchmer from the ground with claw and dragged him away into the morning mist. It was a blur of claws and teeth, cutting back and forth through the shadows. There were biting sounds and more screams in the seconds that elapsed. Herchmer's cries were guttural, managing, "Someone, please help me! Severe! Se…" then they just ended with a bony snap.

Swift Runner was chanting something, winding up, ranting.

Marois shot Taylor dead.

Gagnon turned left and right, eyes wide in terror, gun aimed. "*Tu vas bien*, Fredericke?"

"I'm unharmed." Marois was scanning the fog.

Where is it?

Swift kept screaming madly.

Gagnon barked, "*Ferme ta gueule*, Swift Run—"

The creature shrieked, and a claw came from the fog yanking Gagnon from his horse. Marois shot at it, but it dragged Severe Gagnon away. There was a dull thud, a cry of pain, then grunting, tearing, and the spilling of guts.

Swift Runner let out a mad cry, and the thing screeched back.

Marois turned his gun and shot Swift Runner dead.

Swift slumped over.

All alone now, Marois scanned the opaque, gun ready, eyes wild with fear. He turned, left and right, even looked skyward. "Where is it?" He spun his horse around, gun aiming at nothing. Waiting for the beast's shadow.

"Where is it, Ron?" Marois was looking right at Griffith—but how could that be?

"Where is the beast?"

"I don't know," Griffith said.

Then Marois' face was right in front him, hands reaching out, and shaking him.

"Ron, *mon ami*."

Griffith opened his eyes and sat bolt upright, almost knocking Marois over. He recoiled at first, kicking a foot into the fire, then scrambled up the bank to see them out there on horseback in formation, waiting.

"Easy." Marois took his shoulder. "It's over, we're going home."

A dream? Just a dream!

It hadn't felt like a dream.

"He killed them all, Ron." Marois was weeping. "Little babies. Dear God."

"I know," Griffith whispered.

"You know?"

"I saw everything. I saw you and Taylor too."

"Constable Marois?" Gagnon called from the gathering.

"We're coming, sir," Marois called back and turned to Griffith. "We can talk about that later. Sub-Inspector told me to get you up and moving. He thinks you'll get better, the farther away we get from here."

Griffith said, "Yes, let's go. I want to go home."

"*Moi aussi*," Marois agreed.

V

For Griffith, riding through the morning fog was jarring. He wondered if what he had seen in the vision was a glimpse into their future. As they went south, the fog thinned and the sun burned through the vapor and warmed things up.

They rode for forty-two miles.

During this time, Griffith rode, but Gunner was leading.

Sub-Inspector Gagnon would report no incident going south except for the illness that had beset one of his men. Griffith was monitored by Dr. Herchmer. There was a meeting out of earshot and in darkness when they set up camp.

There had been no sound or sign of the windigo since Swift Runner declared it gone.

"None of us has actually seen it," Brazeau said.

"Gentleman, as I see it, the crime and the evidence we're bringing is far beyond the strange happenings we witnessed in those woods," Gagnon said.

"What about me, Severe?" Griffith asked.

"What about you?"

"What if I don't get better? What if I get worse? What lies will we tell them then?"

"You'll get better," Gagnon said and walked back to the camp.

That night, the talk was mechanical; they fed the prisoner and kept a watch. All of them, including Swift Runner, slept through the night.

On the second day, everyone agreed, including Griffith, that they wouldn't mention a word about the windigo. The story of the death camp and the cargo at Swift Runner's feet was horror enough for them all.

Griffith didn't get better, he got worse, even as the miles between them and the death camp grew in number. Twice along the way, he vomited up the black foamy substance, and he became an even ghostlier pale. He rode behind the wagon, where Swift Runner couldn't see him, just as Crane had.

Griffith looked down at his hands; they were so gray.

I'm losing my color because it's eating me from inside.

He thought the thing inside him was suckling life from the places it was dearly needed—heart, lungs, brain, skin—and his involuntary body was juggling that.

Eventually, I'll die in pain if I don't eat something bloody rare.

And he was tumbling over, catching air, then feeling the full weight of his body slam against the ground. "Oof!"

Then Marois was over him. "Ron! Are you okay?"

"I'm fine," Griffith said, dusting himself off and climbing back up onto Gunner, who had obediently stopped at his human's side. His right shoulder and knee were humming from the impact, but that wasn't a bad thing; the pain cut through the numbness and reminded him that he was still alive.

From that point on, Marois and Herchmer rode on both sides and accompanied Griffith all the way back into Fort Saskatchewan.

They had made it home.

***

Chapter 16 – Blood and Goats

I

Superintendent Jarvis's Office.
Fort Saskatchewan, NWT

Swift Runner hooked two fingers through the eye sockets of the largest skull and declared, "This was my wife," as the spectators looked on in disbelief. Superintendent Jarvis was staring at the bones laid out on a table. Jarvis, who had seen much, gawked as he listened to the killer speak.

Also in attendance were Gagnon, Taylor, and Brazeau.

It was in this room that Swift Runner confirmed that he had killed them all and eaten their flesh, though he blamed the *wihitikow* for the lack of remorse he had during the murders. Not once did he look their way when he spoke of being under the windigo's influence. He divested himself of every gory detail, as his audience listened in horror. Spared the gruesome declaration were Marois and Dr. Herchmer, who had taken Griffith to the infirmary.

Swift Runner also confessed that his favorite, youngest son had shared in the eating of human flesh. His favorite son was the last to die north of Egg Lake.

"It gets into you, takes over," Swift Runner said without a bit of emotion.

When he was done, Taylor escorted Swift Runner back to his cell, while the policemen deliberated over the horror of Swift's deeds. There would be a trial, but the federal government would have to be notified of the charges. As this was a case of murder, the punishment would be death.

After Brazeau and Taylor departed, Jarvis and Gagnon deliberated.

"All this windigo business," Jarvis said. "The press will have a bloody field day!"

"Yes, sir." Gagnon was tired.

"Jesus, he made his own kid eat their flesh," Jarvis said.

"Should we go search for the last child, sir?" Gagnon asked.

Jarvis thought about it. "Swift said he buried the boy, and he'll be charged with the child's murder. I don't see a reason to mount another expedition. After two escape attempts and the charges he now faces, it's not worth the risk, Severe."

"Yes, sir."

"We're going to have to do this again. I'll get Hugh Richardson in tomorrow to record it, and we'll get the bare bones of it down on paper," Jarvis said. "Fucking windigo talk is just what we don't need, Severe."

"Yes, sir."

II

Marois met Corporal Bagley in the yard outside the stables, after checking on his and Griffith's horses.

"I wish I'd gotten the flu," Marois mused.

"Oh no you didn't. I don't think I've ever been so sick. I'd rather have gone north with you boys. That sounded like an adventure." Bagley grinned.

"Wasn't no adventure, Bag's," Marois corrected.

"That bad?" Bagley frowned.

"It was the most awful thing I've ever witnessed." Marois stared into Bagley's eyes. "Be glad you got the flu, Bags. I'll see that bloody muskeg and those tiny skulls for the rest of my days."

"You'll get over it." Bagley patted his shoulder. "You just need time, Fred."

"I hope you're right." Marois didn't think so.

"What is wrong with Griffith?" Bagley asked.

"We don't know,. He might have the same thing Crane has."

"Geez, I hope not. Crane is in the Bin." Bagley was referring to the local lunatic asylum.

"He's in the Bin?"

"He was acting crazy. He killed three goats one night and ate their insides. They put him in a cell, then he kept bashing his head against the door. So, they took him to the lunatic house."

"When did this happen?"

"They took him yesterday." Bagley frowned. "He ain't Danny Crane no more."

Marois thought about Griffith and pushed the obvious away. "I'll talk to you about this later. I really need some sleep. Good night, Bags."

"Goodnight, Fred."

Marois was walking out of the main yard toward the barracks when he saw a silhouette waiting in the darkness. "Horace, is that you?"

Taylor stepped out of the shadows. "I… I couldn't do this in there." His wore a painful grimace, eyes lit with tears. "Am I weak, Fred? Am I a bad police officer because I can't be hard like you guys?"

"No, you're not weak, Horace," Marois said.

"I feel weak. It's tearing me up." His voice was a whimper. "How, Fred? How could he eat his own kids?" He let out a cry. "Those poor little kids. They didn't do nothing, Fred. They was just babies. Was just babies…" He broke down into sobs. "They didn't do nothing. Oh my God…"

Marois stepped forward and placed his hands on Taylor's shoulders. "Horace, I don't know. I'm just as sad as you, *mon ami*." But Marois did know, and so did Taylor. It was the horrible thing they weren't talking about, Swift Runner's accomplice in his crimes. "Listen, Horace, you did a damned good job up there. You thwarted an escape. Some might think crying is weak, but they never saw what we saw up there. You'll suffer no scorn from me. I feel much the same." He let Taylor go. "You're a good Mountie, Horace Taylor. Let's go inside and get some sleep."

"You go on inside, Fred. I'm need to get myself together." Taylor wiped his eyes, and straightened his uniform.

"I understand," Marois said and went inside.

III

The bunkhouse was empty except for an officer named Geoffrey Kirkland, lying awake. Marois lined up on his own cot, which was across from Kirkland's. He stole a glance at the man, who was tall, clean-shaven, and muscular, with ginger hair.

Marois unbuttoned his tunic and hung it up. He sat down on the bunk and pulled off one of his boots, hoping he would get to lie down and forget about the day.

At least until tomorrow.

Then he began to pull off the other boot, and…

"You were up in that death camp?" Kirkland sat up to face him. "With Sub-Inspector Gagnon?"

"Yes," Marois said, pulling off his boot.

"I saw the report, and Taylor filled me in," Kirkland said.

"Taylor filled you in?" Marois was surprised, even a little pissed. It wasn't unusual for officers to talk about cases, and this was the most sensational thing the NWMP had ever investigated. Still, he hadn't expected Taylor to gossip, given his present state.

"He didn't fill me in with any particular glee," Kirkland said. "I read the report, so I just asked him some questions. He answered them, and I told him what happened with Crane and the goat."

"Goat? I thought there were three."

"You must have been talking to Bags," Kirkland said.

"*Oui*," Marois said.

"Bags is two things: a braggart and an exaggerator. There was only one goat, and that was bad enough. I'm the one that found him," Kirkland said. "I was making my way out to relieve the morning sentry. Near the stables, I saw the flickering of light, and I thought there might be a fire." He paused and sucked his lower lip. "There was a small campfire burning in the barnyard, which was unusual. As I got closer, I saw Crane sitting buck naked behind the fire. He was covered with animal blood. A dead goat was lying to his right, its belly open and emptied. Its steaming guts were piled in Crane's naked lap, and he had a helping of goat innards in each hand. He held it up like an offering over the fire."

"An offering?" Marois asked.

"Yeah, like there was an evil spirit in front of him."

Marois thought about Kirkland's choice of words—"evil spirit"—wondering if Taylor had done more than ask a few questions. Perhaps he had added bits about the windigo?

Kirkland continued, "I said to him, 'Crane, you all right?' and even though I was right in front of him, it was like he couldn't see me. He was looking up, fists full of dripping guts, and pleading, 'Please—take it—please!' Then he went quiet for something like ten, maybe fifteen seconds. I thought maybe he was in a daze, but as the seconds dragged on, I realized he was listening. Whatever he was talking to was talking back to him. I just couldn't hear it because I'm not a lunatic. I heard he was sick, but I thought he'd got some blood thing. Then while I'm thinking about that, Crane started screaming, 'I won't! I won't! I won't!' He jumped up, guts in his crotch spilling onto the fire and sizzling, which is a sight and sound I shall not soon forget. He was raving, and when I got right next to him, he turned to me and said, 'Shoot me, Geoff! Shoot me before it's too late!' With all the racket you'd think someone was coming, but nobody did. 'I'm begging you, Geoff, kill me before I can't ask you to do it anymore.' He started around the fire and was coming right at me. 'Kill me, Geoff! Kill me, Geoff!'"

"What did you do?" Marois was leaning in.

"I knocked him out. The man has a glass jaw."

"Were you there when Crane tried to hurt himself?" Marois asked.

"Yeah… After we locked him up, he smashed the hell out of his forehead on the door."

"But only one goat?"

Kirkland sniffed, even smiled. "Bags is so full of shit. He loves embellishing the facts. He's like an old woman. I bet he'll be saying there were five goats by tomorrow afternoon."

Marois chuckled at this.

Taylor came into the bunk house, nodded at them, and got undressed for bed. They were quiet while Marois watched him lie down in his bunk, thinking him smart to do his crying elsewhere. Even after all they had been through, outsiders would have seen the tears as weakness. He had already forgiven him for talking to Kirkland.

Kirkland continued.

"When we pulled him out of the cell, he fought and bucked all the way, and when we were trying to restrain him for travel, he went for my gun. Almost got it too. I had to knock him out again. He was still out when we got there. Hoffman, the medic, was waiting for us, and we delivered him into a room covered in mattresses."

"Mattresses?" At first, Marois didn't understand.

"Yeah, they were on the walls and the floor, nailed or glued down. I've never seen anything like it in my life. They wrapped Crane up in a thing they called a straitjacket. The arms wrap around and are tied in the back. A straitjacket… Have you ever heard of that?"

"Ahh, okay, I understand. I know of these things," Marois said. "The jacket and the mattresses are there to stop him from hurting himself. I was in a lunatic asylum in Paris, about five years ago."

Kirkland raised his eyebrows.

Marois laughed. "Not as a patient! I was there to visit a cousin who was sick in the head. The room that is padded is called *la salle de calme.* The quiet room."

"The quiet room. Hmmm. I'm glad to hear you weren't a patient," Kirkland said. "Anyway, we left him there, and we all felt bad, but he'd gone loony. We didn't know what else to do with him."

"Safe confinement was what he needed," Marois said.

"I don't have much else. But if you check with Bags, I'm sure he'll enlighten you."

Marois laughed, and from his bunk, Taylor also snickered, which made Marois feel a little better.

He gave Kirkland a weary look and said, "I have to sleep."

"Good idea. I'm on watch in four hours." Kirkland leaned back on his cot, and it creaked.

"Goodnight."

"Goodnight."

Marois half dozed, his thoughts mired in bloody muskeg and child skulls. He puzzled over the windigo spirit and its hold on his friends. *If the thing is in Swift Runner, how could it also be down here haunting Crane? Is Crane possessed by the same demon? Is Griffith? How could a single spirit possess the souls of three men simultaneously? And over a range of eighty miles?*

The thoughts fell away one by one, and he thought sleep would never come.

Until there was only one thought.

How do I save them?

Then he was gone.

IV

Fort Saskatchewan, NWT
Sick Quarters

Griffith was lying in a hospital bed and at the foot, sitting in a visitor chair, was the windigo. This was the most definitive Griffith had seen the creature. Before, it had been more ghost-like, an apparition of inky smoke. Every detail of its horror had more definition, from dry and rotted flesh to infected teeth and pinpricks of red glowing in hollow eye sockets.

It sat there, telling him about Crane.

"They took him away," the windigo said. "To a place where he cannot…" It stopped, brought up a claw, and picked at its rotting teeth. "…cannot do anything." It punctured a spot on its gum, and ichor squirted out.

Griffith watched, mouth agape.

"A goat… Can you believe that? He brought me a goat." It ground its teeth, a sound more unbearable than fingernails on a chalk board. "I need sustenance." It rose from the chair, twisting and contorting, stretching up and over the bed, hovering above Griffith, nose to nose. "I am so hungry!" It leaned in even closer. "I need food—they have them all locked up—I must eat—we must eat. It must be you."

"No," Griffith said.

Then it began grinding its teeth. Its lower mandible moved back and forth. Bits of tooth splintered and fell onto Griffith's face but dissipated like gas.

Not real to this world, Griffith thought.

"Oh, I am quite real," it hissed. "Real enough to read your thoughts."

"But not complete," Griffith said.

"You think you know something?" The creature pulled away, floating across the room.

"Yes, I do."

The windigo eased back down into the chair, now the size of a regular man. "Do tell."

"You draw your strength from the acts of murder and cannibalism. But without an actual kill, you're not whole, and the longer time elapses, the weaker you grow."

"Weaker?" It cackled. "You are the one getting weaker, Ron."

"No matter how sick you make me," Griffith said.

"Oh, this is just the beginning," it interrupted.

"I won't do your bidding."

It shifted shape and became Swift Runner. "It must be you, Constable Ron. They are going to kill me for what I have done, and Crane is in a cell. So, it must be you."

"You can go to hell," Griffith spat.

Then it was Danny Crane. "We are already in hell."

The boy from St. Albert. "And so are you, Ron Griffith."

Then Griffith was staring at himself. "We need to get out of bed and find a weapon."

"I won't!" Griffith cried.

"Oh, but you will." It closed its claw into a fist and squeezed.

Griffith felt his guts twisting up in worms of agony, and he cried out. "Ohhh…"

It closed its other fist and squeezed.

The second wave of agony was so unbearable, he curled into the fetal position.

"You need to find a weapon, then you need to decide who..." There was a sound of boots clunking across the boardwalk. The windigo turned its head. "We will finish this later," it growled, becoming smoke and melting into the wall cracks.

The door swung open.

"You okay? I heard a cry," Hoffman, the medic, asked. "You okay, Ron?"

He wasn't looking at Hoffman. He was looking at the wall, feeling the receding pain in his guts and wondering how much worse the devil could make it. When would the pain be so bad that he would give in?

If it comes to that, I'll shoot myself in the head.

"Ron?"

He brought his eyes to meet Hoffman. "Sorry, bad dream."

"You sounded like someone was killing you."

"It was a real bad dream."

V

Marois rose the next morning, tended to his duties, and visited Griffith at the infirmary. He was the last in line; both Superintendent Jarvis and Sub-Inspector Gagnon also visited him in the morning.

"Swift Runner has confessed, but there will be a formal confession today," Superintendent Jarvis said. "Then we go to trial."

"How soon, sir?" Griffith asked.

"I expect it will be less than a week. We're ready to go. We have overwhelming evidence and the killer has confessed. We're going to need your written statement, Corporal Griffith."

Griffith looked confused. "Yes, sir."

"*Félicitations, Caporal.*" Sub-Inspector Gagnon smiled and produced a new set of corporal chevrons. "You're out of uniform, but I'll get it tailored for you."

Griffith smiled and felt his spirits rise some. "Thank you, sir. Thank you, Sub-Inspector."

They left him to write his statement about the expedition.

Marois came in and congratulated him on the promotion. Griffith was lucid, but he still looked sickly pale, and Marois waited until the attending medic stepped out. "What the hell is going on, Ron?"

"You wouldn't believe me if I told you," Griffith said.

"Tell me anyway," Marois insisted.

Griffith told him everything. "The windigo that was haunting Swift Runner spoke Cree to Swift Runner. This thing speaks perfect English, but I think they're the same creature, and I think that Swift Runner is the core of this abomination."

"I want to help. What do I do?" Marois asked.

"I don't know if you can help me," Griffith said. "This thing will probably destroy me. Soon I'll be in a padded room like Danny Crane." He was staring off into nothing.

"Maybe if Swift Runner dies, the curse will die with him," Marois said.

"Maybe," Griffith said, but he didn't believe that.

They were quiet for a long time.
Then Marois had an idea.

***

Chapter 17 – The Last Ride

I

Superintendent Jarvis's Office.
Fort Saskatchewan, NWT

The next day, Swift Runner alerted the guard that he was again ready to confess. Unfortunately, Brazeau wasn't available to interpret. A local farmer named William Borwick was asked to come in and assist. Borwick was a short, scraggly man, unshaven and sloppily dressed, wearing an exhausted cowboy hat, a battered gray overcoat, and oversized pants cinched up with a piece of rope. Jarvis was worried when he met the man but was assured he was fluent in Cree.

In fact, Borwick sounded much more refined than he looked.

They made small talk. Jarvis showed him the previous day's waiver given when Brazeau interpreted, and they worked out how to proceed. Also present at a nearby desk, Special Security Officer Hugh Richardson recorded the confession on paper as it was translated into English.

"Do you understand that anything you say, in Cree or in English, will be written down and can be used against you at any future trial?" Jarvis asked.

Borwick translated.

Swift Runner nodded. "Yes."

"Please proceed," Jarvis said.

Swift Runner spoke in Cree and when he finished, he looked from Borwick to Jarvis.

Borwick translated, "I'm going to tell the truth. I have done a great deal of harm. That is the reason I was backward with telling about it."

Richardson was writing madly.

Borwick said, "I didn't kill anybody else's children, only my own. I told you an awful lie."

Swift Runner continued in Cree, pausing for translation.

Borwick translated, “First, I shot my son, the next to eldest. The eldest died at the camp where men found the bones. I killed all the rest except my youngest son, whom I killed near Egg Lake. I shot him through the back of the head. I shot my wife through the breast. The two little girls I knocked in the head with an ax. I choked the baby girl with a line.”

Swift continued in English...

“I know nothing about my brother and mother. My second boy I shot at the camp I did not show. A few days after my eldest boy died of starvation, I shot my woman and killed all the rest, except my last boy, at the same camp the same day.”

Then he continued in Cree.

“After eating the last boy, I came on to Egg Lake, where I stayed a little while, then I came on to St. Albert. My wife said nothing when I killed my second boy. I never threatened before to kill and eat my wife,” Borwick translated.

Swift Runner looked at Jarvis and said in Cree, “I told you everything I have done.”

II

August 20, 1879
The Trial

With confession in hand, the Mounties charged Swift Runner, and the trial was speedy. The jury consisted of six White men, four of whom spoke Cree. There were no Indigenous people in attendance at the trial. Had they been in attendance, it wouldn’t have been in support of Swift Runner. The Cree were equally repelled by the crime of the accused, windigo madness or not, and thought death was the only remedy for an act so wicked.

The jury viewed the evidence and heard the testimony from the officers involved. This included Sergeant Richard Steele, who had been in the arresting party. Taylor and Marois also gave testimony, as did Dr. Herchmer and Brazeau.

An older Cree man who identified himself as Kis Sie Ko Way, testified, "I know the prisoner and was his father-in-law. The prisoner married my daughter, whose name is Charlotte. They were married fourteen years ago. They lived together and had five children. Three girls and two boys." The old Cree recounted how he had met them at a place called Long Lake near Athabasca, and that they looked healthy enough. "The prisoner and his family were not so far away that they or the children could not readily got into the Hudson's Bay post at the river landing without risk of starvation even if no game could be found."

Sub-Inspector Gagnon gave the most compelling evidence in the chilling recounting of the death camp. That and the skulls and bones made Swift Runner a monster in the eyes of all present.

Especially the children's skulls.

Swift Runner had reviled himself, albeit with the qualification the windigo had taken over in the times of murder and cannibalism. But in the official confession known as "Paper A," Swift Runner confirmed that he had murdered and eaten his family. This was the most damning piece of evidence, but it was far from the whole truth, as any mention of *wihitikow* was omitted or disallowed. "Paper A" sealed Swift Runner's fate, bare bones confession or not.

Outside the small courtroom, they deliberated for twenty minutes.

They returned with a guilty verdict and Swift Runner was sentenced to die.

III

September 20, 1879
Fort Saskatchewan Asylum for Lunatics

Having suffered an extensive mental breakdown, Daniel Crane was now being treated at the Fort Saskatchewan Asylum for Lunatics, also known to NWMP officers as "the Bin." Dr. Herchmer wrote in his report: *This constable has been exposed to a crime of extremism beyond those seen by regular duty officers or even soldiers. He has been remanded to the mental hospital for treatment.*

Crane was being taken from the padded room, a man on either side of him. One big and one small, both very strong. They gripped him like a vise. Crane wasn't walking; they were carrying him down the hall to an adjacent room in the house. The walls were mucus green, the wood floor white, splotched here and there with blood, feces, and urine. They reached a door and the bigger man pushed it open.

They carried him into the room and walked him straight to a waiting tub.

Crane was beyond language but not comprehension, and he blubbered and snarled when he saw it through bars of the cage around his head. His legs were wrapped in three belts, at the thigh, knee, and ankle.

"Ready?" Small asked.

"Ready," Big said.

They lifted him horizontally and walked him, face up, over to the tub. Below him, shards of ice winked in the dim oil lamp light, as the water, black and hungry, waited.

Crane twisted, jerking his head left and right, snapping at them, but they held him firmly.

"Now," Small said.

When they lowered him into the bath, he fought harder and shrieked so loudly that both men let go of him to cover their ears. Crane sank below the ice like a rock, still screaming, as the cage around his head disappeared into the black water. The two attendants removed their hands from their ears and looked down at the bubbles as the tub hummed from the underwater scream.

"Should just let him drown," Big said. "That'd shut him up for sure."

"Can't do that," Small said.

"Why not?"

"Doctor Keach says this one is special. He's got some new techniques he wants to try."

"All right," Big said. He plunged a hand into the tub, grabbed the cage, and brought Crane's head above the icy water. "There you go, Daniel, that should calm you a little. Let the cold water pull out all your aggression."

Crane lay there panting, eyes red-rimmed. He caught his breath, snapped at them, then he took a deep breath and began to shriek again.

"Looks like he needs another dunk," Small said.

"He does so," Big said and pushed the cage below the surface. "He'll come around."

Crane bucked, and the ice rolled the tub's length in several black waves. When he stopped, they brought him up for air. Once the patient was sufficiently calmed, they returned him, soaking wet, to his padded cell and locked him in. Over the last three weeks, Crane's ice baths average was upgraded to three a day. After the treatments, he barely resembled a living man. But every night he would return to ranting and raving like a lunatic.

IV

September 22, 1879
Fort Saskatchewan, NWT

Griffith lay in the infirmary bed, worn out from the windigo's nightly visitations. They were sessions with a single purpose: absolute possession. When there was nothing left, it would get what it wanted. Tonight, it was hanging over him, talking about Crane.

"He is pretty much useless now. They have him all tied up, and he cannot do anything except scream and bellow. He is much further along than you; he is ready to serve. If I could just get him out of his bindings, he would murder everyone in that place and the hunger would—"

"Would just return," Griffith said. "Leave Danny alone."

"I can do that, but first you need to kill someone! Maybe Marois or Taylor."

Griffith turned over and vomited into the bucket. "You're making me sick."

"Sick? Oh no, not yet. When the hunger has eaten your soul, you will come to the fire on your knees with an offering and beg me to let you eat. You will kill them all. You will kill children if I ask."

It withdrew to the chair. "Are you ready for your nightly treatment?" it asked.

"No, please."

"Begging will not help, Ron." It held up its bony, rheumatoid hand, palm open, which tonight had six fingers, each crowned with a jagged talon. It wriggled them, looking like an upturned spider and one by one, the fingers began to fold over in a fist. "Everyone begs, and I always say, there is an easier way. You only gotta kill one person and this does not have to happen."

"Never," Griffith said.

"Your choice." The windigo closed its misshapen fist and squeezed.

Griffith felt agony in his belly. He cupped his stomach and rolled onto his side, contracting into the fetal position, barely managing, "Oooohh." His guts were full of broken glass and iodine.

It was beside him again and said in whispering, reeking breaths, "Just one soul and then it gets easier."

Griffith pulled in a couple short breaths and gasped, "I reject you."

It leaned closer.

"You cannot reject me. We will be one, just as Swift Runner and I are one. You will get your ass up out of that bed and stop hiding from who we are. You will do as I say, Ron. Everyone does."

"Go back to whatever hell you came from," Griffith said weakly.

"You are the one in hell." It clenched its fist even more.

Another contraction of agony. Griffith rolled his head over the side of the bed and vomited out a glut of black.

"This will all stop when we eat," the windigo said.

Griffith had neither strength nor enough air in his lungs to speak, so he glared instead.

"I will give you this, Ron Griffith. You have a strong will." The windigo's words had an air of respect in them. It might even have smiled but was unable, for its lips had long ago been chewed off. "But not stronger than me." It balled up its fist and squeezed again.

The third wave of agony knocked Griffith out, and he remained so for hours.

When he next awoke, the windigo was gone, but it was still dark. The thing was getting stronger with each visit, it was vampiric, feeding on his misery instead of blood.

It's getting stronger and I'm getting weaker.

The treatment was devouring his empathy and morality, replacing them with resentment and hunger. He had begun to entertain lurid thoughts. If he could get away from the fort and find a stranger to sacrifice, that would sate the windigo and the cravings. Griffith thought about the word "sacrifice," and how he conveniently exchanged it for "kill." Soon the windigo would possess him completely.

I can't wait for that, he thought.

Griffith succumbed to exhaustion and fell back asleep.

When he next awoke, the sun was shining through the window.

"Morning, Ron." Taylor was sitting in the windigo's chair.

Griffith gazed up at Taylor. "Morning, Horace."

"Are you feeling any better?"

"I'm afraid not. Please go and get Sub-Inspector Gagnon," Griffith said.

"Okay, I'll get him," Taylor said. He got up and went out the door.

Taylor found Gagnon.

"I'll speak to Griffith. You go and find Marois," Gagnon said.

"Yes, sir," Taylor said, and they went in separate directions. Gagnon walked briskly across the yard and into the infirmary where he said to Griffith, "You want us to take you to the Bin?"

"Yes, before the men see the change in me," Griffith said.

"All right." Gagnon had seen the change in Crane. He was an incoherent madman now, and if he were in Griffith's position, he would likely ask the same. "How do you want to proceed?"

"I'm still an officer of the NWMP. Please allow me the dignity to ride into town on Gunner in my uniform," Griffith said. "Rather than be delivered as a prisoner."

"Of course, *Caporal.*" Gagnon faltered, he turned away, collected himself, and patted Griffith on the shoulder. "I'll have the men ready your horse."

"Thank you, Severe."

V

Half an hour later, Taylor and Marois showed up at the infirmary and helped Griffith get dressed in his uniform, which was adorned with two newly sewn on corporal chevrons. Getting his boots on had been especially difficult. He was physically exhausted and tried to help, but Taylor and Marois did most of the work. Boots on, Marois moved behind him, centering the crease on his pants, while tucking them in. During this, Taylor stood beside Griffith, steadying him. Marois stood up, examined his handiwork, and said, "*Fantastique.*"

"Sharp as a razor's edge, Corporal Griffith," Taylor said, his voice shaky.

"Thanks." Griffith gave a slight smile and a nod to the man whom he had threatened to beat into a bloody pulp only a few weeks before. "I think we're ready."

"One more thing," Marois said, setting the pillbox hat on Griffith's head.

"Let's go," Griffith said.

Dressed in their best bib and tucker, they walked together out of the infirmary and made their way across the yard to the stables in the cadence of military men with purpose. As they did, a looming shadow stood over them. Griffith looked up to see the gallows, and on toward the stables. When he saw Gunner, he smiled, eyes blurred with tears.

Gunner let out a whinny.

Marois placed something hard and round in Griffith's hand. "He's missed you, *mon ami.*"

Griffith looked down, saw the apple, and brought his gaze up to see Gunner standing there. Not just a horse, a friend and confidante, hearing things he wouldn't even tell Marois. He turned to Taylor and Marois. "Give me a minute with him." They let him go and he walked toward his horse. "Hey, Gunner."

Gunner snorted and flapped his lips.

Griffith smiled, brought his hand up to the right side of the horse's face, and stroked his neck, whispering, "I need you to take me for one last ride, my friend."

Behind them, Marois and Taylor wiped their eyes.

The moment passed and he surrendered the apple. Griffith checked out his riding gear while Gunner obliterated the gift. Satisfied, he mustered everything he could, put his foot in the stirrup, grabbed the saddle horn, and pulled himself up onto the saddle on his belly. He hung there, gathering himself, wondering if he would be able to get the rest of the way into a sitting position.

Taylor made a move to help him, but Marois stopped him.

"No," he whispered. "Let him do it."

They watched Griffith lift himself and straighten, left foot in the stirrup, right dangling in the air. He took a deep breath, grabbed the horn with both hands and swung his right leg over, hanging on the saddle at an awkward angle. Finally, Griffith pulled himself up and got himself straight on the horse.

"Good afternoon, *messieurs*," Gagnon said, leading his own horse around the stable. He was also dressed to ride. "It's a nice afternoon for a ride in the company of gentlemen."

"It is at that, Sub-Inspector," Griffith agreed.

They mounted up and gathered in a circular orders group.

"*Caporal* Griffith, Constables Marois and Taylor, it's my great honor to ride with you today," Gagnon said, but he was looking at Griffith. "As we exit the fort, we shall ride like Mounties. With NWMP pride, heads high, and *esprit du corps*."

They all nodded.

"Once out the gate, we ride as friends." Gagnon smiled. "You got that, Horace?"

"Yes," Taylor said. "But I don't know if I can call you by your first name."

They all laughed.

"Today you can call me Severe."

"Yes, sir. I mean, Severe."

More chuckles.

"Form up!" Sub-Inspector Gagnon called. They got into a formation of two by two, Griffith and Gagnon leading. "Forward, march!" They rode slowly through the yard. The officers working in the fort stopped what they were doing, came up to attention, and saluted them as they went. Sub-Inspector Gagnon returned those salutes while the remainder of the group kept their head and eyes front.

They went out the gate.

VI

From his window, Superintendent Jarvis watched them go. He had signed off on Griffith's voluntary admission to the lunatic asylum, although he was indifferent to the suggestion of Indian demons by the condemned Swift Runner. Jarvis had built Fort Saskatchewan, along with Steele and Gagnon and the handful of settlers who had come west. Jarvis had hired locals to build the fort at a significant cost for labor. The government was especially unhappy when that labor cost could have been absorbed by able-bodied Mounties on their way to the fort.

His service record saved him, but they would have no problem replacing him if he started talking about Indian spirits possessing his men. The official diagnosis was blood poisoning and that was what it would remain. Not a drop of ink would be wasted on Indian legends. Nonetheless, he believed that the source of their problems emanated from Swift Runner, and he silently wished the government would move a little faster on the execution date.

"Keep me abreast of their status, Severe," Jarvis had said.

"Yes, sir," Gagnon said.

"One other thing, Severe."

"Yes?"

"I don't want any of our officers repeating the lunacy coming from that cannibal Indian's mouth. Understand?"

"Yes, sir."

"That includes the word 'windigo.' The bureaucrats are still looking for a reason to fire me. Commissioner McLeod is scrutinizing our expenses. If I hear the word 'windigo' from a single NWMP officer's mouth, that man will be punished under the Queen's Regulations and Orders."

"Yes, sir," Gagnon said, but he really didn't know what regulation could be used.

VII

They had stopped along the way to talk about the things the CO had forbidden them to speak of. In this moment, they weren't officers of the Northwest Mounted Police, but friends taking a ride together. They talked about everything, including the death camp, and Griffith was forthcoming with them all.

"It's with me every night," Griffith told them.

"Oh, *mon ami*." Marois brought his hand to his mouth, heart breaking.

"So, we drop you off, and that's it?" Taylor asked.

"I guess you could visit me." Griffith smirked.

"We will do that daily," Marois said.

"As duty allows," Gagnon corrected.

They discussed a few more things. Griffith asked if he and Marois could have a moment, and they talked until Marois objected about something and Griffith calmed him. They talked a little more and rejoined the group.

They rode a beaten path along the north side of the North Saskatchewan River. The ride was quiet except for the clopping of hooves. They came to an open iron gate with a small sign affixed.

Griffith read aloud, "Fort Saskatchewan Asylum for Lunatics."

The building was constructed mostly of red brick and had a shingled roof. There was no porch, just a three-stair riser that led to a blistered, rust-red door. The door swung open, and a gaunt-looking man with ginger hair, wearing a suit and white robe, stepped onto the landing.

"Good afternoon, officers, my name is Doctor Stephen Keach. I run the asylum."

There was a collective of murmured greetings.

"Which one of you is Constable Ronald Griffith?" Keach gazed around, eyes finding Griffith.

"That would be me, Doctor."

"I understand that you are also unwell," Keach said. "Like Constable Crane?"

"Yes, Doctor." Griffith saw a shadow in the woods and wondered if it was the windigo.

Two men in white uniforms stepped out from behind Keach and came down the stairs. One of them was big and white-haired, the other small and thuggish.

"Constable Griffith, please dismount your horse so that we may admit you," Small said.

Keach remained on the landing.

Griffith dismounted, and the other officers started to do the same when Dr. Keach said, "Admitting is a solitary process, gentleman. Visiting hours are mornings between ten and twelve and afternoons between five and seven. Only one visitor at a time."

"His uniform is to be hung and stored," Gagnon said.

"Of course," Dr. Keach said.

"Why can we not come in?" Marois asked.

Dr. Keach turned to Marois. "You can come in during visiting hours. We need to prep the patient, process him, and hang and store his uniform." He gave a patronizing smile to Gagnon, who didn't reciprocate.

"Ron," Marois called.

Griffith looked up.

"You will have a visitor, morning and afternoon," Marois said. Then he turned to Dr. Keach. "He is a corporal in the Northwest Mounted Police and our friend. Please take care of him."

"Of course, officer. It will take all day to process him." Doctor Keach smiled. "Come back tomorrow for a visit." He nodded at the two attendants, and they aided Griffith in climbing the stairs.

When they reached the top, Griffith turned to Marois and said, "Take care of my horse."

"Like he was my own, *mon ami*," Marois said. "I will be here tomorrow."

"Thank you, Horace. It was an honor to ride with you."

Taylor smiled, but it was a sad smile.

"Severe, thank you," Griffith said.

"We'll bring Gunner back to bring you home to the fort when this is over," Gagnon said.

"When this is over," they all echoed.

"Goodbye," Griffith said, and they took him inside.

The steel door closed, leaving a fragmentary feeling in all their hearts. They sat there awhile, waiting for nothing, and finally Marois climbed from his horse and set up a follow for Gunner. His face was flushed, holding it in, tying the knots, and when he was beside his own horse, he stopped, jammed his fist in his mouth, and let out a single strangled cry.

No one said a word.

Taylor looked away, fighting his own tears.

Gagnon's focused on the steel door. "*Au revoir, Caporal* Griffith," he said and when he turned, Marois saw the contortion of his face. That only deepened the mood. Gagnon wiped his tears and yelled, "Forward! March!"

They rode back to the fort without a single word.

Marois took care of both horses.

"Tomorrow," he muttered.

VIII

Tomorrow came and Marois visited Griffith, and they talked, but with each successive visit, there was less of Griffith. His normal calm demeanor was replaced by shaking, convulsing, and screaming of profanities, until he became a violent lunatic just like Crane.

They moved him to the second quiet room, finished only that week. Marois watched through an angled periscope window that was eight feet up the wall in the cell and the adjacent room. There, they had rigged a seven-foot wood scaffold to stand on when viewing the patient's activity.

Marois watched Griffith, who was up on his feet, arms restrained in the straitjacket. He moved from corner to corner in the lumpy white box they kept him in. Griffith reminded Marois of a tiger he had seen at a traveling show in his home of Calais as a child. The giant cat was penned in a ten-foot-square cage, following a pattern back and forth, keeping the muscles warm, eyes trained, and waiting for the opportunity to strike.

Standing beside Marois was a man built like an oak tree, named Garry Van Sloane. Van Sloane and the smaller attendant, a man named Clive Shore, were the ones who had brought Griffith in that first day. Van

Sloane was clean-shaven and had short, naturally white, not gray, hair. He was an albino. His sidekick, Shore, was bald and clean-shaven. Standing a hair over five foot six, he was muscular from hand to toe.

Both men looked like goons.

Marois got a bad feeling from them.

"This is good behavior. They get worse," Van Sloane said.

"Worse?" Marois watched Griffith stop and turn his eyes up toward the little window. They were bloodshot and cloudy, and when they met Marois's eyes, they reminded him of that hungry beast he had met back home in France. He held Griffith's stare, searching for his friend somewhere in that vessel of madness below, but found none.

Griffith broke the stare and went back to pacing.

"At night they go off at almost the exact same time. Arguing with themselves," Van Sloane said.

"Can you understand any of it?"

"No. Not a word."

Both men had stopped responding even after mandatory ice baths and, in Crane's case, they went as far as shock therapy. Neither man had responded to treatment, though treatment continued.

Marois visited both men.

His presence calmed them some; the raving for suicide, for death, for blood, subsided during his visits. Marois didn't see the windigo in the lunatic asylum, but he knew it was present. He felt it watching from the shadowy corners of this awful place, and he smelled it.

After the visit, Marois found himself overcome with grief. Before returning to the fort, he visited Gertrude, and she took him to her bed. The sex was passionate and rough, but for all her prowess, Gertrude couldn't give Marois what he really needed.

Next, he visited the ugly one.

But she wasn't ugly at all. Flora was a thirty-one-year-old Scottish widow, not thin, but not lumpy. She carried her weight well, had a mother's heavy bosom and childbearing hips, and wore no makeup or was bothered about her hair. She wasn't mean, but maybe a little dominant. She was portrayed by Marois as the "ugly one" only because of all his maidens, she was the least fair and the one who had gotten to him.

He was standing at her door, holding it all back, trying to smile, but his face was distorting, eyes welling up with tears. "I thought I'd drop in for a visit."

"Come in, love." Flora let him in, held him through the tears, and took him to her bed.

IX

November 27, 1879
Fort Saskatchewan Lunatic Asylum

Marois had just returned from a three-week patrol and, upon visiting, he found Griffith and Crane both adorned in straightjackets, but removed from their quiet rooms. They were chained to the wall at separate ends of a common room. Less dangerous patients wandered the corridor, one man who had soiled himself moving freely and smearing the joy on the wall as he did. There were only nine inmates, but the house was too small for its purpose. There was talk of a modern hospital that could house up to a hundred lunatics.

"They have an execution date. December 20." Marois was sitting beside Griffith, filling him in on the aftermath of the trial, "Father Leduc is coming from St. Albert, before the execution day. He was quoted in the paper saying if he can't save Swift Runner's life, he'll try and save his eternal soul."

Griffith sat mute, eyes fixed in some purgatory between reality and nightmare.

Marois leaned in and whispered, "Once this business is done, you and Crane will get better." He looked over at Crane and then back at Griffith. "I'm coming back for both of you to save you from of this ghastly place.'"

Marois returned to the fort and Sub-Inspector Gagnon asked the same question he had of all the officers in the fort. "I've been asked to request a volunteer to pull the lever in Swift Runner's hanging?"

"Hangman?" Marois thought the idea was appalling.

"We have the gallows, but no hangman. This is the first hanging in these territories." Gagnon frowned and added, "You're under no obligation, nor will you be judged by your answer." Then he leaned in and said in French, "It's okay to say no, Freddy."

Constable Fredericke Marois had killed five men in his lifetime—two in the military and three during his police career—and he believed that all were justified. He knew Swift Runner and wanted no part in his demise. Even if he hadn't objected, he had been instructed not to involve himself.

Along with every Mountie, Marois respectfully declined the duty of executioner.

None of them wanted to do it.

It wasn't just because they knew Swift Runner; many felt the duty of an officer was to deliver the criminals to the courts, and the matters of state vengeance should be left with jailers and bureaucrats.

"Let them find their own hangman," Gagnon grumbled.

"We're out of it, then?" Marois asked.

"All of you are. I have one duty." Gagnon was frowning.

"And what is that?" Marois asked.

"I get to walk him to the rope." Superintendent Jarvis had assigned Gagnon the duty of walking Swift Runner from his cell to the gallows. He would be sharing this duty with an outsider named Sheriff Edouard Richard, who would be coming from the city of Battleford, the capital of the Northwest Territories.

The ride was seven days in good weather.

The sheriff was coming in December, and winter had already been cruel to the prairies, with heavy snowfall and temperatures dipping into the minus thirties.

"Any change with Crane and Griffith?" Gagnon asked. "I heard you went to visit them today."

"I did. No change. They aren't speaking," Marois murmured. "They're shut down, like…"

"*Comme quoi?*" Gagnon asked.

"Like they're waiting."

"For us or the windigo?" Gagnon hadn't spoken of the windigo since their return. Even in the months following the trial, the word "*wihitikow*" or its English translation never crossed his lips.

"Waiting for Swift Runner to die and take the curse with him to hell," Marois said.

"He's not going to hell. The Catholics are coming to save him." Gagnon smiled sardonically.

"All the better," Marois said.

"What if it doesn't work, Fred?" Severe Gagnon asked in French. "What if they're still possessed after Swift Runner dies? I told Ron he would get better."

"I'm working on that part, Severe," Marois said.

"Let me know when you have it thought out."

Marois nodded.

He had a simple contingency plan. If they couldn't be cured, Griffith wanted to be killed and had told Marois so on that last ride. Crane had been too far gone for such discussion, but Marois decided that if he was to kill Griffith, he would also end Crane's life. He prayed it wouldn't come to that, but he was ready to do it.

***

Chapter 18 – Death Clock

I

Fall, 1879
Fort Saskatchewan, NWT

The last months of Swift Runner's life were spent in solitary suffering. He was the object of revulsion and fury over his crimes. Many of the guards had harsh words for the cannibal, saying if they had their way, they would fix his wagon. He was taunted and threatened. There was plenty of talk in town from folks who also lamented what they would do with the monster if they could get their hands on him.

Reprisal was in thc air, and it was infectious, yet not one of the wagon fixers had ever seen the death camp. The men who had seen it, who had carried the bones south, profoundly wished they hadn't. Additionally, they had lost two comrades to the asylum. While they were equally repulsed by the crime, they also understood that a force of darkness had taken possession of Swift Runner and two of their comrades.

Daily, from outside his cell, came whispered threats and condemnation. Swift Runner was breaking down, and he often vomited into the same pail in which he relieved himself. The cell stank like gangrene. He was beaten down verbally in the daylight and nightly, the windigo came and did the same.

Sub-Inspector Gagnon spoke to Superintendent Jarvis about the officers making threats against the condemned. Incensed, Jarvis immediately drafted up a new standing order regarding conduct while Gagnon put together a death watch. Corporal Bagley, who already had a friendly rapport with Swift Runner, was made death watch commander and assigned three officers.

Bagley was pleased to do it.

Marois and Taylor were kept out of it.

Sub-Inspector Gagnon's approach of using Bagley had worked before. Gagnon had Bagley form the three officers up and read the standing order on conduct penned by Superintendent Jarvis.

"Any questions?" Gagnon asked.

There were none.

"Organize a watch, Corporal." Gagnon turned the detail over to Bagley, who dismissed them and posted the standing order on the cell door. "Make sure every man reads it again. No tolerance."

Bagley copied the order down in his field notepad. "Yes, Sub-Inspector."

From there, the watch ran relatively smoothly.

Without the outrage, a dark gallows humor floated in, and Bagley joked, "Are you eyeing me up for a snack, Swifty?"

"You would be good eating, Corporal," Swift Runner joked back.

"More tender than a prairie chicken," Bagley chirped.

"I would have to think about that," Swift Runner said.

The other guards picked up on it and joked with Swift Runner.

While tasteless, it was better than the former. Swift Runner had accepted his fate. It all went smoothly, except for those offended by Bagley and the other guards making light of Swift Runner's horrible crimes.

II

December 19, 1879
1800 Hours – Temp -41 F
Fort Saskatchewan, NWT

It was cold enough to freeze exposed skin in five to ten minutes. Officers in the yard were dressed for the elements, moving with the single purpose of getting out of said elements. In contrast, the cold northern lights painted a section of the moonless sky to the north. Twisting curtains of green, yellow, blue, and magenta swayed in the night sky, but it would be a short performance. Snow-charged clouds from the west were coming to smother the tempest of light.

Just off watch, Bagley was following one of several paths, tramping through the layers of snow that blanketed the yard over December. On his way to the barrack block, Marois was coming from the mess hall on another trail that intersected with Bagley's

Marois was now at his back.

Bagley saw three silhouettes waiting ahead of him. He sensed something was off when he reached them and said, “It’s rather cold for loitering, don’t you think?” They just sat there, dumbly processing what he had said, so he added, “Is there something I can do for you?”

“Why are you being so nice to that murderous Indian?” the biggest of the three asked.

“Barring his culinary leanings, he ain’t so bad.” Bagley pulled down his scarf to reveal a smile. There was a tense pause, but he didn’t budge or stop smiling.

“That isn’t funny,” the biggest officer said.

“Corporal,” Bagley said.

“Huh?”

“That isn’t funny, Corporal,” Bagley said, and the smile melted into a scowl. “If you’re going to question my wit, you best use my rank.” He waited. “What’s my rank, Gibface?”

The man looked back at his two friends.

“They can’t help you. Say it! Say it or I’ll toss all three of you twat waffles into the brig for insubordination!”

“Corporal,” Gibface relented.

“Everything okay, Corporal Bagley?” Marois had caught up and was walking up from behind.

Bagley turned and smiled. “Why, hello, Fred. Give me a sec, I’m just finishing something up.”

“Carry on, Corporal.” Marois stepped back and watched.

“I intend to.” Bagley gave Marois a wink, spun back and roared. “All of you. Get in file and up to attention! Attention! Attention!” It sounded more like, “Atten—shuh! Atten—shuh!”

They lined up and snapped to attention.

Gibface was on the right.

Bagley reached into his pocket, pulled out his field notepad, and said, “I copied down the Standing Order for Death Watch, so open your fucking ears.” He flipped the pad open and read, “As the order of execution is set for the twentieth of December 1879, let it be known the condemned, Ka Ki Si Kutchin, also known as Swift Runner, is to be treated with respect and dignity until his day of judgment. I will not, under any circumstances, accept abuse of the condemned. Signed: W.D. Jarvis, Superintendent, NWMP."

Bagley folded the pad, stuck it in his pocket, and said, "If I hear another word from any of you, I will have you charged with disobeying a direct order. I will also charge you with insubordination."

They were still at attention.

"You understand, Black?"

"Yes, Corporal."

"You understand, Poss?"

"Yes, Corporal."

"What about you, Clarke?"

"Yes, Corporal," Gibface said.

"You heard what I said, but I'll say it once more. I better not hear a single bellyache in the barracks. Does everyone understand?"

Collectively, "Yes, Corporal."

He waved them off. "Get out of my sight. Dismissed!" Sounding like, "Dis—missed!"

They did a quick right turn and marched off into the darkness, deflated bullies cheated of their outrage. Gibface and the wagon fixers were lucky. Insubordination wasn't tolerated in the NWMP, even if it was toward a malarkey-slinging corporal like Fred "Bags" Bagley.

Bagley watched them go.

Marois came up beside him. "Never seen you pull rank before."

"Never had to," Bagley said. "Until now."

"If you leave me out of the story, I won't dispute the number of potential mutineers you put down," Marois said.

"Hmmm, I'll think about it." Bagley pointed. "Oh look, here comes the Church."

Marois turned his eyes in the direction Bagley indicated. Father Leduc and a younger priest were walking from the nearby parish for another session of Swift Runner's conversion to Catholicism. Father Leduc was much older than the young priest, whose name Marois had forgotten.

Ramus or Remas?

The pair had been coming for a week now.

At first, Swift Runner had declined the invitation of conversion, but he eventually softened after Father Leduc read the History of the

Passion of the Savior to him in Cree. Each day, they came and prayed with him, withdrawing to the parish nightly. Two days previous, he had joined hands with the priests, confessed his sins of murder and cannibalism, and accepted the sacrament. They were now preparing Swift Runner for his final hours, before the judgment.

The priests met them on the same path Bagley had been following.

The sky was black now, the first flurries blowing in.

"Good day, Fathers," Bagley said.

"Good day, Fathers," Marois parroted.

"Good day, Corporal. Constable," the young priest said.

Father Leduc dropped his scarf, revealing cheeks scarred from his work during the smallpox outbreaks in the region ten years earlier.

"One more time before the big day?" Bagley asked.

Marois let out a chirp, then faked a cough as cover.

"We are all children of God," the priest said.

Father Leduc said, "We must cheat the Devil of his prize."

"His prize?" Bagley asked.

"Ka Ki Si Kutchin's *ahcâhk*," Leduc said in Cree.

Bagley said something in Cree and in English added, "Let me escort you to the jail."

III

Marois hung back; he had been avoiding any contact with Swift Runner. He watched them go and pulled down the peephole of the scarf. The brisk air pinched his cheeks. He would have lit it in the barracks, but he got the sense Bags wanted him to wait. He plugged a cigar in his mouth and took five matches against the wind to light it.

He was watching Bagley speaking with them and the guard, and they disappeared through the door. A few minutes later, Bagley emerged, wrapped up his face, and returned.

"One more time before the big day?" Marois laughed.

"What can I say? Sometimes it just comes out, Fred… Say, can I have one of those?"

Marois handed him a cigar. "Not a religious man, Bags?"

"Actually, they've made my job easier. He's lonely and they help with that. The old man wants him calm. They give him comfort." Bagley put the cigar in his mouth, lit it, and took a few puffs.

"What did the father say in Cree, when you asked about the prize?"

"He said the prize was Swift Runner's soul."

"What did you say?"

"I thanked him." Bagley sneered.

"You don't believe?"

"I believe one thing, Fred."

"*Oui*? What is that?"

"No matter what those priests do, how much they pray, take his confession, say the Hail Mary and Amen… They'll never save his soul."

"You don't think so?"

Bagley took another puff and contemplated, "Whatever devil it is that possesses Swift Runner, it's impervious to priests' prayer or dogma."

"You've seen it?"

"No, I haven't seen it, but it comes at night, when those two holy men are tucked safely in their church beds. It torments him. I've heard him screaming at it in Cree, and unlike most of you, I understand most of what he's saying." Bagley said.

"What does he say?" Marois asked.

"He wants to die, he's ready, and the tormentor will have none of that. I came upon him one night, and I heard half of an argument in Cree."

"Tell me," Marois urged.

Bagley said, "In Cree, he said, 'I killed all my family for you. What more can I give?' After a long pause, he said, 'I am tired and must rest,' and 'I can kill for you no more.' Then, 'I will come to my end in two moons.' Then there was a heated argument in a language not even close to Cree, but Swifty spoke it, argued, and even begged. Yesterday, after his conversion, he was all smiles with Father Leduc and Remus, and—"

"Remus," Marois interrupted. "That's it. Father Remus."

Bagley stopped. "Huh?"

"I couldn't remember his name. Sorry, go on."

"Well, if he's a Catholic and saved, nobody bothered to tell the demon that torments him every night. If I were Swift Runner, I'd be running up that stairwell to get it over with. That's the only thing that will save him from the Indian demon."

"The Church doesn't support suicide."

"This ain't Church business, Fred, it's Indian business."

"But the Church is involved."

"They won't be after tomorrow." Bagley took another puff, and they walked quietly, smoking, until they came to another junction. "Thanks for the smoke, Fred."

"You're welcome."

Bagley stubbed out his cigar, tucked it away, and turned to Marois. "Five."

"Five?" Marois didn't understand.

"Five mutineers, and I'll keep your name out of it.

"Deal."

IV

The Egg Lake Cree
1900 Hours – Temp -51 F

The snow was riding a steel breeze out of the north, and the temperatures had dipped even further. The elder, Chogan, brought with him a contingency of Cree men who performed ceremonies and dances of death. In addition to the ceremonies, a death drum thumped around the clock. Chogan met with Superintendent Jarvis and interpreter, Brazeau, who had returned for the execution. Brazeau said he had come in pursuit of another job with the Hudson's Bay Company, but he was here for the same reason as the rest of them.

To see it to its end.

Chogan proposed that Swift Runner should be lashed to a high tree and die by repeated knife cuts. The reasoning for the height was to make it easier to jump from this world into the happy hunting grounds, while the agony of cuts would beg forgiveness of the Great Spirit. He didn't like the idea of a rope around his neck, as it would stop him from crossing over.

"He'll be high, but he'll die on the rope," Jarvis told Brazeau, who repeated it to Chogan in Cree.

"*Kakepâtis*," Chogan grunted with a snort of disapproval and went back to the death ceremonies.

"He called you a fool," Brazeau said. "Or maybe us?"

"I've been called worse," Jarvis said.

There was a knock at the door.

"He's back." Brazeau chuckled and opened the door.

An older gentleman stepped inside, and Brazeau closed it behind him. "I'll be ready for my duties in the morning, sir," the old guy said in a heavy British accent.

"Good, we'll be bringing him at ten a.m.," Jarvis said.

"I'll be there, sir." He gave a short salute and departed.

"Who was that?" Brazeau asked.

"That is our executioner," Jarvis said.

"Geez, I hope he doesn't die before the execution," Brazeau said.

Superintendent Jarvis, not wanting further controversy, had done his best to accommodate the Egg Lake Cree. While in agreement on the sentence, cutting a man into pieces wasn't going to happen. Outside, the death drum continued its cadence, and the Cree prayers and chants sang through the night, but fuel for the fires was running low.

"I'll be glad when this business is done." Jarvis peered out the window; the executioner had gone. The gallows loomed, partially obscured in the shadows as snow sliced the darkness in hard, white streaks. Jarvis thought he saw the elder Chogan walking back toward the stables, but he couldn't be sure. He spun back around to face Brazeau. "Colder than a witches tit out there, George."

"That's one way of putting it," Brazeau laughed.

V

December 19, 1879
2032 Hours – Temp. -53° F.

Sheriff Edouard Richard arrived on a horse-drawn sled with another man. Their faces were covered in scarfs, their gloves and boots wrapped in rags, and they were sugared like abominable snowmen. A duty constable brought them to the stable, where they met Sub-Inspector

Gagnon. After brief pleasantries, Marois and Taylor unhooked their horses from the sled while Gagnon escorted the sheriff and the other man to meet Superintendent Jarvis.

After the horses were put away and the wagon was unloaded, Taylor and Marois found themselves standing alone in the stable. Taylor had looked over both horses and spotted some patches of frostbite on their ears, and he was applying a balm to those spots.

"Nothing but the waiting now," Taylor said.

"Yeah," Marois agreed. "The waiting."

More silence.

"You ready for tomorrow?" Taylor asked.

"No, but it's coming anyway," Marois said.

"I guess so."

More silence.

"Fred?"

"What?"

"Do you think it will work?"

Marois had his arms crossed. "I hope it does."

They left the stable.

VI

December 20, 1879
0100 Hours – Temp. -54° F.

When Bagley came back on shift, Father Leduc and Remus were departing for the parish to clean up, change, and prepare for Swift Runner's first and only Holy Communion.

That last night, Swift Runner had been spared a visitation from the windigo, giving him relative peace. He stirred in his cell, mumbling in Cree, uttering the names of his wife and children, and crying. It wasn't peaceful, but it was all the condemned was afforded.

"I am afraid to die, Corporal Bagley," Swift Runner said.

"It will be quick, Swifty," Bagley said, ditching his dark humor for sympathetic listener. "You've confessed your sins, asked forgiveness, and given your soul to God. Tomorrow, you meet your maker."

"People hate me for what I have done, but you have been nice to me. Why?" Swift asked.

"Your quarrel isn't with me, Swifty. I don't agree with what you did, but judgment comes from a higher court than here on earth. I'm kind of sad it's come to this, but I think you're ready."

"I am ready, Corporal Bagley." Swift got up, his cot creaking. Then he was rummaging around in the darkness.

"What you doing in there, Swift?" Bagley was leaning over, listening.

"You are my only friend. The *wihitikow* has taken everyone else. When I meet the Creator, Father Leduc says I can take no possessions with me." Swift came the cell door and said, "I want you to have these." Then he passed the items through the bars.

Bagley took the objects and stepped back to examine them. There were three items—Swift Runner's smoking pipe, a small stone war club, and his *tapiska'kun*. The *tapiska'kun* was made of leather and fur and had a center square plate of beads. Swift normally wore this around his neck, and it wasn't lost on Bagley that the Cree neckpiece had likely been crafted by his murdered wife, Charlotte.

"Ka Ki Si Kutchin, I accept your *mekinawewin*," Bagley said. "Thank you."

Swift Runner went back to his cot and sat down. It creaked under his weight. He was quiet while Bagley looked over his gift, thinking about the stories he would tell and feeling slightly guilty about it while accepting that it was his nature.

In Cree, Bagley said, "I thank you again, Ka Ki Si Kutchin."

"Will I be forgiven, Corporal Bagley?"

"Yes," Bagley lied.

VII

December 20, 1879
0627 Hours – Temp. -50° F.

They gathered in the mess for breakfast, and the mood was sober and quiet. It was anticipated that many people would be braving the weather to spectate the first hanging in Fort Saskatchewan. Beyond the audience of Cree and Mounties, they expected a large crowd to include some women and children.

Jarvis expected newspaper reporters.

Taylor was passing by the gallows when something caught his eye. He stepped under the walk and peered up through an empty hole. "Shit… Someone stole the bloody trap door from the gallows!"

Then Sergeant Steele was there, looking up through the square hands-on hips, barking orders. "We've only got three and a half hours, and this is already turning into a dog and pony show. Go get the carpenter! Tell him to bring everything he needs to construct a new trap door."

The carpenter also happened to be the veteran hangman.

Taylor got on his horse and headed for town. He got there just as the old man was readying his own horse for the ride. "We have a problem."

"What would that be?"

Taylor told him.

"Did they take the hinges?"

"I don't know," Taylor replied.

The old fella scratched his head. "Fook!"

"We only have so much time. I'll help you gather whatever you need."

"I'll need to cut some lengths of plank and bring my tool bag and the rest of the rigging. You'll have to help me, Officer."

"Tell me what you need."

They gathered planks and Taylor helped cut twelve lengths of board, which they broke into two equal bunches and wound in twine. He scooped a can of nails and handed it to Taylor. As they loaded the two horses up, the old man scratched his head.

"We need to go," Taylor said.

The old man looked around wearily. "All right, then."

When they got back to the fort, the old guy looked up at the missing trap door.

"Well, that's going to be a fooking joy in this scat."

"I'll help you," Taylor said, and they got to work.

VIII

December 20, 1879

0830 Hours – Temp. -51° F.

Father Leduc began the final phase of Swift Runner's conversion, which was Holy Communion. The priest spoke, and Swift Runner commiserated on the afterlife and God's forgiveness of even the foulest of sinners.

There was confession.

There were prayers.

Swift Runner accepted the priest's comfort, and they conversed in Cree. Outside, they heard the sawing of wood and hammers banging away, followed by a curse and then another's laughter. In those last hours of Swift Runner's life, he prepared for death, while distracted by what was still nesting in his bones.

Will I be saved?

"Ka Ki Si Kutchin, let us pray," Father Leduc said.

He prayed and watched shadows on the wall flicker against the dull oil lamp's flame.

Fathers Leduc and Remus took each of his hands, while Remus continued the prayer.

"Open your mouth," Father Leduc instructed.

Swift Runner kept his eyes closed and opened his mouth.

Leduc placed the communion wafer upon his tongue. "The body of Christ," he said in Cree.

They finished Holy Communion, and then they prayed again.

A knock came at the door.

Father Remus opened it. "Yes?"

"Sorry to interrupt, Father," Bagley said. "We need to cut Swift Runner's hair."

The grooming of the hair was to ease interference on the rope.

They vacated the cell and took Swift Runner to a waiting chair, where the fort barber cut his hair above his ears. Bagley, along with the two priests, were stunned by the transformation and the pile of hair on the floor.

"He cleans up well," the barber remarked.

December 20, 1879
0920 Hours – Temp. -54° F.

When they returned to the cell, a plate of cold duck and a cup of steaming hot coffee were waiting. Next to that, woolen pants, shirt, overcoat, and the moccasins his wife had made him. Swift Runner stared at the plate of food.

Father Leduc nodded and smiled. "Go, enjoy this indulgence, and we will speak of God."

Swift Runner ate and drank.

The priests continued their prayers.

When Swift Runner finished eating, Corporal Bagley unshackled him and stood guard as he changed clothes, while Father Leduc recited the Rosary.

Outside, a crowd grew in anticipation of Fort Saskatchewan's first hanging.

Once Swift Runner was dressed, Bagley re-shackled him and excused himself.

December 20, 1879
0945 Hours – Temp. -54° F.

The guard unlocked the outer door to Swift Runner's cell, and Sub-Inspector Gagnon and Sheriff Richard were standing there.

"It's time, Swift Runner."

"Yes, Sub-Inspector Gagnon," Swift Runner said, voice wavering. The artery on his left temple throbbed in congruence with his pounding heart. "Thank you."

Behind him, Father Leduc brought up a shaking hand and placed it on Swift Runner's shoulder.

He turned, fear in his eyes, lower lip quivering.

Leduc said in Cree, "God is with you now, my son."

Sub-Inspector Gagnon read Swift Runner's Order of Execution, finishing with, "Please stand up." Outside were the waiting crowd, distant chatter, and the death drum keeping its slow cadence as it was passed from hand to hand.

They emerged from the jail and stepped outside.

Richard and Gagnon were on either side of him, the priests falling in behind.

There was another cry from the carpenter/hangman. "Fook it all, I've got the wrong ballast!"

"Wrong ballast? I thought you said you had everything?" Taylor asked the old guy. Then, to the approaching Bagley, he said, "He brought the wrong rigging."

Bagley went back. "The old man brought the wrong rigging."

They were standing around, everyone at their place, and now Superintendent Jarvis came over. "What the blazes is going on?"

"The hangman brought the wrong rigging," Gagnon said.

Then Sergeant Steele was there, giving orders. "Taylor!"

"Yes, Sergeant?"

"No, Sergeant Steele, send Corporal Bagley with the hangman," Jarvis ordered.

"Corporal Bagley, accompany this gentleman to town and make sure you've got the proper gear so we can get on with the queen's business," Steele barked.

"Yes, Sergeant," Bagley said, and he and the old man rode back to town.

Taylor felt somewhat slighted in Bagley being his replacement, but Steele came over and said, "Don't take it personally, Horace." Given the circumstances and what lay ahead, he didn't.

Word ran through the crowd, and there was mocking laughter.

A newsman from the *Manitoba Free Press* was shouting, "How old is your hangman?"

There were jeers and cheers.

The senior officers left Swift Runner with the guard while they waited for Bagley and the hangman to return. Jarvis was afraid that Commissioner McLeod, the head of the NWMP, would catch wind of this and come for his job. He was already scrutinizing Jarvis's expense reports and the previous commissioner, French, had sicced McLeod on him.

As Swift and his guard waited, a newsman stepped up and asked to take their photograph. The guard was hesitant, but he agreed after the newsman said, "This is the photo that everyone will remember."

They posed, the young officer's face serious, his hair short, dark, accompanied by a mustache. He wore his pillbox hat in the unforgiving cold, bare hands clasped in front of him. Beside him, Swift Runner held the iron ring attached to his leg chains by a three-foot chain. The overcoat he wore was buttoned to the neck. His weight loss and haircut further articulated his flat forehead, empty eyes, wide nose, and square jaw.

"Thank you," the newsman said.

Neither Swift Runner nor the officer would see the photo in their lifetime.

December 20, 1879
1001 Hours -Temp. -56° F.

Swift Runner was removed from his shackles, and his hands were bound behind his back. He was escorted to the gallows by Gagnon and Richard. Fathers Leduc and Remus followed, as did Superintendent Jarvis. When they reached the stairwell, Jarvis and the two priests took their place as the hangman, who had refused an executioner's mask, waited at the trap door.

Swift was afraid, shivering as the noose was slung over his neck. The snow cut into their faces, as Gagnon and Richard stepped back.

"Swift Runner, do you have any last words?" Jarvis called.

"I have killed no one's children, only my own." Then he asked forgiveness in Cree, though most didn't understand it. "I would like to thank the officers of the Northwest Mounted Police, who have treated me well." Swift Runner faltered, looking into the crowd as the *wihitikow* stared back.

It wore his face, then the bag went over his head.

The hangman tightened the noose.

The drum fell silent.

Even the wind had stopped to listen.

Superintendent Jarvis nodded to the hangman, who pulled the lever retracting the bolt, and the trap door fell silently. Swift Runner disappeared in a blur, until the rope ran out. The crack of his breaking neck was comparable to a tree branch snapping in a windstorm.

Then his body jerked upward and snapped once more.

There was a hush in the crowd.

Some looked away, but most looked on as he began to twist slowly around like an ornament.

Sheriff Richard looked down and said to the hangman, "Well done."

"The trick is in the knot," the hangman said solemnly.

Sheriff Richard left the platform to rejoin Superintendent Jarvis.

"I want the body down and in its burial cart immediately," Gagnon said.

"But…"

"But nothing, Superintendent Jarvis wants this to be done now."

"Seems a waste not to leave him for a while," the hangman said.

"My officers are ready now, so start prepping," Gagnon ordered.

The hangman produced a knife and cut the rope, which disappeared down the trap. They heard Swift Runner's body hit the frozen earth with a cold thump. There were more cries and another hush in the crowd.

"He's prepped," the hangman said.

"How many years did it take you?" Gagnon asked.

"Take me to what?" the hangman asked.

"To perfect being an asshole," Gagnon said and began back the way he came.

"It's my job," the hangman called after him.

"I know." Gagnon went down to meet his men.

IX

Marois and Taylor brought the wagon and loaded Swift Runner's body into a wooden coffin, pounding nails into the lid. As they prepared to lift it into the wagon, the crowd had already begun to disperse; even the Cree were withdrawing.

"Bury it where no one will find it. I want no mark of his memory," Jarvis told Gagnon.

"Yes, sir," Gagnon said.

They set out into the snow.

The burial party consisted of Gagnon, Marois, Taylor, and Brazeau. They were taking Swift Runner back to the wilderness, pulling the coffin behind them in the same Red River wagon they had used to transport him to the death camp. They rode for two hours against the merciless cold, until they came to the agreed upon spot.

***

Chapter 19 – Sacrificial Bonfire

I

December 20, 1879
Somewhere Northeast of Egg Lake, NWT

Upon arrival, they were met by Chogan and three Cree men waiting on horseback. The location was north of Egg Lake. The snow had relented while temperatures hadn't. They didn't dismount but faced each other, Mounties on one side, Cree on the other.

In Cree, Chogan asked, "Where are the other two?"

Brazeau translated throughout.

"They're too sick to travel," Marois said.

Chogan listened to the translation. His face tightened and in Cree he spat, "They should be here!"

"They couldn't be here," Gagnon said.

Chogan complained in Cree, "Because you didn't bring them. I can offer no surety."

Gagnon nodded. "I expect none."

Chogan nodded at Brazeau and Gagnon and said something else in Cree.

Brazeau translated, "We must make camp. Then we begin."

"Where?" Gagnon asked.

Chogan didn't wait for the translation. He pointed toward an opening in the woods and in English, he said, "There." Then he turned his horse and motioned for Gagnon to join him in the ride, and the procession paired two files, Indigenous on the left and Mounties on the right. Behind them, Taylor pulled the wagon that held the combined purpose of their mission. They entered the opening and followed it for twenty yards, passing into a large, oval-shaped grass harbor. The surrounding trees cut the winds and once the wagon reached the center of the harbor, Gagnon ordered, "Burial party… Halt!"

They halted.

Then Chogan and Gagnon both issued orders. They set up camp on the south side of the harbor. A teepee was erected next to a lean-to. Brazeau and Taylor constructed a field stable sewn from tanned hides lashed to trees, offering overhead shelter. Several fires were lit, one each at the teepee, the lean-to, and by the makeshift stable. Behind the fire, Taylor constructed a five-foot wall of snow. As it melted and iced over, it radiated heat back at the horses, who appeared comfortable.

In the center of the harbor, the burial wagon waited.

But they weren't ready yet; there was wood to gather.

Brazeau and Gagnon watched one of the Indians unwrap his face and use the covering to blot away the sweat. His face wasn't as old as Chogan's, but it was weathered and pocked by the journey that had brought him here. He looked to be in his mid-forties, and what differentiated him from the others was his dress. He was wrapped in a blanket decorated in wide, vertical gray-and-white stripes.

"Severe, it was probably best you couldn't bring those boys," Brazeau said.

"Why?"

"That man there isn't from Egg Lake. He's a nomad Indian, has no tribe."

"Who is he?"

"*Omâcîw*," Brazeau said. "He's a windigo hunter."

Gagnon stiffened. "Are you thinking?"

"He might have come to dispatch your boys?"

Gagnon's face darkened. "*Bon sang*!"

"Easy, Severe, they're safe in Fort Saskatchewan." Brazeau pointed at the wagon.

"I'm glad they are," Gagnon said.

They stacked the wood around the wagon, every man bringing a bundle, dropping it, and returning to find more. Gagnon and Chogan arranged the wood beneath the wagon and around it for an even burn. When they could stack no more, they built a pile close by. They soaked rags in kerosene and stuffed them in the cracks all around the fire.

Marois made nine torches and soaked the wicks.

Chogan spoke with the *Omâcîw*, who nodded, pulled out a large knife, and began to scale the woodpile. When he reached the top of the wagon, he used the knife to pry the lid from the coffin. He chanted and waved his hands, encouraging the windigo spirit to depart.

The others came in to watch.

He raised the long blade and, chanting, brought it up as if to strike.

Taylor gasped. "He's going to cut out his heart!"

Marois, who had heard decapitation was a cure for the madness, grabbed Taylor's arm. "Hush."

The *Omâcîw* didn't cut out Swift Runner's heart or remove his head, but he finished the prayer, sheathed the blade, and climbed back down and spoke to Chogan in Cree.

Chogan motioned for everyone to pay attention, and they formed a semi-circle around the elder.

He spoke to all of them in Cree.

Brazeau translated, "The fire will take some time to eat Swift Runner's flesh. The Spirit hides in the bones and only when they are ash will the *wihitikow* spirit depart."

The *Omâcîw* said something to Chogan, who repeated it.

Brazeau translated, "When the bones begin to crack, the *wihitikow* will show itself. Don't touch eyes with the *wihitikow*, it will poison you with its stare."

Chogan said, "*Kakwêcihkêmowin.*"

Brazeau translated, "He wants to know if we have any questions."

"How long will it take to burn the flesh away?" Gagnon asked.

Chogan responded.

The Cree men laughed.

Brazeau translated, "I don't know, I've never done this before."

The Mounties laughed.

Chogan gave Gagnon the faintest smile, which was returned.

Uninterested in jokes, the *Omâcîw* barked, "*Kwâhkotêw.*"

Chogan nodded to him and repeated, "*Kwâhkotêw.*"

Brazeau translated, "Time to light the fire."

Gagnon picked up a torch and lit the end. Chogan came and lit his off Gagnon's, and the others followed suit. Only the *Omâcîw* was without fire, and it he who directed them to circle the wagon. Chogan gave the order, and they brought their torches down. Each kerosene rag burned bright orange and yellow as tendrils of oily smoke began licking the tinder.

Before long, the fire crawled over the wood, and they had to back away from the heat. The scent of burning kerosene and wood were shouted down by the sizzling stink of human flesh and fat being cooked. Most of them covered their mouths and backed even farther away from the stink and heat of the bonfire, which was now in full blaze.

The *Omâcîw* never left the blaze, chanting, occasionally dozing, praying, and chanting again. The chants, although foreign, were clear in their purpose. He was banishing the windigo spirit, ordering it back from whence it had come. During the prayers, he rocked, while around him the rest of the men took shifts feeding the blaze.

When the sun began to rise, the wagon, Swift Runner's coffin, and most of his flesh had gone to ash. Mostly bone remained, protruding from the ashes and buried beneath burning wood.

They stacked more wood, and *the Omâcîw* continued.

"Is something supposed to happen?" Taylor asked.

"I don't know," Marois said.

By late morning, something did happen.

The bones began to crack, and there were whistling shrieks as the gases were released below the flames. It was an unnerving sound, Marois thought, not a language but distant cries and moans from lost souls in the depths of hell. He investigated the fire, thinking it did indeed look like the pits of hell.

Brazeau grumbled. "How long does it take to burn a body?"

Gagnon pointed at the *Omâcîw*. "We keep the fire going until he says we're done."

They stacked more wood, and the *Omâcîw* continued his prayers.

They took shifts, and Chogan brought the *Omâcîw* food.

The day passed, the sounds in the fire changing to a buzz, but still the bones weren't gone.

They added the last of the kerosene, stacked more wood.

The blaze continued.

Just after midnight on the third day, they heard a mad whistling, sounding like a weapons cache ready to explode.

The *Omâcîw* was up on his feet, shouting.

Chogan was shouting.

Brazeau yelled, "It's time! Surround the fire, it's time!"

They surrounded the fire just as the thing began to rise. Oily smoke dampened the flames, climbing from the ashes, twisting back and forth. It was man-like, but it had a devil's red eyes burning against the infinite night of its silhouette.

Chogan shouted a warning in Cree.

Brazeau translated, "Don't look at it!"

They all lowered their eyes.

Only the *Omâcîw* glared at the windigo.

It turned from man to man, probing for weakness, demanding in Cree and in English, "Let me in," the words echoing through their heads. Marois was between Taylor and Gagnon, eyes fixed to the ground, as it hung over him, looking for a doorway in, wheezing, "You cannot help them. They are mine and they will always be mine. Even after they are dead, they are mine."

Marois almost said something, then he felt Gagnon's hand take his and squeeze. He kept his eyes down, and the windigo moved to Taylor.

"They still think you are an imbecile." The windigo's voice changed to Griffith's. "I should have dragged you into the woods and beat you senseless. They are not your friends! They laugh at you."

Marois took Taylor's hand and squeezed.

It skipped Chogan, spoke to one of his men, and skipped the next, until it landed on Brazeau. Marois brought his eyes up; the windigo had its back to him. No longer was it just shadow, but a skeletal form below papery rot. On its back, faces of death formed, of women, of children, of those it had cursed, its prisoners and its victims.

Marois saw Brazeau bringing his eyes up, his mouth unhinging.

The thing sucked in a whispery breath. The tortured faces of Crane and Griffith formed on the thing's back, and Marois heard himself cry out, "George! Don't look at it!"

Brazeau cried out and dropped his eyes.

Furious, the windigo spun back and lunged at Marois, who lowered his eyes. He knew that if it found its way into one of them, then this would all have been for nothing. "Don't look at it!"

The *Omâcîw* raised a bony finger directly at the windigo and roared his demands in a language unknown. Whatever he was demanding came out as scathing as it was fearless.

The faces melted away, and the windigo turned toward the *Omâcîw*.

It screeched again, but this time in pain.

Marois stole another glance at the creature and understood.

"The fire is devouring it," Gagnon whispered.

Marois stood and the others followed suit.

They tossed on more wood.

The windigo spun back and forth in agony. It had vanished below the torso and was floating above the consuming flames. It twisted, writhing in agonized rage. The fire was eating it from within. Its crimson eyes were dulling, flames flicking from its eye sockets. It was gone to the breastbone, floating above the fire like a macabre Chinese lantern. They were staring at the dying monster as it thrashed in agony, the last of its hiding place becoming ash.

The *Omâcîw* was still making demands.

Then the fire exploded.

Everyone, including the *Omâcîw*, ran for cover. Hot coals rained down, dotting the earth with hundreds of glowing embers that burrowed into the snow, sizzling all the way. All the men were peppered, but Brazeau got the worst of it. His long coat caught fire and had to be put out. Two of the horses broke free and fled into the forest. When the firestorm was over, they went back to the fire where the last of the windigo's face burned away like rice paper.

Then nothing.

They waited, afraid to turn their backs.

A minute passed, then two.

Marois looked at Gagnon, who smiled cautiously.

Taylor said, "Is it over, Fred? Is it finally over?"

"I think so, Horace." They cried and hugged.

Gagnon nodded at Chogan, who almost smiled back.

Then the *Omâcîw* said something in Cree.

Brazeau translated, "We must bury the ashes."

They spent hours breaking through the frost line right beside the fire. Taylor and one of the Cree men went after the horses, who were spooked and skittish but, thankfully, unharmed.

They worked in shifts, and it was hard going. The earth below the frost line was clay and proved an exhaustive chore shared by all except the *Omâciw*, who was performing his own ceremony over the ashes. Nobody talked about Swift Runner or the fact that it was his ashes they were burying. Marois tried not to think about that part. They finished burying the ashes late in the afternoon. Then they gathered their supplies and left the harbor. Once outside, they spent an hour stacking deadfall and tree branches to veil the entrance.

"It will have to do," Gagnon said.

Chogan nodded. "Yes."

They pushed south to the meeting point and a parting of ways.

Gagnon spoke to Chogan through Brazeau and when finished, he called, "Fred, he wants to speak to you."

Marois rode over.

Brazeau translated.

Chogan said, "You came to me for help."

"Yes," Marois said.

"Maybe no good will come. If the plague is lifted, your friends will begin to awaken, but the awakening will be slow," Chogan said. "They should return to themselves."

"How long?" Marois asked.

"One or many moons."

Or maybe none, Marois thought sadly, feeling the elder's eyes on him.

Chogan reached out, touched his hand, and gave a sympathetic smile.

"Thank you for helping us," Marois said.

Chogan removed his hand and nodded. Behind him, the *Omâciw* grunted impatiently.

The elder rejoined his party, and they rode off.

"Let's go home," Gagnon said wearily.

Faces covered, they pushed on, under the glow of a quarter moon and the icy pinpricks of winter starlight. Without the burial wagon, they made better ground. Nobody talked through their frozen scarves as the temperatures again dipped into the minus forties. Even the horses seemed determined given the extreme temperatures, and when they saw the glow of Fort Saskatchewan, they pushed a little harder.

II

December 24, 1879
Fort Saskatchewan, NWT
0420 Hours – Temp. -44° F.

Gagnon, Marois, and Taylor returned to the fort after parting ways with Brazeau on the perimeter road. "I'm going home to see the missus," he told them.

"Come for a hot meal," Gagnon invited him.

"No, I'm going to go." Brazeau shook hands.

"Goodbye, George," Gagnon said.

"Bye, George," Taylor said.

"Thank you for coming to help us, George," Marois added.

"I hope it helps your boys," Brazeau said and rode off into the darkness.

Gagnon turned to Marois and Taylor and said, "Not that anyone would believe us, but I recommend this never be spoken of again."

"I still don't believe it," Taylor said, "and I was there."

"We need to get our stories straight," Marois agreed.

They took their horses to the stable and worked out a simple story. All three of them were too tired to head for the barracks and fell asleep alongside their equally exhausted mounts.

Gagnon awakened first, wiped the sleep from his face, and went to work. He groomed himself and before breakfast, he reported in.

"After spending a full day of riding, we found a remote burial spot. The entire day was spent chipping through five feet of frost line in four shifts. We buried Swift Runner's body and took shelter from the storm and the cold. We got caught in a storm that left us blind. We made a camp and there was no dry wood. I gave the order to burn the burial wagon to survive," Gagnon explained.

"I'm glad you're back." Jarvis grinned and squeezed Gagnon's arm. "We'll get another wagon. Give your men time to recuperate. Four days' leave of absence for all of you."

"Thank you, sir."

"Get yourself a bath, Severe, you stink of fire."

"Yes, sir."

They all smelled like fire.

III

All of them were physically and mentally exhausted. Marois skipped breakfast, cleaned up, and collapsed into his bunk. A while later, Taylor came in and did the same.

Both men slept until Christmas morning.

Gagnon slept as well.

Marois and Taylor met Gagnon on the path to the mess hall. When they entered the yard, Taylor looked up and said, "Where did it go?"

Marois realized what they hadn't noticed as they moved about the camp. "I didn't even notice."

The gallows had been erased from the yard.

"The old man had them tear it down," Gagnon said.

"What if they need to hang someone else?" Taylor asked.

"I guess they'll build a new one." Gagnon laughed.

"That could get expensive," Marois said.

When they entered the mess hall, it was a full house, standing room only. Superintendent Jarvis stood, raised his morning coffee, and toasted them. "These three men have followed the bloody trail of this tragedy from beginning to end," he said. "Stand with me now and raise a toast."

Mugs were raised, and there was a cheer.

Marois watched as they milled about, speaking, then lining up for breakfast.

He stood in line, absently holding a plate, waiting his turn.

Dr. Herchmer was talking with Jarvis and Gagnon, who were waiting for the men to get their food. Plates were filled with eggs, ham, and what Bagley coined "twat waffles."

A couple officers laughed.

Marois got his food and joined Taylor at the table. Once he cut into the ham, his appetite was voracious. He gobbled down every bite.

"I don't think I've ever eaten this good." Taylor was wiping his plate with his finger and licking the yellow yoke off it.

"Go get some more before you make me sick," Marois scolded.

Taylor stood and went for more.

Marois finished his last mouthful and washed it down with coffee as Jarvis, Gagnon, and Dr. Herchmer sat down at the table with him. Their faces were unreadable at first, until Gagnon smiled and said, "Merry Christmas, Marois." Then their eyes were brightened by newborn smiles.

"*Joyeux Noël, messieurs*," Marois greeted them back.

"Doctor Herchmer has something to tell you, Constable Marois," Superintendent Jarvis said.

Marois looked at Gagnon, who nodded toward the doctor.

"I received a message from Doctor Keach this morning saying that both officers have responded miraculously to the treatments and are recovering," Herchmer said.

"Miraculously? What does that mean?"

"They're awake, Fred," Gagnon said.

"They're talking," Herchmer said.

Gagnon squeezed his shoulder, leaned into his ear, and whispered, "You did it, Freddy. You saved them."

Taylor came back with a fresh plate.

Marois stood up. "You can have my seat, Horace."

Taylor sat down. "Why is everyone smiling?"

"They're waking up! They're waking up, Horace! Merry Christmas! They're waking up!" Marois cried happily. Everyone was looking but he didn't care; his friends were waking up. He was out of his seat and moving toward the door. "Merry Christmas! *Joyeux Noël*!"

Then he was gone.

IV

Gagnon excused himself and followed Marois out. He called after him in French, "Fredericke, *attends*!" Marois stopped and turned. "Wait. I'll ride with you."

"I'm coming too," Taylor called as he came down the steps.

"Let's go, then. Let's ride." Marois laughed and waved them on as they chased him into the stables.

Ten minutes later, the officers emerged, three men riding horses side by side and two saddled, unmounted, on a follow. They didn't know whether Crane and Griffith would be able to come back today, but Marois brought the horses just in case.

When they arrived, they dismounted and tied their horses off. Then Gagnon led them to the front of the brick house and rapped his knuckles on the rusty steel door.

There was the sound of movement until the rusty door swung open and there stood Dr. Keach squinting at the daylight. "It's still early for visiting hours." He removed his spectacles and cleaned them as his attendants, Van Sloane and Shore, appeared behind him.

"Doctor Keach, I am Sub-Inspector Severe Gagnon, and we have come to see Officers Griffith and Crane."

"I appreciate that, and I happily report that both patients have improved considerably. But this is a hospital for the brain-damaged, with specific rules to meet schedules for treatments."

"Doctor, it's Christmas Day," Gagnon said.

"Come back in two hours," Van Sloan said.

"And just one at a time," Shore added.

"Please, come back at ten." Dr. Keach began to retreat into the doorway, but stopped when Gagnon snapped.

"*Tabarnak*!" Gagnon leaned into the doctor's ear. "Doctor, you either invite us in, or we come by force."

"Oh my, no need for that." Keach turned to the attendants. "Bring Griffith and Crane to the common area." The two men stared back at him dumbly, so he barked, "Go!" They scurried away like rats. Keach turned back to Gagnon and said, "Please follow me."

They entered the building, following him down the hall, and passed an old man sitting on a wooden chair. He had pulled up his hospital gown and was masturbating and humming, "O Holy Night." Next, they passed a sickly-thin woman crying. In her hands were clumps of her brown hair and on her head bald patches.

"Nobody loves Chester," she sobbed. "Nobody loves Chester. Nobody!"

After that, a man bumped along the wall, dragging his cheek, one eye on them as he passed. Dr. Keach led them out of the long hall and into the common area, where chairs lined the walls.

Keach said, "Both of the patients Griffith and Crane were volatile and violent, but we treated them for that aggression."

"My constable informed me of this. What is the purpose of ice baths?" Gagnon asked.

"It knocks down the aggression," Keach replied while looking at Marois. "It may seem extreme, but it is a very effective treatment."

"Effective…" Gagnon hung on that word, looking past Keach at Marois, who shook his head.

"Soon they should be able to go home," Dr. Keach said.

A door slid open and Griffith stepped through it. He looked weak but healthier, his color no longer sickly gray. He glanced around, catching Doctor Keach's gaze, and said, "I thought you would never get here, my brothers."

"Officers, I will leave you to your visit." Doctor Keach stood up and left the room.

"*Joyeux Noël, mon ami,*" Marois said.

"Hi, Fred," Griffith said and reached out to take his hand.

They hugged.

"It's good to see you, Ron," Gagnon said, shaking his hand, tears in his eyes, but smiling.

Then Crane came in, and there were more greetings and smiles.

Dr. Keach and his ghoulish staff had hidden, giving them relative privacy, but for the face dragger making a pass in the hall.

"How do you feel?" Taylor asked Crane.

"Better, but when I woke, it was like I was coming off a six-month whisky binge," Crane said.

"What about you, Ron?"

"Get us the hell out of here," Griffith said.

Crane nodded, "Yes, we want to leave."

"Can you ride?" Gagnon asked.

They nodded.

"We brought your horses," Marois said.

Gagnon stood up, went to the open door, and stuck his head through. "I know you're down there. Get these men their clothes. They'll be returning to Fort Saskatchewan with us."

Dr. Keach didn't come out of his office to protest.

The albino attendant named Van Sloane brought Griffith's uniform and a wooden box with civilian clothes, and a long coat and a pair of flat leather shoes for Crane.

Marois peeked into the box and asked, "Where is his uniform?"

"He was admitted without clothing," Van Sloane said. "These are from a patient who died."

Crane grabbed the box and hissed, "Get out of here."

Van Sloane scurried out the door.

They dressed quickly, neither man near the standard of their usual dress and deportment. Crane's civilian pants were too large and the jacket too small. "The man must have been a pear," he said.

"You can burn those when we get you home," Griffith said.

Crane looked at Griffith's uniform. "When did you get promoted to corporal?"

"I'll tell you later."

"Everyone ready?" Marois asked.

"Let's move," Gagnon said.

Gagnon leading, they went down the hall single file. Their boots thumped on the wood floor, their footfalls synchronized in unconscious military cadence. They passed the room with the crying women, the masturbatory old man, and the face dragger. Marois was bringing up the rear with Crane in front of him. When they reached the door to Dr. Keach's office, Crane stopped suddenly.

"Huh?" Marois bumped into Crane.

Crane placed a hand on the door and said in a low snarl, "Doctor, this is Daniel Crane speaking. Can you hear me?" Muted cowardice hid behind the door. "You or your stooges see me anywhere, well… Let's just say you would be best to run the other way." He patted the door with his hand. "Goodbye, Doctor."

And they were moving again.

Gagnon opened the door, and winter's blinding light crashed into the hallway, bringing with it a blast of sub-arctic cold into their faces.

It looks like a door to heaven, Marois thought. Gagnon, Griffith, Taylor, and Crane became silhouettes and vanished into the white rectangle.

Then it was his turn, and Marois went into the light.

***

Chapter 20 - The Unshakable Dread

I

December 25, 1879
Fort Saskatchewan, NWT

It was Christmas Day, and the men of the NWMP gathered in good spirits at the return of Griffith and Crane, now cleaned up and in uniform.

They were seated at the head table, on either side of Superintendent Jarvis and Sub-Inspector Gagnon. Griffith was to the right of Gagnon. Crane to the left of Jarvis. They were conscious and cognizant, but on the mend. Neither man was fit for duty; both were undernourished and though the color of their flesh had returned, they still had a long journey of healing ahead of them.

"It's good to have you boys back!" Corporal Bagley was making a toast. There were cheers and raised glasses. Bagley made a joke and the group laughed, but it was lost on Griffith, who was watching Marois and Taylor chatting and smiling.

The world seemed foreign, his friends, strangers.

Superintendent Jarvis rose. "Sub-Inspector Gagnon."

"Yes, sir?" Gagnon said.

"Corporal Marois is out of uniform," Jarvis said, producing two cloth chevrons from a pocket.

Marois stood up from his seat, approached the head table, and snapped to attention.

They presented him with his chevrons, followed by applause and gleeful calls.

Griffith was happy for Fred, but he was still in shock. There were other presentations and commendations. After the meal, the senior officers got up to mingle, allowing Griffith to see Crane, who stared blankly into the crowd. He had a thumb-sized scar that crawled from his left eyebrow two inches up his forehead. Griffith didn't know if that was self-inflicted or from the shock treatment Dr. Keach's ghouls had administered. Treatment? It was torture on top of misery.

Poor Danny, they kicked the hell out of him in there, Griffith thought.

Sensing he was being watched, Crane turned to face Griffith.

"You look tired," Griffith said.

"I am," Crane said.

Marois approached with a smile. "Ron, Danny, it is so good to have you home."

"It's good to be home," Griffith said.

"Yeah," Crane said.

"Congratulations, Corporal Marois," Griffith said.

"Why, thank you, Corporal Griffith," Marois replied, already showing an spiritous glow. He looked into Griffith's eyes, held them for a second, then turned to Crane and produced a bundle of cigars. "George Brazeau gave me these. Can I interest you gentlemen in an after-dinner smoke somewhere less crowded?"

"The stables," Griffith said.

"Yeah, let's get out of here," Crane agreed.

Gagnon joined them as they rose from their seats. He was well on his way to being drunk, a drink canted in his left hand while his right tended his beard. "Are we going for a cigar?"

II

Griffith spent some time with Gunner, feeding him three rum balls liberated from the mess hall. "Soon we'll take a nice, long ride, old friend," he said.

Gunner snorted approvingly at this.

Or maybe it was the rum balls.

Then Gagnon and Taylor were there.

They gathered in a circle, puffing away and choking the horses out. A bottle of port wine appeared and was passed ceremoniously from man to man. Griffith took a finger of port in his field cup, the cigar burning absently.

"God bless George Washington Brazeau," Gagnon declared.

"These are fantastic cigars," Taylor agreed.

"The best," Marois said.

Griffith smiled and nodded, but he felt outside it all. He had always loved Christmas, especially as a Mountie. It was a time when everyone joined in celebration and the seriousness of their business was forgotten. It was also a rare moment when rank was relaxed, and they drank and laughed together as men.

For these men, who had gone to hell and back, this was their leave of absence—except for Griffith and Crane, who hadn't just reached the Devil's town line but had taken up residence in the bowels of its horror.

That wasn't going away any time soon.

They gathered around, and Griffith and Crane thanked them.

Griffith spoke first.

"My friends, I barely have the energy to celebrate with the men who saved my life." He stumbled, licked his lips, and chose his words carefully. "After falling ill, I descended into a state of suffering I can't… Can't possibly relate." He cleared his throat. "In my darkest hour, as the sickness was eating into my soul and pulling me into its black heart, I was given hope from my dear friend Fredericke Marois, who I heard say, 'Once this business is done, you and Crane will get better, and then, I'll come back for both of you and save you from this ghastly place." He raised his cup, eyes glassy with tears, and clinked it against Marois's cup. "In our darkest hour, you gave us hope, Fred. That is what we held onto." Then he paused and wiped away a tear. "Thanks to all of you, we're here on Christmas Day rather than in that fucking torture bin."

Crane nodded, his eyes also tearful, and gave his own speech of thanks.

Griffith drank his finger of port and placed the cup where nobody could refill it. He wouldn't be staying long; he needed sleep.

Taylor said, "I'm glad you guys are okay."

"Thank you for what you did, Horace," Griffith said.

"Yeah, thank you, Horace," Crane said.

Then came Gagnon who put a hand around the shoulders of Griffith and Marois. "*Caporal* Marois, *Caporal* Griffith, it is my duty as your sub-inspector and *superieur* to inform you"—he hiccupped—"that you both owe the men, *et moi*, a drink."

He handed Marois the bottle.

To Griffith and Crane, Gagnon said, "Mark my word, gentlemen. I'm not done with that fucking torture bin."

They both nodded, and their private party was interrupted when Bagley came through the door in the company of Sergeant Richard Steele. A few minutes after that, Hood followed, propping up an inebriated Superintendent Jarvis, who had an unopened bottle of port in each hand.

For Griffith and Crane, it was enough.

"I'm going to my bunk," Crane said.

"I'll go with you," Griffith said.

Griffith and Crane dressed for the walk to the barracks. Saying goodnight was a slow affair because Jarvis kept telling them how proud he was of them and how happy he was to have them back. Then Bagley was there, cracking jokes. Hood and Steele hung back, and Marois came over last.

"I'll come with you guys," Marois offered.

"No, Fred, this is your night. You've been promoted. Enjoy it," Griffith said.

"Yeah, we're just going to sleep anyway," Crane said.

"You're sure?" Marois wanted them to say yes.

"Yes," Griffith said while Crane nodded.

"*Joyeux Noël*." Marois hugged both men. "It's so good to have you home."

They went out into the night and heard the party rising, men yammering in liquored mirth. They were quiet, except for their feet crunching in the snow. Tonight was warmer, only minus thirty-eight. The sky had opened, curtains of the aurora were twisting to the north. They followed the path, clouds of vapor coming from their wordless mouths.

Griffith didn't know if Crane was going to speak or not. If he didn't want to talk about it, he would be okay with that. Griffith was beat down; he supposed this was what a liberated prisoner of war felt like.

Then Crane broke his thoughts.

"Did it die with Swift Runner, Ron?"

They stopped and Griffith said, "I hope it did."

"What if it didn't? If it comes back."

"I don't know." But Griffith did know.

"If it comes back, we're done," Crane said.

"Yeah. Let's hope it doesn't come back, Danny."

"Oh, I'm doing that, Ron. Hoping and praying."

They walked a while longer toward the barracks in silence. The aurora continued its emerald dance as each man stewed in their own thoughts and nightmares. Griffith had so much swimming around in his head that he hadn't yet processed—Swift Runner's death, the least of it. He couldn't think about Swift now.

Crane was tapping him, and he looked over.

"Here we are," Crane said.

"Here we are," Griffith said and gave a small grin.

"What if this is a dream, and when we wake up nothing has changed?" Crane was shaking, on the verge of tears.

This thought had also occurred to Griffith, that the days of waking up, the rescue from the asylum, and the Christmas party were all an illusion.

What if?

"I'm scared to go to sleep," Crane confessed. "I have wandered so far from my…" He cocked his head, searching for the word. "I've wandered so far from my humanity, how could I—we—possibly make it back?"

"Danny, we didn't do anything wrong. We never hurt anyone," Griffith said.

"I wanted to, Ron. I wanted to do what it said, and I would have happily ripped those two stooges and their doctor to pieces if I wasn't all tied up. I wanted to taste their flesh."

"I know, Danny, I wanted to as well." Griffith sighed. "But we didn't hurt anyone."

"What if all of this," Crane said, "is simply a place where we're hiding from the darkness? What if this is just a room we picked in our heads to hide from the daily horror?"

For Griffith, the daily horror meant the craving of violence and blood and meat, and being unable to act upon it. The windigo had continued its visits at the Bin, and in conjunction with the asylum staff had administered each man with a regular treatment.

"Swift Runner is dead, Danny. They burned his bones, and the windigo burned with them. If this is the room in which we must hide to escape the madness, I would rather be here than there."

"I wish that made me feel better," Crane said.

"It's all we have, Danny. Which was better than it was."

They entered the bunkhouse, which was empty as most of the officers were still into their cups.

Just five days after Swift Runner had dropped from the end of a rope into the abyss, and it was business as usual at the NWMP.

But for Griffith and Crane, it would never be the same.

III

January 20, 1879
Fort Saskatchewan, NWT

It had not been a dream wrapped inside a nightmare as fearfully contemplated by Griffith and Crane. The Windigo did not come back and dissolve their illusion of reality. Nor drag them back to the horrible nightmare of its collective madness.

Their madness.

Both men were riddled with apprehension, making them unfit for field duty. The demise of that unease could only be remedied by two things, time and acceptance. Both medicines were slow and invisible, and not always inevitable.

One marker in time was the end of the Fort Saskatchewan Asylum for Lunatics. An unofficial investigation into Dr. Keach's Fort Saskatchewan Asylum for Lunatics was initiated by Inspector Jarvis. Gagnon, Marois, Taylor, and Corporal Bagley were sent to the asylum.

The ride in was short, and even before they reached the brick building, they were welcomed at the iron gate by the frozen, naked corpse of the face-dragger. There was no evidence of bullet or stab wounds. No marks at all, just exposure.

"Just walked out here and died?" Bagley shook his head. "Really?"

"I remember him," Marois said.

"Let's go!" Gagnon unholstered his firearm and they hurried down the drive at a heavy gallop.

A minute later, they found the steel door open.

They got off their horses, guns drawn, and entered the building. They explored the house and found no sign of Dr. Keach or his ghoulish assistants, or anyone at first.

"Gone like thieves in the night," Marois cussed.

Of the seven patients, they found five in a large room, all huddled together, beneath heavy curtains torn from the windows. There were five heads riding the seam of that curtain, their faces putty white from the cold. A woman in the middle of four men, vapor randomly puffing from each. They looked like puppets, hair frosty, but at least they had survival instinct to huddle together as the fire dwindled.

Marois remembered her as the crying woman.

She started crying again, and said, "We are cold and hungry, and nobody cares!" Then she started screaming, "Nobody cares!"

"Frannie, you shut up," the man to her right barked.

"My name's not Frannie," she whined. "Nobody cares!"

"I missed my bath," the man to her left said.

The other two just watched.

"Nobody cares! Nobody cares! Nobody cares!"

"Frannie!"

"Why didn't you go get some wood?" Marois asked them.

"Hey, policeman," the man on the far left said to Marois. "Norman went for firewood and never came back. Then Birdy went and never came back."

"Was Birdy the old man?" Marois asked.

"Yeah, Dirty Birdy," the man said.

"How long?"

"A year ago, maybe two? They didn't let us have time."

"What?" Marois shook his head.

Behind him, Gagnon sighed. "Officier Marois."

He turned.

Gagnon pointed to the stove. Marois and Taylor went back out the door and looked around for Birdy while grabbing wood off the pile.

He came back in and with the door closed and a lit stove got the temperature up in the room.

All the while, "Nobody cares."

"Shut up, Frannie."

"Go and get Dr. Herchmer," Gagnon ordered.

Taylor went for the doctor who returned forty minutes later. He checked them out, there was some frostbite. The survivors were kept at the Asylum until arrangements could be made for them to be moved to the hospital.

Dirty Birdy was never found.

Nor were the likes of Keach, Van Sloane or Shore.

IV

Winter gave way to spring, and members of the NWMP were scattered to the many duties of frontier policemen. Spring also brought tragedy.

George Washington Brazeau remained a guide and interpreter for the NWMP until May 25, 1880, when the rifle he was cleaning discharged and killed him. The matter was thoroughly investigated, and his death was ruled an accident. He was buried in St. Albert, survived by his widow, Marie Descheneau.

Some thought he might have been drunk when he picked up the weapon. An investigation ruled the shooting an accident, but there were doubters. Brazeau had been well acquainted with rifles, and it seemed unlikely he would make an amateurishly fatal mistake such as this. Others suggested he might have taken his own life. But why? Why would Brazeau take his own life? Was it the horror of Swift Runner's death camp?

Or had the windigo found its way into his mind?

By mid-June, Severe Gagnon was on assignment in Manitoba. Horace Taylor had been posted south to Fort McLeod. Marois was posted to Fort St James in British Columbia. They were being pulled apart, not on purpose, it was just the business of being a Mountie.

V

Inspector Jarvis hadn't wanted controversy, but the newsmen thought otherwise, and the headlines were as dreadful as they were taunting. Stories detailing the gruesome crimes of Swift Runner ran in every paper from local to national.

Father Leduc had obtained Swift Runner's permission to publish the confessions he made during his conversion. Some of those excerpts further sensationalized the story.

The Death Camp of Swift Runner
Mounties bring back evidence of monstrous crimes.
--The Redwater Moose

Court Sentences Indian Cannibal to Die!
Fort Saskatchewan first execution set for December 20th.
--The Edmonton Post

Indian Cannibal Killer Dead!
"The Purdiest Hanging," declares 49er, Jim Reid.
--St. Albert Tribune

A Cannibal's Confessions!
The Memoirs of Father Hippolyte Leduc
--Montana Mountain News

Did Cannibal Indian Have More Victims?
"Yes," says unidentified source within NWMP.
--Manitoba Prairie Times

There were more stories, leading to animated discussions across kitchen tables, sewing circles, barrack rooms, and along the trail. It seemed everyone loved a good cannibal story, and there were plenty of off-color jokes about cannibalism. Even though it was Swift's mother who perished in the massacre, the joke played better as, bumping off and eating your mother-in-law was a tough piece of business to chew.

Overall, the consensus was that Swift Runner had gotten what he deserved. One life for eight was a bargain for the Devil, no matter what the Catholics thought.

No love lost—burn in hell.

Except for Griffith, who mourned Swift Runner, the man before the madness, the man who had saved his life. He truly hoped Swift was at rest. Forgiveness was another matter altogether. He didn't think he could ever forgive Swift for what he had done, not just to his family, but to Danny Crane and him as well.

VI

Spring became summer, and there was a shift of postings for new corporals. Marois visited Griffith one last time before leaving for Fort St. James, and they spoke about his new adventure.

"I hear the West Coast is breathtaking," Griffith said.

"I wish you were coming with me, *mon ami*," Marois said.

"I'd just hold you back." Griffith appeared healthier, except for the look in his eyes that Marois had only seen in war-weary soldiers. Griffith knew he had the look, although he never remarked about it. They talked about the good times, they laughed, but there was a feeling of finality in that meeting.

Then they talked about the what if?

That conversation was difficult.

They shook hands and shared a hug.

Then Marois was gone.

VII

By the end of the summer, it seemed only Griffith and Crane remained at Fort Saskatchewan. Neither would ever return to full active duty with the Northwest Mounted Police. They were on light duty work around the fort, and new constables arrived as other old ones departed.

Crane said, "I feel like a stranger here."

Griffith nodded. "I know. I feel the same way."

"They look at us differently," Crane said. "They think we're sick, lame, and lazy."

"We are," Griffith said sarcastically, but he thought Danny was right. Maybe not malingerers, but they were considered weak-willed, unreliable. It wasn't paranoia, and both men knew that their days in the NWMP were ending.

"I can't stay here, Ron," Crane said.

"Where will you go?" Griffith asked.

"Back home."

"To England?"

"Yes, the farther away, the better," Crane said. "Everything about this place is a reminder."

He knew that Danny didn't just mean the fort, he meant Griffith too. "I don't blame you, Danny."

That was the beginning of the end.

A month after Marois departed, both Crane and Griffith were given voluntary honorable releases from the NWMP. Upon retirement, Griffith was awarded a horse and an acreage of land. But not just any horse. Gunner.

Griffith built himself a small cabin on the north side of the South Saskatchewan River. He was building a barn for Gunner but was assured by Superintendent Jarvis himself that the stables were his to use until he finished the barn. Both his and Crane's retirement was low-key.

VIII
September 27, 1879
Fort Saskatchewan, NWT

Crane was gone by mid-September, putting an ocean between himself and Fort Saskatchewan while Griffith decided withdrawal was his only option. He worked on his homestead, finishing the small barn and a fenced exercise yard.

He went to the Fort for the last time to retrieve Gunner and say goodbye to Superintendent Jarvis, who came out to see him at the stable.

"You take care, Ron," Jarvis said, shaking his hand.

"Thank you, sir. For a being a good leader, and for letting me keep Gunner here."

Jarvis smiled. "I gotta get back, the Commissioner is coming, but if you need anything, the fort is always your second home."

"Thank you, sir."

Jarvis went back to his office and Griffith finished saddling Gunner.

He mounted up, and a young Mountie waved to him as he rode out. He did not know the Mountie, but he waved back and that was it. He was an outsider now, no uniform to speak of, and it made him sad, but he pushed it away.

"Let's go home, Gunner."

Halfway back, Griffith saw the dog bounding through the field to his right. It was a yellow Labrador Retriever, but not a pure lab. Once closer, it became clear that this dog was over halfway through its life. The dog was a female and bore innumerable scars. She was missing part of her left ear, likely bitten off. She also had crisscrossing slashes on the bridge of her nose, and her left eye was blind and hazy. Despite this, she paced them, keeping out of Gunner's space, wagging her tail as though they were old friends.

Griffith laughed out loud. "You just tagging along?"

The dog glanced up, tail wagging enthusiastically. Griffith decided that if the mutt followed them home, he might just let her stay. His exile was from man, not from animals, and that was reason enough for another sentry to raise the alarm.

He called the dog, Sandy, and she became a part of his family.

Despite her battle scars, Sandy was friendly and thoughtful. Griffith was sure she had been around horses before. She understood about keeping her distance, and staying away from hind quarters. She slept inside, by the door from that point on, posting sentry. She was a tough old girl, and Griffith would grow to love her. He had heard somewhere that sometimes the dead send animals to protect the living. When he looked at this dog quietly sleeping by his door, listening to the darkness, he thought of Penny and wondered.

At least now he could speak to someone.

Part of his fear was that talking to himself might draw out the old madness. He remained monk-like until he was with his horse or his dog. Griffith tended his trapline and kept mostly to himself. He grew a beard, and his hair, once cut short, now covered his ears. He rode Gunner every day, and Sandy tagged along enthusiastically. His animal family along with the letters was almost enough. He had stayed away from Fort Saskatchewan for most of the winter and came in on the tail end of the melting.

He had mail from both Crane and Marois.

After returning home, Griffith stabled Gunner and the dog followed him back into the house. He sat down at his table and felt her lick his hand. He gave her a pat and she went to her spot by the door.

He watched her momentarily, trying to guess her age and thinking about Penny and her sweet promise, "I'll watch over you, David."

He pushed the thought away and examined the envelopes.

He opened the letter from Crane first.

Letter
From: Daniel Crane, 11 Mitre Square
London, England

30 November 1880

Dear Ron,

I hope this letter finds you in good health. I can tell you that leaving and returning to England seems the remedy that I needed. It did not happen overnight, as I spent many nights tormented by the unshakable dread we spoke of. But time and distance contributed greatly to my healing. The fear has finally faded, and I am ready to start my new life.

I sincerely hope that the same applies to you, my friend, please write and let me know.

Maybe they really did kill the thing out there with those Indians. I think about them sometimes, and how they helped us and what happened to them. Are they still in Egg Lake? I am also pleased to report that I have successfully applied and been accepted into the Academy for the Metropolitan Police Department. I begin my training in two weeks, and I am very excited to get back to police work.
But enough about me. How are you? Did you finish your homestead? How is Gunner adapting to living in the country?

That is all for now.

Danny

After finishing the letter, Griffith sensed something he hadn't felt in quite some time, and that was happiness. Not for himself, but for Danny Crane, whom he believed had suffered far longer and worse than he had himself. He remembered watching the windigo torturing Danny when they were chained up in the bin.

He was getting better.

That was good.

He liked Danny Crane and wanted him to be happy, free of the unshakable dread stated in his letter.

Am I free of the unshakable dread?

No. He could function, but his self-imposed solitude enabled the dread to remain. He stayed to himself, his horse and dog, no soulmates or cellmates to counsel or prop him up. No one to reassure him that the windigo would never come back.

I can't risk it.

Griffith had always been a social man, and that need to interact with others had cemented his friendship with Marois.

He folded Crane's letter, replaced it in the envelope, and set it on the table.

He could smell a faint odor, as he brought the second envelope up to his nose and sniffed.

He shook his head and laughed quietly.

"Fred's perfume."

Marois had scented the envelope with a drop of whisky. Even though Griffith had abstained from drinking since Christmas of 1879, he was still delighted by the sentiment.

He feared alcohol might lower his defenses and summon the windigo. He remembered Swift Runner saying it wasn't the alcohol, but the madness itself. He wasn't confident in a man who had touched him with madness. He would die a sober man, always looking over his shoulder.

They had moved on and he had not.

Why?

He opened the envelope and removed the letter.

Letter
From: Corporal Fredericke Marois
c/o Royal Northwest Mounted Police, Fort St. James, BC

15 October 1880

Bonjour, mon ami,

I hope this letter finds you well. I spoke with Horace about your decision to leave the NWMP and understand and support that decision. Horace Taylor has been promoted to corporal. Our young charge has turned out to be a solid officer in lieu of our earlier experiences. Haha. I told him I would be writing you and he mentioned that he isn't much for writing letters. He did ask that I say, "Hi," so consider yourself greeted.

There are rumblings of promotion for me as well, but we'll leave that to rumor.

The area around Stuart Lake is densely forested and mountainous. The air is always fresh because it rains here almost every day. Well, not every day, but a hell of a lot, mon ami. I will say this; it is the prettiest country this new world has to offer.

I will be away for a while; we are escorting a mine payroll in from the coast. It will be good to get out of the fort, but I expect we could be gone a month.

That should leave some time to write back.
Be well and safe,

Fred

IX

The letters were his salvation from loneliness, and he wrote back, living vicariously through written communications. There was only the veiled suggestion of the question nobody was asking. "I hope you are well," really meant, "Are you still okay? Is there anything skulking around inside your head? Did it come back?"

Did it come back?

He tended his traps and hunted, and shared updates, mail gave him an excuse to go to town. A neighbor farmer became an occasional acquaintance, and he had Gunner and Sandy

Still the unshakable dread endured.

***

Chapter 21 – Letters – Grief - Death

I

1881 - 1886
Fort Saskatchewan, NWT

Superintendent Jarvis, who had obsessed about career killing controversies, had differences of opinion regarding expense reports with NWMP Commissioner James McLeod. He would retire from the force in 1881 at the rank of superintendent.

Corporal Bagley would be reassigned and posted to numerous duties. Stories of his exploits were many, some grander than others, especially those told by Bags himself. He was often quoted in articles about Swift Runner and his crimes.

By 1885, the Government of Canada was carving out a nation, and it rolled over anyone who got in the way of that vision. A rebel leader had been taken into custody and was awaiting trial for high treason.

His name was Louis Riel.

The uprising, later called the North-West Rebellion, saw Superintendent Severe Gagnon moved to Fort Carlton, NWT, as post commander. His mission was to gather intelligence that would thwart any discontent that might turn violent.

There was discontent, and it did turn violent.

By the spring of 1886, Severe Gagnon was reassigned to the NWMP Training Depot in Regina as an instructor, and though there was mention of his activities throughout the ranks, Griffith only heard about him through Marois.

Gagnon had no communication with Marois or any of the men who had worked the Swift Runner case. Stories about him came only through Mountie gossip. Severe never offered to write or talk about what had happened or what they had done. He said goodbye and was gone. Griffith supposed Gagnon had put his career between himself and the dark secret they all shared.

II

June 2, 1886
Fort Saskatchewan, NWT

Griffith remained mostly to himself except for his many correspondences with Marois and Crane. His hair was long now, onto his shoulders in dark curls, and he had a full beard falling to his chest. He had dealings with a farmer three miles down the road whom he bartered with, and he occasionally went into town, mostly to mail letters.

He never returned to the garrison of Fort Saskatchewan.

He was a stranger there now, his friends scattered and swapped for new generations. He missed being a Mountie, his friends, having purpose, but that all ended after the expedition to find the camp. He still had his friends Fredericke Marois and Danny Crane, and their letters meant so much to him. They were a lifeline to a world from which he was now an exile. Self-inflicted *wepinikewin.* Griffith could never trust himself. Not after the things he had seen, the horrible thoughts he had contemplated. Would Fred write to him if he had known the thoughts that swam through his mind?

He'd never talk to me again.

Griffith would always be on his guard, unable to trust himself around people. At least he had Gunner and Sandy. Not only companions but protectors.

He tended his homestead and his trapline on the South Saskatchewan River for a little over five years, and Sandy slept by that door listening to the darkness. Griffith wasn't sure of her age, but he thought she was over ten years old. Her face was almost completely white, the brownish yellow fur retreating and fading on her head and ears. Her scars had gone from pink to gray.

She was feeling her age, no longer bouncing around happily as she had the day she charmed her way into his life. Now she moved with an ache in her hips, and she could no longer accompany them to the trapline.

"Not feeling so well, eh?" Griffith patted her gently, sitting beside her bed. She looked up at him with her once good eye that was now hazy. Her tail knocked against the wall, she licked his hand and nestled her head into his arm. Griffith felt a pang of sadness in his heart, but couldn't bring himself to end her pain. It was selfish, but he just didn't want to be the instrument. "Go to sleep Sandy, I'll be okay. Go back to Penny."

The next morning, he rose to find Sandy dead.

He wrapped her up in the blanket and buried her on his property.

Griffith never got another dog.

III

August 15, 1886
Fort Saskatchewan, NWT

No dog, but Griffith again had two animals on the homestead—his horse and a donkey. He had purchased the donkey from the farmer acquaintance down the road. He bought the donkey for two reasons. Gunner was a social horse and had been lonely since leaving the stables in Fort Saskatchewan. The second reason was that after Sandy died, a pack of coyotes had come around, harassing his horse.

The farmer was a French-and-Cree man named Michael Mercier. He was a tall, lanky man, over six foot, tough and wiry-looking, and he had a wife whom Griffith had only seen from afar. She waved at him once and he awkwardly waved back. Two months back, Mike had dropped a pantry off at the end of the property with a note: "I built the Missus a new one, thought you might find a use for the old."

He accepted the gift and reciprocated with meat.

They would stop and chat on the road during Griffith's trips to town. On this day, Mike brought the donkey out on a tether for Griffith examine him.

"He'll kick the coyotes' heads in if they come sniffing around," Mike said.

"Oh, yeah?" Griffith wasn't sold, Sandy kept the coyotes away.

"Everyone thinks donkeys are stupid, but they're pretty smart and plenty tough."

The donkey was handsome in a funny sort of way. He was almost completely brown, except for ears, eyes, and nose, which were all black.

The tip of his muzzle as well as his short, shaggy mane were white, giving him a jester's smile.

"How much do you want for him, Mike?"

"He's worth a hundred," Mike said.

Griffith inhaled and let out a long dramatic breath. "That's a bit high for a donkey."

"He's worth it. He can be used as a work donkey."

"I hear Tedd Hill down the road has cougar hound pups he's giving away for free. Maybe I'll go see him?" Griffith felt guilty bluffing the farmer. He had no interest in another dog.

"Ah, poop, I'll let him go for eighty," Mike said, that being his magic number in the first place.

"Seventy-five, and I'll be back in the summer for your hay," Griffith said. "I might even buy that wagon I always borrow and you never use."

They shook on it. Griffith paid him, set up a follow, and took the donkey home.

He named the donkey "George," after George Washington Brazeau. He was worried that Gunner might be jealous of the donkey, but gave him more attention than he gave George.

The rest just fell into place.

Gunner and George became fast friends, and Griffith took great pleasure watching them play together. Horses and donkeys were such personable creatures. They ran around the fenced yard, George braying with delight as Gunner chased him in circles. Once finished their game, they moseyed like lifelong pals.

"Gunner has a friend." Griffith enjoyed the show.

Letter
From: Corporal Fredericke Marois
c/o Royal Northwest Mounted Police, Fort St. James, BC

15 October 1880

Bonjour, mon ami,

I am afraid I must open this correspondence with tragic news. Our friend and fellow officer, Corporal Horace Taylor, has died in a terrible mishap. At the beginning of April, a boy fell into the swollen Stuart River. Horace was about a hundred yards downstream with another officer named James Barnes, when they saw the boy fall off the bank. Without a second thought, Taylor dismounted and ran down the bank, yelling at Barnes to take the horses downstream and ready a rope.

Both men acted with great urgency.

According to the testimony of Barnes, Horace waited on the bank until he thought he had the right timing and dove into the muddy rapids. He swam all the way to the boy and even had him in his grasp. Barnes waited downstream on shore with a rope ready to cast out to them. He saw them bobbing in the rapids and then they went under the water and did not resurface. Barnes said he cast the rope multiple times hoping, by some miracle, Taylor might grab it, but to no avail.

Their bodies have not been recovered.

If there is any comfort to be taken from this sad tragedy, is that our friend died in the commission of a heroic act. God bless Horace Taylor, and that of the boy he tried to save.

Enough bad news. How are Gunner and his newfound friend, George, doing? I found the name George curious for a donkey. GWB? Have you planted an apple tree yet? You will certainly
need them with two beasts to spoil.

I miss you, mon ami, especially on the trail.

Take care, be well.

Fred

Letter
From: Daniel Crane, 11 Mitre Square
London, England

31 August 1887

Dear Ron,

I was truly sad to hear about the tragedy that befell Horace Taylor. He, along with the others, saved our lives. I will be indebted to these men for the rest of my life. It seems almost preordained that Horace would make the ultimate sacrifice in a mission to save another. His debt was paid in full when he crossed over. I bet St. Peter just said, "Come in, Horace, we've been waiting." I was not as close to Horace as the rest of you, but he was a good man, and he will be sorrily missed.

On a happier note, I have been promoted to inspector. I am with the Metropolitan Police. If I haven't already mentioned it, which I probably have, they call us the Metro. The Metro and the London Police oversee the Whitechapel District, which is an extremely rough part of London. It is a filthy slum filled with tramps, thieves, prostitutes, the scourge of humanity. Six months ago, we went in to deal with riots, and we were pelted with bricks, and stones, and bottles. We had to withdraw and reinforce. Two of my officers were taken to the hospital for serious injuries. One lost an eye, the other sustained a laceration in his arm to the bone, inflicted by a drunken, bottle-wielding whore.

How are Gunner and that new donkey getting along? George? I can't picture you out in the wilderness with a horse and a donkey. I still see you in your uniform, atop Gunner, riding the trail. I will say this for the prairies; they are cleaner than the bowels of London. I am discouraged by the slop, the filth, and the loose deviance of the district. But I am happy to be an officer of the law.

Don't you miss being part of it?

Daniel Crane

V

It was George's braying that alerted Griffith, who arrived at the shelter in time to see Gunner stumble and fall. The horse had begun to twitch in a seizure. Griffith fell to his knees, placed his hand on the horse's shoulder, and saw the fright in Gunner's eye, reaching through the darkness.

He looks afraid. So afraid!

He felt Gunner shudder, trying to hold on, slipping, then falling. His eyes calmed, then went still.

"What, no…" Griffith put his head on the horse's chest, listening.

No heartbeat. Nothing.

"No. Please, no." His face bunched up, and he felt grief tear through him—along with anger and sorrow and victimhood. "I have only them. I have only them." He raised a fist and screamed at the sky, "I have no one else! He was only thirteen, he was only…" He sobbed. "I have only them! Damn you! Don't you understand? I have only them." Then he lay there with Gunner, broken-hearted, moaning on and off, oblivious of time, until he was brought back by George's mournful braying.

He sat up and wiped his eyes.

"George. Come on, George."

George came to him and stopped. *Hawww! Hawwwww!*

"I'm going to miss him too, George." Griffith stroked George's neck and started sobbing again.

George brayed, *Haw, haw* .

Griffith had never felt so completely empty, but he couldn't just lie down and die. If not for George, he might have grabbed his revolver, sat down next to Gunner, and put an end to the isolation.

But he had a grave to dig.

He led George to the front of the house, tethered him, and went back and dug the grave. It took him six hours to carve out a hole wide and deep enough for Gunner.

He rigged George up to pull Gunner into his grave.

"Come on, George," Griffith said.

George pulled Gunner's body only a few feet, and it tumbled into the hole with a heavy thump. At the same time, the ropes wrenched George back, and he brayed in complaint. *Hawwwww*!

"It's okay." Griffith was there, right beside him, and he eased the donkey back, slackening the harness, and unhooked the rigging. "Good boy, George."

He took George back to his spot beside the house.

Two hours later, Griffith was patting down the earth with the shovel. Beside the grave there was still a small pile of dirt that would have to be added as the earth sank. He stabbed the shovel into the pile, removed his shirt, and shook it out. He was soaked in sweat. He used the shirt to wipe his face and beard. He still had to get George into the shelter.

Griffith went and got him and led him to the threshold.

George stopped and refused to cross.

"Come on, George, I'm exhausted."

That night George stayed next to the house.

The next day, Griffith built a new gate that didn't cross Gunner's grave. Later, he marked the grave with a cairn of stones.

Griffith never got another horse. He walked everywhere. When he ran the trapline, he used George to carry his gear. He was seven miles from the town of Fort Saskatchewan; a hike in and out of town only happened once a month and took most of the day. He fished the South Saskatchewan River. He salted the fish and dried it in the smokehouse he had constructed. It wasn't the size of a real smokehouse—only a shed, really, six feet high by four feet square—but it served its purpose. He also made jerky from venison. There was no shortage of wild game, even if the bison were gone.

Another year passed.

He received and sent more letters. Griffith and George got on well, and Griffith thought that walking with a donkey was good for his joints.

Through the years, he watched and waited.

Marois wrote, Crane wrote, Griffith wrote.

Life marched on.

Until the windigo came back.

***

Chapter 22 – London Calling

I

1888 - 1889
Griffith's Homestead
Near Fort Saskatchewan, NWT

While Griffith and Marois continued to correspond, Crane's letters stopped without explanation, the last received by Griffith in August of 1889. Letters were exchanged monthly; sometimes they were late, but mostly they weren't.

Undaunted, Griffith continued to write to Crane, but no response came.

Maybe he's just moved on?

Crane had crossed the ocean to escape Fort Saskatchewan, so maybe he was severing the final tie as Severe Gagnon had? Plausible as that was, Griffith was still worried. He combed older letters for signs of something Crane had written that would indicate anything.

He found nothing.

Griffith kept his routine with George, hunting and trapping, going to town to drop letters written to Marois and another reaching out to the Metropolitan Police Department in London, regarding the whereabouts of Inspector Daniel Crane.

II

December 7, 1889
North Saskatchewan River

The temperatures around the frozen river were unseasonably humid, and vapor rose from the icy surface. Griffith was checking his trapline, while George waited on a path 100 yards from the riverbank. Surprisingly, every trap lay bare, bait untouched.

He spent the morning moving the traps and re-baiting them.

Setting the last trap, he opened the jaw, raised the plate, and set the dog pin. Then he slowly pulled his hands back and picked up his rifle, because he heard something.

He pivoted to see a small deer moving between the trees, coming down the snowy embankment. It wasn't a fawn, too late in the season for a deer that young. Its growth had been stunted; it wasn't more than four feet long, head to tail. Despite its small size, Griffith thought about his empty traps and brought the rifle up. Staring down the sight, he waited for the creature to clear the trees.

Griffith released the trigger and lowered the rifle. The deer, if that's what it had been, was a walking corpse. It wore a crown of broken antlers atop a moss-encrusted, deformed, and fractured skull devoid of its lower mandible. From neck to skeletal frame to bony stilts for legs, it was wrapped in a hide lacerated and tanned to leather. It made no sound, but Griffith saw the vapor rising from its half mouth, and for a moment he mused whether he was back in the asylum being readied for another ice bath.

The creature turned its gaze upon him and stopped.

Griffith brought up his gun.

Then it turned and continued its rickety trek, stabbing each decaying, stilted leg into the snow until it reached the river ice. Griffith watched it disappear into the haze, his hand still wrapped around the rifle.

Then from behind, he heard, "Hello, Constable Ron."

Griffith spun around, rifle up, to see Swift Runner's ghost standing on the bank five feet away. He didn't float, nor was he transparent, but a ghost he was, dressed in his execution clothes, his hair cut short. Griffith had never seen him like this.

"Swift?" He brought his eye up from the rifle slightly.

"Yes, Constable Ron." Swift Runner smiled.

"What are you doing here?" Griffith held his rifle at the ready.

"It is you who is here, Constable Ron," Swift said.

"Where is your friend? The one you set upon me?"

"The *wihitikow*..." Swift Runner's smile faltered. "The *wihitikow* is near."

"So, you're here to do it all over again?" Griffith asked.

"No, Constable Ron, I am here as your friend."

"As my friend?" Griffith's voice wavered as he implored, "Why did you do this to me, Swift? Was it because you thought I betrayed you? Because I banished you, like Chogan?

"I am sorry for what I did. I am sorry I helped the *wihitikow* spread its sickness to you and the others. That is why you are here, Constable Ron."

Griffith heard its distant shriek and immediately thought of George.

"Your animal is safe," Swift Runner said.

The only thing Griffith cared about more than himself was George. "I should check on him anyway."

"George is not in this world, Ron. Only us."

"World?" Griffith looked from Swift to his own hand, to the trees on the bank. No more color, his world black, gray, and white. When did that happen? It had been color only… When? Before the deer?

"This is not your world," Swift Runner interrupted his thoughts.

Griffith looked around. "Are you here all the time?"

"No, just here with you now," Swift Runner said. "It is not my world either."

"Why am I here?" Griffith asked, knowing he wasn't going to like the answer.

"The *wihitikow* has risen." Swift reached out and offered Griffith his hand. "We have much to discuss."

Griffith took his hand.

III
December 20, 1889
Fort Saskatchewan, NWT

On the tenth anniversary of Swift Runner's hanging, Griffith ventured back from town. He had wanted to stay at the post office, but they were closing early. It was minus thirty-five, so he wasn't going to stand around. His pace was a forced march, winds beating mercilessly against him, shin splints chopping at his legs. Regardless, he marched through it, carrying two letters in his pocket—one from Marois, and one from England.

An hour and forty minutes later, he was greeted by George, braying from his barn.

"Hi, George," he called and went into the cabin, removing his boots, gloves, and coat.

He got a fire going.

He thought about his talk with Swift Runner and had been waiting for the creature to come back.

Two days ago, as he tended to George, he'd had the feeling he was being watched. He walked his property and saw no man or thing, but the unshakable dread wrapped its icy claw around his heart and hung inside him, the weight of a church bell.

It was out there, waiting for him.

He sat down and opened the letter from England.

From: Inspector James E. Bath
Metropolitan Police, Whitechapel District
London, England

6 November 1889

Dear Corporal Griffith,

Thank you for your recent query regarding the wellness of one Daniel Crane. I must inform you that we have no record of any such person with that name serving in the Metro, let alone the Whitechapel District. But thinking you might have mistaken us for the London Police Department, I reached out to my colleagues in London, and they also have no record of an inspector or even an Officer Daniel Crane.

We do have a couple of constable Cranes, but not a single Daniel and none who claim to have been in the Northwest Mounted Police.

I suspect you may have been the victim of an unsavory hoax. At least that is what I hope, taking you at your word as a retired member of the Northwest Mounted Police.

If you have any further information, please contact me.

Sincerely,

Inspector James E. Bath

No record? How could that be?

Griffith read the letter twice more.

How can there be no record? He had years' worth of letters from Crane talking about his career, his advancement. Had it all been a ruse? He read the letter again.

He picked up the other envelope and tapped it on the table.

Would Danny create that elaborate of a lie?

He tapped the envelope again.

It appears he's done exactly that.

Then the envelope broke in two.

Huh?

He looked down.

It hadn't broken in two.

There was a smaller envelope stuck to the back of Fred's letter. He lay that envelope down and picked up the other. It bore no return address, but had a London postmark.

Danny, he thought.

He opened the envelope, expecting a letter, instead unfolding a full page cut from a London newspaper.

He spread it out on the table.

"Oh Jesus, no," Griffith whispered, eyes transfixed on the paper. There was no denying or pretending anymore. "Oh, Danny."

IV

December 21, 1889
Near Fort Saskatchewan, NWT

Griffith took George out to Mike's farm and asked if he could watch him. "I have to go away, and I wanted to make sure George is taken care of," he explained.

"For how long?" Mike asked.

"For a long time. This should take care of all his boarding needs." Griffith handed him a wooden cash box. "You can keep the box."

Mike looked inside. "Ron, this is too much."

Griffith said, "Keep him until he dies, Mike."

Mike stared back, contemplating, and said, "Okay, Ron. I'll take care of him."

"Thanks, Mike."

"Come on, we can put him in the barn."

They put George in a barn, and Griffith spent a minute talking to George while Mike gave them some privacy. He never heard what Griffith said to the donkey, but he understood the bond. Mike knew nothing of Griffith's other issues, but they shared a kinship regarding animals.

Two minutes later, Griffith emerged, wiping tears as George brayed sorrowfully from the barn.

Mike pretended not to notice.

Griffith was looking down, fumbling for something inside his coat. "I need one more favor."

"What's that?"

"I need you to mail this on your next trip to town." He held up an envelope.

"I'll be going to town day after tomorrow."

Griffith handed the envelope over, staring across the snowy field, and saw a gray silhouette watching from a stand of birch trees. He turned back to Mike and said, "Please don't forget the letter, Mike. It's very important."

"I won't forget, Ron. I'll take good care of George until you come back." Then Mike reached his hand out and touched Griffith's arm. "Ron, you don't have to go away."

"I'm afraid I do," Griffith said. He turned and began walking. "Take care of George and remember the letter."

"I will," Mike called after him.

Griffith disappeared into the fog.

V

Griffith could only see a few feet in front of him during the trek, but he felt the windigo moving parallel to his right, whispering his name. He wondered if this was how it had taken Crane in England. He could feel it leeching from his bones, again calling for him to do unspeakable things. He tasted blood in his throat, felt its black blood diluting his own, understood that his descent would be faster this time.

When he reached the cabin, he didn't bother to remove his coat and boots. He could hear it coming through the woods. He collected the letters, replaced them in the box, and returned them to the pantry.

Behind him, the door eased open.

The room temperature plummeted.

Griffith didn't turn.

The smell of death filled his nose. He saw its reflection in the glass door on the pantry, framed in the open doorway: demon eyes burning red, chewed off lips, teeth scraping together.

"Hello, Ron, I'm back," it hissed. "Ready for your treatment?"

Griffith turned to face it, gun in hand.

"What are you going do with that?" It cackled and then it knew. "No… No! Nooooo…"

He brough the gun to his temple.

Squeezed.

He heard the windigo screaming.

Hammer struck primer.

He heard thunder.

Then nothing.

***

Epilogue – The Promise

I

February 15, 1890
Fort St. James, British Columbia

Fredericke Marois's lover, Annie, whom he believed would become his wife, slept soundly as he contemplated his options. Annie was a thirtyish blonde with a petite build except for an ample bosom which Marois adored, along with everything else about her.

She wasn't perfect—her smile was slightly crooked, and she had a tiny scar on her chin from a tumble as a child. He loved those imperfections more than he loved her boobs. He also loved her voice, which was angelic, and the way her blue eyes seemed to brighten when she smiled. Marois had come late to the concept of love and marriage, but at the age of thirty-five, he was giving it serious consideration.

Serious because she was carrying his child.

He had written Griffith and spoken of his love and how he wanted Griffith to be his best man at the wedding. Late that afternoon, he had gone to drop that letter and picked up a new letter from Fort Saskatchewan. The envelope meant that Ron was still alive, a worry that plagued Marois. He wanted to get him out of Fort Saskatchewan. Everyone else had moved on, but Ron had chosen to remain there in solitude.

Marois intended on reading the letter when he got home, but Annie was waiting with dinner and wearing nothing else. He set the letter on the table, went to her, and she began undressing him. They made love, then they ate, then they made love again, and they talked and laughed and fell asleep in each other's arms.

Just before midnight, Marois awoke, dressed, got his pistol, and went to use the outhouse. This was something Annie had suggested they would need and so he had built it last spring. It wasn't as convenient as a bucket, and there were risks. Once, during a morning constitution, a rather large grizzly had come around while Marois was armed only with the paper to wipe his bum. He could hear the weight of its paws on the earth. It snorted and bumped against the structure. Marois pulled up his pants, hearing the bear chuffing and whining. It bumped harder against the right side of the outhouse, knocking a board loose. Marois was reaching for the door, readying to make a dash for the house, when he heard the familiar crack of his old Winchester, followed by a heavy thump.

"Freddy? Are you okay?" Annie called.

He opened the door, stepped out, and saw her standing twenty yards away, holding his rifle. To his right, the bear lay dead, a single hole between its eyes. If she had missed, or hit it anywhere else, the grizzly wouldn't have given her time to reload the single-shot rifle.

"*Tu es la femme parfait pour moi,*" Marois said.

She lowered the rifle, smiled, and said, "Yes, I'm the perfect woman for you—and don't you forget it."

"No, *mon amour*, I'll never forget."

They butchered the bear and made a rug from its hide, which they made love on at least a dozen times. Marois thought the pistol probably wasn't enough for another grizzly, but it was better than a mittful of bum wipe.

After finishing his outdoor business, Marois returned to the house, fed the fireplace, and sat down at the table. That was when he noticed the envelope sitting next to a candle on a tea saucer.

He rubbed his eyes and lit the candle, and picked up the envelope. Thinking about the letter of invitation he sent left him wondering what Ron's next correspondence would be.

Would he accept the invitation?

He hoped.

He tore open the envelope and began to read.

From: Corporal Ronald Griffith (Retired)
General delivery
Fort Saskatchewan, NWT

20 December 1889

Dear Fred,

As I mentioned in my previous letters, Danny Crane stopped writing. I sent four letters and received no response. That's when I began to worry, so I sent a letter of concern to the London Metropolitan Police. Two and a half months later I received a reply from an Inspector James Bath, and he stated that they had no Inspector Daniel Crane at the Metro Police.

No Daniel Crane at all.

I have letters monthly from Danny since he went to England. I could memoir his career with the Metropolitan Police. I have over eight years' worth of letters detailing Danny's promotions, his exploits, just as I have with you. Was he lying about being a police officer? The inspector from the Metro Police suggested it was likely a hoax. I thought possibly he might have worked a lesser job but why lie to me? I'm living like a hermit. I am just a shadow of who I was, so why would I judge?

Along with the letter from the Metro Police, there was one from you, and another envelope with no return address postmarked from London. At first, I didn't see it because it was stuck to the back of your letter. I opened that envelope, and the mystery was solved in an article torn from a London newspaper.

The newspaper article recounted a series of hideous unsolved murders against ladies of the night, occurring in a part of London known as the Whitechapel District. This was where
Danny Crane claimed to be working for the Metro Police, Freddy.

Coincidence?

According to the article, the perpetrator was initially dubbed Leather Apron, because a witness had claimed to have seen the suspect wearing such. That nickname is no longer used after the killer sent a series of letters to a local vigilante named George Lusk along with part of a kidney from one of his victims while claiming to have eaten the other half. It was in his correspondences with the press and Lusk, that the killer christened himself with a far more nefarious name: Jack the Ripper.

I don't know if Danny Crane is Jack the Ripper, but even if it isn't him, he may have infected others by spreading the windigo plague to England. I cannot explain almost a decade of letters filled with lies about his career as a police officer. The only thing I am certain of is that the newspaper article was sent by Daniel Crane because written across it were two words penned in blood: **Wihitikow Lives!**

The windigo came back for Danny, and now, me.

Even before the letters, I began to feel something was off. I thought it might be a seasonal bug. Denial, of course, as the familiar venom began leeching from my bones, poisoning my blood, ravaging my heart, and seizing my will. Danny called it the unshakable dread. This feeling was followed by glimpses of the windigo shadowing me, watching from a distance, waiting, for the influence of its madness to take hold on me.

I can feel it getting stronger, its icy black blood diluting mine.

Prior to the letters, I was on the North Saskatchewan checking my trapline. I had that heavy feeling all morning and was moving my traps when all color drained from my vision. Then I spotted what I can only describe as a deer-corpse emerging from the trees. It was stumbling through the snow, and I almost shot it but instead watched it struggle out across the ice-covered river. What I was witnessing was a sad creature of the windigo's parallel world. A world I had been again pulled into.

Then I heard Swift Runner's voice behind me say, "Hello, Constable Ron."

I asked him why he did what he did, and he said, "I felt the wihitikow watching me, drawn to the poison in my heart. I knew it was there but denied what would happen. If I had taken my life, it would have been over, but I was a coward, and it took my whole family instead."

I asked Swift, "Why are you here? To put it on me again?"

Swift said, "I am here as your friend. The wihitikow has risen. You remember what I told you, Constable Ron? Once it's inside you, it never comes out. You must end your life to end the curse, then the fire must finish it."

Without another word, Swift Runner turned and walked away and then there was a flash and a pop.

I blinked and when I opened my eyes, I found myself lying on my side staring at my open trap in color, and heard George braying from the nearby trail. I got up and looked around, thinking it was a dream. Maybe? Like Swift, I wanted to deny it and would have continued doing so until the letter came from England.

I cannot explain the decade of normality. I can only speculate that when you, Horace, Severe, and George went into the woods with Chogan and his men and burned Swift Runner's body, the windigo must have gone into a state of weakened hibernation. The fact is, it was never really gone, and I'm never going to be cured, nor will Danny Crane, or anyone else that this vile curse has touched.

I can't go back to that, my friend. I simply do not have the will nor the strength to repeat this nightmarish process and even if I did, whose bones would you burn this time to save me? The windigo sickness is already warping my thoughts, dissolving my humanity. I have seen it watching from afar, getting stronger as I grow sicker. It will take me faster this time, and I will do the horrible things it demands. I have already had dreams about harming a neighbor.

Time is running out.

By the time you read this letter, I will be dead, but the burden of your promise still holds.

Come quickly, Fred.

Ron

II

"Fredericke, why are you crying?" Annie was wrapped in a blanket. She moved around his chair and wrapped her arms around him. "What happened?"

Marois told her about Griffith's death withholding the grim details. He folded and replaced the letter in the envelope. She knew of their friendship, the letters they shared, but nothing else. Marois had planned on dying with those secrets. He didn't want Ann knowing anything about what happened in the Fort Saskatchewan.

She held him for a long time, and he finally told her, "Go back to bed, Annie. I'm gonna stay up for a bit and think about my friend."

"Okay," she said and went back to bed.

But she didn't go to sleep, instead she lay there worrying about him. If he sat up all night, she would stay awake, and their baby wouldn't get any sleep. Marois got up off the chair, "Annie, I'm going out for a smoke."

"Take your gun," she said.

"I will." He dressed and grabbed his pistol.

Marois went out onto the porch and leaned on the rail looking out over the lake. The sky was clearing. There had been rain, and a mild breeze carried forest scents of cedar, pine, lichen, moss, and moist earth. He extinguished those fragrances with a cigar, thinking about Griffith and their friendship. They'd had a lot of fun as young men and thought the world their oyster.

Marois took a puff, exhaled, and breathed in the night aromas as he thought about his plans. He was retiring from the Mounties and was going to try his hand at prospecting gold. He and Annie had already staked a claim on the other side of Stuart Lake. He loved her deeply, and he thought they might make a few more kids on top of the one he couldn't wait to meet. His life was good. He was happy.

He had hoped that Ron would accept his invitation as best man, come for the wedding and stay for a lifetime. They could have worked the claim together, as partners, and he could have introduced him to some local women and…

"And nothing." He took another puff, considering the cruel unfairness of it all. Not only was Ron dead, but so were Horace and George. Crane was missing, possibly a maniac killer in England, and Severe Gagnon was hiding from what they had done. Marois had written to Severe several times, but the letters went unanswered. God only knew where he might be.

Marois's thoughts came back to the letter and the promise he had made before saying goodbye.

He could hear Ron in his head, "Come quickly, Fred."

And Swift Runner, "…the fire must finish it."

And now, it's left to me, he thought.

He took a puff on the cigar, exhaled.

He would tell Annie of his plans in the morning.

III

Marois told Annie that he had been named executor of Ron Griffith's estate, and he was needed in Fort Saskatchewan to dispense with his will. It was a lie, but a plausible one, and one worth telling, given the circumstances of his real mission. "The trip will take about three months, and I'll be back before the birth of our child."

"Why not wait until spring, and we can go together?" Annie asked.

"*Mon amour*, I don't want you traveling through the mountains in your condition. If something were to happen to you or our child, I would never forgive myself." Marois placed a hand on her belly and kissed her on the tip of her nose.

"Is there something you're not telling me, Fred?"

"I made a promise to my best friend, and I must keep it."

"Okay, my love." She pulled him closer and he held her.

It took until the end of February to process his release from the Mounties. He readied himself for the ride east while working out what he could do.

There were long silences in which Annie watched him staring off into the distance.

She lamented, "You promised me a wedding, Fredericke Marois."

"Yes, I did," he agreed. He took her to the chapel, and they were married by the Catholic priest.

"Now you are Mrs. Fredericke Marois," he told her.

They made love in their bed, as husband and wife. She held him tight, weeping softly and whispering, "Promise me you'll come back, Freddy."

"I promise," he said and pulled her closer.

Morning came, they stood on the porch, and she hugged him. "I love you, Freddy."

"I love you too," he said and patted her belly. "And I love you too."

She kissed him and watched him ride off into winter's dark.

IV
April 7, 1890
30 Miles West of St. Albert, NWT

Almost all of March had been spent escaping the brutality of the Rockies and an endless tempest of storms of snow and wind. Marois broke through at the end of the month and found himself on the final leg of his journey.

Throughout, he had been in varying states of denial, anger, and overwhelming sorrow. The anger was because he was all alone and didn't have time to wait for the mail system. He penned a letter to Gagnon, explaining his intentions with an invitation to help. It was a letter he saw no use in mailing until he arrived in Fort Saskatchewan. Once there, he would find Griffith's homestead and figure out where he was buried. He hoped it was on the homestead, but if Ron was buried in a local cemetery…

Then I guess I become a grave robber.

He was nearing St. Albert, and in the fading daylight, he saw a young man standing over another person who appeared to be hurt or in some form of distress. Marois rode up, dismounted, and inquired, "What is happening here?"

"He just stopped breathing," the young man said and stepped back. There was something familiar about him. Marois gazed down at the man on the ground, who was on his belly and older than the young guy, maybe in his mid-thirties.

Marois gave the young guy a more thorough look. "Do I know you?"

Then he felt a hand clamp around his ankle and looked down.

"Now, Olly! Now, Olly!" the guy holding his ankle bellowed.

Realizing the trap, Marois reached for his revolver, but something hit him in the head, and he went down hard. Incredibly, he was still semiconscious and felt them dragging him off the road, down an embankment, and into the woods. His back bumped over roots and rocks and sticks, and it was painful, but he was half unconscious.

What is this? A robbery? The kid's name is Olly.

"Go get the horse, before someone sees," Olly ordered.

"Okay, Olly. Watch him!" The older guy ran back up the bank.

"Don't hurt my horse," Marois mumbled through the pain his head.

Olly had his revolver and said, "Who invited you into this conversation?" Then the butt of the gun came down, and the lights went out for Fredericke Marois.

V

Drifting in unconsciousness, he still felt them rifling through his pockets but was unable to fight back or stop them. The blow from the gun butt had knocked something loose in his head. Now they were pulling off his clothes, and he heard their grunts as they moved him around. Then he was plunging into the darkness, away from the rest of their indignities.

When Marois regained consciousness, it was to the scent and sound of the crackling of a fire. He played possum and kept his eyes closed. There was pain on the side of his head, and he remembered the kid named Olly had clobbered him twice—once with his own gun. His pulse throbbed in his ears and eyes because the blood had rushed to his head.

Marois opened his eyes and saw the bigger guy pacing back and forth in front of the fire, but everything was upside down. Olly was reading the opened letters Marois had been carrying.

Where do I know this Olly from?

"He's waking up, Olly," the pacing guy said.

"What do you want?" Marois croaked.

Olly stood up, came over, and hunkered down in front of him, letters still in his right hand. "I remember you. You were the one who took him away."

"Took who away?"

"The giant."

"Fee-Fi-Fo-Fum!" the older man tittered.

"Not that giant," Olly said over his shoulder. "You know what giant I'm talking about, Policeman?"

"It's time to give an offering, Olly." The older man yelled, "It's time, Olly!"

"Shut up, Mr. Buchanan," Olly barked. "I'm trying to talk to our friend here."

"It's time, Olly," Mr. Buchanan insisted.

"Excuse me." Olly stood up, turned, and yelled, "Mr. Buchanan do you think you're the only one here who is hungry?"

"No, Olly but—"

"Who's in charge here? Who's the smart one here?"

"You are, Olly—"

"Then shut your mouth and wait until I'm done!"

"Yes, Olly." Buchanan sneered at Marois and went back to pacing.

Olly came back to Marois, knelt, and said, "Mr. Buchanan's mind never came back completely after the sickness returned. He's sort of dim now. Where was I? Oh yeah, you came and took the giant but left us to suffer his master. My mother thought the devil possessed me. They put me in a hospital, and that's where I met Mr. Buchanan. He knew about the giant and his monster, and we just got worse, and the creature tortured us until they hung the giant. When we got out of the hospital, my mom was long gone. Fucking whore took off with some market scab named Dumfries. Since then, it's just been me and Mr. Buchanan and we were cured after you hung the giant, but then—"

"I know who you are," Marois said.

"Then it came back, Olly," Mr. Buchanan said.

"Then it came back, Mr. Buchanan," Oliver said.

"I… know who you are… I know about the windigo," Marois said.

"He knows, Olly, he knows!" Buchanan was banging his forehead with his fist.

"What do you know, Policeman?" Oliver Halford asked.

"It took my friend, and we stopped it. I know it's come back, but we can finish it this time. I can help you."

"Help me?" Olly laughed.

Buchanan joined in.

"You don't want to do this," Marois pleaded. "Please…"

"It's not what I want, Policeman… It's what… It… Wants." Olly tossed the letters into the fire, reached behind his back, and brought out a knife. The nine-inch blade looked razor sharp, a jagged edge rode its upper shank, and it was embedded in a handle made of bone.

Marois looked up, terror dawning. They were really going to do this. "I can help. Please… I can…"

"You couldn't help your friend or the dead giant, and you know why, Policeman? Because… There's only one thing that helps."

"Please, I beg of you… I…"

"You beg all you want—we've heard it all before."

"Heard it all before, Olly!"

"Grab a hold of him, Mr. Buchanan," Olly ordered.

"It's time! It's time for the offering! Time for the offering!" Mr. Buchanan came around behind him gleefully, hooked one arm behind Marois' bound arms, and snatching his hair in his other hand.

Marois tried to buck against him, but it was impossible.

"No, please no, please noooo…"

Olly came at him with the knife and Marios felt his belly catch fire and his flesh unzipping. Then came a waterfall of warm, sticky blood flowing down over his chest, shoulders, neck, face, nose, mouth and right eye. It was infernal agony, what hell must be like, only to be interrupted by pulling, tugging, and more cutting.

They took what they had come for, left him swinging, and went to the fire.

"It's coming, Olly!"

"Let us feast like kings!" Olly cried.

Marois felt the cold numbing his toes, feet, legs, and the inferno in his belly was suddenly gone. His heart was slowing, eyesight fading, yet somehow still, he hung on. Even as the lunatics stood at the fire holding up fistfuls of his guts in offering.

He heard the branches cracking, the maniacs raving.

The windigo took its place at the fire, snatching its tribute, feasting on it while turning its fiery gaze to Marois.

Marois had to see. Had to know if this was the windigo they had burned north of Egg Lake? But his hold slipped, and he tumbled backward into the mystic.

The beast's eyes shrank to pin pricks, gone to the endless night. He heard Annie sobbing and the cries of their first born, and then they were gone too. Then he heard the voices of Ron Griffith, Horace Taylor, and George Washington Brazeau calling his name, summoning him back to Fort Saskatchewan.

Then silence.

-End-

Afterword by the Author

—

Okay, so that was fun. Wasn't it? I mean, sorry about Griffith and Marois and especially Gunner. I assure you, it wasn't planned. Do you still like me?

The truth is that Windigo Plague was outlined without an ending. And another confession is that this is the first book I have ever outlined, I usually fly by the seat of my pants.

Either way, I had no idea that it would end like this.

And, you know what? I like it that way. I usually have some idea, but when it's done, I always think to myself, *How the hell did that happen?* And the truth is, I have not the slightest. An outline is just a guide to the madness, because once those fingers hit the keys, all bets are off.

Horror novels should be filled with fun surprises and so I tossed a few in like Leather Apron aka Jack the Ripper. Remember, this is fiction, man, and horror fiction should be about letting go and surrendering to the crazy.

So, what comes next?

Well, as far as the Fort Saskatchewan Project goes, there will be two more novels: **House of Blood** set in 1979 and **Highway Star** set in 2009. Both novels are partially written and outlined. The common denominator is of course, Fort Saskatchewan, and...

And I hope you come back to read the next novel, and the one after that and the one after that. Because without you, dear reader, I am just another inmate in the bin, but fear not! I am neither Dirty Birdy nor the Face Dragger, but remember, "Nobody loves Chester!"

There's few more pages, including the confession of Ka Ki Si Kutchin, acknowledgements and research material should you care to check it out.

Love the one you're with.

MJ Preston

Historical Characters

- **Ka Ki Si Kutchin/Swift Runner** [Accused]
- **Kis Sie Ko Way** [Swift Runner's father-in-law]
- **Charlotte** [Swift Runner's wife]
- **Superintendent WD Jarvis** [Northwest Mount Police]
- **Sub-Inspector Severe Gagnon** [NWMP]
- **Sergeant Richard Steele** [[NWMP]
- **Corporal Fred Bagley** [NWMP]
- **George Washington Brazeau** [NWMP Guide]
- **Dr. Herchmer** [NWMP Physician]
- **Father Hippolyte Leduc** [Catholic Church]
- **Father Remus** [Catholic Church]
- **The Cree Boy** [Swift Runner's favorite son]
- **Sergeant Sam Steele** [Northwest Mount Police]
- **Godfrey Steele** [Northwest Mount Police]
- **Major General Alfred Howe Terry** [US Army]
- **Chief Sitting Bull** [Lakota People]

II
The Swift Runner Murder Case.
Number of Victims

I did a lot of research into this case and visited all the locations mentioned. The original fort is gone, but a full-size replica stands in Old Fort Saskatchewan. As does the original Catholic chapel in St. Albert, built in 1861 which is believed to be the oldest building in Alberta.

To my knowledge, the precise location of the death camp in the Athabasca region is unknown, as is the exact location of the last child victim killed and eaten somewhere north of Egg Lake; now Lake Manawana.

That victim's body, likely returned to the earth, lies somewhere west of my house in a landscape carved up into range roads, forest, farmland, and pumpjacks bobbing like grazing dinosaurs.

Having written a couple crime thrillers, I have delved into the psyche of homicidal criminals in the past, even cannibals, like Jeffrey Dahmer and Ed Gein. Swift Runner was like most mass murderers, in that he blamed others for his horrific crimes: the government, the Hudson Bay Company, and the windigo he claimed possessed him.

The sadistic brutality of the crimes perpetrated against Swift Runner's family included shooting, stabbing, ligature strangulation, and bludgeoning with an axe. My research indicates that by all accounts, the Cree were equally repelled by this man, accused of killing and eating his own family.

There are differing accounts of how many child victims there were. I have read in testimony that there were six children and three adults, but there are also conflicting documents and accounts that say Swift Runner had five offspring. The contradiction left me with a conundrum, but in the end I went with five children victims, though it is likely there were six.

In his book, Swift Runner, the late Colin A. Thomson stated that he could find no record showing the name of Swift Runner's wife, and therefore assigned a fictional name: **Sun on the Mountain.**

After reviewing the trial transcript, [transcribed by author Hammerson Peters] I found testimony from her father, **Kis Sie Ko Way,** who called his daughter, **Charlotte**, and that is the name I used for Swift Runner's wife.

***

Ka Ki Si Kutchin Confession

PAPER "A"

This is the confession known as the Paper "A" referred to in the evidence of **William Drummer Jarvis** and **William Borwick** taken on the trial of **Ka Ki Si Kutchin** in the above charge.

SSO Hugh Richardson
Superintendent GW Jarvis.

Voluntary confession of Ka Ki Si Kutchin, an Indian committed on the charge of having, during the last six months, in the woods at a place south of muskeg river, between the Saskatchewan and Athabasca rivers, in the northwest territories, murdered several members of his family.

Taken before the underside two of her majesty's justices of the peace and in for the said Territories, this 15th day of June in the year of our Lord, 1879, who (said Indian) saith:

I am going to tell the truth. I have done a great deal of harm. That is the reason I was backward with telling about it. I did not kill anybody else's children, only my own. I told you an awful lie. First, I shot my son, the next to the eldest. The eldest died. At the camp where men found the bones. I killed all the rest except my youngest son which I killed near Egg Lake. I shot him through the back of the head. I shot my wife through the breast. The two little girls I knocked in the head with an axe. I choked the baby girl with a line. I know nothing about my brother and mother. My second boy I shot at the camp I did not show. A few days after my eldest boy died of starvation, I shot my woman and killed all the rest, except my last boy at the same camp the same day. After eating the last boy, I came on to Egg Lake, where I stayed a little while, then I came on to Saint Albert. My wife said nothing when I killed my second boy. I never threatened before to kill and eat my wife. I told you everything I have done.

Signed: Ka Ki Si Kutchin

His Mark [X]

Taken and acknowledged before on the day and year above mentioned as Fort Saskatchewan.

Signed and witnessed: **R. Belcher, William Borwick, GW Braytaw**

Acknowledgement and Credit

Nobody writes a novel of this size without help, so I would like to acknowledge those people now.

Karen Preston, aka **Stormy**, my love, my life, who has always supported me. Despite the nightly clicking of keys, from typewriter to PC keyboard, click-clack-click-clack, and still it continues. I love you, sweetheart.

Patricia Holycross, who has been my research assistant and butt kicker since the Highwayman novels. Patti, I know I dedicated the novel to you, but your patience and friendship are paramount to getting it done, and I thank you.

The Late Robert James Steel (Jim), my mentor and dear friend, whom I lost while writing the novel before this, will always be top of mind. From beginning, Jim was there reading every draft, cheering me on, and enjoying the ride. I miss you, Jim, and this novel is one I would have loved to have you on board for.

Other Writers I've met some dynamite writers in my lifetime, and it is a community of artists with one collective passion: Tell stories.

My thanks to authors: **Don Sawyer, R.L. Keck, Kevin M. Sullivan, Gene O'Neill, Gord Rollo, Craig Spector, Kristi Petersen Schoonover, Steve Stred, Frederick Laforge,** and **Tony Tremblay.** I could go on and on because there are so many more, but I digress: I am humbled by your talent, and you inspire me to be a better writer.

Podcasters and Friends, I would also like to thank the Indie community, from fellow writers to podcasters to enthusiastic folks from across genres, from crime thriller to horror: **Philip Perron, Eric**

Webster, **Dan Hunter,** and the whole gang at the **Dark Discussions Podcast.**

Lastly, storytelling is a labor of love, and without your sweet embrace, **Dear Reader**, it would only be a labor.

Thanks for reading my story

Love the one you're with

MJ

Research Materials

—

Swift Runner by Colin A. Thomson

—

When I initially went searching for a physical copy of this out-of-print book, I found it on Amazon for a whopping $ 1,600.00. Taking a breath, I searched eBay and found a copy for about $45.00. Amazon or the vendor came to its senses and revised the price to $80.00.

Thomson's book is full of interesting tidbits, listing names and places along with a map of 35 cases of windigo madness. My only trouble was that the book often reads like a novel, full of speculation and artistic license. That is not something you find in a true crime account or historical book. I considered contacting him to ask about his approach, but sadly, the former University of Alberta professor had passed away. Final note: I'm not criticizing Colin Thomsen; his book is a treasure trove of research and an interesting, informative read.

—

The Trial of a Cannibal by Hammerson Peters

—

Hammerson Peter's is an expert on everything and anything supernatural in Canada and around the world. There is a fascinating video in which the author, Hammerson Peters, transcribes the handwritten trial transcript and confession of Swift Runner and turns them into a video. What a huge help this was.

His many works can be found at:
https://hammersonpeters.com/

Royal Canadian Mounted Police Quarterly

July 1942 – Volume 10

The Last of Canada's Cannibals by Ex-Sgt. Major F.A. Bagley

♦

Wendigo Encounters in Canada

Episode 3 – Swift Runner

https://mysteriesofcanada.com/alberta/wendigo-encounters-in-canada-episode-3-swift-runner/

♦

Murderpedia – Swift Runner

https://murderpedia.org/male.R/r/runner-swift.htm

♦

Gods and Monsters Swift Runner

https://www.gods-and-monsters.com/swift-runner.html

♦

Creative Commons Canada

Picture of Swift Runner with Mountie/skull exhibit is no longer copyrighted as it was published over 50 years ago and the copyright has since expired making it Canadian Public Domain.

♦

Headlines and Prairie Newspapers

While there were plenty of news stories surrounding the Swift Runner case, the ones presented in this story were fictional as were the newspapers. The reason for not using actual news clippings was due to time restraint and ensuring there were no copyright issues.

Language and Translation

Now, I'd like to tell you that I'm fluent in all three languages, but that would be a blatant lie. I used three specific languages in the writing of this book. English, French and Plains Cree.

—

Sources for the Cree Language

The Online Cree Dictionary

—

A web-based translator that is a fantastic resource. I do not have the confidence to construct Cree sentences and therefore used single words with a translation.

https://www.creedictionary.com/

—

A Dictionary of the Cree Language

Based upon the foundation laid by Rev. E. A. Watkins

—

This Cree/English dictionary has been revised and updated multiple times since it's conception. This dictionary, available in PDF, was a secondary source that I use mostly to double check other Cree words.

—

French Language Sources

—

Once I spoke and understood French on a limited basis during my time as instructor in the military. But that was a long time ago. I leaned heavily on **Microsoft Word Translator** and my bilingual editor to fix all the mistakes and gave it a French feel. Many thanks to editor, **Donna Marie West**, for helping me polish up the final story and get the language of my French characters right, along with advising me on horses and dogs.

OTHER NOVELS BY MJ PRESTON

AVAILABLE IN E-BOOK, PRINT, AND AS AN AUDIOBOOK

THE EQUINOX – Stephen Hopper has a secret even darker than the dead children buried in his cornfield. The debut Horror that started it all.

ACADIA EVENT – North of the 60th Parallel, they've found something buried in the ice that will change everything. And it's about to be unleashed!

HIGHWAYMAN - BOOK ONE – Meet Lance Belanger, he has only one ambition. To be the most prolific serial killer of all time. Witness the birth of a serial killer as he murders his way across America, as the FBI pursues the killer they call: "Highwayman"

FOUR - BOOK TWO – Having escaped identification by the FBI Highwayman has been dormant for over a year and he is going crazy. Throwing caution to the wind, he sets his plan in motion and the killers known as FOUR descend on a suburb of Pittsburgh and Massacre four families in their homes with a message. And this is just the beginning.

What does that mean?

This project was created from scratch by me, the author, and that means I did all the grunt work, shouldered all the cost, from research to writing to editing and even publishing.

An independent writer rarely breaks even, but those of us dedicated to the craft of storytelling continue our mission to broaden our audience enough to sustain that next book project.

You are the key to that mission.

If you enjoyed my work, please leave a short review where you purchased this book, but more importantly, tell all your friends and family about me.

Thank you for reading my work.

MJ

PUBLISHED BY

—

PUBLISHED BY
MJ PRESTON THRILLER AND SUSPENSE

—

Story by M.J. Preston

VISIT ME ONLINE

Website
https://mjpreston.net

Join Facebook Group
https://www.facebook.com/groups/mjprestonthrillersuspense

About the Author

MJ Preston is a Canadian author known for his horror, science fiction, and crime thriller novels. Life experiences include soldier and ice road trucker. He is also an amateur photographer and dabbles in art.

His dedication to storytelling has seen him craft multiple novels and short stories, often inspired by his experiences and deep fascination with folklore and the human condition.

His latest release, **Windigo Plague: Fort Saskatchewan Volume I** showcases his distinctive voice in the Canadian horror genre.

Other works include Canadian horror novels **The Equinox** and **Acadia Event**, and FBI crime thrillers **Highwayman** and **Four**. He is now working on a new crime thriller novel, **MAX,** projected for release in late 2026.

He resides , Alberta, Canada, with his wife Stormy and their two beagles, Jake and Milo.

www.ingramcontent.com/pod-product-compliance
Lightning Source LLC
LaVergne TN
LVHW041111080826
845145LV00007B/1773

* 9 7 8 1 0 6 7 4 9 0 0 0 3 *